The Berrybender Narratives, Book 3

LARRY McMURTRY

By Sorrow's River

A Novel

Simon & Schuster

New York   London   Toronto   Sydney   Singapore

SIMON & SCHUSTER
Rockefeller Center
1230 Avenue of the Americas
New York, NY 10020

SIMON & SCHUSTER and colophon are registered trademarks
of Simon & Schuster, Inc.

For information regarding special discounts for bulk purchases,
please contact Simon & Schuster Special Sales at
1-800-456-6798 or business@simonandschuster.com

Designed by Karolina Harris
Endpaper map courtesy of the Library of Congress

Manufactured in the United States of America

1   3   5   7   9   10   8   6   4   2

Library of Congress Cataloging-in-Publication Data
McMurtry, Larry.
By sorrow's river : a novel / Larry McMurtry.
p. cm.—(The Berrybender narratives ; bk. 3)
1. British—West (U.S.)—Fiction. 2. Eccentrics and eccentricities—Fiction.
3. Women immigrants—Fiction. 4. Young women—Fiction. I. Title.

PS3563.A319B9 2003
813'.54—dc21   2003053892
ISBN 0-7432-3304-2

THE BERRYBENDER NARRATIVES *are dedicated to the second-hand booksellers of the Western world, who have done so much, over a fifty-year stretch, to help me to an education.*

Book 3

At the end of Book 2, *The Wandering Hill*, the Berrybender party, as well as the mountain men, have made their way to a great fur traders' rendezvous in the Valley of the Chickens, west of South Pass. A foggy early-morning battle with some attacking Utes leaves Bobbety Berrybender and the Scottish sportsman William Drummond Stewart dead; in this foggy fight the Ute chief Walkura and No Teeth, an old shaman, are also killed. Pomp Charbonneau, near death from an arrow wound, is saved by the unexpectedly skillful surgery of Father Geoffrin, assisted by a dream visit from Pomp's mother, Sacagawea, and by the fierce determination of Tasmin Berrybender, who refuses to let Pomp die.

Contents

Characters

BERRYBENDERS

Tasmin

Bess (Buffum)

Mary

Kate

Lord Berrybender

Monty, *baby*

Talley, *baby*

Piet Van Wely

Father Geoffrin

Cook

Milly

Eliza

Tim

Signor Claricia

Señor Yanez

Venetia Kennet

MOUNTAIN MEN

Jim Snow (The Sin Killer)

Kit Carson

Jim Bridger

Tom Fitzpatrick (The Broken
  Hand)

Eulalie Bonneville

William Ashley

Maelgwyn Evans

Hugh Glass

Bill and Milt Sublette

Ezekiel Williams

Joe Walker

Pomp Charbonneau

Toussaint Charbonneau

Rabbit, *baby*

INDIANS

High Shoulders, *Ute*

Coal

Little Onion

Greasy Lake

The Partezon, *Sioux*

The Bad Eye, *Gros Ventre*

Fool's Bull, *Sioux*

Hollow Foot, *Brulé Sioux*

Draga, *Aleut*

Takes Bones (The Ear Taker),
  Acoma

CHARACTERS

Red Knee, *Pawnee*

Rattle, *Pawnee*

Slow Possum, *Pawnee*

Duck Catcher, *Pawnee*

Thistle-Pricks-Us, *Pawnee*

Prickly Pear Woman, *Laguna*

Corn Tassel, *Chippewa*

Owl Woman, *Cheyenne*

MISCELLANEOUS

Charles Bent, *trader*

Willy Bent, *trader*

Amboise d'Avigdor

Benjamin Hope-Tipping, *journalist*

Clam de Paty, *journalist*

Obregon, *slaver*

Malgres, *slaver*

Ramon, *slaver*

Maria Jaramillo

Josefina Jaramillo

Lieutenant Molino, *Mexican soldier*

Captain Antonio Reyes, *Mexican soldier*

Doña Esmeralda, *duenna*

By Sorrow's River

Who been here?
    Fishprick.

Where you lie?
    Making itch in Sister's thigh.

KISKATINAW BOGEY SONG
(TRANSLATED BY SUSAN MUSGRAVE
AND SEAN VÍRGO)

Pater semper incertus est . . .

OLD WORRY

1

It was a day of fine sunlight.

"*L A   V I E ,   voyez-vous, ça n'est jamais si bonne ni si mauvaise qu'on croit,*" said Father Geoffrin, relaxing, for a moment, into his native tongue. His patient, Pomp Charbonneau—educated in Germany, competent in several languages—spoke good French. Tasmin Berrybender's *français,* while decidedly casual, was probably adequate, the priest felt, to such a common platitude: life was never so good or so bad as one thought—a proposition which no one who had much acquaintance with the French classics would be likely to dispute.

Tasmin, with a flare of her eloquent nostrils and a cool glance at Father Geoffrin, at once disputed it.

"What foppish nonsense, Geoff!" she said. "Are you going to argue that I wasn't in hell when I thought Pomp was dying, or that I shan't be in ecstasy when I know he's out of danger?"

Though Father Geoffrin, no mean surgeon, had very skillfully removed a flint tip from very near Pomp's heart, the crisis caused by the Ute Walkura's well-placed arrow had not ended there. For three days Pomp's fever soared; except to relieve herself, Tasmin never left his side. Monty, her baby, was brought in to suckle. When Pomp's fever rose she bathed his face and neck from a basin of cold river water; she covered him with blankets when he

shivered with chill. Only that morning the fever had at last broken, leaving Pomp calm but very weak. In his dream deliriums he
had several times had visits from his mother, Sacagawea, dead
many long years, who insisted that he heed Tasmin's anxious
whispers and stay with her in the world of the living. His mother
and Tasmin together held him in life—without them he would
have slipped into the easeful shadows. At the height of his fever
he felt some resentment at the two women's tenacity—couldn't
they just let him go? But the women, one dead, one strongly
alive, were more powerful than the fever. So there Pomp was,
weak but still alive, in the big camp in the Valley of the Chickens,
though his employer, the sportsman William Drummond Stewart, had been hacked to death by the invading Utes. Bobbety
Berrybender, Tasmin's brother, was also killed, trampled as he
wandered in the fog by thirty charging horses. Now, in the crisp
air of a sunny morning, Tasmin and Father Geoffrin were quarreling volubly, as they often did.

"I accept that some women are not quite suited to the life of
moderation," Father Geoff told her. "It's why your Shakespeare
is so popular—all that raging. And of course there's opera—
same raging. I fear you're the operatic sort, Tasmin—if you can't
have passion you'll have torment. Personally, I'd be happy just to
buy some nice clothes."

"Not much opportunity for clothes shopping here," Tasmin
told him. The trader William Ashley, frightened of Tasmin
because she had cursed him violently when he suggested that
Pomp was unlikely to survive his wound, had lent them his tent
for Pomp's convalescence. With Tasmin supporting him, Pomp
had just taken a few steps out into the bright sunlight and
the clean mountain air. Once he was settled comfortably on a
buffalo-robe pallet, the two bear cubs Pomp had caught, Abby
and Andy, shuffled up, eager to be petted. Below them, the same
party of Utes who had attacked them a week earlier were placidly
trading pelts with Eulalie Bonneville, William Ashley, Jim
Bridger, and the other mountain men. From the river came the
low, melancholy notes of Venetia Kennet's cello, playing a dirge

for William Drummond Stewart, who had been her lover.

When the Utes, whose village was nearby, had come diffidently back to trade, Tasmin had been too focused on Pomp and his fever to pay attention to what went on in camp, but now that she saw their attackers milling around among the mountain men, exchanging peltries for hatchets, tobacco, blue and green beads, she felt incensed.

"Aren't those the same savages who trampled my brother and hacked up poor Drum Stewart?" she asked. "Why are those fools giving them hatchets, the better to brain us with?"

"Ah, there's your extreme nature getting in the way of good business sense," Father Geoffrin chided. "Last week the Utes were enemies, but now they're customers. Bill Ashley has his profits to think of, after all."

It was a day of fine sunlight. Tasmin looked around the camp but failed to spot her husband, Jim Snow, who had wisely left her to her nursing when Pomp was in danger. She didn't see Kit Carson either, but her father, Lord Berrybender, was down by the river, listening to Vicky Kennet's mournful music—soon, no doubt, he would be trying to coax the tall cellist back to his bed, his dalliance with Milly, their buxom laundress, having quickly run its course.

Little Onion, Jim Snow's young Ute wife—though a wife in name only—sat not far away, keeping an eye on Monty, Talley, and Rabbit. Monty was Tasmin's, Talley was Vicky's, and Rabbit belonged to Coal, Toussaint Charbonneau's Hidatsa wife, who was, at the moment, drying the meat of an elk Tom Fitzpatrick had shot the day before. Rabbit could toddle about uncertainly, while Monty and Talley were still at the crawling stage. All three little boys were extremely fond of the bear cubs, but the bear cubs, far speedier than the three human cubs, either adroitly avoided the boys or licked their faces until they sneezed and crawled away.

Bess, called Buffum, was helping Cook pick berries from some distant bushes, while Mary Berrybender, their sinister and uncompromising sister, was helping her Dutch friend, Piet Van

Wely, chip with a small hammer at some rocks that, Tasmin supposed, might contain interesting fossils.

"I don't see Jimmy. Where could he be?" Tasmin asked. "I
don't see Kit, either. I hope they haven't left, just as Pomp's feeling better."

Toussaint Charbonneau, Pomp's tall, shambling, much-
stained father, had been drinking whiskey and dipping snuff
with old Hugh Glass, oldest and rawest of the mountain men.
Old Charbonneau, officially the party's interpreter, was a tender-
hearted parent; for days he had been shaking with worry, fearful
that Tasmin would come out of the tent and tell him that his son
was dead.

"Why, look, there's Pomp!" old Charbonneau said, tears springing to his eyes as he saw Tasmin ease Pomp down on the comfortable pallet.

"That English girl's got more brass than all of us put together,"
Hugh Glass observed. "I wish she liked me better. Maybe she'd
take the trouble to pull me through, next time I find that I'm
dying."

But Toussaint Charbonneau didn't hear him—he was stumbling up the hill, excited to see his son alive—the son he soon
enfolded in a tight embrace.

"Careful, monsieur—he's weak," Tasmin said. "We don't want
that wound to start bleeding."

"We don't—I'll be careful," Charbonneau assured her, wiping
the tears off his face with snuff-stained fingers.

Father Geoffrin took Tasmin by the arm and strolled away a
few steps, so father and son could have a bit of privacy. Tasmin
had taken to guarding Pomp as an eagle might guard its egg.

"William Ashley has some nice silk shirts," Father Geoff
remarked. "And also a rather well-stitched pair of whipcord
trousers."

"So what? They're *his* clothes, not *your* clothes," Tasmin said.
"You'll have to wait for Santa Fe before you can buy clothes . . .
and who knows when we'll get to Santa Fe?"

Monty, spotting his mother, whom he had not seen much of

for days, began to crawl toward her as fast as his hands and knees could carry him. Tasmin met him halfway, swooped him up, wiped dirt off his nose, gave him several enthusiastic kisses, but then, to his dismay, handed him back to the patient Little Onion—his other mother, so far as Monty knew. Tasmin then walked away, skirting the traders and the Indians, heading for the river, noting as she passed near Vicky and her father that Vicky Kennet's hair was getting long again. Once it had hung in a rich mass all the way to her derriere; then, in a frenzy of dissatisfaction at being always a rich man's mistress, she had insisted that Tasmin cut it off. Tasmin had done as requested—for a few weeks Vicky Kennet had looked almost as scalped as her unfortunate lover, Drum Stewart, victim of the rampaging Utes.

As she walked down to the rapid, shallow, greenish river, which foamed here and there as it tumbled over rocks, Tasmin kept an eye out for her husband, Jim Snow—called Sin Killer by the Indians and some of the mountain men too. It was Jim, as good a bowman as most Indians, who had killed the Ute chief Walkura only a second after Walkura shot his near-fatal arrow into Pomp Charbonneau. Tasmin walked a step or two into the icy water, stooping to bathe her dusty face and throat; washing was a luxury she had not bothered with or even thought of during her days at Pomp's bedside. The icy water felt good—having her cheeks and throat clean felt good also, so good that she felt like stripping off and bathing the rest of her body as well. Of course, she couldn't do that with the trappers and Indians watching; besides, she had brought nothing clean to put on.

Standing in the shallows, the cold waters numbing her feet and ankles, Tasmin realized that she was, on the whole, relieved not to see her husband. Normally, in the course of a day in camp, her eyes sought him out frequently—even glimpsing Jim at a distance would provide clues to his mood. Jim never hid his feeling; vibration of what he was feeling could be picked out of the air, like the notes of Vicky's cello; then, when it came time for Tasmin to be a wife, she knew whether to approach her husband modestly and shyly or boldly, teasingly. Some moods she could slip around, kissing him if she felt like it, avoiding his hands if she didn't—though it was rare enough that she avoided his hands.

She might, she thought, have avoided them today, if he had approached her suddenly and tried to draw her into the bushes for a rut, as he liked to call it. It struck her, standing in the cold water watching the Indians and the trappers casually trading hatchets and beads, that the one thing she really knew about Jimmy Snow was that he craved her. That was good; she craved him too; but she had been with Pomp Charbonneau for five days, intensely with Pomp Charbonneau; she had felt nothing and thought of nothing except the necessity of keeping him alive. Her child she suckled automatically; the rest of her life she stepped away from, compelled by her determination that Pomp not die. Pomp had been her friend, her protector in times when Jim Snow was away. She had not expected the great bird of death to come swooping at Pomp; but when the bird swooped and nearly carried Pomp off, Tasmin had at once thrown her whole self into the struggle for Pomp's life. Death came so close, at times, that Tasmin was even nervous about stepping out of the tent to make water. Except for the thirty-hour struggle to bring Monty out of her womb, no fight had ever been so intense, so crucial, so starkly a contest between life and death; it required her to call up a level of will that had never been required of her before; it had needed her deepest strength, and she had prevailed, but it was well, she felt, that her husband was not there to want her, just at that moment.

Fortunately, the struggle had ended in victory. Pomp was sitting up, talking with his father and scratching the belly of the bear cub Abby. Once his wound was healed he might be exactly the same Pomp: friendly, kind, urbane, amused, amusing, supple of mind. The sight of him with his father and his pet slowly eased Tasmin's mind, where Pomp was concerned. The bird of death had been driven back to its eyrie. But if he was the same, what of herself? What of Tasmin? It seemed to her she had traveled a great distance during the struggle—thus her relief at not imme-

diately having to deal with Jim, to be a wife again suddenly, as
she had eagerly been for a year and a half. Father Geoffrin, at the
end of his successful surgery, had seen something of this traveling in Tasmin's face, and had made a cynical French joke about
it; the little priest, as sensitive to emotions as Vicky was to tones,
had seen in Tasmin's look something unexpected, something
that went beyond a nurse's determination to save a patient.
Father Geoffrin lifted an eyebrow, he made his joke, but as soon
as Pomp's fever broke he moved the conversation into safer
waters—that is, he talked of clothes. It had annoyed Tasmin
slightly. Once more a man seemed to be avoiding an important
question, leaving her to struggle with it alone. *Had* she fallen in
love with Pomp Charbonneau as he lay near death? Had she perhaps already been in love with him, but only dared to recognize
the feeling when it seemed that she might lose him? Now, her
cheeks cold from the icy water of the mountain stream, she wondered what became of deathbed emotions once death itself had
been avoided. Would she again walk with Pomp along the mild
path of friendship? Or had an emotion much less mild been
seeded between them—feelings that would lead to who knew
what tumult? Her husband, after all, was Pomp's best friend. It
was obvious from Jim's brief visits to the hospital tent that he
hoped Tasmin and the priest could save his friend's life. But Jim
Snow assumed that feelings were settled things; Tasmin knew
they weren't. What if she no longer wanted her vigorous young
husband? They had enjoyed a fierce and finally blissful rut only
the day before the battle with the Utes—the pleasure had lin-
gered in Tasmin's body for hours afterward—and yet, what of it?
Even the most passionate conjugal connection imposed no per-
manency. Desire was not a guarantor of much—desire might
fade, perhaps always did fade; besides, she was her father's
daughter, the child of Lord Albany Berrybender, a man who had
scattered his seed liberally enough to produce fourteen legiti-
mate children and perhaps as many as thirty bastards—and he
was by no means through. On this very expedition into the
American wilderness he had already given Vicky Kennet one

child and might well give her more, if she wasn't careful. Tasmin, though now a mother, had never been prudish. What if she proved as prodigal in her appetites as her father?

Only the winter before, when Pomp had insisted on walking from Pierre Boisdeffre's trading post to the tent a mile away where Jim Snow insisted they live, Tasmin had sometimes wondered if Pomp was walking her all that way because he wanted to kiss her. Reckless in mood, she had sometimes dawdled on their walks, holding Pomp's arm and half hoping he *would* kiss her. But he didn't, and Tasmin had not quite worked up to kissing him, although she considered it more than once, in part, perhaps, out of annoyance with her husband, Jim Snow, who calmly allowed her the company of this shy, handsome Pomp, Jim oblivious to the fact that kisses, and more, might pass between them. Pomp had once shyly admitted to Tasmin that he was virgin, a condition that, considering his sweet attractiveness, any helpful woman might wish to alter. When Pomp admitted that he seldom felt lustful, Tasmin took it almost as an insult to her sex. She complained, but she didn't actively set out to *make* him lustful, though she felt quite sure that she could make him lustful, given a little privacy.

So here they were, as summer neared its end, in the Valley of the Chickens, west of South Pass, with the big fur-trading rendezvous winding down and with the rather vague intention of heading off to Santa Fe pretty soon, so that her father might shoot yet more buffalo, elk, moose, deer, antelope, and whatever else might cross his path. Her husband was nowhere to be seen, nor was the helpful Kit Carson, and there she stood in a cold stream, wishing very much that Pomp Charbonneau *had* tried to kiss her at some point, even though, in his eyes, she was the apparently contented wife of his best friend.

Then the pesky Father Geoffrin, who surprised everyone by his competence as a surgeon, had tried to tell her that life was never as good or as bad as one thought it to be. Tasmin was in no mood to tolerate French equivocation; she felt muddled, so muddled in fact that she failed to note the quiet approach of

Mary Berrybender, a girl with unusual powers, capable of sniffing out edible tubers and perhaps also capable of sniffing out nascent loves, such as might be said to exist between Tasmin and Pomp.

"Now that you've saved Pomp, do you mean to have him, Tassie—I mean carnally?" Mary inquired; she had her full share of the Berrybender directness where the appetites were concerned and had sensed the rising feeling between her sister and Pomp long before either of them would have admitted that they *felt* such feelings.

So there Mary stood, a half-wild look in her eye, asking Tasmin straight out if she meant to seduce Pomp Charbonneau.

"Shut up and get back to your Dutchman," Tasmin warned. "And don't be playing nasty games with him, either."

She referred to the fact that Mary had been lashing the pudgy Dutch botanist on his bare bottom with some brambles, an activity the two claimed to thoroughly enjoy.

"Shame, Tasmin," Mary said hotly. "You were no older when you were tupping Master Tobias Stiles in the stall of father's great horse Charlemagne. You *did* do it, you know!"

"Of course I did it, and lucky to get the opportunity," Tasmin replied. "When it comes to forthright tupping, I suspect Master Stiles set a standard your Dutchman would be hard put to match."

"Being whipped with nettles is a common practice among educated Hollanders," Mary reminded her. "I can't think why you'd mind about it, Tassie."

"I've just come through an ordeal—Pomp nearly died," Tasmin said. "I'm not in the mood to discuss our amatory futures, yours or mine. I don't see my husband and I don't see Kit Carson, either. Do you know where they might be?"

"Oh yes, they're gone on a scout," Mary informed her. "It's the Sioux, I believe, that they're investigating. Santa Fe seems to be a great distance away—Jim doesn't wish us to blunder into too many Sioux—they're very irritable at the moment, it seems."

Just then another sister came trailing up, the sturdy Kate Berrybender, aged four. Tasmin was thinking that while her face and throat felt very clean, the rest of her felt soiled and smelly. The desire to be clean all over rose in her; there were bushes thick enough to hide her up the river a ways. She could bathe in discreet seclusion, but would need clean clothes once she stepped out.

"Mary, go find Buffum—I believe she's picking berries. Ask her to have Milly, our amorous laundress, get me a clean shift," Tasmin asked.

Mary, obliging for once, had hardly left to execute this errand when stout little Kate arrived, wearing her usual look of fierce belligerence.

"Mr. James Snow left a message for you," Kate informed her, without preamble. "He says he is going on a scout and will not be back for three weeks, if then."

"Three weeks? And he didn't think it worth his while to say good-bye to his own wife?" Tasmin complained.

"Mr. James Snow does not say good-bye," Kate informed her, with quite exceptional firmness. "When Mr. James Snow wants to go, he just goes."

"So I've noticed, you insolent midge," Tasmin replied. "This is not his first abrupt departure, since taking me as his wife. Inasmuch as you seem to be his emissary, perhaps you wouldn't mind giving him a message from his wife, next time you see him."

"Perhaps—unless it's an order," Kate said. "You are not allowed to give orders to Mr. James Snow."

"The next time he goes heigh-hoing off, he better leave me Kit—that's the message," Tasmin told her. "Little Onion and I could use Kit's help."

Instead of replying, Kate picked up a rock, intending to heave it at her sister—but something in Tasmin's look caused her to check the impulse. She stood, glared, and finally turned away.

Tasmin hurried upriver, got squarely behind the bushes, stripped, and took a chill but refreshing bath. She had goose bumps all over by the time Buffum finally trailed down the slope with her clothes.

2

Tear his throat out? His Vicky?

L o r d Berrybender was nonplussed: Venetia Kennet, long his darling, his pet, his bedmate, mistress, whore, inamorata—a woman whose languid beauty had always quickened his juices, who even employed delicate skills to arouse him when arousal seemed beyond reach—had just flatly refused him. She had made no effort to be polite about it, either. In fact, she had threatened to tear his throat out if he so much as touched her...

Tear his throat out? His Vicky? Of course, when he approached her she happened to be sitting by the grave of her lover, Drum Stewart, whose unfortunate death at the hands of the Utes had caused her much grief. But then, Lord B.'s own son Bobbety had perished too. Bobbety had not, perhaps, been very imposing, yet he might have led a mild life of some sort, collecting fossils and looking up Latin names for butterflies or shrubs. But Bobbety was dead, and Drum Stewart was dead, but he himself was not dead, nor was Vicky, whose long white body he had enjoyed so often. Wasn't life for the living? Mustn't it be lived to the hilt? He was not getting younger—it was no time to allow the juices of love to dry up. It occurred to Lord B. that his hearing was no longer as keen as it had been—perhaps he had misheard his lively friend, whose face seemed suddenly red with anger—but why?

"What was that you were saying, my lovely dear?" he asked, hoping a compliment would help.

"I said I'd tear your throat out if you touch me," Vicky said, in icy tones.

"But Vicky, think for a minute—let's not be rash," Lord Berrybender replied—sweet reason had never been exactly his métier, but he thought he might try it, for once. His experience, after all, was considerable—there had been hundreds of copulations, in several countries; women had been angry with him before, perhaps even violently angry. The Gypsy woman in Portugal, perhaps? The fiery Neapolitan countess who kept a dagger in her undergarments? Would either of them have offered to tear his throat out? Lord B. could not be sure, though he felt quite certain that his good wife, Lady Constance, would never have threatened such a thing. For one thing, though not entirely devoid of temperament, Lady Constance had been singularly inept—she would not have known how to begin to tear a man's throat out. The most Constance had ever done was whack at him feebly with the fly swat when he awakened her too quickly with copulation in mind. No, the worst that could be said of Lady Constance was that after the fourteenth child she had become sadly less ardent; in many cases, if she had too much laudanum and her usual bottle or two of claret, she even dozed off while they were copulating, leaving him to labor to a lonely conclusion. Sometimes, in fact, Constance had even been known to snore while he was laboring, a rather deflating thing for a husband to have to put up with. Their tupping took at most ten minutes—was it asking too much of a wife that she stay awake for such a modest interval? Lord Berrybender didn't think so, but Lady Constance was beyond persuasion or complaint. Her snores became habitual, which is one reason he had transferred the bulk of his attentions to the tall cellist with the long white legs and the raspberry teats in the first place. And yet this same Vicky, a mother now, her breasts heavy with milk but her legs still just as long, had threatened to tear his throat out, though as far as he could see, she had nothing to tear it out with, only her cello and its bow. It occurred to him that the bow did bear watching—he himself had accidentally poked one of Bobbety's eyes out with a turning fork. He was in the American West mainly for the hunting—he could not easily spare an eye.

Prudently, Lord Berrybender retreated a step, meaning to fend her off with his crutch if she came at him suddenly.

"Now, now, Vicky—I've a tough old throat after all," he told her. "You've not got a pair of scissors in your pocket, now have you? You've not got a knife, I hope?"

By way of answer Vicky bared her strong white teeth and clicked them at him menacingly, ending the performance with a hiss loud enough to give Lord B. a start.

"I've got these teeth," she said. "It's only one vein I'd need to nip, and out would pour your lifeblood. Surely Your Lordship has seen a seamstress nipping a thread. A good sharp nip at the jugular and it's done."

Lord Berrybender was shocked, so shocked that for a moment he felt quite faint. His dead son, Bobbety, lay buried not twenty feet away, and yet his sweet Vicky, so delicate in her strokings, had threatened to go for his throat.

It was all so topsy-turvy, this new world he had blundered into; perhaps it was the fault of democracy or some other American sloppiness. Vicky, for all her musical gifts, was merely a servant girl. He now began to see that democracy might indeed be the problem—didn't the system actually encourage servants to forget their place? Hadn't his own cook threatened to leave him and take a position with Pierre Boisdeffre? Hadn't the gunsmith and the carriage maker simply walked away one night, while on a hunt, as if they had every right to please themselves? Of course, the Mediterraneans had come back and Cook in the end had stayed in his service; and yet Cook *had* threatened, and now here was Vicky exhibiting violent defiance.

"I know just where that vein throbs, Your Lordship," Vicky declared, in chillingly level tones. "There you'd be, rutting for all your worth, and not three inches from my teeth that big vein would be throbbing. One nip, I've often told myself—one nip and the old brute is dead and I shall never have to be so bored again."

"Here now, that's damnable, calling me boring!" Lord Berrybender complained. "I fancy I give thorough service, most of the time, though lately I know I've developed rather a tendency to haste. But damn it Vicky! You're acting like a regular Charlotte Corday—kill me in my bath, I suppose—that'll be the next thing!"

"You're safe enough in your bath—but you ain't safe in my bed," Vicky told him bluntly.

"I ought to whack you, you insolent bitch," Lord Berrybender protested. But he didn't whack her—the look in her eye discouraged him. Women, after all, were quick as cats. What if she sprang at him, got her teeth in his neck? A ripped jugular was bad business, not easily repaired. So, instead of delivering several solid slaps, Lord Berrybender turned and made his way up the hill, traveling as fast as he could on an ill-fitting peg leg, a crutch, and half a foot. The more he thought about the matter, the more convinced he became that his analysis of the problem was correct. These damnable American freedoms—this democracy!—were clearly inimicable to sound English order. Democracy could ruin a good servant faster than gin, in his view. Forgotten her place, Vicky had: made threats, gave him mutinous looks; intolerable behavior, on the whole. He meant to speak to Tasmin about it, perhaps get Tasmin to deliver a stern reprimand. Tasmin would defend her old pater, of that Lord Berrybender felt sure. Only, for now, he thought he might just trouble William Ashley for a bit of his excellent champagne; a little bubbly might settle his nerves, which, at the moment, were far from being in a settled state. Tear out his throat, indeed! A shocking thing to hear. In his father's day proud wenches such as Vicky had been flogged at the cart's tail for less—or put in the stocks, where the mob could pelt them with filth. It had been an admirable form of punishment, the stocks. As a boy he had seen plenty of people pelted: low types, criminals, drunken old women. What a pity there were no stocks anymore—Lord B.

couldn't think why they had fallen out of favor. They'd be just the thing to correct a proud wench like Vicky. *Then* she'd bend her head; *then* there'd be no talk of tearing out the throats of her superiors. A day or two in the stocks, with the villagers pelting her with rotten eggs and sheep shit, would soon take the sass out of her. Then the silly wench would be happy enough to accommodate him, he supposed—even if, of late, he had developed a tendency to be rather too quick.

3

Among the wild, undomesticated company . . .

A M O N G the wild, undomesticated company of the mountain trappers, it was generally considered that rotund Eulalie Bonneville knew the most about women. Bonney, as he was called, was no mean gambler, besides. None of the mountain men could recall seeing Bonney actually trapping any beaver, much less skinning them out. The icy ponds and streams where the other trappers waded to set their traps did not tempt him—keeping his feet warm was a first principle with Eulalie Bonneville; yet at the end of the season, through a succession of clever trades and successful card games or dice rolls or random bets, he generally trekked out of the mountains with more furs than anyone—and better furs too; and yet his prowess as a fur trader drew considerably less attention from his comrades than his expertise with women—for it was exactly *that* expertise that few of the others could claim, their amours for the most part being brief and drunken wallows with river-town whores or compliant Indian women, engagements seldom free of anxiety, since several of their colleagues had had their scalps lifted as a result of lingering too long in the toils of Venus with dusky maidens. And yet Eulalie Bonneville, as broad as he was tall, was said to have at least one wife in every tribe from the Kaw River to the

Marias: Minatarees, Otos, Hidatsas, Teton Sioux, Assiniboines, Shoshones, Pawnees, Cheyennes, and Utes. So far only the women of the Piegan Blackfeet were absent from his scattered harem, a fact old Hugh Glass found curious.

"I'd have thought you'd have taken a Blackfoot wife by now, Bonney," Hugh remarked. Hugh and Joe Walker, the Sublette brothers, and young Jim Bridger were all lounging around camp on this bright morning, the bulk of their trading completed for the summer. The bear cub Abby lay at old Hugh's feet. From time to time all the men directed their glances at the clump of bushes near the river, behind which Tasmin Berrybender was assumed to be bathing her lovely body. The bushes were one hundred yards away—even if Tasmin had chosen to exhibit herself naked, the trappers would not have seen much, and yet they couldn't stop looking.

"I wish I did have a Blackfoot wife," Bonney replied. "Marrying into a tribe is the best way to get a little trade started, but the Blackfoot won't have me."

"I figured that was why you collected all them wives," Joe Walker commented. "It was the trade you were after, I expect."

"I don't despise the trade, but I also happen to like a rut, when I can get it," Bonney admitted.

"So how many wives are you up to, Bonney?" Jim Bridger asked. He himself lacked even one wife, and could not but be envious of the chubby trader's progress.

"An even dozen, unless some of my Missouri River wives have died," Eulalie admitted. "I fancy I could handle about twenty wives, if I could keep them spread out well enough."

Just then Tasmin and her sister Bess, both fully clothed, stepped out from behind the distant bushes. Tasmin bent for a moment to shake the water out of her wet hair.

"Now there's a wife and a half, I'd say," Hugh Glass remarked. "Too dern much of a wife for that young whelp Jimmy Snow."

None of the mountain men spoke. Several of them, in their mind's eye, had been imagining Tasmin naked; she *wasn't* naked, but the trappers were reluctant to let go of the exciting images they had been constructing. All of them considered that it had been Tasmin alone who saved Pomp Charbonneau. She had beaten back death, a rare thing. She had also scared the pants off William Ashley by cursing him, and Ashley, though a rich man now, had weathered several desperate Indian fights. One and all, the trappers admired Tasmin; many wondered how it had been possible for a shy fellow like Jimmy Snow to get her to marry him. Kit Carson, of course, was head over heels in love with her, and many of the other trappers a little in love too, and yet her close approach made them nervous. Now here she was, walking up the slope, right toward them, stopping from time to time to squeeze more water out of her wet hair, the droplets making tiny rainbows in the sunlight.

"What do you think, Mr. Twelve Wives Bonneville?" old Hugh asked. "Think you could handle that much of a wife?"

Bonney, as it happened, was deeply smitten with Tasmin, yet he felt a shy uncertainty overwhelm him when she came near or spoke to him. That the mountain men considered him an expert on women did not displease him; but of course, there were women and women. A Minataree girl or a Ute girl might be one thing, Lady Tasmin quite another.

"She's married to Jimmy—I don't think about her," he replied, a comment that drew skeptical looks from several of the trappers. Abby left Hugh Glass's side and went scampering down the slope to meet Tasmin.

"Them grizzlies are growing fast," Joe Walker observed. "I expect they'll eat a few of us, one of these days."

"Suppose Jimmy Snow got his scalp lifted," Hugh Glass remarked. "That girl'd be a widow. Would you court her then, Bonney?"

"I've always been cautious of Englishwomen," Bonney remarked, vaguely. "Besides, I hear the old lord means to make for Santa Fe—myself, I favor the North."

Tasmin, meanwhile, passed within a few feet of the group— she was complaining to Buffum that, once again, her husband had left without troubling to tell her good-bye.

"You *were* rather intent on Pomp, Tassie," Bess reminded her. "I expect Mr. Snow was loath to interrupt."

"He's your brother-in-law, you don't need to call him Mr. Snow," Tasmin said. "Jim's his name, and his habit is to leave when he wants to leave—the rest of us must muddle along as best we can."

She glanced at the mountain men, all of them still as statues and as silent as judges.

"You gentlemen seem rather subdued," she remarked. "I thought you all came here to get drunk and make merry."

The mountain men looked at one another sheepishly. One or two shrugged. Finally Jim Bridger decided to venture a word or two.

"We're all married out," he admitted. "I've 'bout danced my legs off, as it is."

Tasmin did remember hearing a good deal of fiddle playing and general carousing while she was waiting in the tent with Pomp.

"This year's party's about over," Hugh Glass allowed. "Time to get back to the trapping, pretty soon"—a remark which drew from young Bill Sublette a gloomy look. A sociable man, he did not look forward to lonely times along distant rivers.

"There won't be no more parties in the Valley of the Chickens," Joe Walker said. "Ashley says he's done—not enough peltries to make it worth coming this far."

"So this is the end of the big rendezvous, I suppose," Hugh Glass remarked.

There the talk stopped. The men seemed suddenly overcome by gloom at the thought that the free life in the high Rockies—a life made possible by an abundance of fur-bearing animals—might be finished, its end come before their end.

Tasmin and Buffum walked on.

"Taciturn brutes, these mountain men," she said. "It's all I can do to get one to speak."

"It's because you're so blunt, Tassie," Buffum said. "No one is so blunt as you. I fear it scares the menfolk."

"Piffle—I suppose it's just because I don't bill and coo," Tasmin replied. "The male is generally insufficient, wouldn't you say? They all seem to be weak with women."

"Here's Papa, scuttling up the slope," Buffum announced. "I wonder why he's in such a hurry."

"Probably Vicky refused him." Tassie guessed. "Her lover's barely cold in the ground. I don't imagine she wants Papa pawing her just now."

"He'll wear her down, though," Buffum said. "He knows her ways."

"I say, wait a bit, Tasmin!" Lord Berrybender demanded, with a wave. Struggling up the slope on crutch and peg leg had left him very red in the face.

"Yes, what is it now?" Tasmin asked, impatiently. She had just noticed, to her chagrin, that her patient, Pomp Charbonneau, was no longer on his pallet. Pomp was very weak—she had given him strict orders just to rest, yet there he was, walking slowly toward the enclosure where the captive animals were kept, the creatures that were to have gone to Drummond Stewart's great game park in the north of Scotland.

"I say, girls . . . do wait!" Lord Berrybender stammered, very short of wind. "A very bad thing."

"We know, Father—our brother was killed," Tasmin began, but Lord Berrybender cut her off.

"No, damn it, not *that*—we've got past *that*," he protested. "It's Vicky I must speak to you about."

"Well, and what about her?" Tasmin asked. "She's just grieving—we all are."

"No, no! Will you listen, goddamn you!" Lord B. burst out. "She's crazy. She's lost her mind."

"I doubt it, not unless it's happened since breakfast," Tasmin told him. "I had a good talk with her while we were nursing our babies. She's just in no mood to be bothered by the likes of you—for that matter, neither am I. Pomp's wandered off—I have to go get him, if you'll excuse me."

"Don't give a damn for Pomp!" Lord Berrybender said, grabbing his daughter's arm. "You'll stand and you'll listen. Vicky threatened to tear my throat out. Said she'd do it with her teeth, if I came close. You'll have to chide her, Tassie—deliver a sharp reprimand. Can't have servants threatening to tear their master's throat out. Kind of thing that leads to revolution—all that French misbehavior. She deserves a good flogging, that girl, but if you'll just speak to her sharply, perhaps she'll come to her senses."

Lord B. was squeezing Tasmin's arm quite tightly—he was very red in the face.

"Now Papa, Vicky was probably just upset," Buffum began, but before she could complete her plea, Tasmin dipped her head and gave her father's clutching hand a quick, hard bite; His Lordship gave a cry and immediately released his daughter's arm. Blood at once welled up where Tasmin had bitten him.

Lord Berrybender was too shocked to speak, rather as he had been when Venetia Kennet first delivered her threat—his own daughter had drawn his blood.

"Being the weaker sex, we women have to use such weapons as we possess, when selfish men attempt to interfere with us," Tasmin informed him coldly. "A woman's teeth are not to be taken lightly, as you've now discovered."

"But . . . but . . . ," Lord Berrybender stammered.

"No buts, father—just leave Vicky alone," Tasmin told him. "And don't be grabbing me when I have urgent business to conduct."

Then she left, leaving a startled Buffum to bandage her father's bleeding bite.

4

Wounds were given every day . . .

W H E N Tasmin caught up with Pomp she saw to her dismay that there were tears in his eyes. He was fumbling with the rails that enclosed the small pasture where the captive animals grazed: three young elk, several deer, two antelope, four buffalo, and a clumsy young moose calf.

"Will you wait, please! You're not supposed to do that," Tasmin said, with some impatience; she was afraid the wound in his chest might open if he put himself to any strain. But when she saw the tears she regretted her tone.

"Mr. Stewart's dead," Pomp reminded her. "There's no use keeping these animals penned up any longer—they won't be going off to Scotland."

Of course, Pomp was right. Drummond Stewart's frightened horse had carried him right into the invading Utes, where he was immediately killed. The animals he had collected might as well be let go, but dismantling fences was not something Pomp needed to be doing when he was so weak he could barely walk.

Pomp meekly stepped back and let Tasmin take over—it took only a few minutes for her to scatter the light railing that had been keeping the animals in. Two fawns came over and nuzzled Pomp expectantly—sometimes he fed them tidbits, but he had

nothing with him today. His own weakness surprised him—he
had scarcely walked fifty yards, and yet, on the return, had Tasmin not half carried him, he would have had to sit down and
rest.

Wounds were given every day in the West, and yet Pomp himself had never before suffered so much as a scratch; the fevers,
pneumonias, and other ailments that carried off so many, including his mother, had so far spared him. He knew, of course, that
the Ute's arrow had just missed his heart, and that he was lucky
to be alive, and yet he was shocked at how completely he
seemed to have lost his strength. His legs wobbled—they never
had before. His breathing was shallow—he felt unable to get
enough air. He doubted whether he could draw a bow or lift a
gun—and yet, only two weeks earlier, he had won two wrestling
matches, beating Kit Carson easily and even outlasting the wiry
Jim Bridger.

Pomp could tell, from Tasmin's silence, that she was rather
vexed with him; but she stuck with her task and got him back to
the pallet. He tried to smile at her, but even his facial muscles
seemed tired.

"I'm going to insist that you mind me, and mind me strictly,
for the next few days," Tasmin said briskly. She had been not only
vexed but scared: Pomp's face was ashen—he looked again as
though he might die. Fortunately, once he was on the pallet, his
color soon improved. Tasmin ceased to be quite so afraid.

"I'm sorry," Pomp said. "I've never been sick before. I guess I
don't know how it's done."

"Obey your nurse, that's how it's done," Tasmin said, though
his apology caused her to feel less angry. She herself had always
enjoyed splendid health; she had never been sick either; but she
had borne a child, at the end of a long labor, and she too had
been surprised at how exceedingly weak the effort left her—she
could at first barely hold her own babe, and it was several days
before she could walk confidently across a room.

"In a week I'm sure you'll be fine," she told him. "Just don't
rush things."

Pomp's tears had spilled over—there were tear tracks on his face which Tasmin longed to wipe away; and yet, for a moment, she didn't. Pomp might take it wrong—indeed, it might *be* wrong, inasmuch as she was a married woman. One touch, in her experience, was apt to lead to another. She felt somewhat perturbed—why had this question even entered her thoughts?

Pomp seemed sobered from his close brush with death.

"If it hadn't been for you and my mother—and of course, Father Geoff—I'd be as dead as Mr. Stewart," he said.

"Your mother?" Tasmin asked in surprise.

Pomp looked abashed—he rarely spoke of his mother, and in fact had few memories to expose. And yet he felt Tasmin might understand.

"My mother comes to me sometimes in dreams," he confessed. "She gives me advice."

Tasmin waited—it seemed he might consider that what he was revealing was too private.

"In the fever I felt like I was flying," Pomp said. "But then my mother would come and I'd come down."

"What did your mother advise, in this instance, if I may ask?" Tasmin asked.

"She called you 'the woman who whispers,'" Pomp said. Weary, he had slumped against Tasmin's shoulder.

"I was whispering to you, trying to keep you alive," Tasmin told him. "I whispered and your mother advised, and it worked, you see: you're alive, though you certainly caused us both a good deal of worry."

"I was only seven when my mother died," Pomp said. "I didn't know her very long."

Then he gave Tasmin a sweet, dependent look.

"Where's Jimmy?" he asked, as if just remembering that Tasmin had a husband.

Tasmin shrugged.

"Gone on a scout, and he took Kit with him, which is annoying," she told him. "Kit Carson is a very obliging fellow—I can always put him to good use."

"It's because he's in love with you that he's obliging," Pomp remarked. "Nobody else can get him to do a thing."

Then he looked at her again.

"I hope I can know you for a long time," he told her quietly.

"I hope so too," Tasmin said. She looked for their water basin but it was not to be seen, so Tasmin quickly licked a finger and wiped the dusty tear tracks off Pomp's cheeks.

"Hold still, mind your nurse, it's just a little spit," Tasmin told him. It was a small thing, quickly done, but very pleasing to her, the briefest intimacy, which Pomp accepted, though his mind was elsewhere.

"I'm more apt to cry for animals than for people," he said.

Yes, they're trusting, like you, Tasmin thought. The spittle had done no real good; Pomp's cheeks were still a dusty smear, so she jumped up, hurried to the tent, and returned with the wash-basin, so she could wash her young man properly—for already, in her mind, she thought of Pomp Charbonneau as hers—though exactly in what *sense* he was hers, she could not yet say.

5

Besides the mule, there was Jim.

"YOU'VE got longer legs than me—you'd be fine on this tall mule," Kit suggested.

"I'm fine enough on Joe Walker's mare," Jim informed him. It struck him as curious that he and Kit got along perfectly well when they were part of a big encampment but could not manage to advance even five miles without quarreling when they were alone. They had hardly left the Valley of the Chickens before Kit had started insisting that they trade mounts, a suggestion that Jim ignored. Joe Walker himself had warned Kit about the tall, ornery mule, but Kit had chosen him anyway. Jim himself was quite comfortably mounted on the same little mare that had carried him so smoothly, in the winter past, from the Knife River to the Green, a feat so singular that now all the mountain men coveted the little bay mare.

Jim did not expect to do anything particularly challenging on this scout with Kit; he mainly wanted to have a look at some of the Platte River country before attempting to lead the Berrybender party to Santa Fe. What he didn't need was for Kit Carson—the scout with the keenest eyesight of any mountain man and thus a valuable asset if one were traveling in the lands of the Sioux—to start complaining about his mount before they had even been a week on the trail.

"I'll give you a dollar if you'll trade," Kit said. He had chosen the mule mainly because it was tall—it pleased him to tower over Jim Snow when they rode; Jim, of course, towered over him when they were afoot. The big mule's trot was so rough that it had already caused Kit to bite his tongue. They had a vast amount of country to explore; Kit didn't relish the thought of exploring it on a mule whose trot was a threat to his tongue.

Besides the mule, there was Jim. In camp with the other boys, Jim—though prone to moods—was fairly easygoing. He didn't feel that he had to work every minute—he might laze around with his beautiful wife and his chubby little boy; or he might listen to Hugh Glass tell lies. Jim didn't yarn much himself, but he liked to listen to yarns. But the minute the two of them started to go somewhere, even if it was just a moose hunt in the Assiniboine country, Jim Snow became a demon, relentless and unyielding in his aims. He seemed determined to travel far faster than the accepted norm—fifty miles a day was nothing to Jim, though it represented intolerably rapid travel for a man handicapped by a stiff-gaited mule.

"A dollar's as high as I'll go for a switch," Kit said, annoyed that Jim had ignored what he felt was a reasonable, even a generous offer.

"No thanks, I'm comfortable," Jim replied. "You'll just have to put up with that mule until something better comes along."

"How could anything better come along, when we're out here in the middle of nowhere?" Kit asked, vexed but trying not to let it show.

Jim shrugged. "The Sioux and the Pawnee have plenty of horses," he remarked. "If we run into some friendly Indians, maybe you could trade."

"No, if we run into any Indians they won't be friendly—they'll kill us and take *our* horses," Kit replied. On a scout his outlook was invariably pessimistic, besides which he was still bitterly jealous of the fact that Tasmin had married Jim—in Kit's view the only possible explanation for that union was that Jim was tall. He was unlikely to shrink, either.

"I wouldn't have picked this mule if we hadn't left in such a hurry," Kit pointed out. "You didn't even tell your own wife good-bye, which is rude behavior, in my book."

"She was trying to save Pomp—I hope she saved him," Jim replied. "If I'd told her I was leaving she'd just argue—she always argues when I decide to go someplace. If Tasmin had to take time off to fuss, she might have lost Pomp, and that wouldn't be good.

"When it's time to go, it's better just to go," he added.

Kit's patience, already sorely tried, was further exacerbated by this reply. If he were married to Tasmin he would certainly take the trouble to say good-bye when he left.

"What would it take to get you to switch mounts, you fool!" Kit asked, in hot exasperation.

"Stop pestering me—I ain't switching," Jim said. He glanced at Kit and saw that he was swollen up like a Tom turkey. If they had been on the ground a fistfight would have been hard to avoid, but fortunately, they were mounted. Jim put his heels into the lit-tle mare, who had an easy lope, and went on ahead.

Kit's mule, unlike the mare, lacked an easy lope—in fact, had no true lope at all; he seemed to possess only three gaits, rather than the usual four, though it was true that he could sometimes be coaxed into a gait that was just short of a dead run—a "high lope" was what Joe Walker called it. It was difficult to get the mule, whose name was Brantly, into this high lope, and even more difficult, once he was in it, to keep him from accelerating into a dead run—so the high lope had almost no practical value. The hard trot was Brantly's preferred gait, the very mode of travel that had already caused Kit to bite his tongue.

Now there went Jim, loping off on his little mare, as comfort-able as if he were rocking in a hammock. Kit reminded himself again that he was a fool ever to travel with Jim Snow, since when he did, he invariably got the worst of it. Annoyed, he deliberately held Brantly to a slow, stately walk, which meant that Jim Snow was soon little more than a dot on the prairie, so far ahead that he could be of no use at all if an emergency arose.

Then Jim ceased to be visible, even as a distant dot—Kit was alone on the great gray plain, just the kind of circumstance in which his pessimism was apt to get the better of him. First he might just feel generally low; then he would begin to imagine various ways in which death might come, in which regard Indians usually came to mind first and grizzly bears second. Indians were so good at hiding that they could be hard to spot even on a bare plain: up they'd jump, with their lances and hatchets, and be on him before he could even spur his mule. Grizzly bears too were wily stalkers, able to creep within a few feet of their unsuspecting prey. Kit didn't suppose that his renowned ability to see farther than anyone else would be much help to him in a crisis, since crises usually happened close to hand. Though it pained Kit to admit it, Jim Snow had superior instincts when it came to sensing trouble, and he was very quick to act. After all, it had been Jim who killed the Indian who had wounded Pomp—killed him so cleanly that the man had not had time to yell for reinforcements.

So now what had Jim done? He had ridden off and left Kit aboard a mule nobody liked, with a gun that was unreliable. Kit was about to put Brantly in a high lope, in an effort to catch up, when—as if to prove his point—the old Indian appeared. One moment the plain was empty, and the next minute there the man was, standing over what appeared to be a dead horse. A swell of the prairie had concealed him. Kit grabbed his rifle but then realized the Indian was only old Greasy Lake, a harmless prophet who was apt to show up anywhere there was a gathering of any size, in hopes of delivering a prophecy or two in exchange for presents. Faintly, over the prairie breeze, Kit could hear the old man chanting. He spread his arms to the heavens and shuffled around the horse, which turned out to be not quite dead after all. Now and then Kit saw the horse raise his head, though it made no move to get up. The horse, if it was Greasy Lake's same old nag, was as famous in prairie circles as its master. Mountain men who had first seen the animal twenty-five years earlier and had not supposed it could last a week were astonished to discover that the spavined old nag still hadn't died. Efforts to figure out how old the horse might be revealed only that it had very good teeth for an animal that had been alive so long.

Kit thought he might as well investigate—it was better than riding on alone, thinking gloomy thoughts. At first Greasy Lake, who, as usual, was in a kind of trance, paid no attention to Kit at all. He was rattling some kind of rattle as he chanted and shuffled. Kit politely drew rein; he didn't want to interrupt a religious ceremony. Perhaps Greasy Lake was singing his trusty mount a death song—giving him a proper send-off. To Kit's astonishment the old horse twitched an ear, lifted its head, and slowly got to its feet. Greasy Lake at once stopped chanting. He tucked his rattle into a little pouch he carried and got ready to mount his horse.

"I wouldn't do that, Greasy," Kit advised. "That horse will die for sure if you put any weight on him."

"He's a strong horse," Greasy Lake assured him. "I just have to sing to him in the mornings, to get him up. He's a horse who likes to sleep late."

"That horse is older than me," Kit replied.

The horse did shiver a bit when Greasy Lake climbed on top of him, but no longer seemed to be about to die.

"That horse beats all," Kit remarked. "If I thought he had a year left in him I'd trade for him and let you have this expensive mule."

Greasy Lake ignored that remark—he was not such a fool as to trade for a stiff-gaited mule. It annoyed Kit that he had chosen a mule that not even this old prophet would take. No one had ever been able to pin down quite what tribe Greasy Lake belonged to—his age, like his horse's, was also hard to calculate. He claimed to be the cousin of various powerful chiefs, but no one could be sure of the truth of anything he said. Because it was his habit to wander constantly over the West, he was known to everyone, from the Columbia River to the Rio Grande. No tribe claimed him, yet no tribe turned him away.

"Where are you bound for now?" Kit asked—at least the old fellow was usually good for a little conversation.

"I am on my way to see the Partezon—he is my cousin," Greasy Lake replied. "He doesn't like me but I don't think he'll kill me."

The Partezon, war chief of the Brulé Sioux, was the most feared Indian in the West. It was the Partezon who had destroyed the steamboat the Berrybenders had been traveling on, once it got stuck in the ice above the Knife River. Fortunately Jim Snow had led most of the party overland to Pierre Boisdeffre's trading post on the Yellowstone, but Captain George Aitken, several passengers, and a number of *engagés* had been cruelly butchered up.

"I've heard that old Partezon's mean," Kit said.

"He is not friendly," Greasy Lake admitted. "But now I am on my way to look for some white people who can fly. All the tribes are looking for them. I am going to see the Partezon to see if he knows about these flying men. They fly in a little basket attached to some kind of cloud."

Kit wanted to laugh—white people couldn't fly. Probably the old prophet had gone a little daft.

"I've never seen a white person who could fly," he remarked. "Where are these fellows supposed to be?"

"They are flying over the Platte," Greasy Lake said. "If we watch we might see them."

"How close are we to the Partezon's camp?" Kit asked—even mention of the old warrior's name caused the prairies to take on an aspect of menace—and now Jim Snow was nowhere to be seen.

"The Partezon is always moving," Greasy Lake said vaguely. "He may have gone to see the Bad Eye, to ask him to make a spell that will cause these flying white people to fall out of the sky."

Kit had never seen the Bad Eye, an old, huge, gross shaman of the Gros Ventres—he lived near the Missouri River, in a dwelling called the Skull Lodge, the whole top of which was covered with buffalo skulls. Blind from birth, the Bad Eye was said to have hearing so acute that he could identify different kinds of flies just by their buzzing. He was now so fat that he could no longer stand up; when he needed information about some distant happening, he relied on a dark woman named Draga, thought to be a powerful witch and known to be a cruel torturer who had sent many captives to painful deaths, pouring boiling water over them in a mockery of baptism if they were priests, or draping them in ringlets of white-hot hatchets if they were traders who had not been judicious in the distribution of gifts. Bess Berrybender had briefly been Draga's captive and had suffered many cruelties before she could be ransomed.

Kit hardly knew what to believe about this story of the flying white men—it sounded like a wild lie, but he was experienced enough in the ways of the wilderness to know that it was unwise to entirely disregard the ravings of old prophets, a few of whom actually had powers whites didn't possess. When they were camped in the Valley of the Chickens, the Berrybenders still had their old parrot, Prince Talleyrand, who muttered a few words in the German language one day while Greasy Lake was within hearing. Greasy Lake had announced to all the mountain men that the old bird would be dead within the week. Sure enough, less than a week later, a Ute warrior, come to trade, showed up with the head of Prince Talleyrand, which he said he found under a tree—a badger had evidently carried off the rest of the tough old bird.

The fact that Greasy Lake had predicted the demise of the parrot so accurately convinced Kit that he ought to think twice before rejecting the old man's prophecies. It occurred to him, as he walked Brantly slowly along beside the old man's decrepit horse, that there could even be something to this rumor of white men who could fly. He had forgotten about balloons. He himself, in his last visit to Saint Louis, had attended a kind of fair in which a magician of some sort went quite a ways up in the air beneath a hot-air balloon. The balloon went higher than any church steeple in town, but the trick had ended badly when a wind came up and blew the balloonist over toward the Mississippi; when the man finally descended, he plopped straight down into the mudflats and emerged covered with mud. Nonetheless he *had* flown, riding beneath the balloon in a basket of some sort. Greasy Lake, not being a city dweller, had never witnessed a balloon ascent—what he took to be a cloud was probably the balloon itself, but of course that didn't explain why people with the ability to make a balloon go up would want to fly it over the Partezon's country, where there could be few paying customers and a fair chance of being subjected to serious tortures. Could the balloon have been blown off course, as in the case of the Saint Louis magician? After all, a flying basket with some silk puffed up above it could not be particularly easy to control. Maybe the balloonist had had the bad luck to be blown into the Partezon's hunting territory.

One result of having to think all this through for himself was that Kit became even more annoyed with Jim Snow for leaving just at a time when two heads might have been better than one.

"Aren't you with the Sin Killer? I thought I saw the tracks of that little mare of his yesterday," Greasy Lake inquired.

"I was with him, but he's gone off—we'll be lucky if we catch up with him in a week," Kit said.

He had no sooner said it than he was made to feel foolish—Greasy Lake was pointing at something.

"I don't think it will take that long," he said. "Isn't that him skinning an antelope, over by those rocks? He must have killed the antelope with an arrow. I didn't hear a shot."

Sure enough, there was Jim, plain as day—Kit had been looking in every direction but the right one.

"It looks like a young antelope—young and tender. We'll have a good supper," Greasy Lake said.

Of course, it was just like this old rascal to invite himself to the feast—Kit supposed Jim would be annoyed when presented with a guest.

"There's some men out here flying—I suspect they've got a hot-air balloon," Kit blurted, when they arrived. He hoped this startling news would distract Jim from the fact that he had arrived with an uninvited guest.

But Jim Snow, to Kit's surprise, smiled at the old shaman.

"Get down, Uncle, and rest your horse," he said. "We got fresh meat."

The remark stumped Kit completely. He had seen Jim chatting with the old fellow once or twice when they were camped at the rendezvous, but had never supposed Jim was *that* friendly with him.

"How'd he get to be your uncle?" Kit asked, when he dismounted.

"He kept me from starving when I was with the Osage," Jim told him. "So I adopted him, once I got grown."

"I never knew that," Kit said, in a reproachful tone.

"No, but I could fill a barrel with things you don't know," Jim remarked.

"Your friend almost rode past me," Greasy Lake said. "My horse was laying down at the time."

"He's got good eyesight but sometimes he don't pay attention," Jim allowed, with some amusement in his look. "He could be building a fire right now, so we could cook this meat, but I guess he's feeling sleepy because I don't see no fire."

"I just got here," Kit pointed out, annoyed. Jim Snow was every bit as bad as his sometime tent mate Jim Bridger; both of them seemed to feel that he had been put on earth expressly to do their chores.

Greasy Lake was not listening to this irritating palaver. He was giving the antelope skin a close examination.

"I can use this skin, if you don't need it," he said. "My old pouch is wearing out. I could make a nice new one with this good piece of skin."

Kit looked around at the bare prairie—he was beginning to wish he had had the good sense to stay with the big group in the Valley of the Chickens, where he would at least have had the beautiful Tasmin to look at. His gloomy feeling was getting worse—there was Jim Snow, an unbending kind of fellow, expecting him to build a fire in a place where there were very few sticks lying around. Of course, there were quite a few buffalo chips, but they yielded a poor grade of fuel, in his view.

"Greasy's off to see the Partezon," Kit informed Jim.

But Jim, still busy with his butchering, didn't seem to hear, so Kit, in a lonely mood, took a sack and wandered off to see if he could collect the makings of a fire.

6

The day had begun hopefully, too.

B ENJAMIN H OPE - T IPPING , tall and thin, did not much like the looks of the old Indian on the white horse, the one their interpreter, the youth Amboise d'Avigdor, insisted was the dreaded Partezon. Ben looked at his colleague, Clam de Paty, a man who usually bubbled over with French witticisms; he saw that Clam was not bubbling at the moment. And the boy Amboise was plainly terrified.

The day had begun hopefully, too. Clam, something of a dandy, put on his red pants; they had each had a snort of cognac to wake themselves up. Amboise d'Avigdor, a skilled chef, had poached them several plovers' eggs, which they had with bacon and some of the flat bread Amboise baked in profusion whenever they were stopped long enough to allow him to construct a Dutch oven. A fine breeze was blowing, which helped with the gnats and mosquitoes. For a time he and Clam, each on their old palfreys, had ridden along happily, composing articles in their heads for their respective newspapers. Ben Hope-Tipping had just been composing a few paragraphs about hominy, a dish not then known in Europe; whereas Clam, who had been kept awake part of the night by the roaring of buffalo bulls from a herd of many thousands nearby their camp, was attempting to describe, for his Parisian readership, what the roaring of these bulls, angry in their rut, sounded like on a prairie summer night. The two of them discussed whether it might be worthwhile to include a few notes about burial scaffolds—European readers were always apt to be interested in the burial customs of savage peoples.

Their balloon and all their gear was stored efficiently in a small wagon, driven by Amboise d'Avigdor, who, in the weeks they had been traveling, had become an expert packer. If one of the surly wagon horses didn't kick him, Amboise could have the wagon packed and ready in a commendably short time. Of course, one reason Amboise could have the wagon packed in such a short time was that he had become increasingly reluctant to unpack anything at night. They had scarcely left Plattesmouth when Amboise began to argue against the necessity of linen tablecloths and other common amenities, matters which Ben and Clam had long been in the habit of taking for granted.

"No, messieurs, tablecloths are quite unnecessary out here," Amboise informed them, on only the second day out. "Quite unnecessary. Nothing is more likely to cause savages to attack than the sight of a white tablecloth."

"Surely you jest, monsieur," Clam had remonstrated—he hardly proposed to abandon the habits of a lifetime, one of which was to dine off white tablecloths—because of the whims of savages. Liberties might be permitted at breakfast, but dinner, to a Frenchman, was a sacrament.

"I fear I am unwilling to go native quite to that extent," Clam went on, giving young Amboise a look of such severity that Ben Hope-Tipping supposed the matter to be at an end. He himself felt the same extreme unwillingness to lower his standards, which were no more than the standards of any proper civilization. He was not about to betray his convictions by rashly dispensing with tablecloths.

Nonetheless, Amboise d'Avigdor soon had his way, dropping, as they plodded along, whatever linen he felt disposed to dispense with off the back of the wagon; by the time Ben and Clam discovered this treachery, the tablecloths were gone and many of the heavy napkins as well.

"No napkins—we should kill this boy!" the indignant Clam exclaimed. "How does he suppose we are to wipe our faces?"

"Patience, Clam—I don't think we should kill him just *now*, just *here!*" Ben argued. They were in the middle of a vast prairie, hundreds of miles from any settlement. Matters were inconvenient enough, what with the flies and mosquitoes, and no tablecloths and few napkins; but it was certain that matters would be even more inconvenient if they lost Amboise. They were, at present, in no position to dismiss, much less execute, an insubordinate servant, vexing as the silly creature undoubtedly was.

The necessity of somehow tolerating Amboise d'Avigdor was almost immediately driven home to the two Europeans—Amboise himself being Canadian—by the abrupt and quite menacing arrival of the Partezon and his highly painted band. A Brulé Sioux named Hollow Foot, returning from a vision quest, had happened to notice a trail of white cloths on the prairie. Hollow Foot had hastened over to the Partezon's village to inform him of this phenomenon. The Partezon, who considered it his duty to protect the Holy Road—to the whites merely the route along the Platte—was not indifferent to this information. In fact he gave Hollow Foot a nice young wife, for being so good as to make a prompt report. The Partezon paused only long enough to allow his young warriors to paint themselves appropriately. He himself rarely bothered with paint now, but he was happy enough that the boys of the tribe kept to the old traditions.

Even without the trail of white cloths it was a simple matter to track and overtake the travelers, who were possessed of a slow, heavy cart whose tracks were easily followed. When the Sioux spotted the three travelers, the young warriors wanted to race down and hack them to pieces—it seemed to the Partezon that half his energies as a leader were needed just to restrain the young. Being young, they had little patience with well-planned ambushes or mature battle plans. The young just wanted to strike, and would have under a lesser war chief; but when the

Partezon rode with them, they behaved themselves; he had demonstrated many times that he meant to have obedience. Riding with the Partezon was the greatest honor a Sioux warrior could have, but it was also an honor that could be quickly withdrawn.

The fact that thirty savages seemingly popped out of nowhere and surrounded them came as a considerable shock both to Ben Hope-Tipping and to Clam de Paty. The shock did not serve to increase their already shaky confidence in their interpreter, young Amboise d'Avigdor.

"I thought you were supposed to know how to deal with Indians," Hope-Tipping complained, once it became evident that the red men in the war paint were not going to allow them to advance another inch.

"Well, I do possess some expertise," Amboise said. "I know, for example, that these men are Brulé Sioux and that their leader—that's the man on the white horse—is the dreaded Partezon."

"Still, it's quite rude of him to arrive unannounced," Ben pressed. "He seems unwilling to let us pass—why is that? Free country, America, I was led to believe."

"I suppose they've merely come for their presents," Clam de Paty remarked. "Give them a few fishhooks and a few handfuls of beads."

"Yes, quite—that should make them happy," Ben said.

"It *won't* make them happy, monsieur," Amboise remarked, emphatically.

"But why not? They're excellent beads and very effective fishhooks," Ben insisted. "I caught a fish with one of them myself."

"Don't you remember, messieurs, what I told you about the Partezon—he's not your ordinary savage," Amboise insisted.

"Oh, do remind me," Ben allowed.

"Remind *us*," Clam put in. "What's so special about this old fellow?"

"He's the one who sewed Lord Berrybender's butler into a buffalo, chopping off his feet when they extruded," Amboise reminded them.

"Oh, so he's *that* rascal—very regrettable incident," Ben remarked. He and Clam had heard the story of Lord Berrybender's unfortunate butler many times—it was a staple of saloon conversation as far east as Cincinnati. Evidently the valet, Gladwyn, thought to be of Welsh descent, had been left behind on a hunt. He survived the chill of a prairie blizzard by huddling near a dying buffalo cow—when some natives, Sans Arcs in this case, discovered the man, he was so covered with buffalo blood that the foolish natives, in their innocence, supposed that the cow had actually given birth to him. For a time this notion was accepted and the Welsh valet had become a kind of village god; but there were doubters, one of whom was the Partezon, who ordered a buffalo cow to be killed, into whose belly the unfortunate valet was promptly sewn. The Partezon reasoned that if the man were a god he could easily slip out again, but of course he was merely Lord Albany Berrybender's butler, and he couldn't slip out, and in any case was soon dying from loss of blood.

Ben and Clam had discussed this terrible incident many times, agreeing that the fault lay mainly with Lord Berrybender, for being casual with his servants. No responsible Englishman would have left a well-trained valet out all night in such uncertain weather.

"So that's the brute, is it?" Ben said, squinting at the Partezon. He was beginning to feel distinctly nervous.

"If he doesn't want presents, what *does* the gentleman want?" Clam de Paty inquired. "We can't stop here forever."

Clam de Paty had his full share of Gallic impatience—lengthy negotiations with savages put him in a sulky temper.

"But we *might* stay here forever, because he might kill us," Amboise informed them, in a shaky voice. "You see, he *wants* to kill us, probably after a session of fiendish torture."

"Now, now, young man, really," Ben told him. "Neither Clam nor I are in any mood to be tortured this morning. Please tell Mr. Partezon that."

"I dare not! It will make it worse!" Amboise insisted.

What a vexation this will be to our employers, if we succumb,

Ben thought. Many of the warriors simply bristled with edged weapons—lances, hatchets, arrows. Their own weapons, two rifles and a fowling piece, were safely tucked away in the wagon, their precise location known only to Amboise d'Avigdor.

"We must use the balloon," Clam said.

He turned to Amboise.

"Tell them we can fly," he said. "They won't expect to hear it—and besides, it's true."

Amboise d'Avigdor did as instructed. The Partezon remained unmoved, but a great hubbub arose among the warriors.

"That's a handy thought, Clam," Ben remarked. "I suppose we had best unpack our balloon."

"When white people are cornered they'll say anything," the Partezon said, addressing himself to old Fool's Bull, a warrior with much experience.

"Sans Arcs made fools of themselves by claiming that little white man came out of a buffalo," Fool's Bull reminded him. "You and I knew better, of course."

"Do you think these white men can fly?" the Partezon asked.

"Of course not," Fool's Bull said. "Don't be toying with me. I am not a Sans Arc."

The Partezon instructed the young interpreter to tell the two men to go ahead and fly, if they wanted to. Amboise explained that it would be necessary to build a fire first, and unpack a certain amount of equipment.

"They want to warm up their wings," the Partezon remarked to Fool's Bull, who shrugged.

"We need to build a fire anyway, in order to torture them," Fool's Bull said. "Let them build it, if they want to."

"I am not going to torture them here—we'll do that in the camp," the Partezon said. "The people will be annoyed if we don't provide a captive or two. It's selfish to torture them all by ourselves, though I suppose we might singe them a little."

"Okay, I wash my hands of it," Fool's Bull said. "Do as you please—you always do anyway."

"Don't be so cranky," the Partezon said.

While the young interpreter built a good fire the other white men unpacked a kind of vast blanket from the wagon and spread it on the ground, tying it to a kind of basket with several ropes. It amused the Partezon to see what desperate stratagems white people came up with when they were in trouble, though claiming the ability to fly was a new one to him.

Ben and Clam did not allow young Amboise to help with their balloon. Amboise was always ripping things. Ben and Clam—internationally recognized balloon journalists—could not afford mistakes; a leaky balloon meant no end of trouble. They got out their bellows and prepared to inflate their balloon, watched by the curious Indians.

Though the Partezon didn't like whites and didn't want his people to be corrupted by a dependence on the various goods they produced, he recognized that the whites were very ingenious when it came to tools and gadgets. Their weapons were excellent. He himself had a fine rifle that he had taken off a dead captain, but he rarely shot it, or even showed it, lest his people become dependent on the gun and lose their high skill with the bow—a skill that was essential if they were to continue in the old ways, the ways of their fathers, who had flourished with no reliance on white men's goods.

To the Partezon's surprise, the whites didn't make their fire on the ground—they made it in a kind of metal pot—then, using some kind of bellows, they began to pump hot air into the great silk blanket they had spread on the ground. To the consternation of the young warriors, the cloth began to swell, moving as if a great beast of some kind were inside it. This unexpected development frightened some of the young men considerably, but the Partezon gave them a stern look.

The white men pumped and pumped until gradually the great silk cloth assumed a kind of round shape and began to rise off the prairie—it reminded the Partezon a little of the floats boys sometimes made from buffalo bladders, floats they clung to as they frolicked in the river.

But the great sphere that was rising above the white man's

basket was no small float. Suddenly a great air beast of some kind had risen above them, tethered, for the moment, to some stakes the whites had driven into the ground.

The young warriors were becoming very nervous. What if a great bird emerged and tried to carry them away? The Partezon looked at them with contempt, but he didn't speak. If the boys were such cowards, then let them go—he would deal with them later.

Soon the great air beast was straining at the ropes that held it.

"I believe we're ready," Clam said, checking the lines that tied the balloon to the basket.

"We're ready," Ben agreed. "Do try to keep us in sight, Amboise—we'll hope to alight somewhere beside this river."

But Amboise d'Avigdor was shaking and shivering.

"You wouldn't leave me, would you, sir?" he asked Ben. "I won't last long, if you do. I feel quite sure the Partezon will kill me most painfully, if I'm left."

"Nonsense," Ben said firmly—at such times firmness was always the best policy. The young fellow merely needed to buck up.

"Now, now, none of that," Clam said. "Someone has to bring the wagon and lead our palfreys. And that, after all, is your job, my boy."

"Besides, the basket only holds two, plus a few provisions, of course," Ben reminded the terrified interpreter.

Amboise d'Avigdor, seeing that the case was hopeless, said no more. His masters, the Englishman and the Frenchman, clambered into their basket and gestured to him to unloose the ropes that kept the balloon pegged to its stakes. Amboise, moving like the dead man he now considered himself to be, did as directed—performing a last duty, as he saw it.

As soon as it was released the balloon rose gracefully, fifty feet, a hundred feet, higher and higher.

This was too much for the young warriors of the Brulé Sioux, convinced that a great bird would soon swoop down on them, ignoring the wagon filled with treasures, ignoring Amboise d'Avigdor, even ignoring the Partezon.

Only the Partezon and old Fool's Bull held their ground. Soon they could barely see the faces of the two men in the basket. More from curiosity than anger the Partezon notched an arrow and shot it at the two men in the basket. His strength with the bow had always been legendary among the People—he could drive an arrow completely through a running buffalo if he chose; this time he used his full strength, yet his arrow barely reached the basket, high above them. It hung for a moment and then fell back to earth.

"The time of the People is over," the Partezon said, to Fool's Bull. In his heart he felt bitter chagrin. His lifelong discipline and rigor, all his efforts to protect the People from a weakening dependence on the white man's goods, would now be for naught. The white men, in this instance, had not made a false claim: they said they could fly and they were flying. He had been looking forward to a jolly time, torturing the two flyers and the young man too, but in the face of what he had just seen, it all seemed pointless. The white men, after all, were superior, not in heart but in invention. Many of the People were brave, but none of them could fly.

The balloon, now very high, rode the strong wind that was blowing from the east—already the two flyers were well on their way toward the setting sun. The great air beast was moving through the sky, it seemed to Fool's Bull, almost as fast as the great geese moved. Soon the balloon would be out of sight.

"I don't know why you think the time of the People is over," Fool's Bull said, though without much conviction. "It's just two men."

"Oh, there will be some battles yet," the Partezon told him. "We will win some and the whites will win some. But we can't fly, and they can. Who do you think will win in the end? They can rain down fire on our villages—maybe they could even run off the buffalo."

Amboise d'Avigdor scarcely dared move. All the young Sioux had run away—only the two old men remained, but one of the old men was the Partezon. It seemed to Amboise that if he could just stay still enough, he might be allowed to live, after all. He stood as if planted; he tried not to shake; he even took care to breathe quietly.

The Partezon dismounted and picked up his arrow. It seemed to Fool's Bull that he looked older; he looked as some warriors looked when suddenly faced with defeat.

"Do you want me to kill this boy?" Fool's Bull asked. "We could take him—it could be someone to torture."

The Partezon shook his head. He had no interest in the trembling boy, who probably would not last an hour under torture anyway. He had not yet recovered from the shock of seeing the white men fly—what it meant was that the time for idle amusements was over. If the People were to enjoy much more time as free men, certain steps needed to be taken at once, steps that were much more important than torturing a sniveling white boy.

Though reluctant to ignore such an easy victim, Fool's Bull felt it was not the right time to argue with the Partezon, who, no doubt, was disgusted by the cowardice of the young warriors. In such a mood he would not brook argument—he would probably just kill anyone who annoyed him at such a difficult moment.

And yet, Fool's Bull had a fearful feeling—when he was fearful it was hard for him to hold his tongue.

"What will we do?" he asked, in his uncertainty.

The Partezon knew exactly what he wanted to do next—it was something he had had in mind to do ten years earlier but, for various reasons, had delayed.

"We are going to attack the Mandans and the Rees," the Partezon told him firmly. These were the tribes that controlled the Missouri River—they were the tribes that had encouraged the whites to come, bring trade goods, take away furs.

"They are rich and corrupt, those tribes," he went on. "They want all the things the white men bring—guns, cloth, beads, tobacco, whiskey. It's because of them that so many white men came up the river. I should have destroyed both tribes long ago."

It was clear to the Partezon now how he had erred. Foolishly he had let the white men have the river, supposing they would be satisfied with the peltries they got from these weak tribes, these corn Indians, farmers and traders. He had believed the whites would be satisfied with this safe trade and not bother challenging the stronger tribes of the interior—the tribes whose lands two white men were at this very moment flying over. His calculation had been wrong to begin with: even now the whites were trapping in the lands of the Utes and the Shoshones; eventually they would even be strong enough to challenge the Blackfeet. The truth the Partezon now had to face was that the whites were not going to be satisfied until they had all the People's land. They would not be satisfied with the beaver; when those were gone they would want the buffalo. They would want everything—the rivers, the holy mountains, everything. Even now two whites were directing their air beast directly into the heart of his own country. There were only two, at the moment, but there would be more.

Fool's Bull was startled by the Partezon's statement, though he wasn't disturbed at the prospect of war with the Mandans or the Rees, who had long been trading Indians. They didn't produce many good warriors—and yet the thought of attacking the Mandans particularly made him nervous, not from fear of their warriors but from fear of the Bad Eye, the most powerful prophet in the West, a terrible man whose prophecies, some said, could cause earthquakes and floods. There were even some who believed the Bad Eye had the power to raise the dead. What if the Bad Eye summoned an army of skeleton warriors to stand against the Sioux? Even the Partezon, who feared nothing, might quail if he saw an army of skeletons rising out of the earth to fight against him.

"I'm worried about the Bad Eye," Fool's Bull admitted.

"He's blind and he's fat—they say he can no longer stand up," the Partezon said. "Why worry about *him*?"

"Some say he can raise the dead," Fool's Bull reminded him.

The Partezon merely gave Fool's Bull a scornful look.

"Even if he can't raise the dead, he might make a bad prophecy," Fool's Bull insisted.

"If he does, it will be his last prophecy," the Partezon replied. "He can't raise the dead but he might join them."

Amboise d'Avigdor didn't dare move until the two old Indians were almost out of sight. His fear had been so great, his heart pounded so violently, that it was several minutes before he allowed himself to believe that he was safe. He saw his bosses' two gray palfreys, grazing some distance away, and realized that—since he *was* alive—he had better get busy. Though the encounter with the Partezon had scared him out of his wits, there were his duties to attend to, if he didn't want to be cursed or even cuffed when his employers landed. Ben Hope-Tipping and Clam de Paty did not like to be kept waiting. There was cognac and cheese in the balloon's basket, but little else; his bosses would expect dinner when they landed—it occurred to Amboise that the two might drift so far away that he would be unable to find them before dark, a circumstance to be avoided if at all possible. A night without their amenities would make the two of them very angry indeed. And yet, what was the anger of two Europeans compared to the terror he had just faced? Whatever abuse his bosses might heap on him, it would be nothing compared to what the old Partezon might have done.

7

Below them lay the plains . . .

"I S A Y , Clam—handy thing, a balloon," Ben remarked, offering his companion a slice of cheese. Below them lay the plains, an endless expanse of gray grass.

"It startled those red fellows no end—got us out of a scrape," he added. "The dreaded Partezon was forced to turn tail. I believe I'll just write up our little encounter."

"I am already writing it up," Clam assured him, closing his notebook for a moment in order to better enjoy the cheese, which had come all the way from Paris. The tiff with the Partezon had been, in his view, merely a nuisance, the sort of thing that was only to be expected in an uncivilized country.

"Hardly know where we'll post our next reports," Ben worried. "Postal facilities rather scarce out here, I imagine."

So far, thanks to traffic along the rivers, the two journalists had been able to forward a steady stream of reports to their respective papers. In Cincinnati they had been feted; in Saint Louis they were able to interview the famous Captain William Clark himself, who gave them much useful instruction, showing them on his big map how to locate the famous Swamp of the Swans and other well-known points of interest. Their last report had been filed from Plattesmouth, which merely meant that they had handed their pages to a trapper who claimed to be headed downriver.

"I wonder if that trapper actually took our little write-ups all the way to Saint Louis," Ben said. "We didn't pay the fellow much. Wouldn't surprise me if he tossed them overboard. He couldn't read, you know—as illiterate as a pig."

"We have copies," Clam reminded him. "Our readers will get them someday. You should be keeping the lookout, Ben."

"Lookout for what?" Ben inquired. "I can see the Platte River, and lots of grass, but I don't for the moment see anything that could count as copy."

"You must keep the close lookout so we don't float over the people we need to interview," Clam reminded him firmly. He felt obliged to speak rather sharply: Hope-Tipping, though a good journalist in his way, could be at times a bit thick, making it necessary not merely to point out the obvious, but to repeat it frequently as well.

"The prince of Weid is here somewhere—I would like to speak to this prince and also to his hunter, Herr Dreidoppel, who is, I believe, from Alsace. Perhaps they will have seen the grizzly bears. Many people in Paris want to know about the grizzly bears."

"Of course—same's true of London," Ben remarked. "All the same, I hope it's this hunter who meets them, and not ourselves."

He peered down, happy to see that the plain below them seemed to be absent of bears.

"I've heard that the prince of Weid is not a particularly interesting fellow," Ben went on. "Thorough in his way, I suppose, but hardly notorious. We'd do better to find the Scotsman Drummond Stewart, or some rich fur trader like William Ashley, or, of course, the Berrybenders, my own countrymen. Rather hard to say where *they* might be.

"Lady Tasmin Berrybender is said to be a very great beauty," he went on. "And they have a rather prominent cellist with them, a Miss Venetia Kennet."

"May be, may be," Clam agreed. "But we must *find* these people before we can write them up. So far we are not finding anybody except these noisy red fellows—that is why you must keep the lookout."

"Of course I *will* look, as best I can," Ben assured his friend. "Shouldn't have indulged in that cognac, though."

"What's wrong with the cognac? I chose it myself," Clam said—he found that he had constantly to defend French taste against the rather slighting ways of the English.

"No insult intended, my man," Ben said at once. "It's just that when I drink and look down I become rather queasy. The stomach threatens to flop, at such moments."

Clam de Paty made no reply; he wore, as was often the case, a slightly aggrieved look.

"Things really are *so* distant in America," Ben continued. "I fear we still have hundreds of miles to go before we can expect to find these intrepid explorers you propose to write up."

"We should have questioned that old savage at more length," Clam suggested. "Asked him about the more popular tortures. People always like to read about tortures, wouldn't you agree?"

"I agree that people love reading about tortures," Ben allowed, "but I'm not sure it would have been wise to raise the subject of tortures with him—he might have been all too willing to give a practical demonstration. They did some rather shocking things to your Jesuits, I believe."

"Look, *les oiseaux!*" Clam said, suddenly pointing to a flock of very large birds, flapping toward them from the north.

"Why, so they are," Ben said. "What a pity our ornithological books are all in the wagon. What would you say they are, Clam? Herons, perhaps."

"Well, they have long, sharp beaks," Clam began, and then stopped. The birds were closer now, they were very large birds, and they were coming straight toward the balloon.

"Could they be cranes? They're said to be quite large, I believe," Ben said.

"Shoot them, they are going to hit the balloon," Clam said, in sudden panic. "Go down, go down!"

"The gun, I fear, is in the wagon," Ben reminded him, a second before these very large birds, unwilling to vary their course, plunged into the balloon and even into the basket. Great wings beat all around them. Two of the birds, striking the basket, evidently broke their necks and fell to earth. Some hit the balloon and managed a recovery, while two were actually stuck to the balloon, their beaks having penetrated the silk fabric.

"Let us descend at once, monsieur," Clam insisted.

"Oh, we're descending all right," Ben assured him—the two birds stuck to the balloon managed to free themselves and flew on, followed by an audible hiss of escaping air.

"Damnable creatures, why wouldn't they turn!" Clam yelled, his face red with fury.

"Doubt they expected to run into a balloon on their trip," Ben suggested.

"No, don't talk, steer!" Clam demanded. The balloon was deflating rapidly—already its shape had ceased to be spherical. Fortunately they were over the Platte River, broad and shallow at this point.

"We're going to land either with a thump or a splash," Ben declared. "I think on the whole I prefer the splash."

Fortunately, as the balloon descended, the unfortunate collision with the cranes, if that was what they had been, was balanced by a very helpful gust or two of wind, which allowed them to descend directly into the brown river. The splash, when it came, was a rather considerable one.

"There's something worth writing up, wouldn't you agree, Clam?" Ben Hope-Tipping asked, as the two of them waded out of the cold, shallow water. "Pioneering balloonists felled by whooping cranes—if that indeed is what they were. We'll be the envy of every ornithologist in the world, and not a few reporters."

"Also, my friend, I saved the cheese," Clam de Paty informed him. He held it high, in triumph, as they struggled toward the shore.

8

"If I had a wife as pretty as Tasmin . . ."

" I F I had a wife as pretty as Tasmin, I wouldn't be travel-ing as much as you do," Kit remarked to Jim.

They were stopped near the North Platte, considering whether they should go south for several days, to determine an easy route across to the south branch of the river. Greasy Lake ambled along, a mile or two back.

"You've never had a wife," Jim pointed out. "If you ever get one, then you can decide how much traveling you want to do."

"I almost married my little Josie last time I was in Santa Fe," Kit said, in his own defense. The girl he referred to, Josefina Jaramillo, was short but cheerful—she had let it be known, on more than one occasion, that she wouldn't object to a bit of courting from Kit.

"Isn't she the one you said was bossy?" Jim asked.

"She was a little bossy sometimes," Kit admitted.

"Do you think Tasmin's bossy?" Jim asked.

Kit felt trapped. He didn't want to speak ill of Tasmin, which would mean conceding a point to Jim Snow. The one thing all the trappers agreed on was that Tasmin Berrybender was the bossiest female any of them had ever encountered. When they had nothing better to discuss, the trappers often amused themselves by talking about how much Tasmin needed to be taken down a peg—all agreed that Jim Snow was not the man to accomplish this. Tasmin's bossiness had worked out well for Pomp Charbonneau, since she had flatly refused to allow him to die.

Still, Kit didn't want to come right out and admit to Jim what everybody knew: that his wife was bossy.

"She's sharp-spoken, Tasmin," Kit finally allowed.

"No, she's bossy," Jim said. "I've got used to it, but you needn't be complaining about my traveling.

"If you was married to Tasmin she'd have scared you all the way back to Missouri by now," Jim added.

"Are we going down to the South Platte, or not?" Kit inquired.

"I 'spect we better," Jim said. "We've got a passel of people to guide. It wouldn't hurt to know if there's a big bunch of Indians between here and there."

"It's pretty dern hard to get to Santa Fe, whichever direction you start from," Kit admitted.

"We've got three babies and a passel of females," Jim reminded him. "I hope we can get 'em across before it gets too cold."

He didn't want to discuss it with Kit, but in fact marriage and fatherhood had made travel not quite the free frolic it had once been.

Kit could dance around the question of Tasmin's bossiness all he wanted to, but the fact was that Jim missed his son, Monty, more than he missed his wife. A little time off from Tasmin was only a sensible relief. He and Monty were not yet quite confident of one another, but they were slowly forming a sly attachment. With Tasmin he could only be pleasant and hope for the best.

Jim did feel that a certain amount of scouting was advisable—getting the Berrybenders, or most of them, across to Santa Fe would not be a cakewalk. None of the plains Indians were likely to be friendly—and water was no sure thing along part of the route. If all the mountain men chose to accompany them, they could probably bluff most of the Indians, but it was not likely that the mountain men *would* stay together on such a long trek. The West held too many temptations, in the way of valleys never before explored. The mountain men were notably independent. They might start off in a group and then peel off, one by one.

Jim plunged into the Platte and let the little mare pick her way carefully through the shoals. Kit's mule managed to step in a hole—he stumbled, panicked, threw his rider, and splashed on across the river. Once on the south bank he shook himself thoroughly, showering Jim with cold spray—even so, he was a good deal luckier than Kit, who floundered out, soaked, in a worse temper than he had been in to begin with.

"I'm wet as a rat," he complained; it was very annoying to be stuck with such a worthless mule.

They heard a shout and saw Greasy Lake trotting along the bank at what, for him, was a great rate—he was pointing at the sky. When Jim and Kit first looked up all they saw was a flock of cranes far to the north—for a moment, due to the intensity of the white sunlight, the balloon had been invisible. They could just see the faces of the two white men in the basket, high above.

"Greasy Lake was right—there's our flying men," Kit said.

Jim was startled by the sight of the balloon, a phenomenon he had only vaguely heard about—he had supposed it to be mainly a product of Greasy Lake's imagination, but there it was, as real as anything.

"Now that's a fine way to travel," he said. "If we had a few of those we could float right over to Santa Fe."

"I wouldn't know how to steer it," Kit admitted. "If you couldn't steer it proper, there's no telling where you'd end up."

In their astonishment at seeing the balloon and its passengers, the two of them had forgotten the flock of cranes. Along the Platte large flocks of birds were a common sight—campers sometimes camped a few miles off the river, in order not to be kept awake by the quackings of geese and ducks. But as the cranes came closer, the men in the basket became more agitated, and not without reason: the balloon was directly in the path of the cranes—in a few moments, despite all the balloonists could do, the cranes, in close formation, began to strike the balloon. One or two fell in with the men and then flapped out, but at least six struck the balloon itself.

"Uh-oh," Kit said. "You'd think a dern crane could see a balloon that big."

"Two or three's stuck to it still," Jim remarked—very soon it became evident that the balloon was losing air.

High above, the balloonists were trying frantically to keep their balloon—no longer as round as it had been—up in the air.

Greasy Lake came trotting up, very excited.

"You were right, Greasy," Kit admitted. "There's flying men all right."

"They're trying to hit the river—can't blame them," Jim pointed out.

Fortunately the wind came to the balloonists' aid, pushing the balloon directly over the water.

"I hope they can swim," Kit said, forgetting that he himself had just waded out of the shallow Platte. A moment later he realized that he had spoken foolishly.

"If they'd come down in the Mississippi they'd need to be good swimmers," he added, but thanks to the drama overhead, no one was listening.

Greasy Lake began to wail and chant—he thought it might possibly be gods who were descending into the river. An old Miniconjou, a wandering shaman like himself, had first told him about the balloon and the men who flew beneath it; at first Greasy Lake hadn't known what to believe. But as the balloon came splashing down into the brown water, he saw that the sky travelers, after all, were men and not gods. They waded out of the river, holding what goods they could carry above their heads, looking every bit as wet as Kit Carson. One of the men, a rotund man in wet red pants, seemed to be cursing in French, a language Greasy Lake often heard when he was in the North. The other man was taller, and dressed all in black, as men were said to dress whose business it was to carry off the dead. It seemed to him that the fact that cranes had hit the balloon was not without significance. Some of the People believed that cranes were the carriers of souls; they were said to carry off old souls and bring new souls to babies, when they arrived. Greasy Lake himself had seen nothing of particular merit in the cranes he had observed, nothing that would suggest that they could be entrusted with such an important task, but what he had just seen—cranes bringing down a flying boat—suggested to him that he might need to rethink his position in regard to cranes. Perhaps the reason the flying boat had collapsed was that the cranes had dumped too many souls in it. In the confusion there was the likelihood that some of these souls would escape into uncertain territory, the vague, troubling spaces between life and death, where these flitting souls would likely do much mischief. It might be that what had occurred high over his head was some big error of the gods—an error that had allowed many souls to escape. No one had ever claimed that the gods didn't make mistakes. The gods of war, for example, were always getting things mixed up. What occurred in most battles was often the very opposite of what the war chiefs and war parties had expected to happen. Some men died and others lived, all because of errors of the gods.

9

. . . though happy to have saved his fine Parisian cheese . . .

Cㅣ ᴀ ᴍ ᴅ ᴇ Pᴀ ᴛ ʏ, though happy to have saved his fine Parisian cheese and also a warming bottle of cognac, nonetheless, once he was safely on dry land, blew up into a frothing rage and filled the air with curses, none of them exactly directed at Ben Hope-Tipping but few of them missing him by a very wide mark, either.

"You should have descended—it was our only hope!" he insisted.

"Frankly, old boy, an ascent would have been the better strategy," Ben replied, unmoved by the Frenchman's frothing. "The ballast was on your side—if you'd only tossed out a bag or two we might have missed them."

"*Voilà!* Who's these peoples?" Clam asked, having just observed that they had human company: a small, wet man, leading a tall mule; a tall, dry man on a wet bay horse; and an old Indian of some sort, rather blotched in complexion, aboard a horse that seemed about to fall down.

"Extraordinary, isn't it?" Ben said. "People do just seem to pop up out of nowhere, here in America."

"Of course they come from nowhere—all this is *nowhere!*" Clam began—and then he suddenly remembered that all their guns were in the wagon, and where was that foolish boy Amboise, whose instructions had been to follow them closely? Of course, they would need dry clothes, and need them promptly—and yet there was no sign of Amboise, who deserved a good cuffing, at least.

"These fellows seem to be friendly," Ben said. "The Indian looks to be rather past warrior's age. Can't think what's keeping Amboise—wouldn't mind a change—fear he's lagging, as usual—such a pity to have to introduce ourselves in wet clothes—you must speak severely to Amboise, Clam, when the lazy boy shows up."

"I'll 'severe' him—I'll bash him," Clam assured him. He twisted his mustache a bit, in order to appear civilized, and advanced on the strangers, who stood watching them—they did not seem particularly welcoming, but at least did not seem hostile.

"Hello, gentlemen!" Hope-Tipping said loudly, as they approached. "Very glad of your company, I'm sure. I'm Benjamin Hope-Tipping and this is my French colleague, Monsieur Clam de Paty. We write for the papers, and as you see, we come before you freshly baptized."

Jim Snow felt slightly depressed at the thought of having to deal with two more fools or idiots from Europe. The fact that they could fly did not mean that they would be competent to take care of themselves now that they were on the ground.

Kit, however, was delighted to see the newcomers—weeks of traveling with his unsociable old friend Jim Snow and the erratic old prophet had put him in the mood for more talkative company.

"Why, howdy, glad to meet you," Kit said, striding right over to shake hands. "I'm baptized too, but we'll dry. The fellow on the bay mare is Jim Snow and the Indian is called Greasy Lake—he's a big prophet. We've been guiding the Berrybender party—they ought to be around South Pass somewhere by now."

"Why, yes—the Berrybenders—we're very anxious to meet them," Ben told him. He shook Kit's hand but was looking past him, at Jim Snow. Clam de Paty did the same.

"Monsieur, who did you say that was?" Clam asked, nodding at Jim.

"On the bay mare—that's Jim Snow," Kit replied.

"*The* Jim Snow—the man they call the Sin Killer?" Ben inquired eagerly.

"Why, yes—he's the only Jim Snow there is," Kit declared, a little annoyed. "Sin Killer's a nickname some of the boys gave him."

The two men were paying Kit no mind at all—both of them were staring at Jim.

"Clam, we're made—we've found the Sin Killer," Ben exclaimed.

Clam de Paty was scarcely less excited.

"All we need now are dry notebooks," he said. "Where is that Amboise? I'll have his ears."

Watching the two foreigners approach, squishing loudly in their wet boots, Jim had the feeling it was time to leave. Kit could take these two intruders back to the main party, which should be on the move by now. He himself far preferred to scout alone— Kit had insisted on coming along on this trip because he was badly on the outs with Jim Bridger and Milt Sublette over his neglect of camp chores. Jim Bridger had pummeled Kit soundly in their last fistfight, cracking one of Kit's teeth, an injury much resented.

To Jim it seemed only fair that Kit earn his keep by escorting these two men back to the Berrybenders.

"Oh, I say, Mr. Snow," Ben began. "*So* pleased to meet you. I am Benjamin Hope-Tipping and this is my colleague, Monsieur Clam de Paty—we've traveled quite a long way in hopes of meeting you."

"*Oui,*" Clam said. "Splashing down just when we did was a miracle. But for the birds we would have flown right over you."

Jim said not a word. He merely looked at the two men, wondering what they wanted. Why would anyone travel a long distance to meet him? And what did they expect from him now that they had found him?

"We're journalists," Ben announced, with a touch of pride.

Jim sat on his mare—he did not change expression. He seemed, to Clam, neither surprised nor concerned by Ben's announcement. He didn't react at all.

Ben Hope-Tipping was more than a little disconcerted by Jim Snow's calm lack of response to his statement of purpose. It occurred to him that the term he had used—"journalist"—might not be current in this wild empty West. After all, he and Clam *were* pioneers; certainly pioneers insofar as their use of balloons went. The two of them might well be the first journalists the Sin Killer had ever met. There were, after all, few newspapers in the West—only an ugly sheet or two in Cincinnati and hardly even that in Saint Louis. This young man, the famous Sin Killer, feared by the red savages for his violent furies—yet a man who had won the hand of Lady Tasmin Berrybender—a fine subject for jour-nalistic treatment if there ever was one, probably had no clear idea what a journalist was. It might even be that he had never seen a newspaper. His concern, after all, would be survival, not amusement of the sort newspapers were designed to provide.

"We're journalists," he repeated hopefully. "We write for the papers, you see."

"You're the Sin Killer, yes, yes," Clam said. "We have many questions for you, if you'll oblige."

Jim remained silent—it annoyed him a little that his Sin Killer nickname had become such a staple of Missouri River gossip that even these two foreigners had heard the term.

But the fact that they *had* heard it was just a mild irritant—it really meant little to him, nor did it encourage him to linger in their company. It had been a year since he left the lower Mis-souri—whatever the two fellows had heard was most probably wild lies. The two certainly seemed harmless—they did not appear to be armed—but why they would suppose he'd sit still and let them ask him questions, he could not imagine.

He looked at them, nodded as a small gesture of courtesy, and simply rode around them, leaving them looking at him with open mouths.

"Why didn't he speak—is he mute, the young fool?" Clam asked. Had he traveled all the way from France to have some young American ride around him as if he were a stump?

Ben Hope-Tipping had been as startled as his colleague by Jim Snow's blatantly disinterested response. In his shock at being ignored by this legendary fellow—one of the frontiersmen they had most wanted to meet—Ben wondered if they had omitted some ritual or other—the peace sign, perhaps? Trappers and travelers in the West seemed often to speak to one another through hand signs—perhaps that was what the Sin Killer had been expecting. And yet they had been told that he spoke English—what could be the matter with the fellow?

Jim rode over to Kit and shrugged.

"These two fellows are even nosier than Tasmin," he remarked. "She started asking me questions the minute we met, and these skunks are just as bad."

"They sure didn't ask *me* many questions," Kit replied, in a pouty tone. "All they wanted to know about was the great Sin Killer."

"I ain't the great nothing," Jim told him. "And I can't make much of a scout if I have to drag these two fools behind me. You and Greasy slow me down enough."

"Of course you can go faster than anybody else—you got the best horse," Kit said, still aggrieved.

"I think I'll go south for a few days and have a look around," Jim said. "You can handle these fellows, I expect."

"I don't want to handle them," Kit said at once. "I'm glad we got to see the balloon, but it's busted. Why can't these fellows just handle themselves?"

"Suit yourself—I'm leaving," Jim told him.

"You would leave, you selfish fool!" Kit burst out—Jim's habit of doing exactly what he pleased, with no regard for anyone else, infuriated him.

Jim agreed that seeing the balloon *had* been interesting, but some birds had knocked it down, and helping the men fix it was not his business. He turned to leave. Probably the balloonists had a wagon and a servant nearby who would soon arrive and help them out. He wanted to be on his way, an intention which continued to infuriate Kit.

"What am I supposed to do with them?" he asked, a little desperately.

"Take 'em to Ashley—maybe he'll adopt them," Jim suggested. "He likes to blab and puff himself up—I expect he'll give them some yarns they can write in their papers."

"It's a damn big chore to leave your best friend with," Kit announced—he hoped the appeal to friendship would make Jim change his mind.

"They didn't fly all this way without no kit," Jim pointed out. "I imagine their slave will show up pretty soon and help you with them."

Kit suddenly had a thought. Perhaps the two men were eccentric millionaires, out for a long lark in the West. Perhaps they were as rich as or even richer than Lord Berrybender or the prince of Weid. Maybe if some mild danger arose he could hurry them out of harm's way and then convince them that he had been the one thing that stood between them and death. It might be that they'd want to make him rich for performing such noble service. It would serve Jim Snow right if he managed to get rich off these strangers. For that matter, it would serve everybody right.

Kit was so pleased with his new notion that he could not resist trotting after Jim.

"That's right, you go away . . . leave these folks to me," he said. "I bet they make me rich, once I save them."

"I hope they will—if you *do* save them," Jim said. Then he put the little mare in a lope and hurried off, happy not to have to hear any more rattle from Kit.

10

Jim Snow had no sooner ridden off . . .

J I M   S N O W had no sooner ridden off than the two journalists, wearing looks of extreme dismay, came running over to Kit.

"Where does he go?" the Frenchman in the red pants asked—there was indignation in his tone. "When will he come back, this Sin Killer?"

"We *had* rather hoped to speak to him, you see!" the Englishman remarked, as shocked as he was annoyed.

"It won't be today," Kit assured them. "Not unless you can run as fast as that mare can lope."

"This is an outrage!" the Frenchman spluttered—he was very red in the face, though not quite as red as his bright pants. "If we were in France I would call him out!"

Kit found the remark puzzling.

"Why call him out when he's already out?" he inquired.

"My colleague means he would challenge Mr. Snow to a duel," Ben explained—he had calmed a little.

Kit Carson usually managed to maintain a solemn, even dignified demeanor, easy to do when traveling with an unsociable person like Jim Snow, who was out of sorts most of the time anyway. On the other hand, when some absolutely ridiculous notion was expressed in his hearing he was sometimes given to bursts of hilarity—these giggle fits, as he called them, often lasted so long that they became something of a trial to those who knew him.

The notion that a short Frenchman in red pants could be so foolish as to challenge Jim Snow to a duel was just the kind of nonsense that caused Kit's sense of humor to get the better of him. He burst out laughing, but of course there was no one to tell the joke to except old Greasy Lake, who was over by the river, chanting over the fallen balloon.

"Why are you laughing, monsieur? In France a duel is a serious matter," Clam de Paty insisted—he was finding America less and less to his taste, an awkward thing since, at the moment, he was far out in the middle of it.

Ben Hope-Tipping, annoyed himself by the young fellow's unseemly response, nonetheless realized that his colleague's abrupt mention of a challenge to the Sin Killer *did*, under the circumstances, smack of the ridiculous.

"Not sure a duel is quite the wisest course in this case, Clam," he remarked. "It would seem that the Sin Killer is famous precisely because of his facility in battle. After all, you can hardly write the fellow up if you're dead."

The same thought had occurred, though belatedly, to Clam de Paty himself. Fortunately the man who he had threatened to call out was now almost out of sight—there seemed to be little practical danger of a response from that quarter.

"*Pardon,*" he said, in chilly tones, to his more circumspect colleague. "A duel is no mere brawl, no massacre, no mere thing of fisticuffs—it is, like everything in France, a civilized engagement, a contest with rules. With a pistol in my hand, monsieur, I assure you I am not to be taken lightly."

Ben decided to ignore his friend's absurdly puffed-up conduct—they were not, after all, out with their seconds in the Bois de Boulogne. Still, he could not but be irritated by the young frontiersman's giggling, which seemed to cast their whole enterprise in an undignified light. Clam de Paty, despite his rather erratic temperament, was a leading, perhaps *the* leading, force in

French journalism—had he not interviewed Prince Metternich himself, and Czar Alexander, and the empress of France, not to mention numerous Bourbons, generals, and acrobats?

His own credentials, for that matter, were not evidently the poorer. He too had interviewed lords, ministers, Mrs. Jordan, two Rothschilds, a Baring, even the great Wellington himself. It was bad enough to have their fine, expensively made balloon punctured by some wayward American birds—were they now to be reduced to standing around in wet clothes, on the barren American prairies, being laughed at by a young frontiersman and ignored completely by a rather blotchy old Indian? Ben prided himself on his ability to maintain a level temperament—a good, sound Dorset temperament, on the whole, in clear contrast to the frequent oaths and curses his more volatile Gallic companion was apt to burst out with. Just at the moment, though, Ben found that he was becoming rather vexed. After all, the sun was setting, and there was no sign of Amboise d'Avigdor or the wagon, in which were plenty of dry clothes. They seemed to be faced with a long, damp night. Why was this young fool still giggling?

"Do endeavor to control your hilarity, Mr. Carson," he said sharply. "I confess I can't quite figure out what's so funny."

"I just got tickled at the thought of that French fellow in the red pants fighting a duel with Jimmy," he admitted.

"And why is that amusing, monsieur?" Clam asked.

"Because Jimmy would kill you before you could twitch," Kit informed him calmly. "Jimmy don't hold back when life or death's involved."

Jim Snow, already miles to the south, was only visible for a second or two, above the waving grass.

"Will he come back, do you think, Mr. Carson?" Ben asked—obviously there was no immediate hope of an interview, though it was *the* interview of all interviews that would have done most to enhance the authenticity of their great Western expedition.

"Oh sure, Jimmy will show up someday," Kit told them. "He's got a wife and baby back with Ashley and the trappers."

Just then a cloud passed between them and the sinking sun. Though it had been a warm day, Ben felt suddenly chilly. Their not quite fully deflated balloon floated on the river, snagged on a number of stiff branches. The old piebald Indian was still chanting, though not so loudly.

"I suppose we should rescue our balloon, Clam—possibly it can be patched," Ben remarked.

"It's awkward being wet," Clam admitted. "Where could that foolish boy be?"

"He was rather fearful when we left," Ben recalled. "Seemed rather convinced that those red fellows might do him harm."

"What red fellows?" Kit asked, alarmed. He had no idea how far the balloon might have floated before the cranes downed it— with Jim now gone and two obviously helpless strangers on his hands, the thought that there might be bad Indians somewhere near was entirely unwelcome.

"Oh, quite a bunch of painted fellows stopped us," Ben informed him. "Upset our young interpreter rather a lot. An old fellow on a white horse seemed to be the leader. What was it Amboise called him, Clam? The Partezon, was it?"

"That's right—the Partezon," Clam agreed. "No paint on him, though the other fellows were painted up rather grotesquely. That's when we decided to go up in our balloon."

"I believe we rather frightened the savages when we went up," Ben remarked. "They ran off, but the two old fellows didn't."

Kit began to regret that he had burst out so at Jim—if ever the two of them needed to stick together, it was now. But of course, as usual, Jim had left.

"Best think of our balloon," Ben insisted. "Amboise is sure to turn up soon. If a muskrat were to nibble our balloon, it would only be harder to patch. Once we've saved it we can build a roaring fire and get out of these wet clothes."

"No fire tonight," Kit informed them immediately. It was sadly obvious that the two men lacked even the most elementary practical sense.

"I'll help you get your balloon off the snags," he said, "but we can't be building a fire, not with the Partezon around."

"But sir, no Indians *are* around—we flew over several miles of prairie and it all looked quite empty," Ben insisted; both he and Clam were horrified at the thought of a night spent in their sopping clothes.

"How many miles did you come?" Kit asked.

"Ten, maybe," Ben said. "What do you think, Clam?"

Clam de Paty shrugged. Once in the balloon, he had applied himself to the cheese and the cognac—calculations of distance were none of his affair.

"We flew until the birds came," he told Kit. As the guardian of French precision he tried to avoid vague statements.

"No fire tonight," Kit repeated firmly. "Ten miles ain't far enough. An Indian can smell smoke ten miles—*this* Indian particularly."

"But we're very wet, Mr. Carson," Ben reminded him. "And once we wade around saving our balloon, we'll undoubtedly be even wetter. Surely you can't expect us to spend the night in damp garments."

"I should certainly hope not," Clam added. "What business is it of the savages if we enjoy our fire, monsieur? Civilized men cannot be expected to sleep in wet clothes."

"Take your clothes off and sleep naked, then," Kit advised. "If you start a fire I'll be leaving, and the Partezon will probably be coming."

"Sleep naked—in this chill?" Ben asked, horrified at the thought. "Couldn't we make just a small fire, one not apt to roar? What harm could there be in that?"

"The Partezon will come and burn you in it, that's what harm," Kit told them. "He probably didn't think you could really fly off or he would have burned you already."

Without wasting any more time on chatter, he waded into the river and began to disengage the soppy silk of the balloon from the sticks where it had snagged. Darkness was falling and the work was chilling but Kit's imagination had just served up a warming thought. If he helped save the balloon, maybe the balloonists would let him go up in it with them. If he came floating down into Ashley's big camp in a red balloon it would show all the boys—and Tasmin particularly—what a clever fellow he was. None of the mountain men had ever ridden in a balloon. If he returned to the Berrybenders in a balloon his stock was bound to rise—maybe Tasmin would look at him with new eyes.

It was not easy, extracting such a large, floppy object from the snag-filled river. Greasy Lake had no interest in the rescue, but Ben Hope-Tipping stripped off and came in the water to help. He seemed to appreciate Kit's efforts, unlike the Frenchman, who maintained an airy indifference.

By the time they got the balloon safely free of snags and spread it on the grass, a pale moon had risen. Greasy Lake, without a word of good-bye, rode off just as darkness fell.

"Strange old fellow—where do you suppose he's going?" Ben asked.

"He don't know himself—Greasy just wanders," Kit said.

11

Mainly the Ear Taker hunted people . . .

WHEN the Ear Taker was a boy, hunting in the dry
canyons, the People called him Takes Bones, because he was
always picking up small bones or animal teeth from carcasses in
the desert—bones or teeth that he then worked into fishhooks,
awls, spear points; but once he reached adulthood some of the
People began to call him Who-You-Don't-See, because of the
exceptional stealth of his attacks, most of them aimed at lone
travelers, white traders, careless soldiers. Mainly the Ear Taker
hunted people—white or Mexican usually—but when he hunted
animals his stealth worked just as well. He could even surprise
antelope, most cautious of animals. If he saw several antelope
grazing together he would anticipate the direction of their grazing and go flatten himself in the grass, well ahead of the grazing
animals. Hunting naked at times, he flattened himself until he
became as much part of the ground as a lizard or a snake. The
antelope would sometimes walk right over him, coming so close
that he could strike one with a light spear tipped with poison—
the poison old Prickly Pear Woman had taught him to make from
the secretions of a toad. Prickly Pear Woman was actually white,
but she had been taken prisoner as a small girl and had lived
with the People most of her life—some of the People even

regarded her as the grandmother of the tribe. She had dug herself a little room beneath the roots of a great prickly pear—she
had learned to move among the prickly pear so smoothly that
the thorns didn't stick her, a feat not even the Ear Taker could
manage.

The Ear Taker was short, but it was agreed that he could out-
walk anyone in the band. He could walk from moonrise to
moonrise, licking dew drops off sage leaves or grass blades if
there was no water. Old Prickly Pear Woman had told him of the
terrible cruelties the whites had visited on the People long ago—
many grandmothers ago. When the whites came into the lands of
the People they at once began to order people around—the People, having always been free, didn't like this and made a revolt,
killing many whites. But then many more whites came and made
all the People prisoners; to ensure that the People could never
rise up again, an old governor commanded that all warriors over
a certain age must have one foot chopped off—and the chopping
was soon accomplished, leaving the People a tribe of cripples.
For a generation all the warriors had to hobble on one foot, a
terrible humiliation.

To a great walker like the Ear Taker no greater humiliation
could be imagined—even though the chopping had occurred
many grandmothers ago, and the warriors of the People now
walked on two legs again, the Ear Taker decided to devote himself to avenging this old cruelty.

At first he tried to avenge the atrocity precisely in kind, by
sneaking up on sleeping traders or soldiers and chopping off
one of their feet. It was easy enough, in Santa Fe, to find victims,
most of whom had passed out from drunkenness; but the Ear
Taker soon discovered that chopping off feet with an axe or a
hatchet was not easy to do correctly. Twice he struck too high on
the leg and his victims bled to death. Two others he managed to
strike cleanly, so that at least two white men had to hobble
through their lives as the old warriors had hobbled.

In time, though, the Ear Taker thought of a better, more easily
effected revenge: ears. All white men were vain; they fancied

themselves lords of the earth—with an ear missing, a white man's vanity could never be repaired. In the Ear Taker's view, the loss of such a prominent feature as an ear would be a humiliation worse than death to many of the proud white traders.

Once the choice was made, the Ear Taker began to build his reputation. He haunted the caravan routes into and out of Santa Fe to the east or the south, using his great stealth to slip up on unwary traders as they slept and quickly remove an ear—before the victims could even become fully awake, the Ear Taker was gone.

He soon discovered that the first essential for such work was a knife that could be made as sharp as a razor; and by great good luck, he soon found such a knife. The Ear Taker joined with some Apaches to ambush a little bunch of soldiers bound for the City of Mexico. More than twenty Mexican soldiers were killed, including a captain who possessed a very fine knife. The Ear Taker kept the knife and spent many days sharpening it until the blade was so keen that he could cut flies in two in the air, or bees or other flying insects.

The Apaches with the Ear Taker had, of course, mutilated the soldiers in the traditional ways, castrating them, poking out their eyes, disemboweling a few of them—but they had no interest in ears, which meant that the Ear Taker had twenty sets of ears to practice removing. And he did practice. Since ears were mostly gristle, it was possible to remove them—if one's knife was sharp enough—while causing the victims little immediate pain. The pain, for the whites, would come when they awoke and discovered that they had received an injury that was conspicuous and permanent. A man with a leg cut off might get a wooden leg, but no one could get a wooden ear. A man's humiliation would be there for all to see.

By the time the Ear Taker had finished with the twenty corpses, his technique was perfect: with his left hand he grasped the ear, stretched it, and with his right hand, cut just at the juncture of ear and scalp. Soon he could perform the motions perfectly, in only a second—then he would be off, into the desert or the prairie, gone before his victims could even figure out why one side of their head was suddenly bloody.

In two months, by stalking the caravans from the east, the Ear Taker had removed a dozen ears. Soon, horrified trekkers, white, black, or Mexican, began to arrive in Santa Fe lacking an ear. The governor and the military could not fail to take note. This singular but terrifying threat to a man's appearance would soon begin to act as a brake on the Santa Fe trade. Traders from east or south had always had to contend with droughts, blizzards, or hostile Indians—but now they faced a new threat: an assailant whose pleasure was to cut off ears. This fiend, this Ear Taker, seemed to be able to succeed no matter how many guards were posted. In a few cases he had even taken ears from some undisciplined guards who had nodded off for a moment.

To the military's dismay, the Ear Taker had one huge advantage: no one had ever seen him, or had the slightest idea what he looked like. Barefoot, dressed like any other Indian, the Ear Taker could walk around the plaza in Santa Fe in perfect safety—a small man, dark, modest, friendly, never questioned or suspected by any of the soldiers whose ears he might eventually take. Except for old Prickly Pear Woman, none of his own people would ever have supposed that Takes Bones, a modest toolmaker exceptionally skilled at working bones, had become the dread Ear Taker.

By the time the Ear Taker had wreaked his vengeance for a year, several once-proud traders had given up the trade and sought safety in the East. In Santa Fe the governor became even more alarmed—he even delegated a company of soldiers whose one duty was to hunt down the Ear Taker. The soldiers marched off, first east, then south—they caught no one, but while they were marching, the Ear Taker took three more ears. The soldiers got lost near the Cimarron River and almost starved—six were killed in a brief engagement with the Kiowa. The survivors came back to Santa Fe, having failed completely. How were they to find a man no one had ever seen? The governor then thought of trying to tempt the Ear Taker into committing a rash act. He had three condemned men taken a few miles out of town and left to wander—they were, of course, being watched closely from a distance. The condemned men were not bothered, but one of the soldiers who were supposed to be watching had his ear taken off while drunk. No one saw anything and there were no tracks to follow, but a few days later, a trader named Bates claimed to have seen the Ear Taker fleeing in the dawn, having just taken an ear from a sheepherder. Bates described the Ear Taker as unusually tall, though in fact he was a very short man, not even five feet in height.

Though confident now of his skill, the Ear Taker knew that all the skill in the world could not prevent accident. Sooner or later, if he continued to take ears near Santa Fe, someone *would* see him. There were Apache trackers so skilled that they could track anything—one of them might be employed to track him. Old Prickly Pear Woman, whom he visited frequently, often cautioned him about the risks he was taking.

"The spirits don't like it when we learn to do things too good," she reminded him. "They set traps—good traps—it's to remind us that we are only people. You have taken enough of these ears around here—I think the spirits are getting ready to trick you. You better go somewhere else, if you want to keep taking people's ears."

The Ear Taker knew she was right. Lately he had had the feeling that someone clever was watching him. Often he caught rabbits looking at him steadily, which was disconcerting. Sometimes he came quite close to the steady-looking rabbits, but they didn't flee. They merely hopped a few steps and resumed their steady looking.

The next day he spent several hours in the plaza, just walking around, chatting with a few people. No one bothered him, or even seemed to notice him, but when he left Santa Fe and walked out into the country, the first thing he saw was a big jackrabbit, watching him. The traders had no interest in him, nor the soldiers, but every rabbit he saw seemed to be looking at him. This was a worrisome thing.

The next day the Ear Taker climbed to the top of a butte several miles from town. The butte was a holy place; men came
there seeking visions. The Ear Taker waited all day, but only near
dusk did he see anything that might give him a clue about what
the spirits might be planning. As the sun was sinking a great dust
devil blew up, far to the north, the dust swirling high in the air.
Then the sun struck the dust in such a way as to make a kind of
dust rainbow, a thing the Ear Taker had never seen. The dust
devil headed in a northerly direction and finally dissolved. The
Ear Taker believed he had been given a sign, and what the sign
suggested was that he go north. Perhaps if he went north, where
there were also said to be careless whites—trappers, hunters,
families traveling west—the spirits who were annoyed with him
for being so good at cutting off ears would leave him in peace for
a while.

The minute the Ear Taker made his decision and started
north, the rabbits began to run away from him again.

The Ear Taker walked from moonrise to moonrise. At dawn he
walked through a large prairie dog town and was pleased to note
that there were no small owls to be seen, although owls often
occupied the dens of prairie dogs. The presence of owls always
indicated that death was near—the fact that he didn't see a single
owl gave him confidence that he had made the right decision.

Two weeks of strong walking brought the Ear Taker into the
Sioux country, near the Platte River. On his walk he had not seen
a single soul, neither white man nor red man, but he knew that
when he crossed the brown river and traveled along the Holy
Road, he would soon find humans again. On his walk he had
mostly eaten wild onions, plus one porcupine. When he came to
the Platte River he was hoping to find some berry bushes, but
just as he saw the curve of the river he also spotted two antelope.
At once he lay down and made himself part of the ground, for
the antelope were grazing right toward him. He had his light
spear with him, whose poison should be fresh enough to kill.
The antelope had no inkling of the Ear Taker's presence, of that
he was sure, and yet only a moment later they both raised their

heads and at once took flight to the west. He had been flattened against the ground when the antelope ran—soon he began to pick up the vibrations made by a number of horses. As the Ear Taker watched, about twenty Indians came loping out of the south, their object being to capture three white men, two of them mounted on small horses, the third driving a wagon. The Ear Taker assumed that the three whites would either be killed on the spot or else carried off someplace where they would have to suffer the appropriate tortures. Instead, to his surprise, a parley took place—the young white man driving the wagon was obviously making a plea for mercy. The young warriors looked restless; they were clearly eager to hack up the whites, but an old chief, who rode a white horse, restrained them.

Then two of the white men dismounted and pulled a huge red blanket of some kind out of the wagon; then they built a fire in a bucket and began to pump fire into the blanket, causing it to expand and take on a kind of round shape—it rose from the ground and hung like a red moon over the prairie. This sight startled the young Indians very much—it startled the Ear Taker too. A blanket had turned into a kind of moon, with a basket underneath it, which two of the white men climbed into. To the Ear Taker it all seemed like strange magic; but then, he reminded himself, he was in a new country and should have expected unusual things to happen.

Then, immediately, something even more unusual took place. The young white man who had been conducting the parley with the Indians loosened some ropes and the big moon rose into the air, with the two white men sitting comfortably beneath it. Soon the two men were high above the river. The old Indian shot an arrow at them, but his arrow merely hit the basket and fell back. A breeze pushed the red moon west—soon the two men were well out of range of any arrow.

It was all too much for the young warriors, who galloped away, leaving only the two old men and the young white man who had been driving the wagon.

Seeing the two white men fly was by far the most astonishing piece of magic the Ear Taker had ever witnessed. The north country was clearly where the spirits disposed themselves differently than the spirits of the desert. After a bit the two older Indians rode away, not even bothering to kill the young white man, who caught the two horses and soon proceeded on west along the river in his wagon. The Ear Taker would have liked to discuss what he had just seen with old Prickly Pear Woman, but of course that was impossible—he would have to observe the peoples of this strange country a little longer and then draw his own conclusions.

The sun was sinking—it would be night soon, and night was the Ear Taker's element. It occurred to him that he could test the situation a bit by following the white boy, letting him make camp and go to sleep, and then taking one of his ears. He got up from the ground and carefully followed the wagon, though keeping to his side of the river and watching the skies for any sign that the two flying men were returning. He also watched closely for any sign that the young white man had unusual powers—he did not want to allow himself to be tricked, on his first day in the north country. He remembered that he *had* been tricked, not long before in Santa Fe. He decided to take an ear from the famous white trader John Skraeling, known to Indians as the Twisted Hair. Skraeling was a very light sleeper, thus difficult to rob, as many thieves had discovered to their sorrow. Skraeling slept under his own wagon; the Ear Taker thought it would be a good test of his stealth, to sneak up and take one of Skraeling's ears. The trader was a sick man, who coughed a lot; some of his helpers were just waiting for him to die, so they could divide up his goods, but none were quite bold enough to attempt to kill him.

The Ear Taker chose a moonless night on which to make his attempt. He crept up on Skraeling's wagon and listened carefully for the man's breathing, which would tell him where the head was. It was then that the gods played their trick: Skraeling *wasn't* breathing, though surely he had been when he crawled under the wagon. The Ear Taker crept closer, listening. Thirty yards away some trappers were drinking and carousing, making enough noise that the Ear Taker couldn't hear the sleeping man's light breath. Carefully he put his head under the wagon, but still he heard nothing. No living man could breathe *that* quietly, he thought—and then he realized the truth. Skraeling had crawled under the wagon and died of his own sickness; the Ear Taker had waited one day too long to make his attempt. Since he was there, he took an ear off the dead man anyway, but the mischievous spirits had managed to upset his plans.

At dark the young white man stopped and made a hasty camp. It was clear to the Ear Taker that he was a clumsy boy—he had no skill in hobbling horses or making camp. No doubt his job was just to follow the fliers around and do chores for them when they came down.

When dusk deepened, making it easy to move without being observed, the Ear Taker crossed the river, so he could observe the boy more closely. The young man seemed to be a very ordinary fellow. During the hour or more that the Ear Taker watched he became a little annoyed at the thought of old Prickly Pear Woman, who had managed to convince him that the spirits were likely to set traps for him. She liked to stir people up, getting them all worried about disasters that never happened. She told one old man, who had been her lover once, that he had offended the Toad people and would turn black as a result. The old man didn't turn black, but he worried so much about the Toad people that he stumbled into a gully and broke his neck. That very incident had convinced the Ear Taker that it was not wise to believe everything old Prickly Pear Woman said. Probably she was just bored, and had merely been amusing herself when she told him the spirits might be laying a trap.

Once he determined to go on and take one of the young white man's ears, the Ear Taker carefully observed the usual cautions. He waited until the moon was behind a cloud before creeping into the camp. The boy was a loud snorer, making the position of his head easy to determine. Taking the ear took only a second. The young man jerked, but did not wake up. The Ear Taker left immediately, recrossing the river. He walked most of the night and then hid himself in some bushes and slept. The ear taking had gone well, and he felt relieved, but he still had no intention of being careless. After all, he was in new country, where there might be new rules.

12

Amboise felt safe where there were trees . . .

A M B O I S E D ' A V I G D O R was a deep sleeper, particularly so after a day on which he might have died a terrible death. Since the Partezon, cruelest of all Indians, had spared him, Amboise didn't feel he had much to worry about. Of course, his bosses would be in a terrible fury when he caught up with them the next day; they would have expected him to follow their flight, make their fire, cook their dinner, and lay their beds. The dreadful threat posed by the Partezon had not impressed them; they were safe in their basket, applying themselves to the cognac and cheese. It was irritating, but that was just how his bosses were.

Amboise himself was from the Chippewa country, his father a *voyageur* in the land of the *mille lacs*. Amboise felt safe where there were trees; he did not enjoy being alone on this vast prairie. He could handle a canoe better than a wagon, and he much preferred the company of trappers and river Indians to these two rude Europeans.

Yawning, Amboise soon stretched out on a blanket between the wagon and the campfire—he at once began to send his rasping snores out into the night. He slept deeply, cooled by the night breezes—for a moment he felt a sting like an insect bite but did not come fully awake. The sun was high before he opened his eyes and looked about him absently. Then he saw, to his surprise, that the grass near where he had just slept seemed to be red. Surely the grass hadn't been red when he lay down, else he would have chosen a different spot. Then he noticed— what was more puzzling and also more annoying—that his shirt was red too. When he put up a finger to scratch his cheek, his finger came away red. These reddenings of grass, shirt, and finger were quite puzzling to Amboise. He walked off a little distance and relieved himself; time enough to figure out the source of this puzzling redness later. Only when he happened to notice a lot of green flies buzzing over the reddened grass did it occur to him that the redness might be blood. The two palfreys were quarrelsome beasts, always at odds with the sorrel gelding that pulled the wagon. Perhaps while he slept the horses had fought, bitten one another until the blood flowed. But the palfreys were grazing placidly, some distance away, and the gelding didn't have a mark on him. Besides, his own cheek was bloody, which would be an unlikely result, if the horses had fought.

As he stood by the river, perplexed by this odd circumstance, it struck Amboise with sudden force that the blood must be his own. At once he raised his hand to his cheek, and it came away bloody.

Amboise's first fearful thought was that he had somehow been scalped. Perhaps the old Indian who had seemed so uninterested in him the day before had slipped back in the night and scalped him. Astonished that, as a scalped man, he could still walk around and make water, Amboise rushed to the wagon and quickly pulled out Clam de Paty's little shaving mirror, a useful object that he was obliged to locate for Monsieur de Paty every morning when he was ready to shave.

Amboise opened the mirror, which was in a handsome leather case, and quickly had a look at himself, a procedure that only deepened his puzzlement. One of his cheeks *was* very bloody, and yet it was plain that he still had his hair, and looked, on the whole, very like his healthy young self. But what could have

occurred to make him so bloody? His bosses were always berating him for his clumsiness, but could he have been somehow
clumsy enough to cut himself while he slept? Such a loss of
blood seemed to indicate that he had been bleeding most of the
night, and yet, where was the cut? Could he have walked in his
sleep, fallen on some rocks, or perhaps accidentally cut himself
on the axe that he used to chop firewood? None of these expla-
nations really satisfied, since he had awakened exactly where he
lay down. Clam de Paty's little mirror was small—until Amboise
tilted it at an angle, it hardly showed his whole face. When he did
tilt it, what it showed plainly was that one side of his face was
bloody and one side normal, if rather stubbly—unlike his bosses,
Amboise could rarely find the leisure to shave. The more he
tipped and slanted the mirror, the more it struck Amboise that,
after all, something *was* rather odd about his face—something
just a bit off—but because of the abundance of dried blood he
could not at once say what it was. Then he put up a finger, meaning to scratch his left ear, and found that, instead, he only
scratched his temple. Very carefully Amboise tilted the mirror
and made the astonishing discovery that he no longer *had* a left
ear. At first he could not credit his own vision, which was apt to
be bleary and not too precise in the first moments of the new
day. He had gone to sleep with two ears on his head—he felt
quite sure of that fact—and yet now he seemed to have only one,
which defied all the laws of nature, as Amboise understood
them. For a minute he blamed the mirror, a small mirror, inadequate for close inspection; and yet, play with it though he might,
he could not make the mirror contradict his first impression,
which was that he no longer had two ears. The right one was
there, stiff as an ear should be and even fairly clean. But the left
ear was simply not there, a fact so startling that Amboise sat
down and fell into a faint, in which he dreamed that he was
bathing in a cool river. In this dream, a brief one, he definitely
had two ears. He did his best to delay a return to consciousness,
but despite him, consciousness soon returned—a glance at the
mirror was enough to confirm the dreadful fact: he was a man

with only one ear, an inadequacy that was likely to strike his employers as very discreditable indeed. His employers were exacting men, so exacting, in fact, that Amboise found he was worrying more about how to explain the situation than he was about the loss of the ear itself. Bitter as they would be about the fact that he had not presented himself to make the fire and arrange the bedding, they would take one look at him in his altered state and at once draw the worst conclusions. Very likely they would conclude that he had taken advantage of their absence to borrow one of their shaving kits, perhaps had tried to shave using one of their mirrors, and in an excess of clumsiness, cut off his own ear. The fact that he had smeared blood not only on Clam de Paty's mirror but on much of their kit as well would lend strength to such an assumption. Amboise wondered again if he might, somehow or other, have cut his own ear off, conclud- ing that it was impossible. His first suspicion—that an Indian had crept in and cut it off while he slept—was undoubtedly the right explanation. The old Partezon, who seemed so uninterested in him, had had his sport after all. There was no sign of the ear any- where—whoever cut it off took it away. Who was more likely than the Partezon to commit such a cunning act?

Very hastily Amboise took Clam de Paty's mirror to the river and washed it clean of blood. Then he stripped and ducked him- self several times, so that he would be clean too. A quick check in the mirror revealed a hole in the left side of his head, but with no ear to shield it. The gristly appendage that had been with him for all of his twenty-one years was now gone.

He carried a bucket of water up from the river and did his best to clean the blood off the various articles in the wagon, making rather a damp job of it. Then he hitched the gelding to the wagon, put the palfreys on a loose rein, and hurried off as fast as he could go to the west. He was anxious to be back with his bosses before the old Indian came back and stripped him of his other ear—and perhaps a few other parts of himself as well.

13

Restraint was not her way . . .

" T H E Y trusted me to keep them safe, and I failed," Pomp
said, in a voice so low that Tasmin could scarcely hear him,
though she stood close to his side in the woods a few hundred
yards below the camp. They stood over the remains of the
friendly bear cub Andy, who, with his sister, Abby, had been
caught by Pomp just before the battle in which Pomp was so badly
wounded. Andy had been clubbed to death, skinned, and cut up,
no doubt by the same Indians who had killed the other freed animals, once they wandered away from the enclosure where they
had been penned. Pomp himself, once he recovered, had freed
the animals—buffalo, deer, antelope, elk, and moose, all half
tame and no doubt easy prey for the Indians, who were coming to
the camp to get in a last bit of trading with William Ashley.

"Damn the Indians . . . they should have seen they were pets!"
Tasmin said—Pomp's sadness affected her so deeply that she had
to say something, even though she knew there was no logic in
her complaint—why expect Indians, who lived by hunting and
whose erratic food supply had usually to be earned by exertion
and danger, to pass up easy meat? Pomp himself, as the young
animals were captured, expressed certain doubts about the
semidomestication of these wild beasts, which Drummond Stew-

art had wanted to put in his Scottish zoo. He knew that the caution wild animals needed would not be easily regained—Andy's death made the point emphatically.

"I know there are zoos and game parks and such in Europe, but out here I think it's best just to let the animals be," Pomp remarked. "Once you interfere with them they forget how to be wild."

As you yourself have, Pomp Charbonneau, Tasmin thought—then she took Pomp's face in her hands and kissed him, a thing she had been wanting to do for weeks and weeks. They were alone in a deep glade, what better chance could she have? Restraint was not her way—she wanted to make Pomp not look so sad. It flitted through her mind, as she drew Pomp's face toward her, that she had done much the same when she could no longer resist the urge to kiss her husband, Jim Snow, now several weeks gone on his scout to the south. He should know better than to leave me, Tasmin thought—Jim knew she was a passionate animal, strong in her appetites; he also knew she cared for Pomp, though perhaps without suspecting in quite what way she cared—she had hardly been certain of the nature of her feeling herself. Jim and Pomp were friends; they had hunted and camped together often. Yet their natures were very different, Jim hard, Pomp soft, and the one not necessarily better than the other. Tasmin had learned to align herself more or less comfortably with her husband's hardness, even if it involved sudden slappings and moments of frightening violence, but Jim's rough masculinity was not the only kind she could respond to. Pomp's shy softness had a deep appeal too. She had thought much about Jim and Pomp and come to the conclusion that she was not likely to find complete sufficiency in any one man. She had seen herself that life was very uncertain—William Drummond Stewart had been a virile man a month ago and now he was as dead as Charlemagne, as was her brother Bobbety. The insistence with which her father, Lord Berrybender, pursued even his most vagrant appetites—which had once seemed the most abysmal selfishness—now, in the light of life's risk, made

more or less good sense. Perhaps it was better to honor one's
appetites while one could. Had Pomp been clearly happy, at ease
in his soul, Tasmin felt she might have chosen to let him be; but
he wasn't serene, there was sadness in his eyes—so she stopped
thinking about it all and kissed him. If Jim Snow beat her for it or
killed her for it, so be it! Her kiss, when she first delivered it, was
tentative, soft, shy—for all she knew it was Pomp's first kiss. She
kissed his mouth, and then, still soft and shy, kissed his cheeks,
his eyelids, his throat just once; and then she kissed his mouth
again, a longer kiss this time, if still a soft one. Pomp did not
withdraw; she even felt his breath quicken a little, and that slight
hastening of breath gave her confidence that she had not mis-
read him or forced on him something he didn't want. Pomp did
want her kiss, and even returned it a little, if awkwardly—it was
no polished seducer she was dealing with. She drew back and
looked in his eyes, in which she saw a startled, boyish uncertainty—perhaps a little fear even. He looked at her alertly, as if
trying to pick up an odor or identify the call of a distant bird.

"I've come to love you—I won't lie—I can't help it!" Tasmin
said. "I hope you're glad."

She seized his hand and twined her fingers in his, waiting—it
seemed that her whole future depended on this soft-souled man
who had not yet learned to lust.

"I'm glad—it's all new to me," Pomp said. "I'm not as good a
kisser as you."

"Don't be a fool, you're lovely, you're fine!" Tasmin burst
out—in her relief she spoke so loudly that she quickly looked
around to see if anyone from the camp might be close enough to
hear.

Then she kissed Pomp again, longer and with a little more
diligence this time, lingering over his mouth. She moved a little
closer, locking her arms around him, aligning her body with his;
at this Pomp stiffened a little, not the erect stiffening of the
aroused male—it seemed merely that he was surprised that anyone would want to be so close to him. She lay her cheek against
his breast, listening to him breathe. Just knowing that he wanted

her kiss was heaven—she asked nothing more at the moment. She wished she could stand close to Pomp, reaching up now and then for a kiss, all day—and yet even as she enjoyed their light embrace she knew that the larger world and its demands were not far to seek. Her child, Monty, would soon be wanting to nurse—motherhood could not be scanted for long, no matter how keenly she wanted to stay in the quiet glade with Pomp, nuzzling and kissing. She had feared that he might mention Jim—but he hadn't.

"Have you never had a woman? I must ask," Tasmin said, blushing. Pomp merely shook his head—if anything his silent confession made her feel all the more shy. Jim Snow had been no virgin when he came to her, and she herself had been well prepared for the conjugal business of marriage by her vigorous couplings with Master Tobias Stiles, her father's head groom. She and Jim, of course, had had their share of awkwardness and confusion when they first met, but these had to do with clashing personalities; physically they had been primed for one another, evidence of which was that Monty had been conceived in their first blissful weeks.

Yet now it was Pomp's deep physical shyness that she found so delicious—out of respect for it her kisses were delivered softly—she did not want to frighten him.

"I've seen chambermaids do this, in Germany," Pomp admitted. "The prince had thirty servants and the young maids were always getting in love."

"Why, you little spy," Tasmin said. "And what did the sight of all this kissing make you feel?"

"Sad," Pomp admitted at once.

"Sad . . . but it's merely life going on," Tasmin told him.

"Because I thought no one would ever want *me*," Pomp admitted.

"But you were wrong. Many women will want you, although I don't intend to let them get past me," Tasmin informed him.

Pomp gave a tired shrug. "My mother loved me so much that when she died I tried to die too—I was always springing fevers," he remembered.

Tasmin remembered the night when they were walking to her tent by the icy Yellowstone, when Pomp had admitted that he rarely felt lust. His polite neutrality had irritated her then—now, in the warm summer, with her arms locked around him, she thought she understood a little better. She had wanted, even then, with her husband not two hundred yards away, to kiss him, to push him toward life, to plant him solidly into it and not allow him to be tempted by the other place, death, the mystery that enclosed the mother he still yearned for.

Frightened for a moment, she kissed him again, more deeply this time.

"Those German girls, those maids and cooks, just weren't bold enough," she said. "You're a shy one, Pomp. You need a shameless English girl like me, who ain't afraid to grab you."

Pomp gave her a shy smile, tempting Tasmin to the longest kiss yet, a kiss that seemed to remove them from the normal sphere of daily activity and lifted them to a place where there was only one another. But it wasn't merely daily activity that Tasmin wanted to banish—what she wanted was for him to be tempted by *her*, not by the other place, the place where his mother was. Yet even after this melting kiss, the shadow remained. Happiness, even the extreme happiness she felt when he accepted her kiss, was no barrier to danger. She felt that she would have to be very alert, very forward, so that this young man, her darling, her breath, would not misjudge some dangerous moment because of his old temptation to the shade. Even as she held him and kissed him she wasn't sure that he was quite won.

"You must watch yourself from now on," she told him solemnly. "You mustn't be careless—you mustn't get killed. It would break my heart. I fear we've many dangers to surmount before we reach Santa Fe."

"Yes, and from what I hear, Santa Fe's as dangerous as any other place," he said. "Most of the Mexicans would as soon kill us as look at us."

"Just don't get killed—will you promise?" Tasmin asked, holding his cheeks in her hands so he would face her.

"We mustn't talk about it—it's bad luck," Pomp said. For a moment he looked scared. Just then, in the distance, Tasmin heard Monty wailing. Monty was fascinated by horses—perhaps he had toddled too close to one and been kicked, or else cut himself with a knife someone had carelessly left in his path. Little Onion was the soul of vigilance where the toddlers were concerned, but the little boys had already proven ingenious at injuring themselves, no matter how closely their keepers watched them.

"Damn it, what's wrong with that child now?" Tasmin wondered, annoyed at having her idyll interrupted. "I suppose we can't just stand here kissing forever, although I'd like to. Come with me—I'll feed the hungry brat."

"You go—I want to bury what's left of Andy," Pomp replied. "Besides, I'd be shy around the boys yet."

"You mean you think it shows—that we're in love?" Tasmin asked.

"The boys don't have much to do but gossip and pry," he reminded her. "I guess most people like to gossip and pry. Back at Prince Paul's castle the servants did so much gossiping they barely had time to get the meals cooked, or the horses groomed."

Tasmin was reluctant to stop holding him—she kissed him one more time.

"What a nuisance society is—even *this* society, which is hardly elevated," she said. "I think we deserve a little more time to ourselves, with no comment encouraged."

Pomp smiled.

"You're the most beautiful woman in the world," he told her. "People are going to have something to say about everything you do."

"Oh hush—how many women have you seen, that you should pay me such a compliment?" Tasmin retorted, though she blushed. What with the Indian attack, and her nursing, and her mothering—all the general press of life—it had been weeks since she had had a moment in which to consider her looks. On the boat up the Missouri she had amused herself in all the usual ways: redoing her hair, trying on dresses and jewels, looking in the mirror, worrying that the American climate might affect her complexion. She had also had a bit of time to study herself at Pierre Boisdeffre's trading post. But once on the trek, she had no time for looks—it seemed to her that looks might as well be left out of the equation until they returned to civilization. What she saw the few times she did look was a sunburned, windburned, freckled girl, scratched by weeds and bushes and so pressed by the need to keep her baby well and her husband satisfied that looks hardly seemed worth worrying about. For the moment, energy seemed to matter more, and so far, her energies were still equal to the hundred tasks of the day, whether the tasks were motherly, wifely, or miscellaneous. Still, that Pomp considered her the greatest of beauties was very satisfying.

"I expect there are fine beauties in London or Paris or even New York City that might dispute that comment," she told him. "Of course, there are few of them out here—I suppose I profit from an absence of rivals."

Pomp smiled again—in the distance Monty's wails had intensified.

"I've not paid many women compliments," Pomp said. "I'm just now starting—with you."

"Oh, damn! What could be ailing that child?" Tasmin complained. "I hope you won't be long at your tasks—I want you to come back soon."

"I expect your sisters will be curious, too," he reminded her. "They're always watching, those girls."

"Yes, and they'll be slapped, unless they're careful!" she declared hotly, before she turned away to see what could be the matter with her sturdy child.

14

Tasmin had guessed it: horses!

T A S M I N had guessed it: horses! A large one belonging to William Ashley had stepped on Monty's toe. Little Onion had already made a poultice for the damaged digit, but Monty still sobbed and choked, great tears rolling down his plump cheeks, while the two other toddlers, Talley and Rabbit, looked on in shocked wonder. Seeing his mother, Monty immediately flung out his arms to be taken, and Tasmin did take him, though of course there was not much to be done for a mashed toe that Little Onion had not already seen to.

"Little boys should avoid big horses, if they value their toes," Tasmin told him; she then sat down behind a wagon and gave him the breast, which he attacked greedily, as if, by sucking noisily, he could avoid his hurt. The wagon was theirs, purchased from Ashley by Lord Berrybender—it was already half packed with a mélange of their possessions. The Berrybenders, like the trappers, had been inching toward a departure for several days. But with the Ute danger passed, life in the Valley of the Chickens was on the whole pleasant and no one could quite work up to resuming the hardships of the trek, though William Ashley had hurried off finally that very morning, going north to catch a steamer at the mouth of the Yellowstone. He

had sold Lord Berrybender four horses and what little champagne remained.

Tasmin had marched through the trappers without giving
them a look—a mother hurrying to her injured child was not
likely to attract much comment. In her opinion the mountain
men would have needed to be a good deal more expert in the
ways of women to suspect that she had been enjoying the first
blushing kisses of her new, unsanctioned love.

In fact the mountain men were mainly debating which way to
go once they left the rendezvous: south with the Berrybenders to
Santa Fe, north with Ashley to the Yellowstone, east into the
Black Hills of the Sioux, where there were said to be many
beaver still, or west over the mountains to California. Tasmin and
Pomp were often together anyway—all the mountain men reck-
oned that Pomp would be dead but for Tasmin's nursing. If he
was sweet on his beautiful nurse, that would be only natural.
None of them had ever known Pomp to take a woman—the common opinion was that if he ever *did* take one, he would be
unlikely to start with Jim Snow's formidable wife. In the end the
mountain men who decided on Santa Fe did so at least in part
because it meant they'd have the Berrybender women to look
at—in their minds no small benefit.

Tasmin had hoped for a few minutes alone, in which to
soothe her child and collect her thoughts, but even the modest
privacies attendant on the performance of bodily functions
were not always easily secured in such a large camp. The bear
cub, Abby, who liked to inject herself into every crisis, followed
Tasmin around the wagon and thrust her cold nose into Tasmin's hand. It was a lovely, clear day—near the river Tasmin saw
her father, in argument with Vicky Kennet. Vicky's violent threat
to tear his throat out if he touched her had caused only the
break of a day or two in the old lord's pursuit of the long-
legged cellist.

Tasmin was just shifting Monty, a little boy who would soon be
passing from hunger into sleep, onto the other breast, when his
two little friends, Talley and Rabbit, followed the bear cub and

stood watching the proceedings solemnly, as if waiting for a chance at the teat themselves.

"Go away, boys . . . you've got the wrong ma," Tasmin commanded. "This fountain will soon be empty."

A moment later Little Onion, who had been drying jerky, swooped over and picked up a little boy under each arm; she carried them, unmoving as logs, back around the wagon so that Tasmin could finish her nursing in peace.

She had scarcely gone when Tasmin's sisters came trailing over, Buffum looking subdued and Mary, as always, looking combative.

"Pa's determined to have Vicky—I doubt it will be long before he wears her down," Buffum remarked.

"Mr. Bonneville fancies her too," Mary remarked.

"Mr. Bonneville is said to have twelve wives, which would mean little time for Vicky," Tasmin said. "Perhaps he merely likes her fiddling."

"The pater is tired of Milly," Mary informed them. "And he does know Vicky's ways."

"Vicky's merely a servant, you know," Buffum reminded them. "Servants finally have to do what masters say—even if reluctantly."

"Where have you hidden Pomp?" Mary asked, giving Tasmin one of her not-quite-sane but nonetheless penetrating looks.

"He's burying the other bear cub," Tasmin said. "The Utes made short work of that friendly little beast. Pomp feels badly about it."

"Our Pomp's too softhearted by half," Mary replied. "I suppose you've been soothing him, Tassie, in your insistent way."

"Suppose all you want," Tasmin replied. "Why don't you go flog your fat botanist and leave the rest of us in peace?"

"Such a careless brat, Monty," Mary said. "Letting a vast horse step on his toe."

Tasmin made no answer. She did not propose to talk to Mary, a skilled interrogator who proceeded by indirection but, in the end, usually managed to extract whatever kernel of information she was seeking. It was better to ignore her than to outwit her, although Tasmin did mean to outwit her when it came to her own relations with Pomp. Since Pomp had not reappeared she thought she might use the time, once Monty finished nursing, to do a bit of packing herself. Jimmy, her husband, always kept his possessions neatly, in one place, a habit that irritated her, since her own managed to get themselves scattered over an acre or two.

By the river her father and Vicky still seemed to be faced off. Tasmin was rather fearful that violence might erupt—and it did erupt, but not from the riverside. It came in the form of a loud fit of sobbing, the source being Buffum, who flung herself into Tasmin's arms.

"Oh hell . . . now what's wrong with you?" Tasmin asked. Buffum, usually wan and quiet, if capable of distinctly sharp sarcasm, had been looking unusually cheerful, even beautiful, for the past few weeks, and had even offered, on more than one occasion, to tend to the little boys for an hour or two, while Coal and Little Onion performed prodigies of labor about the camp.

For a time Buffum sobbed so hard she could not get breath to speak, while Tasmin made soothing sounds and occasionally stroked her woeful sister's hair.

Mary, who hated to see her sister Buffum get even the most cursory attention, soon showed her impatience with Buffum's lachrymose fit.

"Do make her hush, Tassie," Mary insisted. "Nothing is as boring as listening to a rich girl cry."

"Rich girl?" Tasmin said. "What possible good's it being a rich girl here? Show a little sympathy for your sister—for all we know she's grievously ill."

"Not a bit of it!" Mary insisted. "The mater spoiled her outrageously and now we must have our conversations interrupted by all this wailing."

"I don't recall that it was much of a conversation anyway," Tasmin remarked, still stroking Buffum's hair, which was rather lank. "Why can't you just go and beat your boyfriend? Bessie here may not wish to reveal this sorrow, which is likely a profound one."

"It *is* a profound one!" Buffum declared, glaring at Mary. "The fact is I'm in love with a Ute and I don't wish to leave, tomorrow or ever."

"Miscegenation—I suspected it," Mary said. "Father will be most distraught."

"Well, first things first—which Ute are you in love with?" Tasmin asked.

Four Utes still wandered around the camp, hoping to pick up a few last presents. Buffum pointed to a tall, handsome youth who was in conversation with Jim Bridger. Tasmin had noticed the boy herself, several times—his looks were indeed striking, and he wore nothing but a loincloth.

"His white name is High Shoulders," Buffum informed them. "I find him singularly beautiful and I shall love him till I die."

"You evil slut, now you've lain with our brother's murderer!" Mary hissed.

"Oh, do leave off," Tasmin said. "Our brother was run over by a horse. I will admit that if I were inclined to copulate with a Ute, young Mr. High Shoulders would be the most likely candidate. It would no doubt be a good deal more normal than flagellating a Dutchman with brambles."

"Oh, Tassie, he is *so* beautiful!" Buffum declared. "I was by the river when he came to me the first time. As you can see, he doesn't wear much—just that little flap, which he quickly removed. I confess I could not look away—Tim, as you might suspect, is a rather stubby lad. High Shoulders at once presented himself to me and we began to fornicate to the most blissful lengths—I even suspect that I may already be with child."

"They must have been blissful lengths, if you're already pregnant," Tasmin said, not unkindly. She remembered her own blissful lengths with Jim and her surprise at how quickly Monty was planted in her—apparently the famous Berrybender fecundity had not been at all affected by vigorous travel in the West.

Lay down with a Berrybender and a child will soon enough arrive, Tasmin thought.

"You are evil hussies, both of you," Mary declared. "I far prefer Piet's mild hygienic practices, myself."

The half-insane light was once again in her eyes.

"Now Buffum will give birth to a wicked little half-breed, further debasing the Berrybender escutcheon," she continued.

"Pomp's a half-breed—surely you don't consider *him* wicked?" Tasmin replied.

"No, but it's plain that you hope to be wicked with him," Mary said. "Perhaps you have been already, even though joined in holy matrimony with Mr. Jim Snow."

"Let's take one imbroglio at a time, if you don't mind," Tasmin said lightly, well aware that a direct or too emphatic denial would only fan Mary's flame. Besides, the fact was that Buffum's dilemma *was* immediate. The company's departure was imminent. What *was* to become of Buffum and her handsome Mr. High Shoulders? Was he to travel with them, far from the land of his people, or was Buffum to be left behind, to live, improbably, as a Ute wife? It was certainly a dilemma Tasmin had not expected to be presented with, but of course such things *would* always happen and a decision would have to be made. She stole another look at the slim youth, High Shoulders—a striking young man in every way. Tasmin could not but wonder whether she would have approved of the union had the Ute been short, squat, and toothless, rather than sharp featured, graceful, and lean. Ugly men might, of course, have fine souls; some she had seen in the London salons, though ugly as frogs, seemed to enjoy clear success with ladies both elegant and highborn. Her sister would not be likely to disregard a fine body, should one present itself.

"This iniquity shall not go unpunished," Mary said, but neither Tasmin nor Buffum paid any attention to her—Mary soon hurried away to make the news known to Piet.

"What am I to do, Tassie? I can't leave him—I can't—and we are to depart tomorrow, Jim Bridger declares."

"Somehow I don't think you'd last long with the Utes," Tasmin told her. "I think we'd better take your handsome savage with us, if he'll go. Jimmy won't much like it—he doesn't trust Utes—but then, who knows when we'll see Jimmy again?"

It was then, as Bess rushed off to her young man, that Tasmin noticed that Monty, unaware of the passion storms swirling around him, had dropped off the breast and was sound asleep.

15

"Stop calling me a wench . . ."

T A S M I N found herself secretly pleased that her sister Bess had been so enterprising as to take a handsome lover. This development would give the trappers something to talk about for a while, so that they were unlikely to take any particular notice if she were to wander off in the woods with Pomp Charbonneau, known, in any case, to be her very close friend.

Where was he, though, her Pomp? She found that she could not keep from throwing glances at the glade where they had recently been embracing. Tasmin was not exactly worried, and yet she did wish Pomp would appear—even a distant glimpse of him would be reassuring. When he didn't appear, little by little, anxieties crept in. Was he perhaps having second thoughts—reminding himself, for example, that it was Jim Snow's wife whom he had just been kissing? He had seemed to welcome her kisses—but then, where was he? Being so very inexperienced, perhaps he merely did not suspect how anxious ladies were likely to become, or how insecure they could be, even about long-established affections, and of course, only more so about affections that had only been acknowledged for a few hours.

In Pomp's arms, with his mouth on hers, Tasmin had felt certain enough about his love—though she was not yet entirely sure about his desire. Hadn't he confessed to her himself that he really didn't know *how* to desire? Tasmin considered desire an easy thing, usually; a thing quickly awakened, though perhaps not likely to appear with uniform intensity either among men or women. There were days, after all, when she felt not the slightest desire to copulate with Jim. That need came often enough, and intensely enough, but there were times when it was absent. Pomp had so far been exempt from these rhythms—entirely normal rhythms, in Tasmin's view. After all, if lovers were constantly at one another, how could work get done and children reared?

Pomp, she felt sure, was merely untouched in that way—she considered that it might be delicious work to get him going and bring him up to speed. But at the moment, she would be content with something simpler: she merely wanted him to reappear, to give her at least a look that might suggest that he wanted to continue what they had begun. The fact that he did *not* reappear was beginning to annoy her. Men, she knew, were rather of the out-of-sight, out-of-mind disposition. She doubted that Jimmy Snow, wherever he might be, had given her two thoughts since he departed; perhaps Pomp, a male after all, was merely trying to catch a fish, or something, quite unaware of the anxious flutters in Tasmin's breast. He was not yet quite back to full strength—he might merely be taking a nap in the cool glade. Tasmin deposited her sleeping child with Little Onion and strolled down toward the trees, meaning to look for Pomp, but before she could put that plan into action, matters came to a head between her father and Vicky. Lord Berrybender gave a loud cry—evidently Vicky had rushed in and bitten the old fool. Lord B., wild with fury, managed to deal her a roundhouse blow, knocking her off her feet and into the shallows of the river. The mountain men, always happy to divert themselves by watching fights, gave a wild cheer, though it was not clear to Tasmin which combatant they were cheering for. Vicky Kennet came at Lord Berrybender again, kicking his peg leg out from under him; she then grabbed his crutch and began to beat him with it—her fighting spirit provoked even wilder cheers from the mountain men. Then Lord B. managed to catch her ankle; he succeeded in upending her. The two of them rolled around near the river's edge, neither able to gain a clear advantage. Lord B. cursed, Vicky screamed insults— a few of the trappers began to stroll down toward the scene of the combat in order to watch the fight at closer range. Tasmin thought she had better go too, perhaps attempt to break up this violent tussle before anyone was very much hurt; but before she could reach the struggling couple, Pomp Charbonneau, the very man she had been hoping to see, emerged from the forest, the carcass of a small deer across his shoulders. He quickly waded the river, dropped his dead buck, and began to urge armistice on the wrestling couple. Much relieved to see that Pomp had merely been hunting, Tasmin hurried along; but by the time she reached the river her father and Vicky had given up punching one another; both sat, wet and exhausted, staring into space. Pomp helped Lord B. get his peg leg adjusted.

"What a tussle, Papa," Tasmin said. "I assure you we've all been most entertained by your efforts to subdue a helpless woman."

"Subdue her? I want to muzzle her—you see where she bit me," Lord Berrybender complained, pointing at a tiny spot of blood on his throat. "I won't be able to sleep a wink, for fear she'll slip in and finish the job."

"Now why would our Vicky do such a thing?" Tasmin asked. "I hope you haven't been suggesting improprieties again—I warned you about that myself."

"That's right—you bit my hand," Lord B. recalled. "I ought to muzzle you and this wench too."

"Stop calling me a wench, you old pile of guts!" Vicky demanded, her nostrils flaring.

And yet, a moment later, when Lord Berrybender struggled to stand up, it was Vicky who helped him, returning the very crutch she had been beating him with.

"I never saw such obstinacy," Lord Berrybender remarked, though in a considerably softer tone.

"So it's the altar or nothing—is that the case, my dear?" he added, thoughtfully.

"That's right—the altar or nothing," Vicky said. "I'll be your wife, I reckon, but I won't be your whore."

Lord Berrybender heaved a sigh. Then he put an arm around Vicky's shoulder and the two of them started up the hill.

"It might as well be the altar, then," Lord B. remarked, to Tasmin's complete astonishment.

The mountain men, far from sure what they were witnessing, nonetheless produced a hearty cheer, as the old lord and the young cellist walked away from their combat hand in hand.

Behind the trappers Tasmin spotted Buffum, standing shyly by the side of High Shoulders, her towering Ute, who seemed to be trying to figure out what the men were celebrating.

"There, do you see that?" Tasmin asked Pomp, with a nod at her father and his bride-to-be.

"I guess they made it up—and there's venison for supper too," he said, smiling.

Tasmin, despite her relief that Pomp was all right, felt a flush of irritation. Made it up? Was that all he saw in the situation?

"It's more than that—he's going to marry her—it's what Vicky's planned for since the moment my mother broke her neck," Tasmin informed him. "I thought my father would elude her, but he didn't. She's won . . . and good for her. Don't you see?"

Pomp got out his knife and prepared to butcher the little deer. He heard a note of irritation in Tasmin's voice and looked up, wondering what was wrong. Tasmin realized that Pomp was merely being practical—getting a meal ready—and yet it irked her that he should have been so untouched by the storm of emotion he had just witnessed; if he was untouched by her father's acknowledgment that he was attached to Vicky, perhaps he was untouched, also, by the fact that they themselves had kissed. If he had strong feelings for her, he was evidently willing to let them wait until the task at hand—cutting up a deer—had been performed properly. It irked her so much that she gave the helpless carcass a vigorous kick.

"Wake up, Pomp!" she demanded. "My father's getting married, my sister's taken a savage lover, and then there's *us*. Rather a lot for an afternoon, wouldn't you say?

"There is *us*, isn't there?" she asked, her confidence slipping.

"There's us," Pomp agreed, calmly. "Do you want to sneak off for a minute, once I get this deer butchered?"

"That's exactly what I do want—to sneak off for a minute, once you get this wretched deer cut up," Tasmin told him. "And you might consider hurrying, if you don't mind. I'm afraid that you'll soon realize that I'm a very impatient person."

"I'll hurry," Pomp said, kneeling by the carcass.

With an effort Tasmin restrained herself—it was on the tip of her tongue to explain to the young Nimrod that in her opinion kissing should come first and mundane chores a distant second. Any of the trappers could easily have butchered the deer. She started to make that point, but held back—she had glanced up the hill and noticed that Father Geoffrin was watching the two of them closely, a fact which irritated her mightily. Father Geoffrin, a great reader of risqué novels, was always the first to spot new currents of emotion, should any happen to swirl through the camp. Tasmin didn't want the nosy priest knowing about herself and Pomp—not just yet. So, instead of immediately drawing Pomp into the bushes, Tasmin waded into the river and washed her face and neck. Even a Jesuit couldn't object to that, or conclude that something might be afoot.

All the same, refreshing as the splash was, Tasmin felt a sag of weariness at the thought of the intractability of men. When she met Jim Snow he had known nothing of women except the bare physical facts. Of course, Jim had grown up in a wilderness—how could he have learned? But Pomp had been educated in a castle in Germany, where by his own admission he had observed cooks and chambermaids making merry with their lovers. And yet it was beginning to dawn on Tasmin that Pomp might know even less about women than Jim had. Was she always, then, doomed to have to be the teacher? Would she never find a man who could teach *her*, someone who would dance her off to bed without her having to forever be leading and expostulating? In the whole camp, the discouraging fact was that the only man who did understand her feelings was a little French priest, whose real interest was in romantical novels and well-stitched French clothes. Must she simply flounder from innocent to innocent until, old and jaded, she accepted one of the cynical old frog princes of the London salons, perhaps for no better reason than that she would at least not have to explain to him the realities of love?

Tasmin didn't know—she still meant to take Pomp into the woods and kiss him to her heart's content—but since that was her plan, she thought it might be wisest to give Father Geoffrin a wide berth until the thing had been accomplished.

How irritating that the priest seemed able to read her emotions as easily as he read his Marmontel!

16

"Not for nothing have I read my Laclos . . ."

BUT that's *why* I understand your emotions better than you understand them yourself," Father Geoffrin informed Tasmin—who had at once forgotten her resolve to avoid him until her romance had been consummated—if it should be.

The two of them, having attacked the tender venison with their hands, were licking grease off their fingers.

"Not for nothing have I read my Laclos, my Crébillon, the divine Madame de Lafayette, my Restif, and all the others," he went on. "I am so well schooled in the subtleties of love that a peek into your own feelings requires not the smallest effort."

"I suppose what you're saying is that I ain't subtle, like your powdered French ladies," Tasmin grumped. "Is that what you're saying, Geoff?"

She was watching Pomp assist Jim Bridger in doctoring a mare who had something amiss with her foot.

"Would you say that a sledgehammer hitting an anvil is subtle?" Geoff asked, with a wicked smile. "That's about how subtle you are, my beauty."

"It's hardly a flattering metaphor, and I'm not your beauty," Tasmin told him. "I feel like crying and you're not helping, even though that is generally thought to be a priest's duty."

"Tasmin, you can't make Pomp Charbonneau into what he's not," Father Geoff told her affably. "He's not a lecherous man. Perhaps you can maul him into what you want him to be—but perhaps not. After all, not all love succeeds—if it did, think of how monotonous life would be."

"Shut up! I'll make this succeed," Tasmin said. "I'll make Pomp want what I want. Why shouldn't he?"

Father Geoffrin shrugged.

"He's a very calm fellow, Pomp," he observed. "Perhaps he prefers his calm—he won't have much of it if you succeed in entangling him in your lusts."

Though Tasmin had sought the priest out—where else was she going to get an informed opinion about matters of the heart but from this smart celibate? But now she found that she hated everything he was telling her. Why would Pomp Charbonneau, the man she meant to have, possibly prefer calm to passion? He hadn't really even known passion yet.

"If he's as innocent as he looks, you might consider giving him a little time to reflect," Geoff advised.

Tasmin put her face in her hands—in a moment warm tears were dripping through her fingers, tears mainly of self-reproach. She was beginning to fear that she must, after all, be a bad woman to want this young man when she already had an excellent husband. It must be sinful to want two at once—and yet that was the fact: she did want two at once. Whatever he might have observed the German chambermaids doing, Pomp Charbonneau *was* as innocent as he looked; yet now she was determined to besmirch that innocence, and as soon as possible. She *did* want to entangle him in her lusts. She was bad—she knew it—and yet she couldn't change. She meant to have her way—the greedy, sensual way of the Berrybenders. Were her appetites, after all, as selfish and unrestrained as her father's? What had he done, for the last forty years, except seduce every comely woman who caught his eye, in the process betraying his marriage vows as casually as if he were eating a peach? She was younger, but was she any better? She knew she wasn't. Even in England she had scorned ladylike behavior—now, far out on the American prairies, it could only be a nuisance. There were social customs—and then there was one's real nature. What *was* her real nature?

"Cry, you'll feel better," said Father Geoffrin, putting an arm around her shoulders rather tentatively. "Although personally it's the one criticism I have of women—they *will* cry—and then men feel so bad."

"Well, you needn't feel bad," Tasmin told him, flinging off the arm. "I wasn't crying about you."

"But you might, mightn't you? After all, I'm a needful person too," the priest told her. "I cry about myself every time I remember how far I am from Paris."

"That's not important," Tasmin said bluntly—she needed to take out her irritation on somebody. Why not Geoff, her understanding friend?

"There you sit, day after day," she went on, "reading about love in your ill-bred books, and yet you never do love with anyone at all. At least I try to grapple with the thing itself, although I always seem to fail."

"You don't always fail—no self-pity now," Geoff reprimanded. "Sometimes you appear to be *very* happy, as you were this morning when you emerged from your first little rendezvous with Pomp."

"How did *you* know that I was happy?" she asked, for it was true: she had been very happy that morning.

"By your blushing—you reddened like a rose," Geoff told her. "It's mainly happy women who blush to the roots of their hair."

"You spy!—sometimes I hate you—no one else saw me blushing," Tasmin retorted.

"Not so—your sister Mary noticed even before I did."

"The sinister brat, what did she say?"

"She said, 'The fat's in the fire, Tasmin has had her way with Pomp,'" the priest quoted.

"But I *haven't* had my way with him—why are you all so convinced that I'm bad?" she asked, feeling very discouraged.

"*I* don't think you're bad," Geoff assured her. "You're merely very impetuous, and rather forward at times."

"I confess I did kiss Pomp—just kissing, no more," Tasmin admitted. "And you were right—I *was* happy, and I did blush. But it was only kissing."

"Fine—though kissing has been known to lead to even more intimate behavior," Father Geoff reminded her. "And then you went back in the woods with him after he butchered our deer. That was for more kissing, I assume."

Tasmin put her face in her hands again, too upset to voice her disappointment.

"It was like kissing a brother," she confided, when she felt able to speak.

"Now I understand your tears," Father Geoffrin said, putting his arm around her again; this time she let it be, and even rested her throbbing head against his shoulder.

"The kisses of a brother are not always what one wants," he said.

"It was so sweet this morning," Tasmin told him. "But this afternoon it just didn't work . . . he wouldn't even allow me to hug him as I wished to."

"My, my . . . it's so complicated," Father Geoffrin said. "Do you suppose you'd ever want to kiss me? You needn't worry that I'd feel brotherly about you."

Tasmin fairly jumped away—she could not have moved more quickly if she had discovered that she was standing on a snake.

"But Geoff, you're a priest—you can't kiss anybody, much less me," she told him.

"I'm not much of a priest—you yourself frequently remind me of that sad fact," Geoff said. "Besides, there's a whole school of literature based on the unchaste and disorderly behavior of priests and nuns."

"I'm not literature, I'm a woman," Tasmin said, indignantly. "You of all people—trying to catch me when I'm discouraged."

"A catch is a catch," Father Geoffrin said.

Tasmin looked him in the face. His was a thin face, intelli-

gence popping off it like sparks. In his eyes she saw unmistak-
able desire, the one thing she had not been able to arouse in her
sweet, handsome Pomp. A shiver ran through her—she was
about to tell Geoff quite firmly that he had better mind his man-
ners when Monty came waddling in their direction. The confusion inside Tasmin was so great that she merely jumped up and
hurried toward the river, passing her son without even giving
him a pat, a lapse that startled Monty so that he opened his
mouth to protest but then forgot to wail.

Father Geoffrin sighed; he thought there might yet be at least
a glimmer of opportunity, though opportunity was not likely to
present itself anytime soon. As a second best he helped himself
to another bloody slice of the excellent, tender venison.

17

In her confusion she first blamed Jim . . .

W H E N dusk fell, Tasmin hurried down to the river and
walked along it until she found some concealing bushes; then
she sat down and sobbed until she was empty of tears. In her
confusion she first blamed Jim—why would he just go riding off
and leave his wife the opportunity to develop so many unfaithful
feelings? There were several competent scouts in the company—
why couldn't two of them have conducted this scout, if it was so
important? Wasn't the real reason Jim left that he simply got tired
of dealing with her? Of course, their matings were still lively and
satisfying—it was her talk, the incessant flow of opinions that
poured out of her, which seemed to tire Jim. Indeed, her talk
seemed to tire everyone, except perhaps the smart little French
priest, whose sudden declaration of interest had just shocked
her so. If only Jimmy wouldn't indulge in such lengthy absences
she would have much less opportunity to daydream of love with
Pomp.

But once she was cried out, which left her calm if tired, content merely to listen to the river rush over its rocks, Tasmin knew
that blaming Jim Snow wasn't really fair. She had had just as
many daydreams of romance with Pomp Charbonneau while
Jimmy was still in camp. Nor could Pomp be blamed, particu-

larly—he had told her months before that he wasn't lustful, a confession she had felt free to ignore, confident that she could make any man lust a little if she applied herself to the task. Young virgins often became old lechers, in her opinion. Pomp Charbonneau simply didn't know what he was missing—once she was able to show him, surely he wouldn't want to miss it anymore.

Sitting concealed behind her bush, Tasmin felt exhausted—a whole day of the surge and ebb of feeling had worn her out— and for what? Here they were, hundreds of miles from Santa Fe, with summer ending, the temperament of the Indians uncertain, the way hazardous, Jimmy gone, herself with a young child to care for, a task that would have usurped all her energies had she not been able to count on the loyalty of Little Onion, a young woman who had nothing in particular to be happy about, that Tasmin could see, but who was unfailing in her devotion to the various little boys while still managing to accomplish a myriad of chores.

Tasmin knew she should have been grateful enough just to be alive and healthy, with a healthy baby. She should be capable of concentrating on just the task of survival, and not go around kissing one minute and sobbing the next, allowing herself to be prey to the sort of hothouse emotions that might better have flourished among the bored nobility of London or Paris, Venice or Vienna, rather than in a remote and rugged valley by a mountain river. Why bother loving, kissing, seducing, desiring, failing, or succeeding in the rare sublimities and frequent disappointments attendant on the attempt to love any man, much less the two intractable specimens she had fixed her feelings on? Why didn't she just stop it, pack up her kit, yell at the trappers until they sprang into action, get the whole company on the road— any road?

She knew she didn't lack character—it must be that her character was just bad, selfish, even brutal. She couldn't stop wanting the pleasure of being loved by a man—even the sneaky little priest had looked at her in such a way as to make her shiver. The first soft kisses she had exchanged with Pomp that morning *had* made her blush to the roots of her hair. She *was* reckless and she couldn't help it—she was going to make trouble for men. Those who didn't welcome trouble would do better to stay out of her way.

Just as Tasmin was reaching this uncomfortable conclusion, she happened to notice a small, squat figure watching her through the bushes. Kate Berrybender, unobserved, had found her out.

"Are you crying because you miss Mr. James Snow?" Kate asked, with her customary bluntness.

"I would be glad to see Jimmy—I mostly am always glad to see Jimmy," Tasmin admitted, wondering why, of all times, she now had to be interrogated by a four-year-old.

"So is that why you're crying, then?" Kate asked, in a tone that was surprisingly sympathetic.

"It's not always easy to say why one cries, my dear," Tasmin said. "I cry because I'd burst if I don't."

"I think it's because you miss Mr. James Snow," Kate concluded. "I often feel like crying myself when Mr. James Snow is absent. When he's here I don't feel that the Indians are as likely to scalp me."

"An accurate surmise, I'd say."

"Pomp Charbonneau is rather worried—I believe he's looking for you," Kate informed her.

"You found me easily enough," Tasmin pointed out. "Surely a skilled scout such as Pomp could locate me if he really wanted to."

"I don't know whether to call him 'mister' or 'monsieur,'" Kate confessed. "At times he seems rather French."

Tasmin chuckled.

"Personally, I don't find him French enough," she confessed. "Nor do I find him American enough. It may be that he's stuck in between, which is why he vexes me so."

"That priest is a wily fellow," Kate remarked.

"Wily indeed—but at least he's French enough," Tasmin told her.

"All the same, I do feel better when Mr. James Snow is with us," Kate said.

"I suppose I do too," Tasmin allowed. "If you see Monsieur Pomp, tell him that I can be found sitting squarely behind this bush."

"I don't like it that you cry, Tassie," Kate admitted, in a quavering voice. "Perhaps you could hug me. I'm sure I'd feel somewhat better after my hug."

Tasmin hugged her warmly—despite the child's bossy airs, she *was* a baby sister.

"I think I'll just call Pomp 'mister,'" Kate said, as she was leaving. "Perhaps it will help him be more American."

It was full dark when Pomp came—Tasmin had been sitting, rather numbly, wondering if he *would* come. He moved so quietly that when he put his hand on her shoulder Tasmin jumped, thinking it might be Geoff.

"Kate said you were crying—I expect it's my fault," he said.

"Not at all," Tasmin assured him. "If there's one thing I can't stand it's men who assume blame when no blame has been assigned them.

"I have my moods, Pomp," she added. "Many of them are just my moods—most of them have nothing to do with you."

"But you *were* vexed with me this afternoon," he reminded her, easing down to sit beside her.

"It would be more accurate to say I was frustrated," she said. "I didn't see why I shouldn't kiss you, and yet when I tried I felt embarrassed. Nothing is more sobering than trying to kiss a man who doesn't really want you to."

"It's just that this is new," Pomp said. "I was afraid someone might spot us."

Tasmin didn't believe him, but she found his hand and twined her fingers in it.

"Pleasure has its risks," she told him. "I don't shy from them, but you big strong men certainly seem to."

"I was only trying to explain."

"No use, no use," she said sharply. "Explaining won't get us where I want us to be."

She forced him back until he lay full length on the grass—then she bent over and pressed a kiss on him that lasted and lasted, as their kisses had that morning. She was gentle at first but not girl-ish. Soon she kissed his eyelids, his throat and chest, nipped more than once at his lower lip and his neck. Pomp quivered but he didn't draw away. Tasmin, who had daydreamed about many delicious preliminaries that might be drawn out for days or weeks, as Pomp decreed, suddenly felt such a rush of desire that she felt herself go damp and dewy; she at once abandoned the notion of exquisite preliminaries. Keeping him pinned beneath her, her avid mouth on his, she undid his trousers and grasped his shaft. Pomp seemed to shiver, but didn't protest.

"Just let me do what I want," she whispered. "Just let me."

She put her mouth back on his, so as not to let him spoil things by some clumsy word. Dewy as she was, she had only to flex a few times to settle Pomp just where she had been wanting to settle him. Pomp lay very still; he didn't move but Tasmin moved. Her breath grew hoarse and hot against his cheeks—in only a minute, it seemed, his seed surged, and then seeped and seeped and seeped as, for as long as possible, Tasmin held him inside her, calming, her warm cheek against his. They lay thus for several minutes, neither of them speaking, Tasmin stroking his brow, touching his hair, now and then dipping her mouth for a quick kiss. Little by little the worm of his manhood grew smaller, until it finally slipped out.

"Now then, that wasn't so hard, was it?" she asked. Pleasure was still in her voice, just a little hoarseness.

"It's only happened to me in dreams," Pomp admitted, speak-ing softly. He seemed to be sinking into an even deeper quiet.

"Well, I hope you liked it as much as you liked the dreams," she said. "I assume you *did* like them."

"I liked this more, because I like you," Pomp said. "Only I feel I lost something, somehow."

He didn't say it critically—from the gentle way he held her it was clear enough that he was pleased—and he had spoken hon-estly, rather than romantically. He felt he had lost something; he admitted it.

"You did lose something, but it can easily be replenished," Tasmin assured him. "In fact it's replenishing, even now. But you're mine now—I suppose you could justly say you'd lost your freedom."

She leaned close but could not really see his eyes.

"If you're just going to accuse me of stripping away your innocence, then I'm likely to box your ears," she threatened.

"I wasn't innocent," Pomp insisted. "I saw too much to be innocent, even before my mother died."

"I don't know what you're talking about," Tasmin said, wondering why they were talking at all. Very likely, with the right kiss or caress, they could be making love again.

"Ma said I was born by sorrow's river," he said. "I seem to carry a weight. It keeps me from being quite like other men."

"Stop it! Don't talk so!" she demanded. "What we just did made me quite as happy as I've ever been. I don't want my happiness to slip away, and it will if you continue to talk so sadly."

Pomp said no more. He accepted Tasmin's kisses and kissed back, gently. Tasmin expected that he would begin to touch her—her breasts, perhaps, or the seeping place below, but he didn't. She told herself she had better not rush him. Once he learned more about passion he would surely be more active. She must be patient with him, a hard resolve, because she was by nature impatient. Now that she had had a little of what she wanted, she saw no reason not to have more—yet she knew it might be best to accept his shyness, for a time. She tried to brush away the shadow that dappled her happiness. What if Geoff was right? What if Pomp valued calm more than passion? What if in his depths he just wasn't sensual? His body had responded to her, but even then, his soul he seemed to keep for himself. He was a man without strategies. Even Jim Snow, no very refined seducer, had more guile and much more temperament. She continued to hold Pomp and kiss him but she couldn't quite get his sad words out of her mind. He had been born by sorrow's river—he seemed to carry a weight other men needn't carry. What could these words mean? She hated all such reflections.

They lay together in the darkness for almost an hour, until finally the evening chill drove them back to the campfire. The mountain men, playing cards and drinking, took no notice. In order to stoke her resolution, Tasmin flew at once into a frenzy of packing—she charged into the mountain men and demanded that they put down their cards and see to the wagons and animals. She wanted a dawn departure.

Tasmin had finally had enough of the Valley of the Chickens. She was up most of the night, packing and hectoring, and might have actually had the party on the move not long after dawn had not Vicky Kennet insisted that her nuptials with Lord Berrybender be performed before they left.

"I rather fear she means it—damned stubborn on that point," Lord B. was forced to admit.

"Oh damn! Now?" Tasmin protested, but Venetia Kennet held her ground—she refused even to come out of her tent, insisting that they become man and wife before risking the prairies.

"All right, be quick, then—Geoff, get to it! Marry them!" Tasmin demanded.

"But I've hardly had my coffee," Father Geoffrin protested; but Tasmin was ablaze with impatience. Father Geoff managed to find a prayer book, lined up bride, groom, and attendants, and proceeded to intone what seemed to Tasmin like rather dubious Latin, while the mountain men listened in wonder. The minute he was done the bride and groom exchanged a lusty kiss, the mountain men cheered again, and the company slowly climbed into wagons or mounted horses and proceeded out of the Valley of the Chickens. Old Hugh Glass traveled on foot, the bear cub, Abby, trailing behind him.

As the bright sun shone on the long plain ahead and struck gold glints off the snow on the high peaks to the north, Tasmin felt her spirit suddenly soar. They were moving again, they were on their trip in this wide, sunny land. They had been too long stopped, all crowded up together. No wonder she had become moody; no wonder she had worried too much about what Jim or Pomp might feel. Now at least they were on the go: travelers, adventurers! What a fine life it was!

Vicky Kennet, the new bride, sat beside Tasmin on the wagon seat. Lord Berrybender, much excited to be loose amid the game again, had converted their old cart into a kind of fiacre; he raced ahead with Señor Yanez and Signor Claricia, provided with some new guns he had purchased from William Ashley, eager to shoot whatever beasts presented themselves.

"Well, Vic, I guess you're my stepmother now," Tasmin remarked. "I hope you'll attempt to give me motherly advice when I need it, which is apt to be often."

"I will, but it's not likely you'll take it," Vicky said, with a smile.

"At any rate, congratulations—I thought you had about given up on the old boy," Tasmin offered.

"I did give up on him, several times," Vicky admitted. "But Drum was killed and I came to find that I rather missed your father, odd as that must sound."

"Pretty odd, yes," Tasmin said.

Vicky Kennet didn't feel especially victorious. Mainly she felt tired. The struggle with Lord Berrybender had filled some years of her life, and would no doubt go on being a struggle, and yet the sun was bright and the sky above them vast and blue.

"I expect we're suited enough, your father and I," she remarked to Tasmin. "He knows my ways and I know his."

Tasmin wondered if she would ever be lucky enough to say such a thing. Would she ever know Jim's ways—or he hers? Would she ever know Pomp's ways? Did he even want to know hers?

Before she could slip into a funk again from pondering the imponderables of human love, Monty, too unsteady in the bouncing rig to stand up, crawled to his mother, pulled himself up by grasping her long black hair, and began to make hungry sounds. As if on cue, Vicky's little boy did the same.

Tasmin handed Vicky the reins and pulled Monty into her lap.

"If you drive while I feed mine, I'll drive while you feed yours," she offered.

"Oh Talley won't wait," Vicky told her. "He's as greedy as his father. Perhaps Little Onion can drive—then we can nurse our brats together."

Little Onion, stunned at first to be offered such a huge responsibility, nonetheless accepted the reins and was driving the team
as if she had been doing it all her life. She drove, the two mothers nursed, and the Valley of the Chickens was soon just a blue
shadow, far behind them.

18

. . . two wolves, huge and insolent . . .

J I M   S N O W had just killed an elk—more meat than he
needed, but the only game he had seen larger than a prairie dog
for three days. A week earlier he had been among innumerable
buffalo, but the great herds were being pressed by so many
Indian bands—Sioux mainly—that he had thought it wiser to
leave the buffalo prairies and drift back to areas where there was
too little game to attract many hunters.

It was an old elk—it had been trailed by two wolves, who were
waiting for it to weaken sufficiently that they could attack. The
elk's flesh would be barely edible, but prairie dog made poor
eating too, and Jim had to eat. The two wolves, huge and insolent, only retreated a few hundred yards at the sound of his shot.
They expected to get their share of the elk, and no doubt would.

Jim was just sharpening his knife, preparatory to cutting up
this old, tough animal, when he thought he heard a shout—it
seemed he could just see a moving speck, far to the east. The
speck might be a human or a solitary buffalo—he couldn't yet
tell.

By the time Jim was half done with his butchering, the speck
had grown and divided: two humans were approaching on foot
from the east. It seemed likely that they were friendly, since they

were approaching him directly, making no attempt to conceal themselves. Jim continued his work; he felt little enthusiasm for jerking meat that was almost too tough to chew, but nothing better offered, and a man who was too picky about food could easily starve.

Jim had not seen a soul in six days, as he scouted to the south, enjoying the calm of the great empty country. Very likely the Berrybender party would have left the Valley of the Chickens by then—they would be expecting him to rejoin them soon and lead them to Santa Fe. With Pomp and Kit and Jim Bridger and the others with the party, Jim saw little reason to worry; they were all competent guides.

Then he stood up in surprise: one of the two advancing specks was clearly Maelgwyn Evans, a trapper and friend he had last seen in his camp on the Knife River. The larger speck was probably one of Maelgwyn's sizable wives. But why would Maelgwyn Evans and a large wife be hoofing it across these dun prairies, where there were no beaver to trap?

"Ho, Jimmy," Maelgwyn said, in his lilting Welsh voice, when the couple came in hailing range.

"Hello yourself—this is a fine surprise," Jim said. "I didn't know you was much of a hand for taking long walks like this."

"Well, no, I ain't that much of a walker, and neither is my little bride here, Corn Tassel, who was a maiden of the Chippewas. She's the one gave you that good rubbing with bear grease, when you visited me on the Knife."

"I remember Corn Tassel, but you used to brag that you had six hundred pounds of wives," Jim reminded him. "Corn Tassel's no fawn, but she don't weigh six hundred pounds, either."

"She don't for a fact," Maelgwyn agreed. "I guess you ain't been to the Missouri lately, Jim. So you don't know."

"Don't know what?"

"About the smallpox," Maelgwyn told him. "Water don't burn, but the pox swept up that river like a blaze. I doubt there's thirty Rees left, maybe forty Mandans, and not more than a dozen Otos."

Maelgwyn sighed.

"That's it, Jimmy," he went on. "There's been a raging plague—I expect it's in Canada by now. Bodies everywhere in the villages—wolves feasting. The living too weak to bury the dead. I lost four hundred pounds of wives in less than a week—that's how fast people went."

Jim Snow could hardly credit what he was being told. The Rees and the Mandans had been populous tribes, strong enough to hold their positions as river keepers since long before Lewis and Clark made their trip. Barely a decade earlier, the Rees had turned back William Ashley and a boatload of well-armed mountain men, and the Mandans had been courted by traders from as far away as the Columbia River or the Hudson.

"Only thirty Rees?" he said, shocked—it was almost too much to believe.

"If there's that many," Maelgwyn said. "They may have all died by now. People couldn't die much quicker if you shot them. I seen six dead in a bull boat—I guess they meant to paddle off, but they waited too long to escape."

Jim could hardly get his mind to accept it: as long as he could remember, the Rees and the Mandans had been the powers of the North. If they were gone, what would it mean?

"But you didn't live on the river," he said to Maelgwyn. "How'd it happen to hit you?"

"My smallest wife's sister came to visit, just as the pox hit. She brought it. Most of the Missouri valley's just a land of ghosts now, which is why me and Corn Tassel are moving west."

Jim was still absorbing the shock of what he had been told: the Rees gone, the Otos, the Mandans—suddenly gone. It was hard to accept.

"They say birds carry it—I don't know if that's true," Maelgwyn went on. "I just thought I'd better leave while I still have one good wife. I couldn't do without my Tassel. She's spoiled me, with her good rubs."

The two large, insolent wolves still sat in the distance, watching.

"This is an old elk," Jim mentioned. "I've got what I need.

You're welcome to the rest. Not much game to the west that I can find."

"Tassel and me are bound for the Russian River," Maelgwyn told him. "Then we may go north. I've an urge to learn to hunt the seal."

The sun was low, so the old friends decided to make camp together. There was little wood to be found, but Corn Tassel soon gathered enough buffalo chips to make a fire.

"It's good exercise for the jaws—that's the best I can say for your elk," Maelgwyn remarked, as they were eating.

"I thought you was married, Jimmy—what became of that brash English wife, and the old wild lord?" he asked.

"They've been with Ashley, at the big rendezvous," Jim said. "I imagine they're on the move by now. Kit and I decided to do a little scouting."

Maelgwyn made a show of looking around.

"I don't seem to see Kit," he said. "If he's playing hide-and-seek, I hope he won't jump out and scare me too bad."

"He won't—I left him with the balloon fellows," Jim told him. "Heard about the balloon?"

"Oh, everybody's been talking about that balloon," Maelgwyn told him. "What's your news?"

"Some cranes hit it while those two fellows were flying over the Platte. The two men didn't know their way around, so I left Kit to look after them."

"Bill Ashley's sold the skins of a big number of beavers," Maelgwyn mused. "You'd think he'd be rich enough by now that he'd get out of the country before somebody lifts his hair."

"He says he's quitting," Jim mentioned.

"If Ashley's quitting, then that's about it, for beaver," Maelgwyn remarked. "I might do better to try seals—seals might get popular, for all we know."

"Any news of the Partezon?" Jim asked.

Maelgwyn, yawning, shook his head.

"A day of walking will tire a man out," he said.

He lay down with his large wife and was soon snoring. Jim

liked Maelgwyn but didn't care for the snoring. Most of the mountain men snored noisily, another reason he liked to roam around by himself from time to time.

Usually Jim slept easily—even Maelgwyn's snoring would not have been enough to keep him awake. But he didn't sleep well that night—the story of the smallpox plague unsettled him. What if birds did carry it? If it could wipe out whole villages of Mandans and Rees, it could kill mountain men too, not to mention English travelers. What if it had struck the company? Tasmin and Monty might already be dead. He had traveled away from them happily enough—not a worry had crossed his mind—but suddenly a big worry came. While he was roaming around, enjoying the prairie light, Tasmin and Monty might be suffering. Maelgwyn had lost four wives, all healthy women, within a week.

The more Jim thought about the matter, the more anxious he became. He had scouted enough—most of the Indians were to the east, with the buffalo, getting their meat. Progress to the south should not be too difficult. Maelgwyn's story of whole villages of unburied bodies convinced him that a worse threat was loose in the land.

Jim didn't want to wait. In a minute he had Joe Walker's little mare saddled and ready. Corn Tassel, large and silent, watched alertly. When Jim was ready to leave he put a hand on Maelgwyn's shoulder—the trapper's eyes at once came open.

"I think I better get back to my family," he said. "That news about the pox is bad."

"Sure is—be careful then, Jimmy," Maelgwyn told him. "If you ever get over by the Russian River, look me up."

By the time Jim mounted, Maelgwyn Evans was already snoring again.

19

The cawing of the ravens—hundreds of ravens . . .

T H E cawing of the ravens—hundreds of ravens—made
the Bad Eye realize that the People were dying. He could not see
the festers breaking out on his face and on the vast bulk of his
body, but he could feel them: he called for Draga. He had
become too large to move upright by himself—two stout young
braves helped him out of the Skull Lodge when he needed to
drop his excrement. But both these young braves were now
dead, along with most of the Mandans, Hidatsas, Gros Ventres.
Some had fled, but others lay around the village, rotting—wolves
and dogs, coyotes and ravens pulled or pecked at them. A few
young girls were left alive but they were not strong enough to
support the Bad Eye's weight. One of the girls told him that the
witch, Draga, was not infected—she still lived in her earth lodge
outside the village.

The Bad Eye, blind from birth, could not see the festers, popping out like pods bursting over his body, but he could smell the
smell of sickness, the smell of rot. Stalled on his filthy platform,
unable to do more than sit up, he sent one of the young girls
hurrying to Draga. Near the platform was a big trunk, given him
by an important French trader, long ago. In the trunk were his
money, his beads, his knives, watches, pistols—all the things the

French and English had given him as presents over the years, either in ransom for captives or in hopes of buying his favor. It was a large trunk, but it was full. As he sat on his platform he could hear the groans of dying people, hear the wailing of the grieved and the despairing.

The Bad Eye did not intend to die with them—he wanted the powerful witch, Draga, to come and cure him. If Draga could protect herself from this evil plague, which caused the hot pods to burst out on his skin, then Draga could help him too. She could make the pods dry up, make his skin grow cool again, not feverish, as it had been since the illness came. If Draga would just cure him she could have what she wanted out of the trunk. He knew her to be a greedy woman—it would be easy enough to bribe her with the treasures in his trunk. Then, once the plague passed, the French and English and Americans would return to the river and make him rich again.

At first Draga refused to come—she told the girl to tell him she was busy. This delay infuriated the Bad Eye—he knew that if Draga didn't come and bring him a cure, he *would* die—it would be too late. He sent the girl back again and this time Draga came. He didn't hear her enter but he knew she was there because her presence made the air feel bad.

"I want you to make a spell and cure me," the Bad Eye told her. He did not immediately mention the treasures in the trunk.

Draga only chuckled. She was not a friendly woman—even her chuckle was like a curse.

"You are the great prophet of the Mandans," she reminded him. "You are the prophet all the People feared. Make your own spell."

"There's a great trunk there, full of treasure," the Bad Eye told her—he didn't want to waste time haggling. "If you cure me, I'll give you the key and you can have it all—then no one will be as rich as you."

"Why would I need your key?" Draga asked. "I brought an axe."

The Bad Eye had not considered that possibility. No one of the

People would have dared touch his trunk—but Draga was not of the People. She began to chop into the trunk—he could hear the tinkling of his treasures as they spilled out onto the floor.

"Take it all, but make me a spell," he offered, but again, Draga laughed her evil laugh.

"The whites fooled you," she said. "They knew you were blind so they gave you only the cheapest trinkets. You were a fool to suppose that the whites would make you rich, when they could trick you so easily. And your People were fools to believe you were a prophet. You're just a blind man who got too fat to walk."

"Make me a spell!" the Bad Eye commanded, summoning all his force; but no one answered. He could tell by the feel of the room that Draga was gone.

In the delirium of his fever the Bad Eye slept a little and dreamed of water. In his dream he was floating on the river, whose ripplings he had heard all his life. As he floated, many tiny fish came and nibbled at his sores. He felt them nipping, and little by little, his sores healed and his skin grew smooth again.

When he woke the Bad Eye knew that in his dream he had been granted a good prophecy. The water would save him; the little nibbling fish would cure him. The only problem was that he was in the Skull Lodge—he could hear the river as it flowed past, but he needed to be in it, and there was no one strong enough to help him out of the lodge and into the water. All the warriors were dead—the few children and few old people who were alive had not the strength to support his weight. The Bad Eye felt bitterly angry. He was the great prophet of the Mandans, but the tribe had collapsed and there was no one to assist him in the time of his greatest need.

Then it occurred to the Bad Eye that perhaps there was a chance, after all. He couldn't walk but it might be that he could crawl. Carefully he rolled off the low ledge where he had held court to tribes and traders for so long and managed to heave himself onto his hands and knees. The effort was enormous; sweat poured off him, stinging sweat that mingled with his sores; but he did manage to crawl a few yards before he had to stop and rest.

Three times he had to stop, exhausted, before he was out of

the Skull Lodge. All around him he smelled death—it seemed there must be hundreds of cawing ravens in the camp. But he could also smell the water, which gave him hope. It seemed not far. If he stopped and rested from time to time, surely he could reach it and be saved by the nibbling fish. It was not an easy crawl. Several times he blundered into corpses, or parts of corpses. Once he became entangled in a tree that had washed ashore. But he kept on, convinced that he would be healed if he could only reach the water and give himself to the little fish, the nibblers. For a time it was day—he felt the sun—but the river was much farther than he had supposed it would be, and there were many obstacles in his way. A large creature that he supposed to be a dead buffalo, putrid now, had to be skirted. Finally, after much pushing, he got around it.

Near the river he got into some terrible sticky mud. His hands sunk deep into it when he tried to crawl over it. The water was not far—he could hear the song of its flowing, but his strength was almost gone. Night had come; the mud was cold. Soon he began to shake from fever, shivering one minute and burning the next. Every time he rested it became harder and harder to raise himself onto his hands and knees. The mud was a dreadful obstacle; he could only crawl a few yards before collapsing. At one point, on the slick slope, he slid a few feet and almost rolled onto his back. That wouldn't do: on his back he would be as helpless as a turtle who had been flipped over by a raccoon. Feeling that he was going to be too weak to reach the water, the Bad Eye put all his strength into one last effort, and he did reach water, but it was not the river, it was only a shallow pond near the river's edge. The coolness of the water made him shiver so violently that he felt death might be shaking him. With his hands he raked the water of the little pond, hoping to touch a fish, a little fish, who might nibble the poison out of him. But the only fish in the pond was a dead one, who lent the water a stagnant smell. The Bad Eye felt keenly disappointed. He was in water, but not the right water. He knew he must try again, and he did try, but this time his weight was greater than his strength. He could barely even hold his face out of the water of the pond, even though the pond was only a few inches deep. He tried to crawl out of the pond but water lapped into his mouth and nose when he failed to lift his head. Frightened and bewildered, he began to sputter. His face had never been in water before—except perhaps long before, in boyhood, when his mother had taken him into the river in hopes that it would cure his blindness. All his life he had heard the sound of the river, and yet now he couldn't reach it. When he lifted his head above the water he could breathe the humid, smelly, fishy air, but when he tired, when his neck could no longer support the lifting of his head, his face fell into the water, causing him to choke and splutter. He thrashed, but he could not advance: then he began to drink, swallowing the filthy water, gulping as fast as he could so that it wouldn't cover his face when he rested. Perhaps if he swallowed enough he would finally float, as he had floated in his dream.

It was there, in the misty dawn, still fifty yards from the channel of the great river he had been trying to reach, that the Partezon, riding with Fool's Bull through the camp of the dead, found the great prophet of the Mandans drowned in a puddle so shallow that the water hardly came above the hocks of the Partezon's white horse. A frog sat on the drowned man's head; it leapt into the water with a plop when the two horses came to the edge of the pond.

"Look, there he is," the Partezon said, to Fool's Bull.

"So what? He's just a dead man, let's go," Fool's Bull urged.

But the Partezon was not to be hurried; he sat on his white horse, looking at the swollen corpse of the Bad Eye for what seemed to Fool's Bull like a long time.

"He was supposed to be the greatest man in the world," the Partezon remarked. "And now look: frogs jump off his head. He's just dead, like anybody else."

"Yes, dead—like we'll be in two or three days if we don't get out of here," Fool's Bull remarked bitterly.

"You're always in too big a hurry," the Partezon remarked, but he finally turned his horse and rode downstream.

20

Far out on the prairies . . .

F A R O U T on the prairies, a day or even two days out
from the river, the Partezon and Fool's Bull had begun to come
upon dead people: Mandans, Rees, a few Otos who had fled in
hopes of saving themselves from the great sickness that seemed
to hang over the river. They were now half eaten; they had failed
to save themselves. As the two riders came closer to the river
they saw more and more dead—so many that Fool's Bull would
have much preferred to turn back, hunt a little more, enjoy the
summer prairies. But the Partezon refused to listen—he always
refused to listen. The last thing Fool's Bull would have chosen to
do was ride through a country where everyone was dead or
dying. It made no sense. This plague had already destroyed the
people of the river. Why go where people were dying? The sickness might leave the river and follow them onto the plains, in
which case even they would die too.

Fool's Bull had said as much to his stubborn companion, but
such sensible considerations didn't interest the Partezon at all.
He just kept riding east, ignoring, with his usual rudeness, every
sensible thing that Fool's Bull brought up. Over and over Fool's
Bull vowed to himself that he himself would turn back and leave
the Partezon to his folly; but he didn't turn back. Mainly he kept

riding east because he didn't want to give the Partezon a chance to call him a coward, which the Partezon would certainly do if Fool's Bull pulled out of this strange quest.

"We'll die ourselves if we're not careful," he said several times. They were on the edge of what had been the largest Mandan village, and yet they saw nothing but abandoned lodges, some of them with dying people laying half inside and half out, too weak to go farther. Old people, young people, warriors, babies: all were dead or almost dead; the few who clung to life looked at them indifferently as they rode past. They were too far gone to struggle.

"I expect to die someday," the Partezon remarked. "I don't know why you think you ought to live forever."

"I don't want to live forever, but I don't want to die right now, either," Fool's Bull argued. "I have two young wives, remember. If you had a few young wives, instead of your cranky old wives, you wouldn't be so reckless with your life."

"I am too old for young wives," the Partezon argued—it amused him to see what lengths Fool's Bull would go to avoid certain tasks.

"Your young wives look bossy to me," he added. "I wouldn't be surprised if they wear you out pretty soon."

Conversation with the Partezon was rarely satisfactory, mainly because the Partezon scorned what seemed to Fool's Bull a sensible, simple, reasonable approach to life. Common sense should have told the man that it was foolish to come into a place where all the people were dying of a horrible sickness; and yet, there they were. Only after they had ridden all the way to the river itself, and seen the drowned body of the Mandan prophet, did the Partezon seem satisfied.

"It's a poor prophet who can't even save himself," the Partezon commented, once they had watered their horses and turned back to the prairie.

The Partezon had heard about the Bad Eye for many years; he had hoped to see him and perhaps converse with him a little. The Mandans had always seemed to him a gullible people, easily tricked by the white traders. It would have been interesting to see what kind of prophecies the fat prophet would have come out with.

Fool's Bull, for his part, was horrified by the state of the dead people he had seen. He was long accustomed to seeing men die in battle and had witnessed many captives being tortured; those deaths had seemed clean, in a way: they were honorable deaths, involving defeat but not shame. The dead in the Mandan camp were different: they were foul deaths, putrefying deaths; and there were so many dead that proper burial was out of the question. He didn't want to see any more such scenes.

"I hope the sickness doesn't follow us," he said, several times.

"You should listen when I tell you something," the Partezon scolded. "The minute I saw those two whites fly up in the air, where only birds are supposed to go, I told you that the time of the People was ending. Now that you've seen it with your own eyes, perhaps you'll pay attention when I tell you something important."

"I saw it, but I don't understand it—how can a whole tribe suddenly die?" Fool's Bull asked.

"The whites made the plague, that's why," the Partezon answered. "Maybe they dropped it out of the sky. If they can fly, then it must be easy for them to sow plagues. Maybe they fly over at night and drop the poisons into cooking pots or onto blankets. I don't know how they spread this pox, but I'm sure they do it."

"What if they drop some on us?" Fool's Bull asked, suddenly fearful—the Partezon had voiced an awful thought.

"Then we'll die, as the Mandans died," the Partezon told him. "Only I don't plan to be as foolish as that fat prophet—I won't crawl into a puddle and drown."

"It's all very well for you to be calm about dying—you're old," Fool's Bull reminded him. "I'm a young man with two wives to sleep with. I don't want this pox dropped on me."

"What you are is a liar," the Partezon told him. "We were born in the same summer—they put us in our cradle boards together—it's nonsense to say I'm old and you're young."

Fool's Bull realized he had spoken carelessly. He and the Partezon *were* the same age. And yet he wanted to live a long time and the Partezon seemed indifferent to the prospect of immediate death.

"Even if the whites *can* fly, it doesn't mean the time of the People is over," he argued.

"You're wrong—that's exactly what it does mean," the Partezon told him.

Of course, he himself did not mean to die shamefully, half in and half out of a lodge, as so many of the Mandans had. He had had a full life, killing many enemies, stealing many horses. When it came time for him to pass into the spirit world, he meant to do it in a dignified way. He meant to go alone in Paha Sapa, the sacred Black Hills, and find a cliff high up, where the eagles nested; there he would fast and pray and chant a little until the spirit left him and passed on to the Sky House, the place of spirits, higher than any white man could hope to fly. He had supposed that the life he had always known would last forever, season following season with the old ways unchanged; but that was shallow thinking. Things changed for everything: for the eagles, for the Sioux, for the buffalo.

Even as he was thinking these thoughts he happened to see some dim brown shapes on the far horizon and at once put his horse into a gallop. The brown shapes were buffalo—the Partezon wanted to kill a few more, while his arm was strong and his heart high. The sight of the buffalo excited Fool's Bull too—he forgot to complain. Soon the two men who had hung in cradle boards together, many summers before, were racing full out, bows ready, eager to kill a few more buffalo, in the old way, their way, the fearless and noble way of the fighting Sioux.

21

It was well past noon . . .

I T was well past noon when Amboise d'Avigdor finally caught up with his impatient masters, Benjamin Hope-Tipping and Clam de Paty. At once, of course, they noticed that he now had only one ear, and jumped—as he had feared they would—to the wrong conclusions.

"What? You clumsy young fool! You cut off your ear?" Clam exclaimed. "And I suppose you used my razor to do it—an instrument far too fine for your clumsy hands."

"No, monsieur . . . no, I didn't," Amboise protested, "though I did just borrow your mirror for a few minutes, to inspect my head."

"Rot, I'm afraid, Amboise—it's rot!" Ben Hope-Tipping complained. "The fact is you now have only one ear, and how else could you have lost the one you're missing?"

"I don't know, sir . . . I swear I don't . . . it's a great embarrassment to me, I assure you," Amboise pleaded. "The palfreys were recalcitrant, you see, so that I was unable to catch up with you. So I just lay down to rest for a few minutes and when I awoke I was all bloody—quite offensively so—and I am exactly as you see me now, a man with only one ear."

"Now, now . . . stop lying, monsieur," Clam began. "Ears do

not simply remove themselves as one sleeps. Ears are well attached, I might add. Quite firmly attached, I insist. One can box them sharply, as I am inclined to box yours, and yet they do not fall off."

"Well, Clam, accidents happen," Ben said. He saw no point in berating this shivering boy, who had at least arrived with their kit intact. "Never mind about the ear—the thing to do now is shave and get into some decent clothes."

"This wasn't an accident," Kit told them, looking carefully at Amboise's head.

"Not an accident—explain yourself, monsieur?" Clam insisted. "You mean this foolish boy cut off his ear on purpose?"

"He didn't cut it off, the Ear Taker cut it off," Kit said.

There was silence on the prairies.

"Excuse me? The Ear Taker? Who is this Ear Taker?" Ben inquired.

Talking to these men often made Kit feel as if he were traveling in circles. Wouldn't it seem likely that the Ear Taker was just what his name implied: a man who takes ears?

"Nobody knows who he is, but what he likes to do is cut off people's ears," he explained. "White men's ears, mostly. He slips up on people while they're sleeping and when they wake up they're one-eared, like this fellow."

"I believe there's a story here, Clam," Ben remarked at once. "I believe I'd like to get my notebook and jot down a few particulars, if Mr. Carson will oblige us."

"Certainly there's a story—what does this fellow look like?" Clam asked.

"I don't know and neither does anybody else," Kit said. "Nobody's even seen him. He works at night and he's so quick with his slicing that he's gone before the victim even wakes up."

"But why haven't the authorities done something?" Clam asked. "Catch him, garrote him! Rid us of this menace!"

"Who's supposed to catch him? There are no authorities out here," Kit reminded them. "He used to work around Santa Fe mostly, but I guess he's moved."

"But that's most disturbing," Ben told him. "You don't suppose he has designs on our ears, do you?"

"Probably," Kit allowed.

"Then we will have to post a guard in future," Ben told him.

"Where would we get a guard?" Kit asked.

Ben and Clam exchanged glances.

"Well, there's Amboise," Ben suggested.

"I can't guard very well, sirs," Amboise admitted. "Can't seem to stay awake."

"If you nod off I expect the Ear Taker will just slip in and take your other ear," Kit announced.

The two Europeans weighed their prospects in silence, looking apprehensively at the long plain and the waving grass. Clam's blood had begun to boil at the thought of this criminal threat. Nothing of the sort would be allowed if they were in France.

"I'll shoot him on sight," he declared.

"There won't be a sight—he works in the dark," Kit reminded them. "You won't see him."

"What must we do, then, Mr. Carson?" Hope-Tipping asked. "I'm afraid neither Clam nor I can afford to lose an ear—we're much in society, you know. It would not be acceptable in the chanceries, I'm afraid."

"Well, we can hurry up and join the Berrybenders," Kit suggested. "Some of the mountain men are probably still with them—they're pretty fair guards, if they ain't drunk."

"We shall have to insist on sobriety, then—won't we, Clam?" Hope-Tipping said. "If you'll just excuse us while we make a bit of a toilette, we can be on our way."

"You better patch that balloon up, if you've got anything to patch it with," Kit suggested. "It might come in pretty handy."

He had not given up on the notion of a dramatic entrance via balloon, once they located the company—Tasmin would be mighty impressed, if she looked up and saw him flying. The two journalists were thoroughly aggravating—it would serve them right if the Ear Taker got one of their ears—but that didn't mean he was ready to give up on a flight in their fine balloon.

22

Tasmin, primed and ready . . .

T A S M I N , primed and ready, deeply in the mood to enjoy her new love, would cheerfully have spent all her time alone with Pomp Charbonneau; but thanks to the myriad vexations of travel, the Berrybender party had been proceeding east for more than a week and she had so far spent no time alone with Pomp at all, a situation that vexed her very much. With Jim Snow gone; Kit Carson gone; Lord Berrybender newly besotted with his bride, Venetia Kennet; Buffum Berrybender in constant shy attendance on her tall Ute; and William Ashley and Eulalie Bonneville, nominal leaders of the mountain men, departed for the north, it fell to Tasmin and Cook—herself the object of a circumspect courtship with Tom Fitzpatrick—to manage the day-to-day affairs of the expedition. Tasmin found herself saddled with so many duties that she would have had little time for love even if her lover had been assiduous in pursuit, which he wasn't. This too vexed Tasmin extremely. She had given herself to the man and knew that he had been pleased; and yet, instead of coming back for more, Pomp rode off every morning with Jim Bridger to scout the day's route, and sometimes did not return until after dark, by which time Tasmin had her child to feed and the camp to more or less administer. Of course, it would merely have been prudent to wait and come to Pomp well after dark, when they could have enjoyed one another in secret—but Pomp didn't allow her even this. Often it was late when he returned—he usually just rolled up in a blanket and slept by the campfire with the other men.

Tasmin, never one to be passively thwarted, would soon have developed her own strategies for seduction; she would have intercepted Pomp and cajoled him into making love had she herself not been ground down by the exigencies of camp life, which were constant and mostly negative.

First Monty wandered into a bush and was stung nearly a dozen times by wasps. Despite Little Onion's dexterity with poultices, the little boy ran a high fever; he sobbed fretfully whenever Tasmin left him. Then Coal's little boy, Rabbit, managed to bounce out of the wagon, which ran over his foot, causing him to add his wails to Monty's. Were that not enough, Piet Van Wely, while attempting to chip a fossil out of a rock, was bitten in the calf by a rattlesnake; while the babies whined, Piet groaned and sweated. Hugh Glass made a cut in the calf and sucked out most of the poison, but Piet languished for three days, a stricken Mary Berrybender in panicky attendance. Finally Little Onion made Piet a bitter concoction which purged him thoroughly, after which he soon recovered. Mary held the Dutchman's sweaty head as she cooed to him. Intolerant of children at the best of times, she felt no compunction about kicking Monty or Talley or Rabbit if they crowded into Piet's space.

"These brats have all fouled themselves—I smell it!" she insisted. "And soon Buffum will be giving birth to a red brat who will do the same."

"Not too soon—she just got pregnant," Tasmin replied. "You're Monty's aunt—you could take a hand in his upbringing, you know. It wouldn't kill you to wipe a baby's bottom."

Vicky Kennet, the new bride, seldom rode with them during the day—Lord B.'s besottedness had reached such a level that he required Vicky to accompany him on his daily hunts. Revived by the fine high air, His Lordship sometimes felt in the mood for a spot of copulation around lunchtime. He could not bear to be without the services of his bride.

"Why is the pater so gross?" Mary asked, a question Tasmin made no attempt to answer. She was uncomfortably aware that, if she were allowed to indulge her natural inclinations, they might not be much less gross than her father's. More than once Tasmin found herself wishing that Pomp would leave Jim Bridger with the company and take *her* on a scout. She could well have tolerated a spot of copulation around lunchtime herself.

But no such notion occurred to Pomp, whose main concern, when he was in camp, seemed to be with his ailing father, who had been taken with the jaundice and was in consequence so wobbly on his feet that he too had to be allowed space in the wagon. Coal and Little Onion combined their skills and gathered herbs for yet more concoctions, which, though beneficial, did not cure the elder Charbonneau very quickly. After a long consultation with Pomp it was concluded that old Charbonneau would profit from sitting for a time in a sweat lodge, where the poisons could be sweated out of him. This required a half day's break in the trekking—Tasmin hoped it might present her with an opportunity to get Pomp to herself for a bit. Old Hugh Glass not only helped build the sweat lodge but, once it was built, casually stripped off and insisted on participating.

"I've a heap too much bile," he announced. "When I lived with the Rees I was often refreshed by the sweats." He at once crawled in with old Charbonneau.

Unhappily for Tasmin they were stopped on an absolutely open plain, with no deep glades that might be suited for romantic interludes, which Pomp, to her fury, showed no sign of wanting anyway. He spent his time happily giving archery lessons to Jim Bridger, who desired to master the bow but, so far, was a long way from doing so.

The night Tasmin seduced Pomp, Jim had not been mentioned—in fact Jim had never entered her thoughts. The moment was hers and Pomp's; at the time she had hardly supposed it would be their only such moment, but now she was beginning to wonder. Was Pomp *thinking* of Jim—his friend, her husband? Was that what kept him away?

When old Charbonneau and Hugh Glass emerged from the sweat lodge Mary Berrybender watched from the back of the wagon, where she was attending to her Piet.

"How odd, Tassie," she remarked. "Mr. Glass is very tall, yet his organ of generation is no longer than Piet's. You would think it would be longer, since Piet himself is short."

"What are you talking about?" Tasmin asked. Her thoughts had been on Pomp—she had merely glanced at the two naked men.

"You would think a man's organ of generation would have some relation to his size, and yet it doesn't seem to," Mary said.

"Don't be so pompous—just call it a prick," Tasmin advised. "I confess I take very little interest in this subject myself, and I can hardly see why a maiden such as yourself should be concerned with such matters."

Piet, still feverish, raised himself on an elbow and looked at the two old men.

"We Dutch always manage to hold our own," he muttered.

Buffum, newly radiant, caught the drift of the discourse and smiled.

"What *are* we talking about?" she asked, smiling.

"The size of pricks, but I don't want to hear you bragging about your Ute," Tasmin said. "It's obvious from your constant blushing that he's not backward in the services of Venus. But the subject is on the whole a very tedious one."

"You're just jealous," Mary remarked, with a smirk. "You never expected Buffum and me to do better than you when it comes to lovers—and we have."

The fact that there was some truth in what her sister said left Tasmin feeling sullen, and not a little discouraged. Buffum had caught herself a very handsome boy, and Mary had forged a companionable bond with her pudgy botanist—and what *did* she have to put against these conquests? A husband who was frequently gone and a lover who was hesitant, to put it politely. At least in Europe men were willing to do the seducing—had she not spent years fending off unwanted kisses, sudden lecheries and assaults? Yet here in America, women had to do most of the work of love. Jim Snow had soon come round, but only because she pressed him. She had done more than press Pomp and had expected a good deal more return for her effort than had so far been achieved. Now here were her sisters, preening themselves over their lovers, while she spent her days tending babies, driving wagons, and trying to keep her family and its ill-constituted retinue in reasonable marching order. Just when she felt capable of any wildness, there was no one who would even allow her to be wild with them. She was irritated with Jim for leaving and staying gone, angry with Pomp because, she suspected, he was either afraid of her or afraid of what he felt when he was with her. She was even annoyed with her personal whipping boy, Kit Carson, who had casually drifted off just when she needed him most.

"What is it, Tassie?" Mary asked, all alarmed at the look of anger she saw in Tasmin's face.

"I wish I was back in Europe, that's what!" Tasmin said, with sudden vehemence.

"But Europe's *very* far away," Mary reminded her. "I doubt we shall be returned there even within the year."

Tasmin doubted it too—and yet a sudden longing for London streets or green rural dales, with hedgerows and sheep, or mild cattle, was so overpowering that tears started in her eyes. The sight shocked both her sisters, and yet Tasmin couldn't help it—a need for the familiar seized her. She jumped off the wagon and more or less pitched Monty to Buffum; both baby and aunt were shocked.

"Here, get some practice, you'll need it," she said, and then went stumbling off, walking right past Hugh Glass and Toussaint Charbonneau, both of whom hastened to cover their nakedness. Tasmin, shaken by a homesickness the more powerful for being, in immediate terms, hopeless, just kept walking, heedless, into the empty prairies that lay between her and all that she desired: English order, English privilege, English intelligence, English lanes, even English clouds. The great prairie sky that had thrilled her so the first time she beheld it, on that first ecstatic moment on the banks of the Missouri, now seemed a brutal thing, a sky under which the worst barbarities were enacted—indeed, might yet be enacted on herself, her siblings, and her child unless they were lucky. She wanted to be again in a place where men saw themselves as lovers of women, rather than killers or trappers.

Tasmin sobbed, dried her eyes, cried more, wet her cheeks, dried her cheeks, all the time walking farther and farther from camp. When no more tears came she slumped suddenly and sat down. It was only then that she noticed that she was completely alone in the seemingly endless world of grass. The camp was not in sight, and for a few minutes she was too tired to care. In the camp were many able trackers—someone would soon find her, though of course it was possible that hostiles might find her first. She remembered that her sister Buffum and their *femme de chambre*, Mademoiselle Pellenc—now married to a fur trader in Canada—had rushed off into the prairies in an effort to recover Prince Talleyrand, their mother's old parrot, and had been caught and subjected to painful indignities before being ransomed.

Perhaps she would be caught too, but if she couldn't be back in England—a haven thousands of miles distant—she was not immediately sure that she particularly cared. The prairies seemed so empty, so desolate, that merely looking at them increased Tasmin's deep homesickness; hopeless again, she put her head in her hands, feeling such darkness in her heart that she hardly knew what to do.

Then Pomp was there, his approach, as usual, so quiet that she jumped when she opened her eyes and saw his legs.

"Now where were you thinking of running off to?" he asked.

"Why would you care?" she said, so angry that she was ready to bite, if challenged.

"Because I saw some bear sign yesterday and it wasn't Abby's," he told her. "It's not safe to be running off when there's grizzlies around."

"Perhaps not—on the other hand, I'm in the kind of mood that makes being eaten by a bear almost a welcome diversion," she told him, unable to keep bitterness out of her voice.

"I don't suppose *you've* ever been in that sort of mood, have you, Pomp?" she asked, fixing him with a direct look.

"Not me—the first thing my father and mother both warned me about was bears—I give bears all the room they want," he said, more than a little confused by the antagonism he was getting from Tasmin.

"It's very natural that your parents would have warned you about the danger of bears," she said. "What I wish is that they had taught you a bit more about the dangers of women."

Pomp shrugged.

"Ma died when I was too little to need to know much," he said. "And Pa's only had Indian wives. He wouldn't know what to say to a woman like you."

"Do you think there's that much difference between an Indian woman and myself?" Tasmin asked him. "Mightn't it be that at some level we want many of the same attentions?"

"Don't think so," Pomp said. "Pa's married to Coal now—I don't think Coal's like you."

"But she is, for those who have eyes to see," Tasmin insisted. "I know Coal a little—I like her very much. And I would beg to argue that we're more alike than you think."

Pomp didn't reply—he was thinking.

"Well, you both have babies," he ventured.

"That's right—we both have babies, which occurred because we got men to desire us," Tasmin said. "Coal wanted your father to want her—she persisted. I remember how happy she was when she conceived. She thought the swans were a factor—but desire was the main factor, and in exactly the same brute way, I want you to desire me. I thought you did, Pomp—but now I just don't know. I love you—I confess it! I love you! What I don't like is being in thrall to a man who doesn't want me. It sours one, you know. I have a child to raise. I'd rather not be sour."

She reached up, took his hand, and pulled at him, meaning to lay him down as she had before, meaning to kiss him and make him want her. If she was going to have to do everything, then she *would* do everything! She was prepared to reach up and take him out of his pants, as she had done before, only then it had been in darkness. To grasp a man in daylight was a good deal bolder thing—and yet her hands were at his trousers, when she happened to glance up and noticed that Pomp was completely unaware of what she was about. Pomp was looking up into the sky, a very odd thing to do, in her opinion, when a woman was being as direct as she was being about her eagerness to make love. Even a near virgin, as Pomp was, must accept the fact of his own desire, once his desire was made manifest, a thing Tasmin felt sure she could accomplish.

Then a shadow fell on them, caused, she supposed, by a small drifting cloud; but the startled look on Pomp's face caused her to look higher, where, to her astonishment, she saw a balloon floating their way, a balloon, with three men in its basket, making a slow but steady descent toward the prairie.

"Good Lord!" she exclaimed. "How did a balloon get way out here?"

"I don't know, but Kit's in it," Pomp said. "I don't know who those other two gents are—but here comes a wagon too. Maybe there's a circus traveling round."

"That's nonsense—a circus?" Tasmin questioned. "Who would pay to see it?"

Despite the shock of seeing a balloon descending near them, Tasmin's first reaction was anger at Kit Carson. First he had left her without asking permission, just when she had stood in woeful need of him; then he remained absent for weeks; and now here he was, drifting down just in time to spoil her bold seduction attempt on Pomp Charbonneau. No man that she could think of had annoyed her in so many ways in such a short time.

"Who would have thought Kit would ever get up the nerve to go flying around in a balloon?" Pomp asked.

"I don't know, but I can assure you he'll be wishing he was back up in it before I get through with him!" Tasmin said.

23

The tall, thin one looked as if he might be a clerk . . .

KIT CARSON, confident that he would be looked on as a conquering hero from the mere fact that he was arriving in a balloon, was mortified, when he stepped out of the basket, to be immediately seized by Tasmin Berrybender and given a violent shaking, followed by a tongue-lashing so severe and so unexpected that he could only blush with embarrassment. Tasmin too was red in the face but her color came from anger, and Kit's from shock.

"How dare you leave like that!" she said. "You should have spoken to me. How dare you dawdle around ballooning when I sorely needed your help?"

"I wasn't ballooning much—just today, mainly," Kit said, in hasty defense. "Mostly I was helping Jimmy. Then we met these fellows who were looking for your father—and here we are."

Tasmin threw the two startled Europeans a hot glance. The tall, thin one looked as if he might be a clerk from Manchester; the fat one, in the red pants, was obviously French. She still held Kit by the arms, so as to give him a sharp shake when she felt like it. She saw that Pomp was watching with amazement, perhaps even repugnance, as she attacked Kit. Anger coursed through her body, though she had hoped for pleasure; someone had to suffer for her disappointment, and that someone was Kit.

"My husband, Jim Snow, is perhaps the most self-sufficient person on the planet," she lectured her captive, through clenched teeth. "He didn't need you—I needed you. Don't you ever desert me like that again."

"Won't," Kit mumbled, crushed by the failure of his grand return. The day before, he had spotted Jim Bridger scouting alone; Kit quickly hid, and persuaded the two journalists to surprise the party by arriving in their balloon. That it would impress the company he had no doubt, and it *did* impress the company too—or most of it. When Lord Berrybender first saw the balloon he at once began to shout and wave—so did some of the boys.

Hearing Tasmin mention Jim Snow caused Ben Hope-Tipping and Clam de Paty to exchange glances. Could this rare English beauty, at present so out of sorts with Kit Carson, actually be married to the dreaded Sin Killer?

"Excuse me, madam," Ben said politely, tipping his hat. "Did I hear you say your husband's name was Jim Snow?"

Tasmin was cooling a little. An opportunity had been missed—she would have to create another. Now here were these two Europeans, rabbly scribblers of some sort, who had been conveying Kit around the prairies by balloon. Why did they think they were entitled to question her about her husband?

It seemed to Clam that his colleague, Benjamin, quailed a bit at the chill in the Englishwoman's look. It was very English of him, of course; Englishmen rarely knew how to address women of spirit, an area of behavior in which they had had far less practice than Frenchmen—most Frenchwomen, after all, were women of spirit, not cold-blooded like your Englishwoman. He thought he had better trot out his best English and correct the situation.

"Pardon, my lady, but is not Monsieur Snow the one they call the Sin Killer?" he asked, making a suave bow.

"Why should that concern you, monsieur?" Tasmin asked, in her chilliest tone.

Before the man could answer, Pomp came over and bowed slightly.

"Bonjour," he said. "I believe you're Monsieur de Paty. We met in Stuttgart, I believe. You had come to interview my patron, the prince of Württemberg, about some educational reforms he was attempting at the time."

Clam de Paty was thunderstruck: he *had* visited the prince of Württemberg; he *had* written about those educational reforms—a subject deucedly difficult to make interesting to scandal-hungry Parisians; he *had* even drawn the prince out a bit about his adventures in the American West. But how could this young fellow, who looked like an Indian and dressed like a frontiers-man, possibly know of such a thing?

"I'm Jean Baptiste Charbonneau," Pomp said—he reminded the startled journalist that there had been a blizzard on the day of his arrival at the prince's castle.

"I helped dig out your carriage," Pomp remarked.

"Oui, oui! The snows!" Clam replied.

Ben Hope-Tipping, too, was very surprised—how amazing that they had landed their balloon on the one spot on the prairies where there was a friendly young fellow who had met Clam before, in Europe. Even more startling was the fact that the young fellow even knew that Clam had been sent to Germany to write about educational reform, a subject his own employers would not likely have sent him two leagues to investigate.

That same young man seemed to be a friend of the Sin Killer's beautiful but on the whole rather terrifying wife—and now here came Lord Berrybender himself, in a kind of buggy, with a very handsome woman by his side. It added up to such an excess of good fortune, after the travails of recent weeks, that Ben scarcely even noticed the arrival of Amboise d'Avigdor, who at once jumped down and started gathering in the rapidly deflating bal-loon.

"Excuse me," Tasmin said, not impressed by all this flutter, "can anyone tell me why this good-looking young man has only one ear?"

"Yes, it's quite awkward for him—only one remains, madam," Ben told her. "I'm Ben Hope-Tipping, by the way. If you happen to be a reader of the papers you may have chanced on one or two of my trifling reports."

"Stick to the point," Tasmin told him bluntly. "What about this boy's ear?"

"Quite a nuisance, I fear," Ben said. "It seems there's an Indian whose hobby is to slip up on sleepers and neatly remove an ear. Mr. Carson knows of him. About a week ago he took our young servant's—rather mars his appearance, I admit."

Pomp and Clam had strolled over to the deflating balloon, talking quietly in French. Since the whole company was about to engulf them, Tasmin released her grip on Kit Carson's arm, only to have her own arm seized, a moment later, by Father Geoffrin, who seemed to be wildly excited by the presence of his rotund countryman in the ridiculous red trousers.

"Tasmin, don't you know who that is?" the Jesuit gasped.

"No idea, except he looks a fool in those trousers," she replied.

"But it's Clam de Paty, the most famous journalist in Europe," Father Geoff blurted. "He knows all the actresses—intimately, in some cases—at least that's the rumor."

"So what?" Tasmin said. "Shall we all be required to curtsy to some common little French seducer?"

Father Geoff didn't answer—in a moment he rushed over, interrupted Pomp, and began to babble in French, assuring the journalist Clam de Paty that he had long been an admirer of his theater reviews. Geoff even went so far as to say that he had often rushed out at dawn and seized the papers the minute they became available, in order to be the first to read Monsieur Clam de Paty's review of this or that performance. Clam de Paty, evidently not at all surprised to find that his wit was appreciated, even in the wilderness, received Geoff's compliments with a complacency that was not far from rudeness.

Disgusted as Tasmin was at Father Geoffrin's bowing and scraping, she was, a moment later, even more disgusted when her father drove up, to be set upon at once with more bowings and scrapings, cooing and complimenting. Instead of brushing

this riffraff aside, as Tasmin assumed he would, Lord Berrybender immediately began discoursing on his own exploits as a
hunter in America. The journalists were at once at him with
questions. When the former Vicky Kennet, now Lady Berrybender, descended from the buggy she was greeted no less effu-
sively.

"Gad, gentlemen, we hardly expected the papers to pursue us
even into these wild parts," Lord Berrybender said; he seemed
pleased as punch by these attentions, as he attempted to com-
bine the hauteur of the noble lord, the bluntness of the great
hunter, and the graciousness of the squire receiving at his seat.

"Smart of you to come in a balloon—often wished I had one
myself," he said. "We've had some fine adventures, I assure
you—hope you're getting it all down."

The mountain men wandered up, were introduced, gaped at
the balloon—they displayed little interest in the two scribblers.
Hugh Glass and Tom Fitzpatrick, both of whom knew of the Ear
Taker, examined Amboise's head at some length.

"I guess I'll try sleeping with my head in a bucket, if that rascal's around," Hugh Glass declared.

Mary arrived, and Buffum, and High Shoulders; then Cook,
Eliza, Millicent, Tim, Piet, Jim Bridger, all curious to see the gentlemen who had dropped from the sky—they had all seen the
balloon, when it was soaring, and had been amazed.

"It's chilly up there—some dern cranes knocked us down
once," Kit told the awed assembly, neglecting to mention that he
had merely been an earthbound observer of that catastrophe.

Tasmin, who, only minutes before, had been sobbing hot tears
because she missed Europe so much, discovered, now that
Europe had come to her, that she quite despised it. There was
Pomp, who might have made love to her that very morning, and
Father Geoffrin, who had at least declared his interest in making
love to her, both of them babbling in French about politics and
actresses with a little French popinjay, while her father was
expanding about his own adventures to a tall lanky fellow who
might have been an undertaker.

Ben Hope-Tipping and Clam de Paty, though of course making themselves agreeable to everyone—especially to young Monsieur Charbonneau, whose patron was a prince—did not forget what they had heard when they first landed, which was that Lady Tasmin Berrybender was married to the famous Sin Killer, the one man in all the West whom they most wanted to interview. Forward-looking German princes and great peers of the realm were all very well, but after all, what their readers really wanted was blood, the hotter, redder, and more copious the better: murders, gallows, scalpings, tortures, gory battles—that is what the people who bought the papers really wanted to read about.

So it was not long before Clam de Paty politely slipped away from Pomp and Father Geoffrin and the rest—he angled over to Tasmin, who stood alone, staring darkly into space.

"Excuse me, madame—one must be polite to one's readers," he began—suavely, he hoped. "But we have not journeyed to America merely to meet old admirers—it's fresh information we seek. Do I understand correctly that you really are married to this Monsieur Snow, this Sin Killer?"

"I hardly care to discuss my domestic situation with strangers—particularly French strangers," Tasmin replied. "I am married to Monsieur Snow, but I fail to see how that concerns you."

"But it is of the greatest concern to me, madame!" Clam said, coloring a bit at the undisguised insolence in the woman's tone, a tone that suggested quite clearly that he—a citizen, a critic, a wit, a lover of actresses and more actresses—was of no more interest to her than a beetle, a bug, a worm!

"We had the great good fortune to meet your husband," he informed her, "but unfortunately he was in a hurry to be gone. We had no chance to talk to him—it means a grave disappointment for our readers, I assure you."

"Why would Jimmy want to talk to you anyway, monsieur?" Tasmin inquired. "He ain't French, and he ain't nice to strangers."

"But our readers, madame! Our readers!" Clam insisted. "They know of your famous Sin Killer. They *know*, but not enough. We will disappoint all of Europe if we come home with no news of the Sin Killer. In Europe he is more famous than Hawkeye, or Natty Bumpo, or any of the characters of Mr. Cooper. It is said he was struck by lightning and feels it is his mission to wipe out sin. They say he can shoot a bow like an Indian, or the rifle like Hawkeye. So please, Madame Snow—when do you expect him to return?"

"Why, I've no idea," Tasmin said, amused that this puffed-up little French person considered himself indispensable to the readers of all Europe.

"But, madame—you are his wife! Surely you expect he will come back," Clam insisted.

"Oh, I don't know about that," Tasmin told him. "As a Frenchman and a man of the world, you must know that sometimes husbands do stray for rather long stretches.

"I would not be surprised to discover that you have even done so yourself," she went on, looking Clam directly in the eye.

Clam de Paty colored. Damn the impertinent woman! In fact he did have a modest little wife at home in Paris, whom he had not visited for quite some time. After all, why visit a wife when Paris was so full of actresses?

Nonetheless, although the tables had been more or less turned, Clam was determined to press on with his original inquiry.

"Ah, madame, but you are very beautiful," Clam said, trying to summon his old gallantry. "Surely no husband would want to stay away from you for very long."

"All I can say is that if my husband does show up, you would do well to change your trousers," she said.

"My trousers—why?" Clam asked, startled.

"My husband hates red," she informed him—why not toy with this absurd little man a bit?

"It's the color of blood, you know," she went on. "He even denies me my red petticoats. In fact I'm rather surprised he spared you when you met on the prairie. He might have whacked your head off in an instant, on account of those red trousers. Fair warning, monsieur!"

At that she turned and walked away. Of course, Jimmy had no prejudice against red, but she saw no reason not to scare a pompous Frenchman, if she could.

Of a sudden, despite her fever for Pomp, she missed her plain Jim. And the more she listened to the Europeans babble, the more she missed him—it was time her American came back to her arms.

24

*He had been as far north as the prairies
went . . .*

J I M   S N O W was angry with himself for having idly wandered so far from his wife and child. All his life, from the time he
had been able to support himself as a hunter, his habit had been
to wander the prairies frequently, for no other reason than to
look and explore. He had been as far north as the prairies went,
and as far south as the deserts of New Mexico. Sometimes he
merely drifted with the game. Never before had he felt the need
to get back to a particular person. Sometimes he came to the aid
of travelers who were lost—those had mainly been just the accidents of travel. The urgency he now felt as he urged Joe Walker's
gallant little mare to her limits was of a different order. Maelgwyn Evans's report of the smallpox plague frightened Jim as
nothing else ever had. On this scout he had drifted nearly four
hundred miles from his wife—or wives—and son. That was not
an unusual distance at all, as mountain-man rambles went; but
fear of the plague had abruptly changed his way of thinking. In a
normal sense he had left his family well protected. Kit was very
likely back by then—he would help Tasmin with the chores, and
so would Little Onion. Pomp or Jim Bridger or Tom Fitzpatrick
would be quick to sniff out Indian trouble, if any offered.

But even Pomp couldn't sniff out the plague. A sick Indian,

fleeing contagion and not realizing he had brought it with him, could have run into the company. Maelgwyn said it was a quick-acting plague—if they were unlucky enough to contract the pox, then his wife and child might be already dead.

Often Jim had found Tasmin exasperating, gabby, rude, exhausting—but that didn't mean he wanted to lose her. No doubt she found much to dislike in his own behavior, much to criticize in his limitations. After all, he could barely puzzle out a few verses in the Holy Book. He knew nothing of all the things Tasmin talked about with Pomp or Father Geoffrin. He had long realized—and he had said it—that Pomp would make a more likely husband for Tasmin than himself. He was not polished, as Pomp was. He liked silence—Tasmin liked chatter. She was full of questions he couldn't answer; she constantly and boldly criti-cized his behavior, which a good wife was not supposed to do. She was so bad about this and so loose in her language that he had struck her several times—once or twice she had gone so far as to hit him back. Yet now, at the thought that Tasmin might be dead, Jim was deeply fearful, abashed, ashamed of his idle wan-derings. He found himself wishing he could run into the travel-ers with the balloon—soaring above the country would be a lot quicker than pounding over it. Smooth gaited and enduring as the little mare was, she could not cover four hundred miles overnight. She was not his mare—Jim didn't want to ruin her. He camped where there was good grass and he tried not to work the mare too hard, and yet, all the time, he was anxious in a way he had not been before.

Near the end of the sixth day he had been about to make camp when he thought he saw the flicker of campfires, far ahead; who could it be but the Berrybenders and the mountain men? He had seen no game for three days—where there was so little game, there were unlikely to be Indians.

Jim let the mare have an hour to roll, rest, and graze, and then rode on toward the distant fires, glimpsed now and then when he topped a ridge. Once close, he slowed—it could, after all, be Utes, or even Pawnees. But then he saw a white tent, which Lord

Berrybender must have purchased from William Ashley—it was the tent Pomp had been put in while Tasmin nursed him. So he had found the company—he heard a baby cry briefly—it wasn't Monty. The fact that everything seemed normal was an immense relief. Probably there would be a sentry, either Pomp or Tom Fitzpatrick most likely, they being the most reliable sentinels. Kit Carson was rarely allowed to stand sentry because in the darkness his imagination ran away with him. Twice he had roused the camp, mistaking a bush for an Indian.

Jim dismounted and led the mare the last half mile. There was only faint moonlight. He didn't want to blunder into camp and wake everybody up. He looked up but could see no sentries. It annoyed him to think the company had become so negligent that they hadn't posted a guard. Any passing band of Indians could sneak in and steal the horses. But before his annoyance could build, he saw a slight movement and Pomp spoke.

"Well, Jimmy, you're back," Pomp said. "Tasmin will be glad."

"Any sickness here?" Jim asked at once.

"The Dutchman got snakebit and your boy collected some wasp stings—that's it, except for Pa, who's been poorly," Pomp reported.

Looking around camp, Jim saw another, smaller tent, which he didn't recognize—but the wagon of the balloonists stood nearby.

"I guess the balloon fellows made it," he said.

"Yes, but not before the Ear Taker took an ear from that servant of theirs."

Jim didn't reply. One missing ear was nothing compared to a smallpox plague.

"Did they mention the pox?" he asked. "Maelgwyn Evans lost three wives to it—and the river Indians are mostly dead, he claims."

"What river Indians?" Pomp asked. The Englishman had mentioned something about pox amid the Choctaws, but the Choctaws were far to the south.

"Maelgwyn says it's wiped out the Mandans and the Rees," Jim told him. "That's why I hurried back. I thought it might be here."

"No," Pomp said, "just wasp stings and snakebite."

The anxiety Jim had been living with for a week began to leave him—of course, he should have known that Pomp would take care of things—Pomp had always been a trustworthy man.

"There's been a good deal of marrying and mating, though," Pomp informed him. "Old Lord Berrybender married Vicky, and Buffum's pretty taken with that tall Ute boy, High Shoulders. I don't know how much progress Tom Fitzpatrick is making with Cook, but he's still trying.

"The balloonists haven't married anybody yet but they're going to be mighty happy that you're back. All they can talk about is the famous Sin Killer—they're anxious to write up your adventures for their papers."

"I think I'll check on Tasmin," Jim said. "Being married to her is about the only adventure I've ever had."

He slipped his gear off the tired little mare and hurried down into camp.

25

She felt rumpled and sweaty . . .

EXCEPT in wet weather, Tasmin had developed a large dislike of tents. The cold, drafty one Jim insisted they winter in on the Yellowstone she had never liked. On the trek, while sleeping outdoors or, at worst, under a wagon, she had begun to like looking up at the stars. When she went to bed angry or discontent—irked at some obstinacy of Jim's, or else burdened with a fretful child—the unvarying brilliance of the stars had come to have a soothing influence on her.

At night she mainly just rolled up with Monty in a blanket, near a campfire laid well away from the mountain men, so she would not be kept awake by their carousing. When the mountain men slept, Tasmin could not figure—their singing and yarning seemed to go on all night.

She was sleeping deeply when the man eased down beside her and put a hand on her bare arm. The shock of male flesh on her flesh brought her eyes open in alarm. Her first thought was rape—old Hugh Glass had not desisted from his lecherous looks. Her second thought was Pomp—perhaps he had relented in his standoffishness—but by smell more than sight, in a moment she knew it was her husband. "Oh Jimmy," she said, and a hard kiss followed, a hungry kiss of the sort her Jimmy liked to give. Monty, his fever not quite gone, gave a fretful whimper. It caused his father to draw back.

"Is he sick?" Jim asked.

"Not very—not now," Tasmin whispered. "But twelve wasp stings are plenty for a little fellow, I reckon."

"You're not sick, are you?" he asked. Fear of the pox had not quite left him.

"As a matter of fact, I am—sick of you being gone!" she said, with heat. "You mustn't leave me so. Nothing terrible has happened, but aggravations just seem to pile up when you leave— especially if you rob me of Kit. People have been marrying and mating at a furious pace, and now these two wretched scribblers are here with their balloon."

"I met them—I suppose they're harmless," he told her.

"Of course, they're not dangerous as the Utes are dangerous," Tasmin admitted. "But their incessant curiosity about you is just one more aggravation I'm saddled with."

Jim had only wanted to know that she was well. Once convinced of that, he took her face in his hands and kissed her again. Tasmin felt annoyed. As usual, he didn't want her to talk. From the force of the kiss she saw that all the fine feelings she had hoped to develop in her delicate love affair with Pomp were going to be swept aside, in the middle of the night, by a husband eager to at once resume conjugal exercise—never mind how late it was, no matter how long he had been away.

"Let's go somewhere, so we won't wake everybody up," he whispered.

"All right," Tasmin said, half excited but still half annoyed. She felt rumpled and sweaty; Jim had not even had the forethought to arrive in the daylight, when she might have troubled to present a more pleasing appearance. Yet he wanted her now, despite sweat, despite rumpledness.

"I'll just take Monty over to Little Onion," she whispered. "If he wakes up and sees you, there'll be no getting him back to sleep. Poor child, he's handed back and forth so often he must feel rather like a package in the mail."

"Hurry, then," Jim told her.

"Listen—just let me do this in my own way," Tasmin answered. "And please get a blanket. I'm a mass of scratches, as it is."

For a fleeting moment, as they walked out of camp, Jim's hand already busy, Tasmin thought of Pomp. Was he near? Would he care if he heard her cries and sighs? Did he not want what they were about to have?

But once they spread their blanket Tasmin gave all her attention to Jim. He was back, he was her husband, she had missed him, and now it was time to enjoy being a wife.

26

Once the night drew on . . .

P O M P had developed the habit of napping during the
noon stop, and again in the early evening, when most of
the company were busy with their meals or little chores. Once
the night drew on, he seldom slept; this was not merely because
there were dangers to be guarded against. It was at night, alone,
that he felt most himself and most at peace, sitting somewhere
not far from camp, hearing the boys at their singing, listening to
the low sighing of the wind or the occasional rustlings of
beasts—the rumbling roar of the bull buffaloes, when they were
near a herd, or the cough of an elk or moose, the yip of coyotes,
or the deeper howls of wolves.

From his spot slightly above the camp he watched Jim Snow
go into camp and wake his wife, saw Tasmin take her baby to Little Onion, saw the couple make their way onto the prairies to the
west, where, as mates would, they would soon be doing the
thing Tasmin had invited him to do the morning the balloonists
arrived. While he was watching them slip out of camp the bear
cub, Abby, ambled up to Pomp and stuck her cold nose in his
face. Usually Abby bedded down with Hugh Glass, but sometimes, wakeful, she seemed to feel that she should check on
everybody, to make sure the camp was secure.

"Go to sleep, Abby—it's late," Pomp said, scratching her fore-head, a caress she particularly liked. Very soon she slumped down beside Pomp and went to sleep.

Occasionally, at night, Pomp found that he wished his old tutor, Herr Hanfstaengl, were with him so they could examine the interesting questions that arose in the course of a day: for example, that he, Jean Baptiste Charbonneau, had readily caressed a bear but had declined, on more than one occasion, to caress Tasmin Berrybender, a woman he both cared for and admired. They had made love once, he and Tasmin—she had easily drawn his seed into her body, their pleasure very sharp. Most men would have hastened to repeat this pleasure—repeat it as often as possible; and yet Pomp hadn't. In fact he had done what he could, short of insult, to avoid further embraces with Tasmin. Herr Hanfstaengl, possessed of a stout wife and eleven children, would surely have been curious to know why he had declined to pursue this love affair. Was it because Tasmin was the wife of his friend? Was it from morality that he abstained? Or was it merely that his temperament was to stand apart? Herr Hanf-staengl, who had known the great Kant, had also mastered San-skrit and was writing a lengthy study of the Eastern holy books. One conversation Pomp remembered in particular: Herr Hanf-staengl had been explaining to him that the Hindus believed that there should be four stages to a man's life, each lasting perhaps a score of years. The first stage would be given to enjoyment, to women, drink, the pleasures of the flesh. In the second stage a man was expected to be a governor, to work for the people of his community; in the third stage he should become the head of a household; and in the fourth and final stage he was to give away all his possessions and live alone, in a hermitage, in a cave, on a mountaintop, to subsist on as little as possible while meditating on the eternal things, the holy truths.

In Stuttgart, in the prince's castle, Pomp had been happiest playing with the creatures in the prince's small zoo: three goats, an ibex, two gazelles, several monkeys, a gray parrot, and a coat-imundi. Watching Pomp with the animals, all of whom approached him without fear, Herr Hanfstaengl one day observed to Pomp that in his case the stages were happening in reverse, Pomp having little interest in the common pleasures of the sort that had caused Herr Hanfstaengl to father eleven children.

"You are not in a cave or on a peak, but I think you are in a hermitage anyway, my dear Pompey," the tutor told him. "You are at peace in the hermitage of yourself. These beasts, these simple creatures who know no guile, they come to you and stay with you. You win them with your calm. But people . . . I don't know if people can come in. You have turned the stages around, and perhaps that is how it will always be."

Pomp had come back to America, back to the Osage prairies, and then beyond them into the deep West, but he had not forgotten his wise old tutor's words. Animals, like the young bear sleeping beside him, he could still welcome; but Tasmin he had kept out. Not completely out—he had come to love her in his way, which was not her way. Why had he refused Tasmin? It was not because of Jim, who freely admitted that Tasmin was more than he could happily deal with. She wore Jim down, not merely with the peremptoriness of her appetites but simply with a force of personality that seemed to operate constantly. Almost everyone, even the strong mountain men, had a time of quitting, a day when they pressed no issues, trapped no beaver, did nothing special. But Tasmin Berrybender seemed not to know the meaning of quiescence, the ability to just let be.

"You're educated," Jim had said to Pomp several times. "You and her can talk about things I'll never know about. You ought to talk to her more."

"You might learn about some of those things, if you let Tasmin take you to Europe," Pomp told him.

Jim shook his head. He didn't want to go to Europe. The prairies and the mountains, the rivers and streams of the West were in themselves a sufficient world, a world about which he still had much to learn. The things Tasmin talked about with Pomp and Father Geoffrin—novels and operas, palaces and princes—might well be good and worthwhile things, probably were; but he had the land and its millions of details to study, and that was all he wanted.

Pomp couldn't disagree. Jim was a frontiersman, one of the most accomplished frontiersmen in the West. Pomp knew himself to be a competent guide, but in tight situations he had not quite Jim's keenness, Jim's instincts. In the battle with the Utes, Jim had killed, and he himself had almost been killed. In the struggle for survival Jim had a slight edge; but the fact that he could read novels whereas Jim couldn't was not the cause of Jim's problems with Tasmin. Tasmin, when she wanted something, would not be denied. For the moment he had dodged her, but Pomp knew she would be back—she had given no indication that she considered her marriage vows a barrier to whatever else she wanted in the way of romance.

In the pearly dawn Pomp saw Tasmin and Jim slip back into camp. Tasmin went at once to Little Onion and took her child. Jim walked over to where Kit Carson was sleeping and nudged him a time or two until Kit reluctantly sat up. The two seemed to be slightly at odds, Pomp didn't know why—of course, Kit was frequently at odds with somebody and occasionally at odds with everybody. It was clear even from a distance that he didn't welcome being waked up just to hear Jim Snow's complaint.

Abby suddenly woke up, shook the dew off her coat, and went gamboling down into the camp, startling the one-eared servant, Amboise d'Avigdor, who was up early brewing tea for his masters.

Kit Carson turned his back on Jim and walked away. Pomp stood up and stretched—his watch was over for the night. Kit turned in his direction, so Pomp walked down to meet him.

Kit, who had a cowlick that stuck straight up at times, was red in the face from indignation.

"You don't look happy," Pomp remarked.

Kit shrugged. "Tasmin's still mad at me for staying gone so long and now she's got Jim stirred up too. I'm thinking of leaving the whole bunch of them for good."

"You made yourself too useful, and now Tasmin depends on you," Pomp told him. "I'd say you're stuck."

In Kit's heart was bitter confusion. He had not supposed Tasmin would mind his absence, or even notice it, and yet she had. Probably Tasmin had harassed Jim, so now Jim was annoyed with him too.

"I say goddamn them both," Kit said, in a fury.

Then Kit looked abashed. It was the strongest oath he had ever uttered.

"Cook's got breakfast going," Pomp said, putting his arm around Kit. "Stick by me and I won't let them beat you up. I expect you'll feel better after you eat, anyway."

27

. . . it's not got a thing to do with love . . .

" **P** R A C T I C A L copulation, I suppose you could call it," Tasmin remarked to the former Vicky Kennet, now her step-mother. They were bouncing along in a wagon driven by Little Onion, who, proud of her role as driver, now drove with spirit and a certain recklessness when it came to the avoidance of holes, or even small gullies.

"I've not heard it referred to in quite those terms," Vicky admitted.

"Practical copulation—it's what married couples do," Tasmin assured her. "Clears the head, of course, but it's not got a thing to do with love, that I can see."

"I would agree that the practicality of it isn't necessarily deter-mined by sentiment," Vicky said—at the moment she looked rather droopy. "But you've always been luckier than me. There is also such a thing as impractical copulation, I can assure you. I suppose I might be considered to be something of an authority on *that* kind."

"Oh, I'm sorry, Vicky," Tasmin said. "Papa flagging a bit, is he?"

"It's not merely that," Vicky assured her. "It's that the less he *can* do, the more he wants to do. Efforts are made but satisfac-tion is not exactly frequent—despite which I'm pregnant, I fear."

"So that's why you look so wan," Tasmin said—she hoped that Vicky had not seen her vomiting behind a bush that morning, just as she had vomited into the Oto corn when she had been pregnant with Monty—although what good there was in concealing what would soon be obvious to all, she could not have said. She was undoubtedly pregnant too—and just as her husband, Jim Snow, had become an absolute martinet, forcing the party on toward Santa Fe at a pace that did not take into account the problems of pregnant women. He considered that the rendezvous had taken far too long—he wanted to reach the distant city before winter could catch them on the naked plain.

The suspicion lodged in Tasmin's mind that the child inside her was very likely Pomp's, not Jim's. Now that he was back, he was at Tasmin frequently—there would be no reason for him to suspect that any child she bore was not his. And yet Tasmin remembered how deeply she had opened herself to Pomp, how long she had held him, capturing the long flow of seed. Jim Snow, although he had come to like his son, Monty, often rolling him around and tickling him in the evenings, was not, in Tasmin's opinion, particularly attentive when it came to babies. He was not keen, as she and Vicky were, to inspect a baby closely, identifying features that belonged to this parent or that. Besides, the child inside her might well be a girl—in which case neither Jim nor anyone else would have reason to suspect that the child was Pomp's.

"Now Buffum's pregnant too, by her splendid Ute," Tasmin remarked. "There'll soon be a crowded nursery. Then there's our sweet Coal. Do you suppose she'll manage to squeeze another child out of old Sharbo?"

"Oh, but he's so yellowish—if I were Coal I believe I'd take a lover," Vicky said.

Tasmin glanced at Little Onion, their spirited driver, and—though Tasmin sometimes forgot this—her husband's other wife. At once, somewhat to her own dismay, a very wicked thought occurred to Tasmin, a thought so extremely wicked, and yet so logical, that she would have preferred to discuss it with

someone French, ideally her old *femme de chambre,* Mademoiselle Pellenc, to whom no love scheme, however wicked, could
bring a blush. But Mademoiselle Pellenc was no longer a mademoiselle and was far away besides.

Tasmin was so shocked by her own notion that her first
instinct was to slide the whole question of maternity sideways—
she certainly didn't want the watchful Vicky to gain an inkling of
what was in her mind.

"I don't suppose our Mary will really mate with that stumpy
botanist, do you?" she asked.

"Why not? Piet is quite good to Mary, and it cannot always
be an easy task. I believe he loves her deeply," Vicky told her.
"You're such a snob, Tasmin. Just because you caught a fine-
looking man doesn't mean that only handsome people procreate.
Piet and Mary might surprise us someday with a fine little babe.
Just consider Cook."

Tasmin did consider Cook, a forthright woman who had
raised twelve children, in spotless cleanliness and considerable
fear of their mother, while also taking a large hand in the raising
of the many Berrybenders. Yet Cook, a widow, was shaped like a
barrel, and was quite prickly when approached, as old Tom Fitzpatrick was finding out, to his frustration.

"You're right, there's Cook," Tasmin admitted. "If Cook can
produce twelve, I suppose Piet and Mary might manage one or
two."

Tasmin had been heartened by Jim Snow's return. After all,
she liked him, and their ruts, as she put it, cleared their heads.
But there were other, more complex considerations. Why should
Little Onion be childless, while all around her babies were arriving? The advantage to polygamy, as she saw it, was that it spread
around certain chores, the conjugal chore not least among them.
Jim, after all, *was* married to Little Onion, though he claimed it
had only been at the urging of her sister Sun Girl, then his wife,
but now dead. Still, he *had* married her—was it really fair that he
offered her nothing in the way of pleasure after the loyalty she
had given so freely both to Monty and to Tasmin? He presumably

enjoyed her sister; why wouldn't he enjoy Little Onion as well?

"You've a wicked gleam in your eye—a very wicked gleam," Vicky remarked.

"Supposing I do?" Tasmin said sharply, annoyed that Vicky had become so keenly observant of her moods.

"I can't recall that I ever claimed to be a saint," she added.

Vicky's casual comment merely served to remind her of how much more acute women were than men in regard to the intricacies of love. Jim Snow could sit beside her for a year and never have the slightest suspicion of what was on her mind, yet Vicky, newly pregnant, not too well, constantly set upon by Lord Berrybender, had nonetheless a probably not inaccurate picture of what Tasmin was contemplating.

"Read much in the old romances, my dear?" Vicky asked, with a languorous smile.

"If you mean Miss Austen, I don't find her particularly romantic," Tasmin declared. "Can't say that I care much about marriage arrangements among the middle classes."

"No, not Miss Austen," Vicky argued. "I mean the *old* romances: King Arthur, the fair Guinevere, Sir Lancelot, Sir Galahad . . . *that* bunch."

"Nanny Craigie read us a bit about the knights," Tasmin recalled. "I don't know that I believed it. Why, for goodness' sake?"

"I was just thinking that the rule of chastity was rather extreme, in those days," Vicky said. "Much worshiping at a distance. *Very* courtly love. Knights sighing with great passion but never exactly allowed to get down to it."

"Why would I want to read nonsense like that?" Tasmin asked. "It's worse than middle-class marriage. At least in Father Geoffrin's naughty French books, people do get down to it. In fact, they seem to do little else."

"Oh well, don't mind me," Vicky said. "I don't quite know why Guinevere popped into my head. Perhaps I recall some girlish fancy of having a fine brave knight love me eternally, though scarcely being allowed to do more than kiss my hand."

"A fine vision, but that's hardly Papa," Tasmin reminded her.

"No, it's not," Vicky admitted.

They bounced on, saying no more about the matter. Jim had led the party onto the plain east of the mountains, but a few great peaks, snowcapped and hidden in cloud, were visible to the west. Jim Bridger, Tom Fitzpatrick, and the Sublette brothers frequently spent their days in the foothills, hoping to find streams that still had beaver. Game had been scarce, but that morning Lord Berrybender, dashing ahead, had managed to kill a buffalo and an elk. The journalists, following on their palfreys, scribbled industriously whenever the company halted for any reason. In this instance they stayed behind to watch the buffalo and the elk being butchered, the butchers on this occasion being Pomp and young High Shoulders. Pomp, his shirt off and his arms bloody to the shoulders, seemed to be doing most of the cutting. Jim himself had told Tasmin that none of the mountain men were as skilled at taking every usable part of an animal as Pomp Charbonneau.

"He was trained not to waste a scrap, and he don't waste a scrap," Jim told her.

Pomp, seeing the ladies bouncing past, gave them a friendly, if bloody, wave. Signor Claricia and Señor Yanez stood disconsolately around the rapidly shrinking carcasses, while Cook, somehow spotless, received the bloody slabs on large platters acquired, like the wagons and much else, from William Ashley.

The two journalists stood over Pomp, who politely pointed out to them the variously named cuts as he removed them. While the ladies watched, he carefully cut thin slices from the buffalo liver, squeezed a bit of bile on them, and handed them to the journalists—a prairie treat to sample.

Ben Hope-Tipping seemed none too pleased with this raw meat, but Clam de Paty, with a great, all-embracing gastronomic tradition to defend, ate his with apparent relish.

"It's rather like liver of aurochs," he said, with a touch of pomposity.

Tasmin gave Pomp only the briefest wave—it was clear that

Vicky had her suspicions. She tried her best to pretend coolness, though dissembling in the matter of the emotions was not something she did particularly well.

"If you want to know a secret, Vicky, I'll tell you one," she said. "My husband won me with a slice of deer's liver. I woke with the most terrible hunger, so he killed a nearby deer and presented me with a slice of the liver, barely scorched. I can't say that I've ever tasted anything better."

But a glance at Vicky convinced Tasmin that the cellist was now well off the scent of herself and Pomp. Vicky looked white, sick—too unwell to be concerned just then with Tasmin's wicked notions.

"It was the sight of that blood—all that blood—and the men drenched in it," Vicky said, weakly. "I fear I may have to hop down and be sick."

The mention of blood put Tasmin suddenly more or less in the same state as her stricken stepmother. She felt faint.

Vicky made good her vow, jumped down, and stumbled away a few steps before kneeling down, after which she was sick.

Tasmin's queasiness at once increased—it had been that great pool of blood beside the dead buffalo. She felt more than a little quaint herself. A moment later she too was forced to step down and stumble off, quite as sick as her stepmother.

28

Probably the Cheyenne had just been feeling good . . .

T H E seven Pawnee boys were out on a lark when they heard the popping of a rifle and noticed a strange party of whites, strung out on the prairies a mile or so away.

"There's some whites, let's go kill them," Red Knee ordered, in his usual rude, impetuous way. Red Knee had been the one to suggest that they break off from the tribe's big summer hunt and go steal some horses, a thing they had not yet managed to do. Only the day before they had tried to run off some horses from a small Cheyenne encampment, but the Cheyenne were too wary—their guards saw the Pawnee boys long before they were close enough to the herd to run off any horses. Then a very hot pursuit ensued—too hot for Rattle, the oldest and most experienced of the group. It was Rattle's misfortune to have the weakest horse of any of the Pawnees, a horse whose wind easily gave out. Two of the Cheyenne warriors who pursued him were almost close enough on his tail to count coup; but they pulled up and let the little raiding party go. Probably the Cheyenne had just been feeling good; probably they were more amused than anything that these reckless Pawnee youngsters thought they could actually steal horses from the mighty Cheyenne. If the pursuers had been in a different mood, less happy because of a poor hunt or perhaps bitter because one of their own warriors had been killed, then all seven of the Pawnee boys might have been run down and killed—of this Rattle was sure, but when he said as much to Red Knee, that wild one just looked at him as if his remark was too stupid to deserve an answer.

"No puny Cheyenne is going to kill me," he said smugly.

They all knew that Red Knee was impossibly vain—in fact there were plenty of Cheyenne who could have killed him easily, but there seemed to be little point in saying that to him; now, without even counting the white people or trying to determine just how strong they might be, Red Knee was ready to ride right into battle.

"Wait a minute," Rattle insisted. "I think that's a bunch of those trappers. They are terrible fighters, those men—better than the Cheyenne."

Various of the other young Pawnees looked uncertain, too, at the prospect of attacking a party of whites. Slow Possum, particularly, had a few objections. He had come even closer than Rattle to being killed by a Cheyenne—a Cheyenne warrior on an extremely fast horse had actually counted coup on him, but instead of killing him, the Cheyenne had merely whacked him on the head a few times with the flat of his hatchet. Then he pulled up, laughing. The Cheyenne simply refused to take the Pawnee boys seriously—they had laughed at them, when they might have killed them.

"We don't have any guns," Slow Possum pointed out. "Those white people probably have a lot of guns. I think it's a hunting party, and the whites don't hunt with bows."

"The Sin Killer hunts with a bow," Rattle reminded them. "He's around here somewhere—old Greasy Lake said so."

This reminder sobered Red Knee a little. Though privately he considered himself a match for the Sin Killer, or any other of the trappers, he knew that if he said as much the others would just laugh at him and then probably turn and go home. Everyone knew that the Sin Killer had eaten the lightning and thus could not be killed by conventional means. Only someone in league with a powerful witch would have a chance against the Sin Killer.

Of course, Slow Possum had just been guessing—he had no way of knowing whether the Sin Killer was with this party of whites.

"I don't think he's here—it's just some hunters—and I see some women," Red Knee remarked, pointing. "Maybe we could catch a woman, or at least scalp one."

It usually fell to Rattle to make the case for conservative behavior. They had been lucky with the Cheyenne, but they might not be lucky with the whites.

"It's too risky—let's just watch them for a day or two," he suggested. "At least we could crawl a little closer and try to get a count."

"He's right," Slow Possum counseled. "There's whites all over the place. There might be some hiding—maybe they spotted us."

He and Rattle and the others waited anxiously—it seldom did any good to try to talk Red Knee into behaving reasonably. He took all such counsels as affronts to his courage. Red Knee would only restrain himself if an older, proven warrior reined him in. Of course, raiding was always a little dangerous; even very great warriors were sometimes killed, usually because their courage propelled them into hopeless situations.

Rattle was hoping that, for once, Red Knee would be sensible and spend a few hours scouting the white party to see how many men it contained. But Rattle knew this wasn't likely. If Red Knee charged the whites, the rest of them would have no choice but to follow him. Not to support a comrade would be the blackest cowardice.

Red Knee didn't want to hesitate, to think it all out. He was a warrior—and in no mood to wait, or plan. The fact that there were several women in the group convinced him that these white scalps would be easy picking. What glory that would mean when they got home—whereas, otherwise, only derision awaited them, for they would be returning without a single stolen horse. He had no interest in sitting around arguing with Rattle and Slow Possum.

"Maybe if we wait until tonight we can steal *their* horses," Rattle suggested, though he doubted that Red Knee would accept this sensible compromise.

His doubt was accurate.

With a high, echoing war cry Red Knee raised his lance and charged.

29

. . . Tim and Milly were required to wander . . .

T I M , the three-fingered stable boy, and Millicent, the discarded laundress, had much to commiserate about. Buffum Berrybender, for long Tim's main source of fornication, had now fallen in love with a tall Ute who carried a lance and a big hatchet. Tim now rarely even so much as said good day to Buffum, for fear that her lover, High Shoulders, might poke him with the lance.

Millicent had fared no better. For a few months she had been Lord Berrybender's favorite, had drunk claret with him and indulged him in all manner of hot practices, both day and night; during this period of eminence she had come to rather look down on the other servants, formerly her peers.

But Lord Berrybender cooled where Milly was concerned; before she could much more than blink, the capricious old lord had married Vicky Kennet—Millicent, without so much as a word of thanks, was back doing laundry again, and Cook, who had been mightily offended by Millicent's brief elevation to mistress rank, quickly set out to humble her as a means of reminding her not to look above her station. Chores were piled on chores; Cook closely examined every garment Milly washed to be sure she was not cutting corners when it came to doing the Berrybenders' clothes.

Thus, scorned by nearly everyone, Tim and Milly found that when they wanted to bemoan their lot they had only one another to apply to. During the day, usually, Tim and Milly were required to wander here and there, gathering what firewood they saw—if no wood was to be found, they had to drag around big sacks, filling them with buffalo chips, numbers of which Cook burned when she set about preparing the evening meal.

So Millicent and Tim wandered the prairies, often at considerable distance from the company, each dragging a large sack. Now and then, despondent, Milly so forgot herself as to permit Tim small liberties—fumblings, probings, a breast revealed here and there. A few times even, in order to take her mind off her disappointing existence, Millicent had been persuaded to open Tim's pants and pull him off, an action she performed efficiently, knowing that the slightest trace of spunk would at once be pounced on by the vigilant Cook.

Tim, of course, sought even greater intimacies, but these Millicent continued to refuse. After all, she had her pride. The great Lord Berrybender had been her lover—where those noble loins had worked, Milly could not permit a mere stable boy to follow.

When they saw the Indians coming they had proceeded, with their sacks, some distance from the rest of the company. The plain around them was absolutely bare and flat—even if Milly had been in the mood for a little carnal stimulation, there would have been no way for them to conceal themselves. She was just stooping to pick up half a dozen large, flat buffalo chips when the strange cries first reached her ears.

"Oh, lordy, Tim—I believe it's savages coming," she said, very startled.

Tim glanced at the racing Indians but did not feel particularly alarmed—Indians seemed to prefer to travel at top speed most of the time. Probably these were merely having a race, thinking that whoever arrived first at the wagons would receive the best presents. His time at the rendezvous had convinced him that savages mostly wanted presents.

"They're in a hurry for booty, I expect," he said. "Or maybe they're friends of that one Buffum likes."

"Pardon me, Tim, but you ain't to call her by no nicknames," Millicent insisted. "She's Miss Berrybender to you, if you don't mind."

"I do mind, you ugly tub!" Tim yelled, infuriated that a laundress would presume to correct him.

"Wasn't it me afucking with her in the stables?" he reminded Milly. "I guess I can call her Buffum if I please."

So outraged was he that Milly, who was no more than a laundress, would presume to question his references to his old lover that he forgot, for a moment, the issue of the Indians, until the cries got very loud and the sound of pounding hooves very close.

"Oh lordy, Tim! Lordy!" Milly cried, in terrible panic. She was suddenly so scared that she could scarcely force the words out of her mouth.

Tim turned and was shocked to see that the Indians, who had been quite distant only a moment before, were now not distant at all, nor did they seem to be bearing toward the wagons, where the trade goods were. On speeding horses, kicking up a cloud of dust, they were coming straight for himself and Milly, neither of whom had a weapon of any sort.

"Oh lordy, we're kilt!" Milly cried; then she screamed at the top of her lungs, but the scream rang only for a second across the prairies before Rattle, startled by the piercing quality of the woman's cry, stopped it for good and all by splitting her head open with his hatchet; Milly died even as she sagged. Tim turned to flee but made it only two steps before Red Knee stuck him in the throat with his long lance. Slow Possum and the others, angry because they had not got to count the fatal coup, hacked and hacked at Tim, nearly severing his head. The latecomers, four boys on slower horses, jumped down and effected such mutilation as they could. The large woman was scalped, no easy job with her brains spilling out; then the dead stable boy was scalped too, quickly castrated, had his eyes poked out and legs slashed, as the triumphant Pawnees vented their fury on the two lifeless corpses.

"They won't laugh at us in the village now," Red Knee said.

Rattle had to admit that Red Knee had been right to charge; here they had two easily taken scalps to make up for the mockery they had endured with the haughty Cheyenne.

"Let's get some more of them—I see some in a wagon," Slow Possum cried, pointing to where Lord Berrybender, with the two Europeans holding his guns, bounced over the prairie, uncertain at what was happening.

After taking a last few satisfying cuts at the two corpses, the Pawnees raced off to intercept the wagon.

Ranging a mile or more to the south, Jim and Kit heard the high war cries and whirled at once, though they were too far away to see clearly what was happening. Kit, on the big mule, didn't wait to speculate but broke at once for the scene of combat, with Jim Snow following as rapidly as he could on the short-legged mare.

Tasmin and Vicky, both sick to their stomachs, heard the cries and looked up in time to see a number of Indians hacking at something on the ground—at first neither could see what. Little Onion knew, however—she started to turn the wagon, so as to cluster with Cook and the others, but before she could finish turning, Pomp and High Shoulders ran up and quickly cut the wagon horses loose. Pomp mounted one, High Shoulders the other, and they raced away in the direction of Lord Berrybender.

"What? Are we to be killed?" Tasmin asked; she and Vicky quickly grabbed their babies. Toussaint Charbonneau hurried up, rifle in hand, Coal and Rabbit just behind him.

"What is it, monsieur? Are they coming to kill us?" Vicky asked.

"Not us, but I fear Tim and Milly are lost," he told her. "I make it seven raiders—they look like Pawnee boys to me. I expect we can hold them off."

Pomp saw that the Pawnee youths were galloping straight for Lord Berrybender—it seemed that Ben Hope-Tipping and Clam de Paty, not yet aware of the danger, were still trying to interview His Lordship. Pomp fired at the lead Pawnee, hoping to hit his horse and slow the charge, but he missed and could not stop to reload.

"I say, gentlemen—do you think we could be under attack?" Lord Berrybender inquired. The day was very bright. When he attempted to stare across the sunlit prairie, his eyes had a tendency to water, as they did, inconveniently, at this moment.

Señor Yanez and Signor Claricia were both napping, as they often did in the dull spaces of these daylong hunts which Lord Berrybender so enjoyed. Hearing shouts, they both attempted to struggle up to wakefulness.

"I say, Clam, now there's a fine sight," Hope-Tipping remarked. He could see several savages, racing magnificently flat out, right toward them, with Pomp and High Shoulders riding to cut them off. All in all a great and colorful chase was under way—a spectacle arranged, he assumed, by Pomp for their entertainment.

Ben sensed no danger. He turned to Clam, who had drawn an old saber he liked to practice whacking with, from time to time—Clam was looking rather bellicose, on the whole, it seemed to Ben.

"I say, Clam—something to write about, what?" Ben declared.

"You fool, you idiot! They are coming to kill us," Clam exclaimed. Determined to sell his life dearly as a Frenchman should, he raised his saber and waited.

Lord B., too, soon realized that danger was approaching them at the speed of a fleet horse.

"The Belgian gun, the Belgian gun!" he yelled, shaking Señor Yanez furiously. Señor Yanez blinked and at once handed over the weapon.

Ben Hope-Tipping turned back to survey the spectacle of the wild race.

"But surely," he protested, just as the first arrow struck him in the stomach—three others followed immediately, piercing his arm, shoulder, and chest.

"Hide man, hide!" Lord Berrybender urged, astonished that the tall journalist was merely standing there calmly, allowing himself to be turned into a human pincushion.

Lord Berrybender fired the Belgian gun at almost point-blank range, killing the oldest of the raiders, a youth named Thistle-Pricks-Us, who was famous for his stinging remarks.

Lord Berrybender at once reached for the other rifle, only to watch in astonishment as Signor Claricia fired it straight up into the air.

Red Knee tried to get his lance into the fat man in the red pants, but only succeeded in giving him a poor cut. The man struck out with his saber, missing Red Knee but spooking his horse so violently that the horse whinnied, reared, and fell.

"I say, Clam . . . don't you think this is most irregular?" Ben Hope-Tipping remarked, as he looked in amazement at the arrows protruding from his body. Then he quietly sat down.

Angry at the attack on his horse, Red Knee jumped up, ran at the wagon, and thrust his lance deep into the little man who had handed the old warrior a gun.

"Why damn this fellow, now he's killed my gunsmith," Lord Berrybender yelled, whacking at Red Knee with the empty rifle.

Rattle was doing his best to get his hatchet into the fat man with the long knife, but the man resisted agilely for one so round. It was Rattle who first realized that the easy fighting was over and a fast retreat advisable. Two men were coming from the north, and two more from the south—any one of them might be the Sin Killer.

"Come on, let's go, jump on my horse," Rattle urged Red Knee, who was trying to pull his lance out of the dead man. All he managed to do was yank the small man out of the wagon—in a rage, Red Knee quickly scalped him and then, reluctantly abandoning his lance, he jumped on Thistle-Pricks-Us's horse—he wouldn't be needing it anymore—and followed Rattle.

"Here's two men coming—I want to kill that Ute!" Slow Possum yelled.

"No—we have three scalps, let's go," Rattle urged, turning quickly.

Pomp saw that the Pawnees were through—they were ready to flee, all except one, who was fitting an arrow to his bow and yelling insults at High Shoulders. Pomp tried to get High Shoulders to stop while they were still out of arrow range, but the young Ute, hot for the challenge, raced right past him. Pomp jumped down, reloaded, and killed the Pawnee archer, but not before he put an arrow in High Shoulders's hip. Infuriated, High Shoulders ran on and poked the dead Pawnee with his lance several times.

When the five remaining warriors broke for the open prairie, Kit and Jim swung east to attempt to intercept them. Kit's mule was exceptionally hard mouthed—once he got his speed up, there was no stopping him. When he was nearly into the fleeing Pawnees, Kit suddenly realized he no longer had control of his mount—the very thing that had caused the death of Drum Stewart was now happening to him. He pulled back on the reins with all his might but it had no effect on the mule at all. In fact, he increased his speed to a wild runaway's, which very quickly carried Kit straight into the midst of the fleeing Pawnees.

Jim Snow was doing his best to catch up, but knew it was hopeless. The mare wasn't as fast as the big mule. Jim also saw that Kit had lost control of his mount and was fast approaching a collision point. It occurred to Jim that he could shoot the mule, but Kit might be injured in the fall, in which case he would be an easy kill.

Kit himself, as he got closer and closer to impact with the Pawnees, thought of shooting the mule himself, but that would leave him with an empty gun, so he held off.

Rattle was the only one of the fleeing raiders to notice that a collision was coming—Red Knee, flushed with his triumph, was merely running for the fun of it, and the other boys, happy to be alive, were whooping and hollering, giving no thought to the white man on the mule. Rattle thought he might get an arrow into the foolish white man whose mule was running away with him, but to his great annoyance, his horse jumped a bush and he dropped his arrow just as he was ready to string it. Before he could ready a second, the huge mule plunged right into the midst of the surprised Pawnees. Rattle's horse and two others were knocked down. The mule fell to its knees, tried to recover, then fell and rolled over one of the Pawnee boys just as Kit Carson jumped free. Rattle was knocked into the melee but clung to his bow and, as soon as he could scramble to his feet, readied an arrow to fire at the foolish white man whose erratic mount had knocked down and possibly damaged three Pawnee horses.

Kit saw Rattle notch the arrow and fired at him from the hip—the arrow, when released, flew over his head. Two of the Pawnee boys whose mounts had been knocked down were staggering around with the wind knocked out of them. Red Knee and a boy named Duck Catcher because of his skill with snares were the only raiders whose horses were not affected.

Highly annoyed that this white man had spoiled their triumphant departure, Red Knee turned back, meaning to kill the man—whose gun was empty—with his hatchet. He leapt off the horse he had taken from the dead Thistle-Pricks-Us and ran at the white man on foot, hatchet raised.

Jim Snow, in easy range now, saw that Kit—faced off with Rattle—had no notion that he was being menaced from the rear. Jim fired—the bullet took Red Knee in the side, startling him so that he promptly sat down—but that reaction only lasted a second. In a moment Red Knee got to his feet, remounted, and joined Duck Catcher in flight.

Pomp, Kit, and Jim all knew that the battle was won, but High Shoulders, one leg covered with blood from the wound in his hip, raced in and lanced one of the winded Pawnee boys before anyone could wave him off. Rattle, winded too, and wounded in the thigh by Kit's bullet, was unable to find the arrow he had been about to shoot; he began to sing his death song—so did the other young Pawnee, who faced the white men armed with nothing but a knife. Jim came riding up, rifle at the ready, but he held his fire. Red Knee and Duck Catcher, having ridden off a certain distance, pulled up, uncomfortably aware that the battle was not over and that two of their comrades were facing death. They sat on their horses indecisively, trying to decide what to do. Matters that had at first looked simple were now very confused.

For a moment, both sets of warriors were poised in tense

indecision; they were ready for blood and death and yet did not feel quite compelled to push matters to a conclusion. The excitable High Shoulders was ready to kill both Pawnees, but Pomp waved him back and Kit merely stood where he was, his gun empty. The conflict could have been rejoined and finished in a few seconds; and yet, no one moved or spoke until Pomp realized that there was something familiar about Rattle.

"But you're the son of Skinny Woman," he said. "My father was married to her sister once. Aren't you called Rattle?"

Rattle, surprised that Pomp, or Six Tongues, had remembered him—they had met for only a few minutes after a buffalo hunt—merely nodded.

"Dern, your pa's been married to more women than Bonney," Kit said. "It's hard to go anyplace without running into some of his kin."

Rattle left off his death song—it didn't seem that the whites were in the mood to kill them, though it annoyed him that Red Knee, who had started the whole thing, was just sitting there watching from a safe distance.

"We tried to steal some horses from the Cheyenne, but they were too much for us," Rattle said—suddenly he felt very tired.

"Yes, it's hard to steal from those Cheyenne," Pomp agreed. He tried to speak very carefully—such situations were tricky to get through. If any one of the combatants, on either side, felt that their courage or honor was being slighted, knives and hatchets would flash and it might be necessary to kill all the young Pawnees, something Pomp wanted to avoid if at all possible. They were just boys, raiding a little; if it became necessary to kill them all, the tribe would certainly attempt to avenge them. The company might be facing a hundred warriors this time, instead of these few youths.

Rattle knew that the whites could easily finish them off, but it seemed their blood had cooled—it might be possible for them to leave.

"We would like to take our dead," he said, addressing himself to Pomp. The Ute, he knew, would have liked to fight on, but the whites did not seem in a mood to support him. Even the Sin Killer was no longer leveling his gun.

Once Jim heard Pomp talking calmly to the young Pawnee he knew that there needed to be no more killing. It was screams and war cries that kept battles going. Once there was even a little friendly conversation, the war mood usually died; unless someone jumped in the wrong direction or accidentally fired a gun, there would be, for a time, an end to slaughter. After the terrible effort of violence a calm seemed to enfold them all. Even Lord Berrybender, who was approaching cautiously in his buggy, a gun across his lap, seemed to feel it.

"There's no calm like the calm of a battlefield, once the killing's over," he remarked, looking around him with composure. There was the great sky, and the light, waving grass—there lay the dead. The living, no longer locked in struggle, had a moment of quiet, of gratitude. After all, they were alive. Even High Shoulders had calmed down.

One horse had a broken leg. It was a Pawnee horse, and it was agreed that the Pawnees should have the meat. When the horse was killed, High Shoulders even helped with the butchering, which was accomplished in a very short time.

In the distance, the apprehensive women watched. Father Geoffrin and Clam de Paty were talking calmly to Ben Hope-Tipping, who still sat upright. Pomp hurried over—just as he arrived, Ben lay back in the grass and died. The Pawnees were now trotting slowly away, with their three dead and their fresh horse meat. Soon the prairie swallowed them up, as a boat is lost in the curving distance of the sea. Pomp's father came ambling over. Clam de Paty was sobbing, bitterly remorseful because he had not managed to warn his friend in time to save him.

"Skinny Woman's son was not hurt badly," Pomp informed his father. "Kit just wounded him in the fatty part of his leg."

Toussaint Charbonneau shook his head, in general regret.

"Those boys are too young to be out raiding on their own," he remarked. "Too young to have any judgment. They thought we'd be easy pickings, but we weren't."

"Dern if I'll ever ride that goddamned hard-mouth mule again," Kit declared. "That big ugly fool nearly got me killed."

"You don't need to be cussing, let's just dig these graves," Jim told him.

"Jim Bridger and the Sublettes would go off just when we needed them," Kit said. He was so happy to be alive that he felt he could indulge in a few complaints.

"I guess you'd complain if you were in heaven," Jim told him. "Only if you don't stop that cussing, you won't be in heaven."

"You could be wrong about that," Kit told him, angrily. "You ain't God—you could be wrong."

30

She had armed herself with an axe . . .

W H A T do they think just happened, a fox hunt?" Tasmin asked, with considerable pique. She had armed herself with an axe, which she still gripped tightly. Coal and Little Onion had skinning knives, Cook a great cleaver, Vicky, Buffum, and Mary sharp hatchets, Eliza a rolling pin. Unlikely Amazons though they were, they crouched behind the wagon, ready to mount a spirited defense of their lives and their virtue; yet abruptly the crisis seemed to pass. The combatants had become more or less at ease with one another. Jim and Kit were helping the Pawnees tie their dead on horses; High Shoulders helped cut up the horse.

"It was the same with the Utes," Tasmin reminded them. "Enemies one day and customers the next."

"I suppose it's merely the frontier way, Tasmin," Vicky remarked.

"More likely the military way, I guess," Tasmin replied. "If battles were fought to the last man, then there would soon be no more battles and the only masculine thing our silly males would have to do is fornicate, and I'm sure they'd soon tire of *that* simple pleasure."

"Not High Shoulders," Bess observed, with a blush. "High Shoulders never tires of fornication."

"Well, then ain't you lucky," Tasmin told her. "Many of us are forced to endure lengthy stretches of abstinence. I suppose we had better go attend to Milly and Tim—or what's left of them."

"And Mr. Hope-Tipping and Señor Yanez," Mary reminded her. "Fortunately my good Piet is safe."

During the anxious moments of battle the babies had been piled in the wagon and enjoined to keep still. Tasmin had looked at Monty so sternly that he opened his mouth in dismay. His mother's stern looks, which came without warning or explanation, usually had the effect of freezing Monty in his place, which was just what Tasmin intended.

Eliza, Cook's clumsy helper, who had only been allowed a rolling pin by way of a weapon, for fear that if given anything sharp she would probably only injure herself, was sobbing hopelessly, in grief at Milly's death. Though lately they had fallen out—Milly then a nobleman's mistress, Eliza just an unwanted servant girl—Eliza wept because she had now lost her one friend, a girl, like herself, born into the service of the Berrybenders. Milly was dead, and where would she ever find a friend in this violent place, America?

Tasmin, Buffum, and Mary, carrying some worn blankets that might be suitable for shrouds, trudged off into the prairie toward where Milly and Tim had last been seen.

Jim and Pomp came hurrying over, anxious to divert this burial party if they could.

"I wouldn't go look," Pomp told Tasmin. "Me and Jim can tidy them up."

"I'm going to go look," Tasmin informed him bluntly. "Who were those Indians, Jimmy? Why did they attack us?"

"Pawnees—just boys," Jim told her. "They couldn't manage to steal any horses from the Cheyenne, so they decided to try and kill a few of us."

"They didn't merely try—they succeeded," Tasmin pointed out. "Are Señor Yanez and Mr. Hope-Tipping both dead?"

Pomp nodded.

"They killed four of us—how many of them did we kill?"

"Three," Jim said.

"Then it's a narrow victory for the savage Pawnees," Tasmin declared. "We women weren't frightened out of our wits for nothing."

Gripping her axe, she had been so scared that she was trembling, but as soon as she saw Jim racing back to join the battle, her wild terror diminished. Her husband might not understand her, but Tasmin had absolute confidence in his ability to protect her.

"Why do you want to be looking at those dead folks?" Jim asked. "They're apt to be chopped up bad."

"That's precisely why I want to see them," Mary told him. "Piet thinks I'm progressing rather rapidly with my anatomical studies—I'm sure a close look at poor Tim and Milly's remains will be most helpful."

"You hush," Tasmin said. She had no real answer for her husband's question. Why *did* she want to see two badly mangled corpses? Pomp and Jim gave up the effort to stop them; soon they were looking at the remains of two servants who, for all their lives, had been entirely familiar: Tim and Milly.

"It's exactly as it was with Fraulein Pfretzskaner," Buffum informed them. "They cracked her skull and then seemed unable to stop chopping."

"The human cranium must be little harder to crack than a coconut," Mary said, staring sadly at the remains of the girl who, for most of her life, had washed and ironed her clothes.

Buffum suddenly burst into deep, gulping sobs—the sight of the mutilated girl brought back hard memories of her own brief but painful captivity by the Mandans. She remembered the terrible cold at night, with herself and Mademoiselle Pellenc huddling under a bit of deerskin they had snatched from the dogs. Then the men had been at her; the terrible witch woman, Draga, had beaten them with hot sticks. Now there lay Milly and Tim: the former she had often abused, the latter was a lover who, though not especially gifted, had done his best. Both were now so gashed about that they might indeed, as Mary suggested, have been cadavers there to be examined by an anatomy class.

Tasmin put her arms around her sobbing sister. The two corpses already had a waxy look, as if figures in a wax museum had been crudely disassembled. Their remains had already become unhuman. Once there was no life in the flesh, only an absence of life, a sort of unhumanity, what was there to say?

"I don't know why they refer to dead bodies as mortal remains—of Lord this or that, of Jack and Jill for that matter," Tasmin told them. "We're only mortals while we're alive. Once we aren't alive, what does remain—these scraps of flesh, these bloody bones—hardly seems worth fussing over."

"Oh, don't be icy, Tasmin," Buffum sobbed. "Don't."

"Sorry," Tasmin said. "I very much regret that those Pawnee boys chose to attack us, the result being that neither Tim nor Milly, nor Mr. Hope-Tipping nor good Señor Yanez, will ever be among us again. But they're *gone*—and their husks don't interest me.

"We'll all leave husks someday, somewhere," she added. "Let's just bury them and go along."

"I suppose they always remove the genitals of the male," Mary remarked.

"Not always—in some cases there is no time for such embellishments," Tasmin told her.

Buffum, still sobbing, still distraught, stumbled off to find High Shoulders, but Cook—an expert with shrouds—soon arrived, accompanied by Tom Fitzpatrick, who had just missed the battle, though he claimed to have had intimations of it.

"I seen some birds fly up, and some antelope start running," he said. "If you've been in as many Indian fights as I have, things like that get you wondering."

Tasmin left the corpses to Cook and wandered back to the wagon where the children were. Her mind was on the anxious minutes when she had stood behind the wagon, gripping her axe. What *would* she have done if the battle had gone the other way—or if the Pawnees had passed up Tim and Milly and come straight for the wagon? Suppose Pomp had been killed? Suppose

Jim and Kit had been out of earshot, and her father too slow to mount a defense? Could she and the women have somehow fought off these racing warriors with their flashing lances and deadly hatchets? Would old Charbonneau have been able to sway the attackers? Should she and the women have done better to fight, or to submit? After all, Buffum had survived *her* capture. What if the Pawnees had simply filled them all full of arrows, as they had Mr. Hope-Tipping?

Tasmin stopped for a moment—her legs suddenly became jelly at the thought of what might have happened. She sank to her knees, feeling a throb of relief deeper than any she had ever felt before: the relief of one who had been within a minute of death and yet had been left alive. The plain around her had never seemed more vast and merciless, the sky above never so filled with light and brilliance. And yet, in this place of light, the darkness of death was not more than a minute away. Her survival had not been due either to the craft of men or to the bounty of the gods: it had been absolute luck. Tim and Milly, dragging their fuel sacks around, had blundered right into the path of the warriors—without the brake their deaths provided, the Pawnees would have been at the wagon in only a minute more. Even Pomp and High Shoulders, though they had been quick, might not have been quick enough. The memory of an old book of Greek fables she had had as a child came to her. In it was a picture of Zeus and Poseidon looking down on earthlings through a hole in the clouds, pointing their fingers in an arbitrary way at this mortal or that, far below.

So it might have been that day, Tasmin felt. Señor Yanez and Signor Claricia had been sitting next to one another. Ben Hope-Tipping had been no more than an arm's length from Clam de Paty, yet now the Frenchman and the Italian were alive, the Englishman and the Spaniard quite dead.

She had survived, and so had her child, her sisters, father, husband, lover, and most of the company—and yet the deadly combat had been the work of only seven restless boys. Were not there thousands of Indians somewhere on the plain? What if twenty came, next time, rather than seven? Suppose a hundred came?

In time strength returned to Tasmin's legs; she walked on to the wagon, where her hungry child was waiting. The burials were accomplished without ceremony, Father Geoff merely mumbling a few *Requiescant in pace*s. No one wanted to linger in this spot where death had caught them. Jim Bridger and the Sublette brothers, returning from a fruitless search for beaver, got back just as the company pulled away from the four mounds of earth on the long prairie.

"Was it the Partezon?" Jim Bridger asked.

"Of course not, you fool!" Kit responded angrily. He and Jim Bridger were currently not on good terms.

"I ain't a fool, I just asked a question," Jim replied, doing his best not to inflame the volatile Kit.

"It was just some Pawnee boys, out practicing raiding," Pomp told him.

"That dern big mule nearly got me killed," Kit said, attempting to produce a friendlier tone. He didn't really like being cross with Jim Bridger, his old pard, but for some reason he often did feel distinctly cross with him.

Jim Bridger spat a goodly chew of tobacco juice onto the prairie.

"If them Pawnee sprouts killed four of us just practicing, I don't think I want to make their acquaintance once they get practiced up."

"Amen to that," Billy Sublette remarked.

31

In a while she might be more welcoming.

W H E N Jim put his hand on her, Tasmin angrily knocked it away. It startled him—she sometimes refused him when she was very sleepy, but now she lay beside him wide awake. Jim could see her staring upward. Of course, if she had been violently angry with him, as she sometimes was, he would have known it and kept his hands to himself. But she did not seem angry, merely stiff and distant—indeed, more stiff and more distant than he had ever known her to be.

Of course, Tasmin was changeable. In a while she might be more welcoming. He let her be for a bit, but when he advanced his hand, Tasmin, who had been waiting for just such a move, knocked it away with even more emphasis.

"Stop it," she said. "Can't you tell when I don't wish to be pawed?"

"Not till I try," Jim replied.

"It would be a good thing for you to learn—when to leave well enough alone," Tasmin told him.

Jim was silent. He had hoped to make love, not argue. Tasmin had shown plenty of courage during the fight that day, from what he had seen. She had grabbed an axe, and been ready to use it. But the big fight was over. Why did she think she wanted to fight him?

"I guess it's good night, then," he said.

But Tasmin clutched his arm. To his surprise her hands were shaking, and there were tears on her cheeks. She clutched him hard, crying silently, her body shaking, but not with passion.

"I'm scared . . . I'm scared . . . that's why I don't want you, can't you tell?" she said.

Jim relaxed a bit and held her until her shaking stopped. He felt that for once he did understand her mood. In sudden battle there was no time for fear—it was act or die. But afterward, once the issue was settled, strong men sometimes took the shakes, just as Tasmin had. No doubt it was the recollection of how close death had been. He himself had once had an Osage arrow part his hair: a fraction of an inch had been the difference between living and dying. He had paid no attention to the arrow at the time, though he chased and finally killed the Osage who shot it. But the next day, watering a horse, he recollected that something had zipped right across his scalp, even drawing a few drops of blood. He sat at the water hole a long time, not shaking, but thinking. Once he left the water he forgot about the arrow. Prairie life involved so many close calls that experienced men learned not to dwell on them—surviving them was enough.

"You might get your pa to loan you a gun or two," he suggested. "Indians won't pay much attention to a bunch of women with axes and knives."

"I suppose not," Tasmin admitted.

"What if you and Kit had been farther away?" she asked, sitting up. "What if Pomp had gone off with the trappers, as he meant to do? What if High Shoulders had been hunting?"

"Try not to be thinking about it," Jim said—only to receive a sharp dig from Tasmin's elbow.

"Jimmy, I *am* thinking about it!" she said, pounding him twice on his chest with her fist. "I *have* to think about it. If you can't be persuaded to stay close, then I need to know what to do if some restless Indians show up again."

"I'll be staying close," Jim assured her. It wasn't a chore he looked forward to—he was fond of roaming far ahead, out of range of the squabbles and arguments of the company. But the Pawnee boys, once they got home, would be sure to mention the big party of whites traveling through their country. In the party were several women who might be captured and sold, and also some fine horses. The Pawnee elders might decide they were a tempting target.

"Just tell me what to do if they come and you're not close," Tasmin plead. "Do I fight, or do I submit?"

Jim did not answer immediately. All the whites along the line of the frontier had to ask themselves that question. Buffum had survived a few weeks of captivity not too damaged, but she had been held at the great trading entrepôt of the Mandans, where captives were traded regularly and seen as a valuable source of profit. Women taken into the deep plains by the Osage, the Comanche, or other roving tribes, seldom fared as well—it depended on the speed and the intentions of the captors. Husbands searched for years and never found their lost wives, or fathers their lost daughters. Unless ransomed quickly, captive women became wives—even if rescued, these were seldom able to return successfully to their families or their communities.

"I'll be staying close, for now," Jim promised. "If they took you women they'd probably kill the little boys—raiders won't usually be bothered with children on the teat."

"In that case I'll fight," Tasmin assured him. "I'll not stand by and watch our babies butchered like Tim and Milly."

They were silent for a time, but it was not a restful or comfortable silence. Jim felt resentful. Here he was trapped in a situation that had no particular purpose.

"Your pa's drug you all out here and put you in danger," he reminded her. "For what? Just so he can shoot a lot of critters?"

"I agree completely," Tasmin said. "He's endangered several blameless womenfolk, and for no good reason."

"He should have taken you all back on the boat with Ashley," Jim said. "He's shot plenty of buffalo already."

"Not enough to suit him," Tasmin said. "Papa plans to shoot for at least another year."

Jim knew that. He had heard the old lord talk of crossing the plains of Texas, an intrusion that was sure to rile the Comanches, who were usually riled anyway.

Tasmin lay back in a dark, confused mood. But little by little, lying comfortably in her husband's arms, her mood slowly lifted. Some of the relief she had felt that afternoon on the prairie surged through her again. After all, she wasn't dead, her son was healthy, and she was married.

"Most questions have two sides, I suppose," she said. "If my foolish, selfish father hadn't brought us to America I'd be safe enough, but I wouldn't have met you."

Jim didn't answer—of course she was right.

"You *are* glad we met, aren't you, Jimmy?" she asked, in a warmer, breathier tone.

"I'm glad," Jim said.

"Jimmy, you're the Sin Killer," she said, reaching up to tug gently at his beard. "You used to be terribly hard on sin—as, sinner that I am, I remember to my sorrow. But lately you don't seem so hard. You've not slapped me for a while."

"You ain't cussed for a while, either."

"Not in your hearing," she told him. "But I'm not always in your hearing, and when I'm not, I could be cussing fervently for all you know."

"If you do you're a fool to tell me," Jim said.

"I notice you didn't kill those Pawnee boys, though I expected you to," Tasmin reminded him. "After all, they killed four of us. Isn't murder a sin?"

"A big sin," Jim agreed, though he wished she'd shut up.

"Then why didn't you kill them all?"

"They were young boys," he said. "If we'd killed them all, it would have brought the whole tribe down on our heads—and then they'd kill *us* all."

Tasmin began to caress his bare stomach. Some need to gamble, to dare, had almost made her ask what his position was on adultery—she was tempted but she held her tongue.

When Jim put his hand on her again, Tasmin didn't knock it

away. He was cautious, perhaps expecting a rebuke, which didn't come. This time Tasmin opened her legs and accepted him, though quietly, almost passively, with less than her usual ardor. It was affection she had been seeking, not passion, but husbands had their needs. She pulled his beard a time or two, so as not to forget who she was with—when her blood rose a little the thought of Pomp kept slipping into her mind. When Jim was finished Tasmin locked her legs around him and held him in for as long as she could.

"It's a funny thing, Jimmy," she whispered, with another tiny tug of his beard. "You aggravate me so that there are times when I don't much want you to come in—but then once you're there I don't want you to come out. Is that not perversity for you, my sweet?"

But Jim had dozed. He didn't hear her, which, once she slipped out from under him, Tasmin decided was just as well. Why risk making the silly creature vain?

32

*. . . traveling south on a plain burnt
brown . . .*

A   W E E K   later, traveling south on a plain burnt brown,
under a cloudless, white hot sky, Tasmin and her siblings and all
the Europeans were introduced to a new sensation: thirst. The
company had but one small water barrel, which Jim and Pomp
were quick to fill brimful whenever they came to a water hole or
crossed a flowing stream. But a day came when they passed no
flowing streams—the route became much drier than it had been
when Jim crossed it only a few weeks earlier.

Never in their lives had Tasmin or any of the Berrybenders
been more than a few minutes from abundant sources of cool
water. Not only had there been plenty of water to drink, there
had been water to bathe in as often as they liked, water for
Cook's great stews, and water for all the laundering of clothes
that days of sweaty travel made necessary.

Then one morning, with the plain stretching before them,
vast, baking, treeless, waterless, brown, almost sandy, Jim and
Pomp called them to the wagon and explained to them that the
water they had left would have to be severely rationed.

Pomp held up a tin cup.

"A cup a day it will have to be, until we can find a spring or a
running creek," he told the startled company.

"That's *all*?" Tasmin said. "Even if we can moderate our drinking, what are we to wash with?"

Pomp and Kit looked embarrassed, but Jim Snow was matter-
of-fact.

"The washing's over until we get to a wetter place," he
informed them, wondering why he had to mention such a self-
evident truth.

Clam de Paty, who had been subdued and morose since the
death of Ben Hope-Tipping, suddenly colored and began to
shout.

"But this is an outrage!" he said loudly. "Of course we must
make our toilettes—don't you agree, Lord Berrybender?"

To his shock Lord B. did not support his protest.

"It's deuced inconvenient, I admit," Lord Berrybender said. "I
enjoy a washup as much as the next man. But it's clear that we've
come to a rather dry place—drier than Castile, and Castile is dry
enough."

"But Jimmy, surely . . . can't we change directions, head for a
river or something? Or perhaps the snowy mountains?" Tasmin
asked.

"Wouldn't help," Jim said. "Wasn't much snow in the high
passes last winter—that's why these little creeks ain't running."

"But I'll just send Amboise off with a bucket," Clam proposed.
"He's a good servant. He'll find us a stream."

"No, he'll just get lost and starve," Jim told him, thinking that
it would be hard to exceed the stupidity of Europeans. He
turned and walked off with Kit and Jim Bridger. Pomp understood Europeans—let him explain. He had merely said they had
to be careful of water, a commonplace of prairie travel. The company would just have to travel dirty for a while, as the trappers
had always traveled.

"When in Rome, do as the Romans do," Pomp told the group.
"I'm sure you've heard that old saying."

"When I'm in Rome *I* do as the French do—I do," Clam said. "I
hardly think I wish to alter my habits to accommodate a bunch of
garlicky Italians."

Signor Claricia, insulted, at once flung himself at Clam de Paty, who, surprised, tripped and fell over backward, Signor Claricia on top of him. They rolled over and over in the dust until Pomp, with the help of Amboise d'Avigdor, stepped in and separated them. Both men were covered with dust from head to heels, a circumstance so untimely, in view of the no-wash order, that Pomp had to hide a smile.

"Jimmy didn't mean to say we'd starve," Pomp told them. "There's water here and there, and we'll locate it. But certain habits will have to be given up until we strike a river."

"And when will that be, monsieur?" Clam demanded to know.

"Three weeks, maybe, if we don't have to trouble with the Indians," Pomp speculated.

The mere knowledge that they couldn't have a bath awoke in several of the Europeans the desire for exactly that, the one most affected being Cook. Though stoic in the face of most calamities, Cook had always been sustained by the principle of absolute cleanliness. The prairies had already offered a challenge, and yet there had usually been rills and streams, rivers and ponds, and she availed herself of every opportunity for a vigorous scrub—besides which she had always pushed Millicent to keep up with the laundry—nothing worse than a filthy garment on a clean body. Now Millicent was dead—that very morning Cook had had a slight tiff with Mary Berrybender over the issue of laundry.

"Since Milly is dead, Eliza is all we've got," Mary pointed out, in her cool way. "She may indeed be a clumsy girl, but after all, a dress isn't much like a plate. If she drops a dress it won't actually break."

"Oh, but here we are amid the weeds and brambles, miss," Cook replied. "I fear there will be rips and tears."

Indeed, in the few days since Milly's death, Cook had thought of little else *but* laundry, which was already piling up so fast that it threatened to crowd the babies out of the wagon—and now there was no stream in sight in which it could be properly soaked and beaten.

To the dismay of the company, and especially of her suitor,

Tom Fitzpatrick, Cook suddenly burst into loud sobs, startling Lord Berrybender so that he came near to dropping his beloved Belgian gun.

"Good Lord in heaven, our Cook is in tears!" he exclaimed. "I've known the woman fifty years and she's never dripped a tear, that I can recall. Do help out, Tasmin—hate to see a woman cry."

"You may hate to see tears, Papa, but if we'd only collected all the tears you've caused to flow, we could all enjoy several baths and probably do the laundry as well," Tasmin told him, acidly.

"I wouldn't wish to bathe in tears—too salty," Lord B. replied, before stumping off.

"It won't be that bad," Pomp assured them. "Look at the trappers—they never bathe, and yet they're healthy men."

Tasmin did look at the trappers, who were standing in a group some distance away, discussing where to look for water. The only clean animal in the group seemed to be the bear cub, Abby, a real animal. All the mountain men were filthy, their clothes smeared with grease and dust.

"I don't think I want to be as filthy as those trappers, however healthy I might be," Tasmin told Pomp.

"Let's go," Jim Snow directed. "From now on we need to travel early, rest in the heat of the day, and push on till moonrise."

"All right, but those of us who are being required to change a whole way of life might like a few minutes to adjust to it," Tasmin replied.

"This is some of that droughty country I told you about when you first wanted me to take you off to Santa Fe," Jim reminded her. "I wouldn't take you because of this big dry."

"Santa Fe was only a ruse," Tasmin told him. "I mainly wanted to copulate with you, my sweet, which, thanks to my own great perseverance, I did succeed in doing."

"You're talking too loud—Pomp will hear," Jim said.

"Ah, but young Monsieur Charbonneau is not much afflicted by the torments of lust," Tasmin said.

Actually she hoped Pomp *would* hear her talking about copulation—perhaps the carnal impulse would stir in him if she teased him with provocative words.

"We had rather a lively courtship, at least," Tasmin mentioned. "The day I tried to get you to take me to Santa Fe you seized me and shook me like a rag, as I recall."

"Yes, because you were cussing," Jim said.

"Yes, and since filth is all I now have to look forward to, I may drop a few more filthy oaths," Tasmin said.

Jim left immediately and spent the day watching for birds or game, in hopes of finding a herd or a flock that would lead them to water. All the mountain men had fanned out on the same quest. The only birds Jim saw were hawks, riding the hot air, and he saw no game at all, not a deer, not an antelope, not even a jackrabbit. It was not a good omen. Gameless places were often waterless places. In a day or two, if they didn't find a spring, there would be no water to drink.

Kit, a mile or two to the west of Jim, drifted over to discuss the situation. He and Jim had twice crossed the country they were in while going to their first winter scout on the Green River, and returning from it. Not far ahead he remembered a little creek. On neither crossing had they had trouble finding water. Not far ahead, in fact, there had been a little creek with one or two trees growing along it. The creek had been running, then. They had taken a good-sized trout out of it. Surely it would be running now.

"I was just thinking of that creek," Jim said, when Kit reminded him of the trout that had made a fine supper.

But when they found the creek, some three miles on, it was bone dry—Jim Bridger joined them and they followed the creek toward the mountains, hoping to find a pond—but they found no pond. A little later the rest of the party straggled up.

"We might try digging for it," Jim suggested. "If we can get down to the damp sand we might get a pretty good seep."

None of the mountain men had a better idea. When Cook started to draw a little water from the barrel, just enough to make a soup, Pomp stopped her.

"No soup for a while," he told her.

Clam de Paty started to launch into another protest, but something about the look of the mountain men stopped him. They all wore looks of taut concern.

Jim and Kit, wielding two spades, began to dig holes in the center of the creek bed. Lord Berrybender watched this activity with furrowed brow. Like Clam he was subdued, in part by the realization that they had drunk the last of the Ashley champagne only the day before. The company was now without spirits of any kind.

Vicky shared the general concern. She and Tasmin stood by Cook, who was extremely distressed. No baths to bathe in, no laundry done, and now not even soup. To Cook, these were shocking things.

At mealtime that evening the whole company was despondent. Cook, for the first time in her long service, had nothing to cook. The little boys made do with mother's milk—for the rest there was only elk jerky and a little corn they had purchased from the Utes. To the mountain men this was nothing out of the ordinary, but the Europeans were faced for the first time with a total absence of anything that could be called dinner.

"Sure you don't have another bottle or two of that good cognac tucked away in your basket, monsieur?" Lord Berrybender asked Clam.

The Frenchman merely shook his head.

Tasmin realized that she was seeing her father sober for the first time in her life.

"Not sure I've ever seen you sober, Father," she said.

"Bad planning, or I wouldn't be sober now," Lord Berrybender replied. "Life seems rather a harsh business, when one is sober, just as I feared it would. I seem to be married to Vicky now—none too clear as to how that came about."

Then a thought seemed to stir him.

"I say, Clam—you've still got your balloon," he pointed out. "What if we puff it up and you and I go sailing off? If we caught a nice breeze it might waft us to Santa Fe—plenty to drink there, I bet."

Clam brightened at this suggestion—but only briefly. The wind that might blow them to Santa Fe could just as easily blow them into some Indians, as it had once already.

"A thought, monsieur—a thought," he replied.

"Never been in a balloon myself—I'm anxious to try it," Lord B. went on—he brightened visibly at this prospect. "I might even bring my Belgian gun. Could increase my bag considerably, if I'm lucky. Sail right over a buffalo herd and pop away at them."

Clam found that he was not much attracted to the notion of ballooning with Lord Berrybender. On the whole he thought he preferred to stick to the mountain men, who seemed to know what they were doing, even though presently there were hardships. But then, life in the Grande Armée had not all been pretty girls and puddings, either.

"A damn pity losing Yanez," Lord Berrybender continued. "He did keep the guns in good working order, I'll say that for him."

Tasmin felt an anger growing—and just when she had been rather sympathetic to her father. Sober, he looked wan and old, almost pitiful—and yet he had immediately demonstrated that he was prepared to be as selfish as ever.

"You mean you'd just leave us, Father?" she asked, in a quiet tone. "You bring us to a desert where we'll likely either starve or be killed by savages, while you propose to fly away—is that really your intention?"

"Can't see much wrong with the notion," Lord B. replied. In his mind he saw himself killing buffalo after buffalo—or perhaps even one of the great bears—while flying along in the cool air.

"Then you *would* leave us, wouldn't you?" Tasmin inquired, in ominous tones. "You brought us here, far from our customary shores, and you propose to desert us just when our prospects are bleakest—it's rotten behavior, if you ask me."

"But I *didn't* ask you, and why should I, you contentious hussy?" Lord B. said, annoyed. Tasmin's accusations were making it difficult for him to concentrate on his own nice fancies of the hunt.

"Rotten behavior, Papa—I feel the same!" Buffum announced, with sudden spirit.

"And I curse you for a black tyrant," little Kate yelled suddenly. Then, to the surprise and shock of the company, Kate rushed at her father, penknife drawn, and began to stab him vigorously in the leg, striking home at least three times before Amboise stepped in and lifted her off, kicking and stabbing, into the air.

Amboise handed her to Jim, who managed to persuade her to surrender the bloody penknife.

Lord Berrybender was stunned. His wounds were hardly serious, but his lap was now soaked with his own blood.

"I've always known it was a mistake to breed," he remarked, to no one in particular. "But Constance *would* breed, and now Vicky will soon be the size of a cow again. It's a bad business, monsieur."

Pomp, Vicky, and Cook managed to cut Lord Berrybender's trouser leg off; to Cook's shame, there were no clean trousers to produce; they were allowed just enough water to wash the wound. Vicky helped her husband off to their tent, while Tasmin gave the violent Kate a lecture on the evils of patricide.

"I say he's a black tyrant!" the unrepentant Kate insisted.

Tasmin noticed that the mountain men seemed unusually subdued, sitting in silence as a sunset faded to a line of pink along the western horizon. Jim Bridger was whittling a stick, the rest of them merely sitting.

"You seem a dispirited bunch," Tasmin told them. "Surely one of you—well traveled as you are—must know someplace where we could find water."

"We know the country pretty well, I guess," Tom Fitzpatrick told her. "We just forgot something, in this case."

"What?"

"That every year ain't the same," he told her. "Some's wet and some's dry."

"And then some's *real* dry," Jim Bridger added.

"I see. And this is one of the ones that are *real* dry, correct?" Tasmin said.

"The driest I've ever seen," Hugh Glass admitted.

"There's springs, though," Kit Carson insisted. "The Indians hunt out here. They must know places where there's water."

"What they probably know is when to stay away," Tom said. "That's why we ain't seen Indians for a spell."

"It might rain," Jim Bridger pointed out.

"Or it might not," Hugh Glass said grimly.

When told that they must ration water, Tasmin had supposed that the worst that might happen was they would all have to be dirty and thirsty for a few days. Now, looking at the grave faces of the men—resilient fellows all, not easily daunted—she realized that their situation went beyond inconvenience. They were clearly in danger.

"We oughtn't to have let Greasy Lake wander off," Kit said. "If there's a spring anywhere near, he'd know it."

"We've got our animals, at least," Jim Bridger reminded them. "I've drunk horse piss before."

Then he suddenly realized that Tasmin had heard him use a coarse term—he turned beet red from embarrassment.

Jim Snow was so annoyed by this lapse that he stood up and led Tasmin away. The word hadn't shocked her, but the vision it called up was very shocking indeed.

"Drink piss?" she asked, when they were alone. "Could it get that bad?"

"That bad and worse," Jim said.

33

As dawn light spread over the plain . . .

As dawn light spread over the plain, only Cook and one or two others were stirring. Even Jim Snow was still dozing. Tasmin gave Monty the breast and then deposited him with Little Onion. She picked up the axe that she had used to defend herself in the Pawnee attack and carried it to the small wagon belonging to Clam de Paty, who was sleeping under it. It was Amboise d'Avigdor, a friendly boy now known as Ambo to most of the company, whom Tasmin shook awake.

"Get up, Ambo, I need you," she whispered. "I want you to help me get the balloon out of the wagon—and the basket too."

Amboise quickly accomplished what he was asked to do, awakening Clam de Paty in the process—but Clam didn't emerge from beneath the wagon, or offer any objection to what Tasmin was planning.

"If you want a ride we need to make a fire," Amboise whispered. "It only goes up if you fill it with hot air."

"Not what I had in mind at all, thanks," Tasmin said. Then she attacked the padded basket with her axe and soon reduced it to kindling. Clam still lay on his pillow, a pleasant smile on his face.

"Got any shears?" Tasmin asked Amboise. Shears were at once produced, after which Tasmin cut several great holes in the fabric of the balloon; she then folded the cut pieces neatly.

"I expect Cook can find a use for these snippets," Tasmin said, before bending down to address Monsieur de Paty.

"I just destroyed your balloon, monsieur," she informed him cheerfully. "Nothing against you, of course. I'm merely determined that my father shall not be able to exempt himself from whatever torments the rest of us must endure."

"Good work," Clam told her. "I hated that balloon. It was the paper's idea, you know? Balloons over America, you see? Hate heights myself—only managed the flights by drinking lots of cognac."

When Tasmin returned to her own place, only Jim and Kit were in sight—the rest of the mountain men seemed to have vanished.

"Fanned out to look for water," Jim told her.

"We caught a pretty good seep in that creek last night," Kit told her. "Enough to water the horses and the people pretty well."

When Tasmin went with Jim to inspect the holes the men had dug she saw that all of them had liquid in them, but liquid of an extremely muddy nature. One hole, the smallest, was reserved for people, Jim said.

"You expect us to drink that?" she asked. "It looks like mud soup."

"Oh, we'll strain it," Jim assured her.

Two buckets of the liquid were quickly lifted out of the hole. Cook provided a coarse cloth through which the substance was strained—everyone was given a large cup—and by that time everyone was thirsty enough to drink without complaint, although Vicky, still morning sick, had trouble keeping hers down. Tasmin closed her eyes and gulped; she was left with a film of grit on her tongue but she was much less thirsty.

Lord Berrybender, in a shaky state due to the absence of spirits, spat out the first mouthful but then drank his cup. When he saw the wreckage of the balloon he merely glanced at it absently and turned away.

"Impractical notion, I suppose, hunting buffalo from a balloon," he said. "What if I were to drop my fine gun?"

Tasmin didn't like Pomp being gone—although they seldom spoke, during the day she liked to let her eyes rest on him from time to time. It provided her some measure of reassurance; it satisfied some need. She was glad enough that Jim was close at hand, but she didn't derive the same comfort from looking at him as she did from looking at Pomp. Her arrangement with Jim was practical; she trusted him to keep her safe. It was Pomp she distinctly missed; his absence always caused a mild disquiet.

Tasmin and Vicky were just about to climb into the wagon when Jim came over and informed them that, for a time at least, they had better walk.

"Walk? Us?" Tasmin asked, startled. The company possessed three wagons. Why should anyone walk?

"It's hot, Jimmy," she reminded him. "What's a horse for, if not to pull a wagon, and what's a wagon for, if not to ride in?"

"Just walk," he said, irritated. Nothing annoyed him more than Tasmin's almost automatic tendency to question his orders.

"You need to get used to it," he said, and turned away.

"Why should we get used to something unnecessary?" Tasmin asked, but she didn't expect an answer and she didn't get one.

Ignored and annoyed, Tasmin hurried over to Kit Carson, who had managed to run a thorn into his thumb—he had borrowed a needle from Cook and was attempting to push out the thorn—but the thorn was in his right thumb and he was awkward with his left, so progress had been nil.

"Hello, Kit—my husband says we are all to walk, but he won't say why," Tasmin informed him. "You know the man better than I do. What's his reasoning? Why must we walk when it's so hot?"

Kit found that he could hardly concentrate on his delicate task—not with Tasmin standing so close.

"Nobody's seen any game for three days," he told her. "We'll have to start eating horses pretty soon."

His thumb was bleeding a little from his awkward probings.

Tasmin knelt in front of him and relieved him of the needle.

"Would you please let me do this?" she requested, looking closely at the injured thumb. Kit wiggled when she poked it with the needle.

"Hold still there," she said. "No surgeon can work on a moving target."

Kit kept as still as possible—Tasmin, after all, was holding his hand, an intimacy that embarrassed him greatly, even though her purpose was purely medical.

"First drinking mud and then eating horses—not much of a pleasure trip we're having, is it?" she said. The thorn, when she eased it out, was only a tiny speck of green, yet it was evidently quite poisonous, for Kit's thumb was hugely swollen.

"How very ingenious of you, Kit—to get a thorn in your hand in this place where there are no trees or bushes," Tasmin told him.

"There's cactus, though—little mean cactuses about the size of a gold piece," Kit said. "You'll know you're stuck if you step on one. Better watch where you put your feet if we're going to be hiking. The little green ones are as poisonous as a rattlesnake."

"It's sweet of you to warn me—indeed, you are very sweet in general, Mr. Kit Carson," Tasmin complimented. "I expect you'll make a fine mate, if any woman could ever catch you."

Kit immediately blushed, the blush spreading even down his neck.

Tasmin noted this with amusement—here was a young man she could easily work her charms on, to whatever extent she chose to. Young Kit wouldn't turn his back on her, or let her questions and opinions go unanswered, as her husband had just done. Kit would always be her champion, if Jim and Pomp both failed her.

But now there was the heat to be faced. Even before she got back to the wagon, where the women stood in a listless, discouraged group, Tasmin felt the sweat begin to trickle down her ribs.

34

She carefully guarded the cup . . .

"ELIZA, you must drink! You must!" Buffum pleaded. "You must or else you'll die."

She carefully guarded the cup, lest Eliza strike out and spill the greenish, frothy, acrid liquid which Jim Snow had carefully drained from the stomach of the second palfrey, killed only this morning.

"I can't, miss—I can't, Miss Bess—I'll just be dying, perhaps I'll be seeing poor Milly in heaven," the choking girl said, her tongue so swollen that she could scarcely speak.

"Now, Eliza, there is a way to do this," Bess said, with surprising patience—Tasmin and Cook had given up on the girl, who had taken not a drop of liquid through a long scorching day.

"Shut your eyes tight and hold your nose firmly," Bess instructed. "Don't look and don't smell, just swallow. It's very un-Christian to die when you might be saved. It's the Lord who has sent us this trial, Liza, and we must not allow despair into our souls."

"Anno Domini," Father Geoff intoned. *"Anno Domini."* Though his own stomach had all but rejected this same unpalatable liquid, he thought a few words of Latin might strengthen Buffum's case.

"Please, Eliza, just try," Buffum pleaded. "Tassie and Cook will help."

"I'll try—don't mind it if I vomit," Eliza said at last.

Cook at once clasped both hands over the girl's eyes and Tasmin firmly pinched her nostrils shut. Buffum tilted the cup and the girl drank five large swallows, all that the cup contained. Eliza spluttered a bit, but did not vomit.

Tasmin, whose own tongue felt twice as thick as was normal, walked over to where Kit and Jim were standing with Lord Berrybender.

"Well, we got it down her," Tasmin said, tired.

"I'm rather proud of Buffum—she's revealed unexpected resolve," Lord Berrybender said.

"Yes, she has," Tasmin agreed. "She has a child in her and a handsome mate to set against starvation."

They saw Piet and Mary approaching the camp. They had been hunting edibles, but despite Mary's remarkable nose, the hot prairies had only yielded several handfuls of wild onions.

"We've only got three more horses, Jimmy," Tasmin pointed out. "How many days does that give us?"

They were in the middle of a baking, unforgiving plain, so bleak that Tasmin's own feelings were not much more hopeful than Eliza's. Her first fear was that her milk might be drying up— Vicky had the same worry. What would they use to feed the little boys?

"Long enough, I expect, if we're lucky," Jim said, pointing to the north. "What does your smeller say, Kit?"

Tasmin had stopped believing that she would ever see a real cloud again, or feel rain on her skin, but to the north, where Jim had pointed, a dark line of cloud lay on the horizon, with slanting gray lines underneath it; there was even the distant rumble of thunder.

"I can't smell it yet but I 'spect it's coming this way," Kit told them.

"I hope you're right," Jim said. "Sometimes these little sprinkles don't last but a minute. We better set out the pots and buckets—if it does come we need to catch as much of it as we can."

Filled with sudden hope, Tasmin ran back to Cook—soon every pot, bucket, or crock that could hold water was lined up, waiting for the approaching shower, which teased them for over an hour as they waited anxiously. Twice the clouds dissolved and bright sun shone, but then the clouds re-formed and darkened, as the whole company stood and watched, riveted by the drama of water on the plain.

"I hope it don't skip us," Kit said. "Sometimes it'll get close and then skip you."

"It won't skip us—it mustn't," Tasmin cajoled. "Maybe Father Geoff could make a prayer."

"I'll make a hundred prayers and even say my rosary, if I can find it," Father Geoff agreed.

"Try to do better than *Anno Domini*," Tasmin instructed. "That worked for Eliza, but the rain gods probably expect better. They might merely scoff."

Not until the rain was close enough that they could all smell it was the group convinced that the shower wouldn't skip them. The fresh smell of rain as the first drops splattered on the dusty grass was the most delicious smell Tasmin had ever experienced. Even the feverish Eliza's face lit up. The first drops were gentle, wide-spaced, uneven; but then the rain came faster and steadier and steadier. Tasmin realized that here was an unexpected opportunity to be clean. Their bodies were smeared and smudged, black with dust. Was not this their chance? As the shower thickened Tasmin began to strip off.

"Go away, men—go away, hurry!" she demanded; the men, startled for a moment, turned their backs and moved away toward the wagon where the babies were, guarded by Little Onion. The women continued their stripping—soon even Cook, with her tremendous rolls of flesh, stood naked under the pelting shower. From the wagon came a wailing from the babies, shocked and then horrified that they were being rained on. Tasmin could see, through the rain, Coal and Little Onion tittering with embarrassment at the sight of the naked white

women—even the trembling Eliza recovered her spirit sufficiently to disrobe.

Taking their cue from the women, Lord Berrybender, Clam de
Paty, and Father Geoffrin also stripped. Kit, too modest, fearful
that the women might see him, merely removed his shirt. Jim
Snow and the rest of the mountain men remained fully clothed.
Amboise d'Avigdor dithered; he did not feel it quite proper to
strip. Piet Van Wely hesitated; he stood indecisively between the
men and the women, until Mary Berrybender, naked, young
breasts bouncing, rushed over and insisted that he undress.

As the shower intensified, the rain became cold—the women,
burning only moments before, broke out in goose bumps.

Tasmin reveled in the pelting rain, which had swept over them
so miraculously. Only an hour before, they had conspired to
force Eliza to drink a revolting liquid from a horse's belly, and
now the pure liquid of the heavens was washing them all clean.
She slipped over to the wagon and removed the little boy's
ragged garments. All three were crying lustily, thinking that the
world might be ending, but Tasmin ignored their screams—here
was a heaven-sent chance to get them clean.

In no more than ten minutes the shower began to diminish—
sunlight broke through the clouds and, in the distance, a rainbow arched over the plain. Mist rose from the wet grass. As the
last drops splattered down, Tasmin rejoined the women, all of
them faced with the same dilemma. They were clean, but their
clothes, now a sodden heap, were not. Tasmin enjoyed the last
few drifting drops, noticing with amusement that her belly,
Vicky's, and Buffum's had begun to swell. Fertility had not been
lacking in the Valley of the Chickens. Cook would be having to
assist at three births, almost at the same time.

"All my garments reek," Buffum complained. "I do so hate to
put on reeking garments."

Without warning Jim Snow suddenly appeared in their midst,
causing Vicky and Buffum to blush, although he took no more
notice of their nakedness than he would have had they been so
many deer.

"Grab the pitchers and get busy," he instructed. "We've got to collect this water before it soaks in."

Tasmin saw that, indeed, the prairie was covered with hundreds of shining puddles, the rainwater temporarily caught in small declivities. The men were already hard at work, dipping cups into the puddles and emptying them into pitchers and pots. At some the horses drank—Tasmin saw Jim Snow bend down and drink his fill from one of the deeper puddles.

"Look, girls—drink like Jimmy's drinking," Tasmin ordered. "We're saved, I bet—at least we're saved for now. Scoop up what you can."

Soon the women were doing as the men did, scooping up water in whatever containers they could find. Long into the night they worked, locating puddles by moonlight. Tom Fitzpatrick came back and fell to, but the Sublettes, Hugh Glass, and Pomp were still somewhere in the field. Tasmin had become anxious about Pomp, who had not come back for three nights. In her anxiety she conjured up accidents that could have befallen him: snakebite, twisted ankle, grizzly attack. She didn't mention her worry to Jim—he would just have reminded her of what she already knew: that Pomp was a competent frontiersman who could well look after himself.

Tasmin thought the fine shower might be a portent. Perhaps the time of thirst was over, though the fact that the men worked through the night, searching the prairies for overlooked puddles, suggested that they had not yet reached a zone of safety.

At dawn Jim stopped for a rest, stretching out beside Tasmin.

"Do you think there'll be more showers?" she asked. "That one was *so* pleasant."

"Not regular, not this early," he told her. "We're only halfway across the Big Dry. We've still got to be careful about water."

Tasmin put a hand on his arm but otherwise didn't touch him. In the days of constant thirst every feeling except the desire for cool water had left her, and left the others too, she felt sure. The anxieties and titillations of romance were burned away by all-consuming thirst. Passion had stopped—in recent days she would have bartered anything for a good long drink.

When she had been over one of the deeper puddles to drink she had seen her own haggard reflection. And yet no sooner had she drunk her fill than old thoughts, old feelings, began to return. If only she could drink her fill often enough she might one day want to be a wife again.

"Pomp's been gone three days, and so has Mr. Glass and the Sublettes, and even Buffum's Ute," she told him, wondering what he made of these absences.

"I expect we'll see them tomorrow, unless they've spotted buffalo," Jim told her. "There used to be a herd that grazed close to the mountains—Arapaho buffalo, we called them, because the Arapaho took most of them."

Suddenly, across the wide, dark sky, shooting stars began to flash—only one or two at first, but then a burst, a kind of shower.

"Goodness, I've never seen *that* before," Tasmin said, sitting up.

"They come now and then," Jim told her. "I seen a terrible bunch of them the night before Preacher Cockerell got struck by lightning. The Indians get spooked if they see all these shooting stars fall at once. They think it means death to the tribe."

Tasmin lay back beside him. It had been on the tip of her tongue to ask Jim if he was happy about the new baby that was coming—but she held back. At first she had supposed the child was Pomp's—but as time went on she became less sure. Pomp was just so distant; if he *had* made the baby it was because she had forced him to. And what would Jim think, if he knew? Would he attack her violently, in punishment for her undoubted sin? Or would he be indifferent? Jim and Pomp, in their different ways, were very hard to know. Of neither's feelings at a given time could she be sure.

"I hope we're somewhere where there's plenty of water when this baby comes," she said. "It would be a hard mothering if it's still this dry. What if I hadn't good milk?"

Jim, though, had nodded off—when he slept his breathing was even, just like Monty's. It irked her a little, that she was always the one who seemed to be awake—seemed to be pondering questions that had no obvious answers. Then she heard Monty making urgent sounds from the wagon. Monty was hungry—his needs, at least, were definite. With a sigh she got up and went to get her child.

35

Clam de Paty only smiled.

J I M   S N O W and Jim Bridger, food having run very low, were debating whether they should kill their next-to-last horse, when Kit Carson's quick eye saw movement far to the east. For a moment he could scarcely credit his own vision.

"I see an ox and there's a man riding on it," he informed them.

"I doubt you see no ox," the ever-skeptical Jim Bridger said.

"Doubt me if you like, you fool!" Kit told him, hotly. "There's an ox and a man riding on it, and Pomp and High Shoulders leading the way."

Jim Snow kept his own counsel. Usually Kit was right, when it came to faraway sights.

"If you can see so good, who's on the ox, then?" Jim Bridger asked. It went against his nature to back down easily.

Kit took another look.

"All I know about the fellow riding the ox is that he's old," Kit told them. "He could be Methuselah, for all I know."

Tom Fitzpatrick took a long look himself.

"It ain't Methuselah, it's Zeke Williams—why, I thought the Arapaho took Zeke's hair a year ago. It shows you you can't believe everything you hear."

"I don't believe *anything* I hear, particularly not if it comes out of Jim Bridger's mouth," Kit said—he was feeling smug about the fact that his vision had been accurate after all.

There was a mist on the prairie that morning—when Tasmin looked the first thing she saw was the top half of Pomp Charbonneau, seemingly floating on a cloud. At once her spirits rose. There he was, not dead at all. But where had he secured such a noble ox?

To Jim Snow the reassuring thing was not that old Zeke Williams was still alive, but that the ox he rode seemed to be in good flesh, not gaunt like their own horses. That meant there was abundant water somewhere near—oxen sometimes faltered on the Big Dry. For the first time in two weeks Jim felt optimistic about their chances. The sight of a healthy ox suggested that they might survive.

"Hello, Zeke—where have you been this last year, and how did you get so gone that we gave you up for dead?" Tom Fitzpatrick asked.

All of them saw that the old man's feet were swollen and cut— no wonder he had to ride the ox.

"Why the goddamn thieving Rappies caught me," Zeke said— his eyes were bright blue and twinkling.

"Kept me all this time, hoping to sell me," he added.

"Hoping to sell you? Why, who'd pay money for a man your age?" Kit asked. He almost got a fit of giggles at the thought.

"If I was in the market they could sell Zeke to me," Tom Fitzpatrick remarked. He gave Kit a severe frown.

"Zeke came to the Big Horn River with Manuel Lisa a derned long time ago," he said. "He knows every water hole in the West. I'd buy him just for what he knows."

"Got any bacon, boys?" Zeke asked, impatient with the palaver. "I've been on the run from the Rappies ten days—I've mostly et grasshoppers."

Pomp gently eased the old man off the placid ox. Zeke's beard was long and white; he was so bent that, when he attempted to stand, he almost stepped on it. He was almost naked and badly scratched up, but his eyes were lively, and his look, once he spotted the women, was impish.

"Why, look at those pretty gals, what a sight!" he said. "The Rappies don't have that many pretty gals in their whole tribe—and I ought to know. I had to marry up with four of them."

"Four wives?" Jim Bridger questioned. "I thought you were a dern prisoner—why'd they give you four wives?"

"Not enough bucks in the band, that's why," Zeke explained. "The Pawnees killed a bunch off—so they had women going to waste. Women get mean as cats when they're going to waste, and the Rappies know it."

"So they put you to stud, did they?" Lord Berrybender exclaimed. "Clam, you should be taking this down. Put to stud by the Arapaho. It would make rather a good report, I'd say."

Clam de Paty only smiled. In the hard days of hunger and thirst he had lost so much weight that his red pants no longer fit. He had ceased to believe in his own survival, or the company's. He supposed they would either starve to death or be killed in some brutal way, as Benjamin Hope-Tipping had been. Why write anything up? The rain had raised his hopes, but already the day was hot; the horizons shimmered in the distance. Ordinarily he *would* have written up the old fellow's story, made a racy item of it; a lust slave amid the native Eves. It was just the kind of thing Parisians liked to read about over their coffee—but Clam was too discouraged to care. He had fought with the Grande Armée, he had been awarded medals, and where had it all brought him? To a scorching plain, rude company, daily aggravation, even danger. Had he been put on earth so rich Parisians could read racy stories with their coffee? His notebook was in his pocket but he didn't reach for it. Who was Lord Berrybender to tell him what to write?

Clam turned and walked away.

"Moody fellow . . . that's the French, you know . . . can't be bothered," Lord Berrybender observed.

Tasmin had grabbed Pomp and was chattering with him. Jim wanted to know about the ox, an animal in excellent flesh. And he wanted to get the company moving. They could all listen to Zeke Williams rattle when night came.

Tasmin had just started filling Pomp in on the events of the last few days when Jim Snow walked up, looking impatient, practical, and stern. It irked her; why had she married such an impatient person? But there he was.

"That ox don't look thirsty," Jim said.

"He's not—there's a fine spring about twenty miles east," Pomp told him. "A family of travelers found it but the Arapaho wiped them out. Nine dead. Zeke hid in a snake den, or else they would have got him."

"I guess that means the Rappies are still around. But I doubt they'd attack *us,* if we stay bunched up. Seen Hugh and the Sublettes?"

"I saw them—they went exploring," Pomp told him. "Maybe we'll see them in Santa Fe."

Tasmin was annoyed; she wanted to talk. If there was one truth that irked her more than any other it was that men had so little use for women's talk. Even Pomp often looked a little absent, a little bored, when she attempted to expound her views on this and that. Was there any man, anywhere, who really cared to talk to her?

"*I* care to talk to you—surely you'll grant me that modest distinction," Father Geoffrin said, as the two of them plodded beside the slow-walking ox. As a novelty they had sat the three little boys on the beast's broad back, an experience that awed the children into complete silence, afraid to utter a sound in the presence of this great beast god, the ox.

"My husband merely closes his ears—it's as if they have tiny doors—when I start to talk," she went on. "Kit listens, but then Kit is so deeply smitten with me that he hardly counts."

"What about your new love, Monsieur Charbonneau?" the priest asked. "Has he no taste for your enchanting babble?"

Tasmin shrugged. Did Pomp really listen to her? Could he really be expected to, when the trek was so hard, their lives so threatened?

"Sometimes he tolerates it—whether he actually likes it, I can't say. It's goddamn hard to determine what men actually *like,* don't you think?"

"And yet men are open books compared to women," Father Geoff told her. "You know what I miss in America? Frivolity! Out here it's all life-or-death. No time for frivolous kisses, clothes buying, books and plays, *maquillage,* dancing, a little light seduction—all the things that make life so pleasant. No one here will be frivolous with you—I suspect that's your difficulty, my dear."

Tasmin shrugged again. The world Father Geoffrin's words conjured up—a world where women wore rouge and powder, danced quadrilles, went to operas and plays—was so different from the world where she now found herself that in memory it hardly seemed to belong to the same life.

Even on the steamer *Rocky Mount,* not a year ago, she and Vicky Kennet had made themselves up and paid a great deal of attention to their hair. But that had been another time. Only yesterday she had been weak from thirst—they had all faced the prospect of dying, not a situation in which one gave much thought to hair curlers and the like.

"It's the reason we get along so well, I expect, Tasmin," the priest went on. "We both like our fun, and it needn't be particularly serious fun. But your husband is not what I'd call a frivolous man, and neither is your new love, Pomp."

"Stop calling him my new love," Tasmin insisted, glancing around to be sure no one had heard him.

"I find all this rather odd," she continued. "Here we are, inching across a prairie where we might be killed on any given day, and you think I ought to be more frivolous. I don't know that this is very useful advice, if it is advice."

"Perhaps not—but we might return to civilization someday," the priest reminded her. "If we do, I hope you'll remember that I, at least, liked to listen to you talk. It's worth something, isn't it?"

"Of course it is—I'm not ungrateful," Tasmin said.

They had by then jettisoned all but one small wagon, in which her father, old Zeke Williams, and the babies rode. Sometimes Toussaint Charbonneau, still yellowish, was allowed to ride for a bit. But mostly Charbonneau walked, with Pomp at his side, carrying his gun and helping him a little if he faltered.

"I suppose there's no one more dutiful than Pomp," Tasmin said, looking back at the pair. "He's far more careful of his father than we Berrybenders are of our own."

"Of course, and it's entirely admirable," Father Geoff agreed. "And yet I do feel that dutiful men are sometimes rather lacking in spirit."

"What nonsense! Nothing of the sort is true of Pomp," Tasmin said, flaring up. "He has plenty of spirit."

Father Geoffrin smiled and shrugged.

"I'm sure you'd know best about that, my dear," he said, with a smile that indicated that he didn't believe her for a minute.

They strode in silence for a while.

"In my experience women tend to favor rascals," Geoff said. "I've often wondered why."

"You're more than enough of a rascal yourself, if you ask me," Tasmin said tartly. "I believe I've had enough of your saucy talk for now."

"I'm sure you'd know best about that," the priest said, but by then Tasmin had already turned away.

36

. . . tears of pain and frustration . . .

"**B**UT none of us are used to walking, Pomp," Tasmin said, tears of pain and frustration staining her cheeks—minutes earlier she had done the very thing Kit Carson had warned her about: she stepped on a small poisonous cactus, whose thorns pierced her moccasin and stuck deep in her heel. Now Pomp held her foot in his hand as, probing gently with a needle, he attempted to perform for her the service she had performed for Kit. One by one he was working the greenish thorns out of her foot.

"We're pampered gentlewomen, not mountain men," Tasmin reminded him. "Even the grass here is like spikes, and the sun's so bright I can't possibly spot every vicious cactus that lies in my path."

"You best learn to look out for them," her husband advised, politely.

"Oh, shut up, Jimmy—even the experienced Kit Carson stepped on one not long ago—why am I expected to be more expert than Kit?" Tasmin asked.

Jim Snow walked away—any attempt at counsel would only make Tasmin angrier. Let Pomp do the doctoring—she didn't seem to get quite so angry with Pomp.

"Anyway, I'm not the only sufferer," Tasmin pointed out. "Vicky's feet are severely blistered and so are Buffum's."

Pomp had almost finished extracting the thorns—her foot was not really much damaged, but her point was unarguable. Of all the Englishwomen only Mary Berrybender was used to walking—until their feet toughened, there were bound to be problems. But with the company now down to two horses, one wagon, and the ox, there was no alternative to walking.

"It's only about five miles to the springs," Pomp said, hoping to cheer Tasmin up at least a bit. "We can rest for a few days, once we get there."

"Two or three of you could ride on the ox," Kit Carson suggested. "It's big enough to carry two or three of you."

"But we'll soon have to eat the ox," Vicky pointed out. "Jim Snow said so this morning—eat it just as we ate the palfreys and most of the rest of our steeds. Why get used to riding a beast we will then immediately eat?"

Tasmin let out a yelp—Pomp, probing with the needle, went a little too deeply in pursuit of the last tiny thorn.

"This will pass," Pomp assured her. "Your feet will soon toughen up. Look at Zeke. His feet look pretty bad, but he ran nearly a hundred miles on them."

"And I'd run another hundred, if the Rappies got after me," Zeke Williams piped. Since his rescue he spent most of his time staring at the womenfolk with his intense blue eyes. Cook felt strongly that the old fellow required careful handling if lustful assaults were not to occur.

"I can't be much cheered by the thought that my feet might soon look like Mr. Williams's," Tasmin allowed. Then she yelped again, but for the last time: Pomp had captured the final thorn. He rubbed her foot gently, to be sure he hadn't missed any. The last thorn out, Tasmin at once felt the pain diminish. The group began to drift on. Buffum thought she might try the ox and had Jim Bridger lift her up, but just as she mounted, the ox slung its head to rid itself of flies; a string of slobber struck Buffum in the face.

"I do despise ox spit," Buffum said, immediately jumping back down.

Pomp started to set Tasmin's foot back on the ground, but Tasmin kicked at him with it—just a little teasing kick to make him look at her! Notice her! She wanted just to sit with him for a bit, now that the others had gone.

Pomp didn't immediately realize what Tasmin was about. He set the foot down anyway, but before he could stand up, Tasmin kicked at him with the other foot.

"Remember that I'm a biped," she told him. "Don't neglect the other foot."

Pomp looked up then, right into Tasmin's eyes, something he rarely did. In a place where every day's march carried the threat of death, he didn't feel that he should complicate matters by letting this powerful young woman, Jim Snow's wife, fix her feelings on him. But he only had to look into her eyes for a moment to realize that her feelings were already firmly fixed.

"You're such an elusive gentleman, Monsieur Charbonneau," Tasmin said. "I've not been ignored so adroitly in quite a long time."

Pomp didn't turn his eyes away, and he still held her other foot.

"There's no thorn in this foot," he said, giving the foot a light squeeze.

"No, but there's a thorn in my heart," Tasmin told him quietly. "It aches rather as my heel ached before you operated. You could soothe it as easily as you soothed my foot, if you only would."

In the distance she saw Father Geoffrin walking with Clam de Paty—the priest was looking directly at her, an interference that infuriated her.

"There's that detestable Jesuit," she said angrily. "At last I manage to obtain a brief interview with you, and wouldn't you know he'd be looking. I'd like to slap him, and maybe I will."

The fact that Father Geoffrin was watching put Pomp more at ease, a shift that Tasmin immediately noticed.

"You don't care at all, drat you!" she said. "You are such a frustrating man, Pomp. I fell in love with you and I allowed you to know it—a very forward thing. I'm still in love with you. I thought I detected some interest—you returned my kisses, at least."

"I liked those kisses," Pomp admitted. He still held her foot, but felt rather silly. Kit was watching them too, no doubt jealously. The company was inching on, but Pomp and Tasmin had not moved.

"You're such a rational fellow, Pomp," Tasmin said, with a cutting smile. "I suppose my little importunings must seem silly to you. The geography hardly encourages a grand passion. In the days when we had to drink that horse slop I ceased to care whether you loved me at all, but I've had a cool drink or two and now the feeling's back. I thought love was supposed to fatten on obstacles such as these—isn't that what Mr. Shakespeare says?"

At that Pomp smiled, amused despite himself by Tasmin's steely persistence, her wit, her evident determination to do whatever it took to gain his affection—which, of course, she already had. But not many women would call up Shakespeare when they were on a burning plain, with the Arapahos likely to fall on them at any moment.

"I've been gone from Shakespeare for a while," Pomp admitted. "There's probably something like that in the sonnets, though."

When Tasmin saw his shy, astonished smile she knew her gamble had not been wholly in vain. Perhaps he *did* want her still. He was just such a modest young man.

She took back the foot she had thrust into his hand.

"I'm hardly asking you for a wedding cake, Pomp," she remarked. "After all, I'm married, and we have these numerous perils to surmount. But surely a kiss now and then wouldn't be beyond you—or a confiding word, once in a while. I hate being always rebuffed, and why shouldn't I hate it? It's damned vexing to be able to command the attention of everyone except the one person whose attention I crave."

Together they walked back toward the company, Tasmin limping a little, her foot still sore. Pomp took her arm, a gesture of concern that pleased her mightily.

"I'm worried about Pa," he said, in an effort to explain what Tasmin took to be his inattention. "He's sick. He's traveled many a mile. I fear Pa's playing out."

Ahead—far ahead—Tasmin could just see a green smudge on the horizon—it must be the spring Pomp had mentioned. Trees meant water, and water might mean a bath—clean clothes, even. Her thoughts began to fly ahead, and yet she had to admit that Pomp's explanation was just. Toussaint Charbonneau did look as if he might be playing out. Pomp, the good son, would naturally be worried.

"Perhaps we can rest for a few days, once we get to the spring," Tasmin suggested. "Your father might improve."

Pomp didn't answer. He didn't look convinced. But he still held Tasmin's arm—held it firmly, as she limped on, with a defiant look, toward the journalist and the priest.

37

He felt too tired, too sad . . .

" T H I S wilderness has destroy me," Clam de Paty mumbled. He felt too tired, too sad even to make his English precise.
What he had mumbled was the truth: the American wilderness
had destroyed him. He did not want to walk across it—not even
one more mile. He did not want to write about its mountain
men, its savages, its grizzly bears, its mountains. He had come to
America a famous man, a veteran of the Grande Armée, a man
who had won medals; was he not the most famous journalist in
the most civilized country in the world? Yet now, thanks to his
bosses—always greedy for new information—he was destroyed,
broken, finished, ended, afflicted with a numb despair. True,
they had found a good spring, had drunk their fill, had bathed
many times, had rested. And yet, all around them, the wilderness
still yawned. Santa Fe was still hundreds of miles away. The nice
young Monsieur Charbonneau could talk to him all he wanted
about how easy the rest of the trip would be compared to what
had already been endured, but young Monsieur Charbonneau
was missing one big point: Clam de Paty no longer cared. The
wilderness had finished him. All day and all night, as he shook
and trembled, he thought of nothing but Paris, its cobblestones,
its wines, its actresses.

"Of course, it's a dratted nuisance to have no claret," Lord Berrybender allowed. "But aren't you rather overdoing this, monsieur? This wilderness is amenable enough, as wildernesses go. I shot three buffalo yesterday—plenty of meat now for our march. Doubt we'll have to eat horse meat again."

Clam de Paty didn't respond. Why should he? The old Englishman was a fool. A Frenchman would have understood at once that when a man is finished, he is finished. There was no more to be said.

"How vexing," Mary Berrybender remarked. "That Frenchman declares that he will go no further. And now Monsieur Toussaint Charbonneau proposes to leave us and take Coal and Rabbit, a decision Pomp opposes."

There had been a sharp frost during the night—the prairie sparkled as if sown with diamonds, and edges of the green pool had a little rind of ice. Monty had cut his foot on a shard of glass, residue from the family that had been massacred near the spring. Monty, howling, raced off, leaving bloody footprints on the frosty grass. Tasmin was forced to run and catch him, and now had the task of binding up his cut.

"Damn it, why did this child have to cut his toe half off?" Tasmin remarked. She was not very cheered by the thought that she soon would have two children to keep up with. Clam de Paty's despair didn't interest her—if he continued to balk, then he should be abandoned—but Toussaint Charbonneau's departure was a matter for considerable concern. Old Sharbo and his cheerful wife, Coal, had been with them all the way from Saint Louis. The three little boys, Monty, Talley, and Rabbit, had never been separated. And then there was Pomp, whose deep attachment to his father they all respected. Now the old man proposed to quit the company and take his wife and child back to the Missouri River, along whose banks he had lived much of his life.

Little Onion helped Tasmin bandage Monty. Jim Snow and Jim Bridger were devising a harness for the ox, so it could pull the wagon—this meant that their two remaining horses could be used by the hunters.

Tasmin expected long faces—she assumed everyone would be doing their best to dissuade the old interpreter from taking such a dangerous course of action; but instead she found the whole group chatting merrily. Tom Fitzpatrick and old Zeke Williams were advising Charbonneau about the likeliest routes. Old Charbonneau himself, who had been stumbling along, yellowish and tired, seemed suddenly to have a spring in his step—he looked on the whole rather jaunty.

"Why, Monsieur Charbonneau, I'm so surprised that you're leaving us," Tasmin said. "Why this sudden urge to travel alone?"

Toussaint Charbonneau tipped his filthy cap to her.

"It's just that I'm a river man, Lady Tasmin," he said. "I reckon I've been up and down our good old Missouri more than thirty times and I'm longing to make another trip or two before I'm done. Our Pomp was born right on that river, you know—I've just got a yen to see it again. It's a fine, fair river, if sometimes a little muddy."

Tasmin gave Coal a long hug—she was very fond of Coal, who had made Monty the rabbit-fur cap that had seen him snugly through a bitter winter. What Coal thought about the sudden departure, there was no guessing. Her look was stoical. Where her husband went, she too must go. Monty and Talley stood watching, solemn as judges, as Rabbit was put in his pouch. Pomp and his father held a long embrace, and then the Charbonneau family walked off east across the frosty plain, equipped with not much more than a rifle and a blanket. The mountain men gave a cheer and got back to their harnessing and packing. The great sunny distances soon swallowed up the little family.

Tasmin expected Pomp to be sad—it seemed such a risky undertaking his father was attempting. And yet Pomp was in a perfectly good mood; like his father he seemed, if anything, rather jaunty.

"But isn't it risky?" Tasmin asked. "I thought there was smallpox along the river."

"Oh, Pa's bound for Saint Louis, not the Mandans," Pomp assured her. "He likes a visit with Captain Clark every year or two. He'll soon be in Osage country, and Pa gets along with the Osage pretty well."

"I still think it's odd," Tasmin told him. "It seems that among you mountain men the best cure for jaundice or most other ills is just to set out—go to a new place. My Jimmy does it frequently. I don't think I shall ever get used to it, and yet it seemed to have a tonic effect on your father."

"Yes—Pa's not really a trapper or a fighter," Pomp told her. "But as long as he can travel the Missouri he seems to get by pretty well.

"Pa's probably just lucky," he added, reflecting. "Of all the men who went on the big trek with Captain Lewis and Captain Clark, only Pa and two or three others are alive. Most of them were better hunters than Pa—he's never been much of a shot. Most of them were better at handling boats than Pa. All of them were better at tracking. And yet he's alive and they're dead."

"I hope some of his luck rubbed off on us," Tasmin said. "I have a feeling we're going to need it before we get home."

38

Just so, as a boy . . .

CLAM DE PATY, citizen of France, sat calmly by the fine, cool spring, throwing pebbles into the water as the Berry-bender party prepared to leave. His weeping servant, Amboise d'Avigdor, had already stumbled away.

Just so, as a boy, Clam had thrown pebbles into the Seine. Last-minute entreaties were pressed on him, but he maintained a dignified silence. Pomp Charbonneau sat with him a minute; he pointed out that many Indian tribes used these springs, not all of them friendly. Clam might have to fight—he could hardly hope to prevail. Also, bear tracks had been found—an old grizzly evidently came to the springs to water.

All this information Clam ignored. He had explained that he was finished, destroyed; and that, it seemed to him, made matters clear enough. He had no more to say. If a bear came, so be it. If Indians came, so be it. He was under no obligation to travel endlessly on. The Americans and the English were welcome to mind their own business.

It happened to be an exceptionally fine day. The mountain men and the Berrybenders were slow to get off, but finally they departed—the noise of the expedition grew faint in the distance. The only sound was the plop of pebbles, as Clam pitched them one by one into the water. A few crickets sounded. Small birds with skinny legs came and dipped their beaks into the greenish pond. After weeks of loud company, the solitude itself was refreshing.

Clam possessed a fine whetstone—he thought it might be a good time to sharpen his saber, the saber he had used when he fought in the Grande Armée. It was a sword of Toledo steel; he enjoyed keeping its edge keen, attending to it whenever he had the leisure. Now, of course, he had perfect leisure. He had last used his saber in the clash with the Pawnees—the edge of the saber had been dulled when he struck the Pawnee boy's horse. But the whetstone would soon restore an excellent cutting edge. When he finished his work he whacked at a grasshopper, cutting the creature in two.

Clam then napped for a bit in the shade of one of the small cottonwood trees. He awoke feeling rather in a poetical mood, so he took out his notebook and a tiny anthology of poetry containing some verses of Voltaire. They seemed to Clam very bad verses—he himself, he felt quite sure, could do just as well. He thought he might compose an ode to the glory of France. When his body was found, as he hoped it would be, the ode would be there in his notebook, so that his public would know that Clam de Paty had died a patriot.

But poetical composition, once Clam got down to it, proved to be a knotty business. His rhymes wouldn't come, and he had little confidence in his meters. A few phrases seemed to hold promise, in an airy way. He thought he might change the ode to a roundel, a form at which he had once been pleased to consider himself fluent. He had composed some racy verses once to a lady's garter—though the lady herself had been no lady; she was a petite actress named Thérèse whose teeth were crooked, causing her to lisp in a manner that, for a time, won the affections of theatergoers; but jaded creatures that they were, the theatergoers soon tired of Thérèse and her lisp. Clam tired of her too, though his little poem to her garter had been much admired by the beau monde at the time. In despair Thérèse took poison, but didn't die. Her crooked teeth turned black—she was seen on the stage no more. Such was the way of Paris: actors, actresses, journalists like himself, even poets and the writers of satires had but a season; many of them took poison eventually, or flung themselves into the Seine and drowned. And yet that old crab Voltaire had lived to a ripe age, spouting his tedious verses all the while. Clam became a journalist; he placed his faith in facts; he succeeded; he made his name; he interviewed the great; he went to banquets—and it all led inevitably, it seemed, to his present situation. Here he sat, in happy solitude, his Toledo blade well sharpened, sitting by a pool of green water in the American West. He thought he might pass an hour or two versifying about the buffalo, a beast little acclaimed in French verse, so far as he knew. Perhaps a few of the shaggy beasts would come to water, but meanwhile, he took another nap.

So it went all day. His roundel was unsatisfactory—it would take him a few days, perhaps, to hit his stride as a poet. In the meantime, why not take a walk? He might shoot a rabbit, or some other small beast, for his supper. With luck he might get an antelope; he found the meat most flavorful.

Unfortunately, Clam saw no antelope, though he strolled in a great circle around the pool with its fine surround of cottonwoods. As he walked he swished around a bit with his saber, even practiced a few lunges. He was headed back toward the trees when he began to have the uneasy feeling that he was perhaps not entirely alone. The plain seemed quite empty, and yet *something* did seem to be with him—an unseen presence might be drawing near.

Clam tried to shake himself out of this feeling, which, after all, was absurd. Men imagined things. In his time with the Grande Armée he had been prey to dark imaginings. But why would this feeling come on him now, when he had merely been enjoying a quiet stroll?

Suddenly, impelled, Clam whirled and saw the bear, a huge bear with a great brown head, not twenty yards behind him. Clam, so shocked that his hair stood up, froze—and the bear froze too. Clam looked at the bear, the bear looked at Clam, and then, very slowly, Clam raised his rifle, thinking that a bullet in the brain would soon settle the hash of this bear. It was only as he was lifting the gun that an awkward fact forced its way into his attention: his rifle was not loaded. When they killed the second palfrey, Clam had been the one to shoot the loyal beast, his own palfrey. And he had forgotten to reload his gun. Now here was this bear, an easy target, only there was no bullet to hit it with.

Clam knew a moment of intense chagrin. He had always been a disciplined man, and yet he had not had even the elementary discipline to reload his gun—a sign, indeed, that he was finished, just as he had insisted to the company.

Looking at the bear, Clam decided that he felt perhaps a little less finished than he had the day before. The bear had stopped when Clam stopped. He didn't seem angry—perhaps he was merely curious. Probably he had never seen a Frenchman in red pants before, a famous journalist. In his confusion Clam allowed himself to believe that the bear knew he was a famous man, a man of reputation: why else was he being spared?

At once Clam turned and began to walk rapidly toward the spring. He scarcely dared look back, as he walked, but he felt again that a presence was near—when he did look back, he found that the bear was still following him. He was not gaining, but neither was he falling behind. Clam considered speaking sharply to the animal but instead continued to walk on toward the pond. When he reached the water he looked behind him and saw that the bear was rather closer than he had been—he was no more than ten paces back. Clam decided on a desperate strategy—he walked straight into the pond until the water came to his knees; then he turned and presented his saber to the bear, who had stopped just at the water's edge. He thrust out the saber and just pricked the bear with it, right on the end of his black nose.

Startled, the bear sneezed twice, then at once turned and loped away, a response so unexpected that Clam could not quite trust it. All the mountain men had talked to him about the vicious fury of wounded bears. Whole teams of hunters were sometimes put to flight by one enraged grizzly. And yet he had merely pricked the grizzly on the end of his nose and the beast took to his heels. Clam could still see him, far out on the prairie, loping away.

It was a miracle—a wave of relief swept over Clam, relief so powerful that he could hardly command his limbs. He waded out of the water and abruptly sat down, rather muddying his pants. In his mind's eye he replayed this very strange event: he felt a presence, he saw the bear, he walked away, the bear followed, he walked into the pond, he pricked the bear, and the bear turned and fled.

For a few minutes Clam merely sat in the mud, numb with relief. His notebook was in his pocket—it occurred to him that he could write up this extraordinary event, yet, when he went to the small trouble of pulling his notebook out of his pocket, he found that he had no interest at all in writing the adventure up. Clam saw at once that it was far too incredible to be believed. Conquer a grizzly bear by pricking his nose? His editors would guffaw. He would look a fool. The bear had not even snarled, he had put up no fight, there was nothing to write up. If the bear had at least growled viciously, there might have been a possibility to be exploited. A clever journalist could do much with a vicious snarl. But the bear had been a complete disappointment. A story had been lost, even though he himself had been spared.

Clam's relief was great, but also confusing. He was weak in the legs; he could barely walk. He would have loved a bit of cognac, something with a bracing bite, but of cognac there was none, and besides, a chill was falling. Last week it had been hot, this week it was cold. Winter was coming. He gathered a few sticks of firewood and built a fire. As the sun set and the moon rose Clam stared into his fire, a blanket over his shoulders. He did not remember sleeping but he must have slept, because when he awoke his fire was out and the new sun just coming up. It was very cold. There was frost on his blanket, ice at the edges of the pond. The plain was so white with frost that it hurt his eyes to look at it. Though he was shivering and hungry, Clam de Paty felt a sudden, surprising surge of happiness. In fact he had made a mistake: he was *not* finished, after all. He was alive, the sun was rising! The indifference he had felt only the day before—indifference to life, death, starvation, the departure of the company, everything—had left him while he dozed. His encounter with the cowardly bear had changed everything. The bear that might so easily have finished him but chose not to reminded him that there was a value to life—indeed, a very great value. He had been a fool to send his servant away—if he had Amboise he would soon be enjoying a good breakfast, but Amboise, after all, was only a few miles away. The company had been gone less than a day. Without a moment's hesitation Clam gathered up his kit and set out to catch it. The wagon would leave tracks, Amboise would drop things—the company would be easy to find. Already he could imagine their joy when he reappeared. It would be a lesson for them: never count out a Frenchman, a man who had won medals and gone to banquets, a man who had fought with the Grande Armée, a man well known to the actresses of Paris, some of them far better known than poor little Thérèse, with her black, crooked teeth and her lisp.

39

. . . if she was a girl yet, with a fine, springing bosom . . .

"It's as if we've found eternity and it's very flat," Tasmin said to Father Geoff, as the two of them trudged along, well to the rear of the company. "I don't even feel that I'm in a *place* anymore. Places have boundaries or borders, and this goddamn place has neither."

"I like to think of eternity as having a constant temperature, though," Father Geoff replied. "In the great peace of infinity there should be neither hot nor cold—one can't say that of Nuevo México."

"But *are* we in Nuevo México?" Tasmin asked, looking about her irritably. In the very far distance a cloud hovered over an indistinct horizon—otherwise there was nothing to be seen.

Tasmin, bored, had taken to nagging Father Geoff unmercifully, as she had once nagged Kit Carson, but she had grown tired of abusing Kit, who would rarely fight back.

"Do you see a Mexican?" she asked. "Do you see a hut? What announces to your keen intelligence that we're in Mexico?"

"Your husband announced it to me—please don't be so shrill," Geoff said. "He thinks we may soon be arrested."

"Arrested? But where's the jail?" Tasmin asked.

Monty, hanging in a pouch on his mother's back, began to

fret, as he often did when his mother sounded angry. Talley too had been pouched. Lord Berrybender had announced, haughtily, that he didn't care to have a nursery in his wagon. In his state of enforced sobriety, Lord B. had become shaky and petulant, striking out at anyone who displeased him, though, when firmly opposed, he was apt to blubber helplessly.

"Your husband is not given to idle apprehensions," Father Geoff told Tasmin. "If he says we're to be arrested, then very likely we will be."

The weather had turned abruptly from hot to cold. Twice a wind had come singing out of the north, a wind so chill that the women could only huddle in their blankets. Once it drizzled all day and then froze—a sheet of ice covered the prairies, which made for painful walking. Twice it snowed; the women crowded all night around inadequate fires, their fronts warm and their backs freezing. Then the sun returned, melted the snows, and turned the prairies atrickle, so that the women had to flounder through mud and slush.

So unvarying were the prairies themselves that Tasmin had stopped believing that there could ever be an end in sight. Santa Fe, the rich city they were traveling to, came to seem as chimerical as Camelot. Would they ever get there? The mountain men assured her that they would, but the distance remaining to be traveled seemed hardly to shrink. It seemed to Tasmin that it might always be as it was at present, days of walking across endless space, a baby hanging on her back and another growing in her body. The journey they were making seemed almost insanely illogical, based on nothing at all except her father's inclination to pursue blood sports. When pressed to put a time for their arrival in Santa Fe, the men were so vague in their reckonings that Tasmin wanted to slap them.

"Six weeks, I'd say, if the Arkansas ain't in flood," Tom Fitzpatrick guessed—Jim and Pomp thought they might be there a week or two sooner, if Indians didn't impede them.

"Ox travel is slow travel," Jim reminded her—the statement was so obvious that Tasmin wanted to kick him.

"I *know* ox travel is slow travel, Jim—I indulge in it every day," Tasmin reminded him. "I just wanted to know how much farther it is to Santa Fe."

"Getting to Santa Fe always takes longer than folks think it will," he told her.

"I just want to get there before I have this baby," she said. "Four walls and a roof are a great comfort when one is giving birth."

"We'll be there way before then," Jim assured her. "You've got nearly half a year before that baby comes."

"I know—it seems that we've a great deal of time," Tasmin agreed. "And yet one day, to everyone's annoyance, Vicky and Buffum and I will be screeching and screaming as we deliver up our bloody brats. I'd just rather not be outside when I'm doing the screeching."

She realized that such a comment could mean little to Jim Snow, who had spent his entire life outdoors. He could not be in a room—even a large room—without becoming restless. Due to lack of opportunity, indoor life was beyond Jim Snow.

"If we don't make Santa Fe we'll at least make the Bents," Jim assured her—the Bents being a company of several brothers who were said to be building an immense trading post near the Arkansas River. Nightly the mountain men allowed themselves to speculate about all the money they could make if the Bent's big trading venture succeeded. Some were of the opinion that the Bents had paid the Mexican authorities a lavish bribe in order to secure their concession.

"What I like about Santa Fe are the señoritas," Jim Bridger announced one night. "It's been a dern long while since I've danced with a señorita—or done anything else with one."

"Bravo, Jim!" Tasmin said. "And while you're dancing with your dusky señoritas, perhaps we ladies can find some handsome caballeros to dance with. There *are* handsome caballeros in this great capital, aren't there, Kit?"

Kit felt embarrassed—Tasmin's unexpected questions always left him feeling tongue-tied.

"Oh, the Mexicans are always dancing," Kit said vaguely.

"Well, and what about these Bents?" Tasmin asked. "Any dancing to be had at their establishment?"

"St. Vrain, maybe," Tom Fitzpatrick remarked. "He's their partner—flatters all the Mexican ladies. I expect St. Vrain can dance."

"If you're such a dancer, how come you've never asked me for a turn?"

"Well, we ain't had a fiddle, I suppose that's why," he said.

"I suppose a cello is not quite the same," Tasmin admitted. Through thick and thin, despite many abandoned goods, Vicky Kennet had insisted that they must make space for her cello, and they had.

At night Tasmin had taken to sitting up late with the mountain men. Reticent at first in her presence, they soon relaxed and went on gossiping and cussing into the small hours. Jim was at first uneasy about Tasmin's penchant for late hours but he didn't attempt to restrict her. Usually, at night, he was the one to keep Monty, spreading their blankets as far as possible from the sounds of carousing.

Persuading Jim to keep Monty afforded Tasmin her only chance for a little time alone with Pomp—the latter would usually be standing guard just out of camp. Tasmin could sometimes manage a word with him while on her way to join her husband and her child. Pomp was usually cool on these occasions, so cool that Tasmin felt like pounding him with her fists in frustration. His responses were more brotherly than not, a thing that infuriated Tasmin—yet she refused to give up. She loved the man and wanted him. What was wrong? Sometimes, leaving Pomp, she didn't make it back to Jim and Monty. She would sit alone on the prairie all night, crying, confused, tormented. Why couldn't she give up? Pomp didn't want what she wanted—probably he never would. All the wanting was hers. It left her feeling hopeless.

One morning Mary Berrybender, who was often out early seeking specimens for Piet's various collections, found Tasmin sitting listlessly in the grass, not crying, merely looking into space.

"Why, Tassie, Monty is squalling for the teat," Mary said. "Why are you sitting way out here?"

Tasmin lacked the energy for any sort of quarrel with her sister, a girl in many ways so perceptive.

"You're wanting Pomp, I suppose," Mary told her. "Buffum and I and Vicky all think so."

Tasmin shrugged.

"You're a highly professional trio, when it comes to matters of the heart, I'm sure," she said. "If you have all concluded that I'm wanting Pomp, then I suppose I am—it hardly means I'll get him."

Monty's hungry cry, faintly heard, increased her dull irritability. She had once had a fine, springing bosom, and yet now Monty had hung on it for months, with another child soon to take his place at the same milky fountain. Was that the problem? Would Pomp have wanted her if she was a girl yet, with a fine, springing bosom, instead of the mother she had become, whose nipples sometimes dripped with milk?

Somehow she didn't suppose it would matter much to Pomp. Such thoughts were idle. Her husband didn't find her lacking in appeal. Why was she not content with Jim Snow's lively virility? Why had she been obliged to seek another? And why had it to be Pomp, a man too sensitive for his own good?

"Poor Tassie," Mary said. "I suppose it's always hard for great beauties to be happy."

"Great beauty indeed! Don't flatter me," Tasmin said. "I was rather beautiful once, but America has quite scraped that away. Now I'm just a peeling, scratched-up wife and mother. We're all scratched up things. Does no good to dwell on what a beauty I was."

"You're young, though," Mary reminded her. "What's lacking is our gentle English climate. You'd soon be beautiful again if we were in a place that wasn't so dry."

"We've another day's trudging to do—why yap about beauty?" Tasmin asked.

"Because you seem sad," Mary said. "I do believe that Buffum and I are luckier. She's very happy with High Shoulders, and I'm most companionable with my Piet."

"Then my discontent must be my fault," Tasmin said. "My

Jimmy's an excellent man—he ought to be enough. What's wrong with me?"

"It's that you don't have an accepting nature, Tassie," Mary replied. "I don't believe you accept anybody. Even I put up with my Piet's trifling limitations."

At this Tasmin put her face in her hands.

"What I mean to say—it's that you want more than there is," Mary went on. "You want more than there is."

"That's right," Tasmin admitted. "I don't have an accepting nature, and I do want more than there is. How am I to go about correcting these awkward faults?"

"How could I recommend?" Mary said, looking puzzled. "You're my big sister. Buffum and I look to you as to a paragon."

"Rather a muddled paragon, this morning," Tasmin told her. "I used to believe that I was really a de Bury, you know. Mama and Lord de Bury were said to have enjoyed a *petite liaison* before Papa came along. It's hard to imagine Mama doing much copulating without a brat resulting. I used to suppose I was that brat."

"Why shouldn't you suppose it? Perhaps you're right."

"I no longer think so—I'm too much like Papa," Tasmin said. "He also lacks an accepting nature, and I'm sure you would agree that he wants too much. If he didn't want too much we wouldn't be here."

"He's rather had his comeuppance, though," Mary said. "Vicky's got the upper hand now, physically. Papa spends his day cowering, hoping she won't bloody his nose."

"He's greatly altered by a lack of claret," Tasmin pointed out. "Wait till we get someplace where there's liquor—he'll soon be the one doing the bloodying again. Vicky had better enjoy her dominance while she can."

"What will the Sin Killer do if he catches you with Pomp? The thought worries us extremely," Mary said.

"Oh, stop worrying," Tasmin told her. "Pomp's not interested—he's too pure for me. I am going to try to learn not to assault him, if I can."

"But if you're in love with him, how can you stop?" Mary

wanted to know. "It's as if I told Piet I wouldn't whip him with brambles anymore. He would be heartbroken and so would I."

Tasmin saw Little Onion approaching with Monty, who had stopped squalling in expectation of his breakfast.

"Piet's requirements may actually be rather simple when compared to the needs—whatever they are—of the elusive Monsieur Pomp. What does one do with a celibate? I confess I just don't know."

"Piet believes celibacy to be contrary to nature," Mary said. "He plans to make me not a virgin very soon.

"Only he hopes to wait until we're in a more comfortable setting before getting on with penetration," she added.

"Well, that's considerate of him," Tasmin said. "In the end you may be luckier than any of us, Mary."

Little Onion sat Monty down—he began to toddle at his most rapid pace toward his mother, who soon enveloped him in her arms. Here's a person who wants me, Tasmin thought. No doubt about that.

"I wonder if Piet and I will have many brats," Mary mused. "They seem to require such a lot of raising—I really wish Nanny Craigie would have come."

Tasmin's bad mood began to lift—sometimes Monty did amuse her. It was funny to watch such a tiny person making a mad dash over the dewy grass.

Just then she saw Jim Snow, riding off with Tom Fitzpatrick on an early morning hunt. At the sight her spirits lifted even higher. Jim looked so dashing, there on horseback—maybe he'd get them all to Santa Fe, after all.

40

Even the slightest delay had always irked him.

"I AM the one who has been chosen to keep the stories," Greasy Lake reminded the Partezon, who of course knew it as well as he did. But the Partezon was on his way to seek his death place and would not sit still for any long-winded talk. Already the Partezon looked annoyed. Even the slightest delay had always irked him. The Partezon had lived many seasons, and made many people die, but now he was riding into the sacred Black Hills to die—it was important, Greasy Lake felt, that a few things be made clear to the man before he took his journey to the Sky House.

"I am the one who has been trusted with the stories," he said, once again. "That was decided by grandfathers long ago. You know it yourself. Your own mother brought you to me when you were born. Now my horse has died and I can't get around. You are just going to climb up into those hills and die. You have a fine horse. If you take it way up there, it will just get eaten by a cougar or a bear, which is a waste."

"Why didn't you ask Fool's Bull for his horse?" the Partezon countered. "That roan of his is a decent horse. But you let Fool's Bull ride off, and now you want my horse. I could find my death place a lot quicker if I didn't have to deal with people like you and Fool's Bull."

"But I am not a warrior, like Fool's Bull—I'm a prophet," Greasy Lake reminded the Partezon. "You have a fine white horse, and I need the best horse I can get. You are part of the great story I have to protect—give me your horse and I promise to make him last thirty years."

"My horse may last thirty years but you won't," the Partezon said. "Don't bother me with talk about grandfathers. Pretty soon the whites are going to kill all the People, including you. What about your stories then?"

"Now you're being selfish," Greasy Lake said—he was becoming exasperated. "The whites aren't going to kill all the People—and the stories are safe. If the whites knew I was a prophet they would have killed me already, but the whites can't tell a prophet from a fool. I will see that the stories are correctly passed on, but I could do a better job if I had a good horse to carry me around."

"You don't weigh much—you should get a young horse," the Partezon told him.

"I'm not heavy—it's the stories that are heavy," Greasy Lake said. "The stories finally broke my old horse down. I carry all the stories—as many as ducks on the Platte. Soon I will be carrying your story too."

For two turnings of the seasons the Partezon had been passing blood, but lately he had begun to pass more blood, and blood of a vivid red. He told no one—he didn't want the People to know that he was dying—but he himself was convinced of it, which is why he had no fear of the pox that had destroyed the Mandans and the Rees. He had no fear that Fool's Bull would get sick, either, because Fool's Bull was the luckiest man among the Sioux. Fool's Bull had ridden through battle after battle without a scratch. Bullets could not seem to hit him, nor arrows, either. The worst injury of Fool's Bull's life was a centipede bite which caused one of his fingers to turn black.

The Partezon didn't like prophets, particularly, but he knew that old Greasy Lake must be a good prophet because he had been able to intercept him as he journeyed to his death place. After their trip to the Mandans, the Partezon had sent Fool's Bull back to the tribe, with instructions to keep them well away from the river. Fool's Bull had been reluctant to go, but the Partezon had insisted, so he went. He was scarcely even out of sight when Greasy Lake turned up, standing by his dead horse. Of course, he at once started talking about the big responsibility he had, as the keeper of stories.

The Partezon had serious business to arrange—his death—and he did not want to waste much time at the foot of the sacred mountains, talking to a puffed-up old prophet.

Abruptly, he dismounted.

"All right—take the horse—load it down with your stories, if you want to," he said. "But let me alone."

But the Partezon had walked only a few yards before Greasy Lake interrupted him again. He pointed at a mountain that stood alone, well to the north of the mass of hills—that, he indicated, was where the Partezon should look for his death place.

"It's the hill where the rocks face north," Greasy Lake said. "That's the one where the eagles nest."

Somewhat to the Partezon's surprise, it turned out to be good advice. It took the Partezon, who was becoming very weak, almost a full day to make his way to the rocky summit where the eagles circled. There were nine of them at least, he saw. The presence of the eagles convinced him that he had done the right thing when he gave Greasy Lake the horse. There they were, the great soaring eagles, flying far more gracefully than the white men had flown in their clumsy machine.

Climbing carefully, applying his disciplined attention for the last time, the Partezon managed to reach the top of a bare rock spur. He thought he would be safe there—it was unlikely that a bear would try to climb the rock spur just to eat an old man like himself. Instead, the great eagles would eat him—in time he would be part of their fine, sweeping flight. At sunset the Partezon lay flat on the rock. He was very weak, but at least he didn't have to think anymore—a great relief. He looked a last time far away, to the plain where the People lived. In the night, without him noticing, his breath became one with the wind.

41

Both brothers were short . . .

"CHARLIE and Willy, they're going to fight!" Josefina announced. "Every single day since we've been here they fight."

Maria Jaramillo, engaged to be married to Charles Bent, peeked off the parapet where she and her sister had climbed. The man she was to marry, Charlie Bent, stood nose to nose with his brother Willy. Both brothers were short, only a little taller than Josefina, who was not quite five feet tall. No doubt Charlie had given Willy an order Willy didn't like. Willy's habit of objecting to Charlie's orders was cause of many fistfights between the brothers—most of the fights, fortunately, were brief.

Maria and Josefina had climbed up to the parapet of the huge adobe edifice the brothers were building with their partner St. Vrain—a building part fort, part trading post, and part caravanserai—in order to smoke their little *cigallos,* cigars wrapped in corn husks, a popular vice with girls of the better class. On the parapet they would be less likely to be caught in this mildly illicit activity by their aunt and chaperone, Doña Esmeralda, an aging beauty who had spent virtually her whole life in the governor's palace, drifting serenely from one intrigue to another. Doña Esmeralda smoked *cigallos* herself but forbade them to her nieces.

"There they go! With their fists!" Josefina said. Maria looked down and saw that, sure enough, Charlie and Willy were raining punches upon one another, to very little effect. The brothers' fistfights, occurring, as they did, on an almost daily basis, aroused no interest at all in the various people at work in the huge courtyard. Ceran St. Vrain, just back from a trip to their warehouses in Saint Louis, was serenely inventorying goods as they were unloaded from the big wagons. Across the way, at the unbuilt gap in the south wall, the small men who worked with adobe went on shaping their mud bricks and setting them in place. A herd of sheep had just passed out of the wide gates, accompanied by two sheepherders and a woolly black dog.

"The fight's over—nobody won," Josefina remarked. Charlie and Willy now seemed to be in amiable discussion.

"What if he beats you up, Maria?" Josefina asked.

Maria directed no more than a casual glance toward her fiancé, Charles Bent. She didn't fear Charlie Bent—he'd be lucky if she didn't beat *him* up. Even in Santa Fe, where wellborn señoritas were trained to be properly haughty, Maria stood out in her ability to frighten men. Many brave soldiers, some of them even captains, trembled when they asked her to dance. Charles Bent was neither the richest nor the best looking of her suitors, but he had proved the most persistent. When Charles Bent first stumbled into Santa Fe, having hauled his first load of goods across the prairie, a dance had been in progress. Maria had hardly noticed the small, dusty figure watching her from the edge of the crowd. Many elegant young Mexican officers were there, dressed impeccably, their mustaches trimmed and waxed—and yet the short *americano* had hardly waited five minutes before he asked Maria to dance. Everyone was so startled by this temerity that the governor, who happened to be Maria's uncle, was about to have the young fool arrested—but Maria waved him off and actually danced with the newcomer. After all, she could dance with the young officers anytime. To her embarrassment Charlie proved to be a terrible dancer—he knew nothing of quadrilles and could only hop about; to make matters worse, he was much shorter than Maria. In her view men who couldn't dance should at least be tall.

After that beginning Maria refused Charles Bent many times, curling her lip and flashing him looks of scorn. Charles Bent refused to be discouraged—he made her presents of fine silks and even velvet, carefully protected on their long trip across the plains.

Soon her uncle the governor, seeing that there was money to be made from this persistent young *americano,* began to grant the young man and his partner certain privileges, even allowing the construction of the big post on the Arkansas.

Doña Esmeralda opposed these favors; she opposed, even more strenuously, any sort of match between Maria and the American. She even went so far as to hint to the girls that there were vital pleasures that a man of such small stature would be unlikely to provide. Maria was not quite sure what her aunt was hinting at, but it didn't matter, since she had no intention of marrying Charles Bent. She said no to him a hundred times; but then, one day, she found herself in the mood to leave Santa Fe and go out into the world. Instead of saying no she said yes, which is why she and Josefina were on the parapet of the fort, smoking their *cigallos* when they thought no one was looking. Doña Esmeralda was at the moment enjoying a flirtation with a stout young muleteer—at such times she was apt to neglect her duties as a duenna.

"I hope he won't beat you too much," Josefina said.

"If he has any mettle he'll beat me," Maria said. "Auntie says that a man who lacks the mettle to beat a woman is not a man worth keeping." Doña Esmeralda was always warning the girls about the fact that men's mettle varied greatly. Some men didn't have much—those men were to be avoided.

"A stallion is not supposed to be tame when he mounts the mare," she said to her nieces, with a wink.

The well-bred Jaramillo girls had never been allowed to observe a stallion mounting a mare, but it was advice to ponder. Both were virgins; the practices that belonged to adulthood had

not yet been theirs, but they could speculate, they could imagine, they could dream. Where passion was concerned, Maria felt
quite confident of her powers. If she chose to stir a man up until
he struck her, she felt sure she could accomplish that without
difficulty. The bare mechanics of copulation had been explained
to her by a servant girl. Though it sounded a little disgusting, it
occurred to her that *that* must be what Doña Esmeralda was up
to, with her cadets and muleteers.

Maria rarely shared her thoughts with her sister, Josefina, a
pure girl so small and dark that, so far, she had only attracted
one suitor, Kit Carson, a wandering *americano* who had not
been seen in Santa Fe for over a year. No one in Santa Fe liked
having too many *americanos* around. The Bents had been
allowed to build their trading post, but far off, on the Arkansas;
that way the grandees of Santa Fe would not always be having to
put up with a lot of smelly *americanos* at their dances and fies-
tas. Some among the older families looked with disapproval on
the fact that Maria Jaramillo, one of their greatest beauties,
should be wed to an *americano,* a newcomer. Maria herself had
been of two minds at first, but, bored with the formalities of the
capital, she finally said yes to Charles Bent.

"I dreamed of Kit Carson last night," Josefina confessed.
"Maybe that means he'll be coming back soon."

It was rare that Josefina voiced her shy hopes about Kit, since
Maria would be sure to trample on them. She thought Josefina
too young to have beaux. Josefina had never told her about her
most exciting experience: several kisses, exchanged just before
Kit went north with the trappers. They had also held hands, but
holding hands did not feel as important as kissing. There had
even been some whispery talk of marriage, which of course
could not take place until Kit felt rich enough to support her. In
her dream Kit had ridden into the post on a prancing horse. It
seemed a good omen. When Maria wanted to tease Josefina she
tried to make her believe that Kit had probably long since taken
an Indian wife, as Willy Bent had done. Willy's wife was a
Cheyenne girl named Owl Woman, an independent girl who

only rarely stayed at the post with Willy. Mostly Owl Woman preferred to wander with her people—if Willy Bent wanted to see her, he had to search for her on the plains, a fact that led to many quarrels between the brothers. Charles Bent was reluctant to let his little brother miss many days' work—the fact that he wanted to go see his wife, Owl Woman, was not a sufficient excuse.

Maria didn't bother asking Josefina for details of her dream about Kit Carson. She had been watching the muleteers unload the big wagons with the goods they had brought from Saint Louis. Several large trunks were being unloaded—it was exciting.

"Let's go look in those trunks,"she said. There might be ivory combs, or silver-backed hairbrushes in those trunks. Maria wanted to look in them right away—it was far more exciting than listening to her little sister indulge in pretty daydreams about Kit Carson, an unprepossessing *americano* who had been gone for more than a year. Of course, some people considered her Charlie unprepossessing too—and he too made long trips. But at least when Charlie got back he brought wagons full of exciting goods.

"If we see something we want, maybe Charlie will give it to us as a present," Maria suggested.

"He might give *you* a present, you mean," Josefina corrected. Maria was the only person Charles Bent was ever generous with—he had never given Josefina so much as a thimble or a ribbon. Still, even if she didn't get anything, it might be exciting to look. Josefina stubbed out her little cigar and followed her sister down the stairs.

42

He had spotted the dust cloud . . .

"Let's get in the gully quick, and hope those soldiers
don't have eyesight as good as yours," Jim Snow told Kit.

"Well, they wouldn't have to—they could just have a spyglass,"
Kit remarked. He had spotted the dust cloud in the east while he
and Jim were trying to stalk an antelope. They were on horseback, about half a mile ahead of the company. Jim Bridger, afoot,
was also hunting, a mile or two to the west. Jim Snow's plan was
to get the antelope in bow range, but if he failed, maybe the
beast would go in Jim Bridger's direction—Jim Bridger was the
best rifle shot in the company; with any luck he would bring in
meat, and meat was needed.

The distant dust cloud, visible to the keen-eyed Kit, caused
the immediate abandonment of the antelope hunt.

"I bet it's Mexican soldiers—just what I was afraid of," Jim
said. "It's lucky we have this gully to hide in—I doubt they spotted us yet."

"Damn the luck—seems like every time I get close to Santa Fe,
I get arrested," Kit complained.

"You ain't arrested yet, and neither am I," Jim pointed out. "I
think we can skirt 'em if we're sly."

"We can, but what about the rest?" Kit asked. "What about
your wife?"

"Oh, they'll arrest the main party—we can't stop that. Maybe Jimmy Bridger will skirt 'em too—he's pretty quick on his feet."

"He's not as quick as a soldier on horseback," Kit objected. "I expect they'll soon run him down."

He never enjoyed hearing Jim Bridger complimented.

"You and I have to split up," Jim Snow told Kit. "This gully runs southeast. Stay in it as long as it lasts, and then go lickety-split for the Bents'. You can probably be there tomorrow if you ride all night."

"I guess I'll do it if I ain't shot," Kit agreed.

"Stay low and lead your horse until you're past the soldiers," Jim instructed. "Go on. Find the Bents and tell them to send someone to Santa Fe who the Mexicans will listen to. Tasmin's not going to like being in jail."

"I hope that dern Charlie Bent ain't home," Kit said. "I like Willy, but Charlie Bent is not an easy man to hurry. All that money he's got has made him cranky. Last time I saw him he was full of sass."

"You can lecture me about Charlie some other time," Jim said. "Skedaddle."

"What about you?"

"I'll just follow along and keep out of sight," Jim said. "Tom and Pomp can talk to the Mexicans—maybe some Indians ran off some horses and they're out looking for them. I imagine they'll just lead the folks to Santa Fe and demand a ransom—that's what usually happens."

"I hope Charlie Bent don't sass me," Kit repeated. He began to lead his horse along the rocky gully. When he looked back Jim Snow was gone.

43

. . . a serious disability . . .

J I M S N O W had never been able to imitate birdsongs—
a serious disability in the situation he found himself in. Pomp
Charbonneau could reproduce almost flawlessly more than a
dozen birdcalls, and Jim Bridger was almost as proficient. Pomp
would hear a birdcall and mimic it immediately. Jim Bridger, a little jealous of Pomp's ability, attributed it to the fact that Pomp
was half Indian. Jim Snow had no opinion on that question. All
he knew was that Pomp's birdcalling was so good it fooled the
birds themselves.

Now, with what seemed to be a patrol of Mexican soldiers proceeding across flat country, Jim knew he had to move quickly if
he didn't want to be arrested with the rest. For the moment he
was safely concealed in the gully. His first problem was to get rid
of the horse. Most of the soldiers would just be young Mexican
boys, very unskilled in pursuit. Even on the flat prairie Jim felt
confident that he could hide successfully, but he couldn't conceal the horse. Pomp was standing with Tasmin, not far from the
gully. It was morning—there was little wind. Jim tried the one
birdcall he was good at, a quail call—then he repeated it three
times. Jim's imitation was so bad that Pomp immediately looked
toward the gully.

"Your husband's trying to sound like a quail," Pomp told Tasmin. He had just seen the dust cloud to the east—he too supposed it was soldiers. Pomp turned toward the gully—as soon as he did, Jim popped the horse on the rump, sending it over to Pomp, who at once caught it and mounted. He saw Jim Snow in the gully—Jim made a quick sign and then crept away.

Tasmin was puzzled—where was Jimmy, and what was going on?

"I think there's a company of soldiers coming this way," Pomp told her. "I suppose we'll be arrested—it's mostly just a formality. Jimmy probably thinks he can be more useful if he's not arrested."

Tasmin just saw a dust cloud—if there were soldiers in it, she couldn't yet see them. She looked around for Kit and didn't see him, either. After promising her he wouldn't run off, Kit had done exactly that.

"Kit may have headed for the Bents'," Pomp said. "They'll soon send someone to help us out with the authorities."

"But isn't this America?" Tasmin asked. "Don't we have a right to be here?"

"It's subject to interpretation," Pomp told her. "No boundaries have been drawn yet. We think it's America but they think it's Mexico. There's a contest going on."

"A peculiar contest, if you ask me," Tasmin said. "There's nothing here to want. What are we being arrested for? We're merely wandering."

"Spies—they think all Americans are spies," Pomp explained. "The Mexicans think the Americans mean to drive them out and take their land. I suppose they're right. The Americans probably will drive them out, eventually."

To Tasmin it seemed absurd. They were a hunting party, exhausted, scratched, sunburned—they had little to eat and were just stumbling along behind their one ox. What threat could they pose?

Her father was talking with Tom Fitzpatrick, who found this new challenge annoying.

"Damn it, we'd have been at the Bents' in two more days," the Broken Hand said. "They could have arranged matters for us."

"Oh, I suspect this will just come down to bribery," Lord Berrybender said. "I suppose we'll have to chivvy up—won't mind so much if I can get a change of clothes."

"That's right, we're in rags and I'm hungry," Tasmin remarked. "Will our captors feed us, at least?"

"*Frijoles,* maybe. Beans," Pomp told her.

Tom Fitzpatrick, watching the riders approach, had stopped looking indignant. His look had become somber. Pomp too stiffened.

"They ain't soldiers—Jim and Kit made a mistake," Tom said. "They ain't soldiers—or am I wrong, Pomp?"

Pomp studied the approaching riders with more care. A few of them seemed to be in military coats, and carried military muskets, with bayonets. The sun glinted off the bayonets, and off the brass buttons on the coats. But they were not riding in a military formation. He had supposed they were going to be faced with the inconvenience of a polite arrest. But now he wasn't so sure.

"But gentlemen, if they aren't soldiers, who are they?" Lord Berrybender asked.

"Renegades!" Zeke Williams suddenly announced, peering at the company with his hard, blue stare. "They're slavers, I expect. I know that big fellow on the black mule. That's Obregon."

"You know him?" Pomp asked, surprised.

"It's Obregon," Zeke repeated. "He came trading for slaves when the Pawnees had me. Didn't want me, though. Wanted women, when he could get them. Or boys, if he couldn't get women."

Tasmin's mild apprehension turned to a chill of fear. Here was the threat that all the women had talked about when they were still safe on the steamer *Rocky Mount:* abduction, rape, slavery. Even Jim Snow, in the first days of their acquaintance, had warned her about slavers. Now the frightening prospect, which they had once talked about in the safety of their staterooms, had become real.

"I count fourteen of them," Tom told Pomp.

"That's what I make it," Pomp said. "We need the two Jimmys back—with them I think we could put up a good fight."

"I'm sure if they hear shooting they'll come running—Jim Snow's just back in the gully," Tom said.

"Maybe I should try to parley with them," Pomp told the group.

"No parleys!" old Zeke piped up. "Parleys don't interest Obregon—not when he figures he has the advantage. He's gonna see all these pretty women, and he'll be thinking of all the money he could get for them down in Chihuahua."

Pomp considered the advice but felt inclined to disregard it.

"I'll be watchful," he said. "It'd be best if all the women hunker down behind the wagon. We don't want to whet Señor Obregon's appetite."

When Tasmin saw that Pomp meant to ride out and talk to the slavers, she walked over and grabbed his rein, a thing she would not have done had she not felt such deep apprehension.

"Mr. Williams knows these men—why won't you listen to him?" she asked. "They might just shoot you down and overrun us."

"Here, signor, hand me my fine Belgian gun," Lord Berrybender said. "At least we have time to prepare for this fight—not like those impetuous Pawnees."

High Shoulders, alerted to the danger, came running to the wagon with his lance, ready for battle. Just as he arrived, Pomp saw Jim Bridger returning to camp at a casual pace. He carried a prairie chicken and a jackrabbit. Though Jim had clearly seen the advancing party he showed no particular concern—in fact, he was whistling, a practice he was much prone to.

Jim Snow, too, was walking back toward the group. It had not taken him long to revise his first estimate of the situation.

When he arrived Pomp dismounted.

"That changes the odds, pretty considerably," he said. "We'll let *them* send someone to parley if they want to talk. Maybe Kit will come back, too."

"Nope, Kit's bound for the Bents'—I sent him," Jim Snow told Pomp. "If those fellows aren't soldiers, who are they?"

"Slavers, Zeke says," Tom Fitzpatrick told him. "Ever hear of a fellow named Obregon?"

Jim shook his head.

Tasmin walked off—she wanted to be alone. Now that her husband was back she had lost her fear. Jim would see that they weren't harmed—and yet she was shaking because it had been such a close thing with Pomp. If she hadn't grabbed his rein she felt sure he would have loped off and been killed. In her mind she saw the bullet strike him, saw him fall off his horse and lie dead. And yet Pomp must have engaged in many such parleys—why was she so fearful on his behalf? He was a grown man, a famous guide, skilled, alert—she could not say why she harbored such a deep fear of his death. She still believed she would lose him if she didn't watch him close. It wasn't that he was weak—Pomp wasn't weak—and yet neither was he hard, as Jim Snow was hard. Even her selfish old father was harder in some essential way. Was it that Pomp didn't seem particularly interested in preserving himself? In the tent, after he was wounded, when she was trying so hard to keep him alive, she felt that he wouldn't have minded dying then—he even seemed a little resentful that she wouldn't let him. She had forced him to live, when his own inclination was for the shade. Pomp had grace, he had sweetness—yet the harsh plains they were crossing hardly rewarded either virtue. It was not for grace and sweetness that she looked to Jim Snow. Jim could be sweet, he could be amused—but by nature he was suspicious. Before he rode off to parley he would have made very sure of the field, the odds, his chances. When Jim left her, as he had several times, she didn't worry about him in the way she worried about Pomp. Her mind made no pictures of Jim Snow lying dead. Jim might exasperate her; he often did. He might pester her into lovemaking when she was only half inclined; he did that too. But she didn't worry about him and at times felt so distant from him that their union seemed very odd. Why had she married this man whom she

didn't know, except physically? She sometimes found herself forgetting him, even when he was around—but she never forgot
Pomp.

As usual Tasmin's perplexity of spirit was missed by everyone
but Mary.

"So is our lot to be slavery?" Mary asked.

"Of course not—both Jims came back—there's now not much
likelihood of an attack," Tasmin said. "Won't you just go away?
Why must I always have to deal with *you* when I'm upset about
something?"

"Because I know what you're upset about," Mary said,
although she abandoned her superior tone. "It's Pomp—you're
too in love with him."

Tasmin didn't answer.

"I believe you'd make a great fool of yourself, if Pomp would
cooperate," Mary continued. "But I don't think he will cooperate—he's only a *bit* in love, not wild with it, like you, Tassie."

"Mary, if there was a slaver here right now I'd sell you to him,"
Tasmin said.

"Of course—you don't like to hear the truth," Mary said. "You
don't respect it, either. I expect you'd ruin us all, if it meant you
could have Pomp."

Mary gave her a pat on the shoulder and went back to her Piet.

44

In the dark, with his thin knife . . .

" I T ' S those English people who were on the steamboat that got stuck in the ice," Malgres explained to Obregon. "The old man is very rich."

Malgres thought that was the kind of news that might stir Obregon to action. The English party was only two hundred yards away—instead of charging, as Malgres had urged, Obregon had stopped the column. Now he sat on his large black mule, musing about what he wanted to do next.

"I see some white women," Obregon said. "But I see some trappers too—you know how those trappers fight."

Malgres had to admit that Obregon had a point. In the dark, with his thin knife, he thought he could kill any of the trappers—but it was not dark, and except for himself, the men with Obregon were just a ragtag bunch of renegades. The mountain men were formidable; if there was a battle, few of the renegades would survive. Obregon hadn't survived as a slaver for twenty years by rashly pitting himself against well-armed and determined opposition. It was beginning to look as if there would be no battle.

"I'm afraid of the Sin Killer," Obregon admitted casually. He was prone to making frank admissions of that sort, admissions

that did nothing to boost the morale of the bandits who were
supposed to do the fighting.

"If I were small, like you, I wouldn't be such a good target,"
Obregon said. "But I'm a very big target, and the Sin Killer is supposed to be good at shooting arrows. Since I'm the biggest target
he might shoot some into me. I had two arrows stuck in me by
the Sioux and I didn't like it. I'm not a man who likes to be punctured."

Ramon, the tall, skinny *pistolero,* cackled at this remark. If
one worked with Obregon it helped to have a sense of humor.
Obregon wasn't merely afraid of having arrows stuck in him, he
was afraid of everything: lightning, grizzly bears, Sioux Indians,
snakes that lived in water, scorpions—the list was long. He was
even afraid of women with sharp fingernails—a captive girl from
one of the pueblos whom he had been raping jabbed her finger-
nail into his eye. Now the eye, his left eye, refused to look
straight ahead, as an eye should—his left eye looked off at an
angle, a disconcerting thing. Eyes should be set straight ahead,
not angled off to the left.

The injury had much reduced Obregon's appetite for rape,
too. He didn't rape girls anymore unless they were securely held
down by at least four men—if a girl managed to get a hand free,
he might suffer damage to his good eye, which would mean that
his career as a slaver was over.

It was a wonder to Ramon, and to Malgres also, that a man as
cowardly as Obregon had managed to prosper in the dangerous
business of slave trading. Obregon didn't even pretend to
bravado, yet he had a sure touch with the Indians, who were so
amused by his ineptness that they were eager to sell him captives. To the Indians Obregon was a great clown, a man who
sometimes simply rolled off his horse because he had neglected
to pull his girths tight enough. When Obregon arrived in a village or intercepted a hunting band, the Indians got ready to
laugh, and sometimes they laughed so much that they practically
gave their captives away. Obregon succeeded in a hard business
by being foolish, cowardly, and clumsy. Other slavers were bit-

terly jealous of Obregon's absurd success. They knew that if they made the kind of mistakes Obregon made, they would be killed immediately—some did make such mistakes and *were* killed. Yet Obregon slouched on, riding his old black mules, tolerated and even welcomed by his prairie customers.

Sometimes, cautiously, the *pistoleros* argued about Obregon. Some maintained that he just put on a good act to disarm his customers. Nobody could really be that clumsy, that stupid, that cowardly and survive in such a hard place. Ramon argued the other position. Ramon believed that Obregon really *was* that cowardly, really *was* that clumsy. But some of the men remained unconvinced.

"So what are we going to do?" Malgres asked sullenly. He had only joined Obregon's renegades after the death of John Skraeling, the trader he had worked with for some months. In Malgres's opinion they should have charged the English group before the trappers had time to get organized. They might have lost a *pistolero* or two but they might have been able to carry off two or three white girls, captives who would bring huge prices in Mexico, where there were many rich hidalgos. But instead of charging, Obregon had allowed himself to start thinking about how much he disliked having arrows stuck in his fat body; instead of charging, he stopped. The trappers, who had been scattered and disorganized at first, were now concealed, concentrated, and ready for battle. A big profit had been there for the taking, but Obregon had been too cowardly to seize it.

"Hombres, go around that way and stay out of range," Obregon ordered, sweeping his arm toward the east. "Get across that gully and wait for me."

"Wait for you—where are you going?" Malgres asked.

"To talk to the English—why not?" Obregon said. "You can come if you like—Ramon can stay with the hombres."

Then Obregon waved his hands, to indicate to the English that no hostilities were intended. He clucked at his mule and proceeded at a slow walk toward the English group. Malgres hesitated for a moment, and then joined him.

"We can get a good, close look at the women," Obregon said. "It doesn't hurt to have a count. We might meet these English again someday, when they don't have so many good shots to help them. Then we can catch a few women and have ourselves a little fiesta."

When they were halfway to the English company, Malgres suddenly changed his mind. He remembered that he had killed the old Mandan chieftain Big White, who had been with the English for a time. Big White had left the steamer and was on his way home when Malgres and two Poncas ran into him. The old chief spoke rudely to them and a fight ensued. Big White killed one Ponca with his great war club, but before he could catch the other Ponca, Malgres slipped in and stabbed him in the liver with his thin knife. The old man cursed him and died.

That had occurred the previous winter—few knew that he had killed Big White, but the Sin Killer might know it, or one of the other trappers. One or two of them might have been friends of Big White; the sight of Malgres might provoke them to seek revenge.

"I'll go with Ramon—you count those women yourself," Malgres said, turning toward the gully.

"Suit yourself, amigo," Obregon said.

45

When the fat man, still smiling . . .

WHEN Malgres turned away from Obregon and loped over to join the other renegades, Jim Snow was more than a little suspicious. The renegades disappeared into the gully where he and Kit had hidden—Jim thought they might be planning to race through the gully and make a flanking attack.

"That was Malgres—he killed Big White," Jim told them. "Be watchful."

Even as he said it, the ragtag group of slavers trotted up the east side of the gully and stopped. They did not look in the mood to charge. They merely sat on their horses, waiting for their jefe to return.

"Hello, my friends, don't shoot!" Obregon yelled, as he plodded toward the waiting company.

"Why, the fellow looks like a dunce," Lord Berrybender said.

"Agreed," Tom Fitzpatrick remarked. "Are you sure this is the slaver, Zeke? He looks like a fool to me."

Zeke Williams did not appreciate having his information challenged by men of small experience, and he considered that most men younger than himself were men of small experience.

"Did I say he was a professor?" Zeke inquired. "He's a slaver. He trades in boys and girls, when he can get them."

"Oh, what we'd call a pimp," Lord B. remarked. "I suppose it's the same everywhere . . . old rich men like virgins."

When the fat man, still smiling, rode up to them on his scabby mule, Tasmin moved closer to her husband, for there was something peculiarly repulsive about the man, something that suggested rot, decay, an unwholesome softness—all the women felt like shuddering, and yet none of them could say quite why they were so repulsed.

"Don't shoot, let's all be friends," Obregon said, in his shrill voice. "You don't need to point your guns at me, señores. Let's all be peaceful together."

"We took you for soldiers, at first," Tom Fitzpatrick said.

Obregon wore a filthy straw hat—he removed it and made a small bow to the women, his eyes lazily assessing them even as he practiced this courtesy.

"Oh no, there are no patrols out here today," Obregon assured them. "They are all out hunting the Ear Taker—he has come back to Santa Fe. You know of him, I suppose.

"I see you do know of him," he went on, looking directly at Amboise d'Avigdor. "Last week he took an ear from the governor's nephew—I wouldn't want to be the Ear Taker, if they catch him."

Tasmin had picked up Monty—she held him close, her arms wrapped around him. She had never seen a man as disgusting as Obregon. She felt almost queasy, and not from morning sickness, either.

"Do you suppose that's how eunuchs look, in harems?" Mary asked.

"Hush, he might hear you," Tasmin warned—though she thought Mary might be right.

"I'm sorry if my caballeros frightened the ladies," Obregon went on. "We are kindly fellows—we didn't come to harm anyone."

"I suppose you're looking for those thieving Pawnees," Zeke Williams told him. "You were mighty friendly with 'em when they had me captive."

Obregon smiled again—he allowed his gaze to drift over the women, especially Tasmin and Vicky. He remembered that the old fellow who spoke had been a prisoner of the Pawnees on one occasion when he had visited.

"No, we are merely going to visit some Cheyenne who are hunting nearby," Obregon said. "Would you gentlemen have any coffee or tobacco to spare—we are running low ourselves or I wouldn't ask."

"Do we look rich to you?" Zeke piped up at him. "We've got nothing to spare."

"Why, I see the English gentleman has an excellent gun," Obregon said. "Such a gun must be very expensive—all we seek is a little coffee."

Tom Fitzpatrick found the man irritating.

"Zeke's right, we've nothing to spare," he said firmly.

"Where's Skraeling—the man Malgres rides with?" Jim asked.

Obregon smiled again, looking not at Jim but at Tasmin.

"Señor Skraeling, he died," Obregon informed them. "He was not a healthy man. Malgres rides with me now."

There was a nervous silence. The men had become as uncomfortable with Obregon as the women. Yet Obregon continued to sit, smiling blandly, as he let his eyes dwell on this woman and that.

"Could I buy this girl?" he asked, pointing at Mary. A small quirt dangled from his wrist—he used it to point.

"Buy her? Certainly not, sir," Lord Berrybender told him. "She happens to be my daughter, and a very skilled girl she is. Knows a good deal about the sciences. I can't properly be said to own her, but if I did I'd certainly not sell her to a ruffian like yourself. Doubt her chastity would be worth a fig, if you had her."

"Is chastity worth a fig, Your Lordship?" Obregon asked. "She is a fierce one, the young miss. She snarls at me like a wildcat."

Indeed, Mary had bared her teeth at the man.

"I don't like him, Tassie—I think he is very bad," Mary whispered, too loudly. Obregon heard.

"Oh, not very bad, young miss," he said. "I suppose all men are a *little* bad, sometimes."

He pursed his lips and looked around at the men nervously waiting across the gully.

"Perhaps you'll sell me the servant girl, then," Obregon said, pointing his quirt at Eliza, who blanched in shock.

"I buy people—you have no coffee and no tobacco—surely you can spare a servant girl," he said. "Top prices paid, as the *americanos* say."

Tasmin, who had grasped Jim's arm, felt him stiffen suddenly— his face became dark with anger and he moved so quickly that no one, later, could remember the exact sequence of his actions. Suddenly the pole was in his hands—a pole that they had sharpened to make a goad for their slow and sleepy ox. The pole was Signor Claricia's. He used it to jab the ox, when the ox seemed about to stop altogether. He had been holding the pole nervously when Obregon approached. But suddenly the Sin Killer had it; Obregon could do no more than open his mouth in shock when Jim hit him in the face with the pole so hard that he was knocked completely off his mule. The pole broke. Jim threw it aside, caught Obregon by his feet, and dragged him to the gully, across from where the renegades waited. Blood poured from the unconscious man's broken mouth. None of the renegades moved a muscle. Jim pushed Obregon over the edge—he tumbled a few times and lay flat on his back, at the bottom of the gully.

"It's a bad sin, selling people!" Jim yelled. "Tell him that when he wakes up."

Then he came back to the group, such a dark fury in his face that no one, not even Tasmin, dared speak to him as he strode through them. He stood by the horse he had been riding until his face, which had been dark red, became white again.

It took six of the renegades to lift Obregon out of the gully. Once they had him, the youngest of the renegades, a frightened boy, rode across the gully and approached the party.

"Señores, may we take his mule?" he asked. "None of our horses can carry him—he is too large."

"Take the mule," Jim yelled. "And tell that man I'll do worse if I see him again."

"*Sí*, señor, I'll tell him," the boy said. He led the mule back across the gully. Obregon had regained consciousness but could not stand unassisted. His whole front was drenched in his blood. Half the company struggled to lift him onto his mule—as soon as he was settled, the renegades rode away.

Jim still stood by his horse. The men were determined to give him time to cool, but Eliza, who had been more frightened than she had ever been in her life, could not wait to express her gratitude. Trembling and tearful, she stumbled over to Jim.

"Thank you so much, Mr. Snow," Eliza said. "I didn't care for those fellows. I fear they would have misused me, had you let me go."

Jim nodded. "We won't be letting nobody go," he assured her.

Monty had lately acquired the habit of thumb sucking. As Tasmin held him he stared at his father, thumb firmly planted in his mouth.

46

A cold, cutting wind . . .

"Q U I T E a morning," Father Geoffrin remarked, as he walked along with Tasmin. "It's given me a new aim in life— quite the most distinct aim I've ever been able to formulate."

"Nothing salacious, I hope," Tasmin said. "We've had enough of that for one day. What's your new aim?"

"To never make your husband mad, that's it," Geoff told her. "I think Señor Obregon is lucky to be alive. We've seen a good deal of violence on this trek, but *that* was different, don't you agree?"

"Yes, only I wish Jimmy had killed him," Tasmin said. "Then there'd be no chance that we'd encounter him again. I'd rather face Pawnees or Utes than meet that man again. He didn't touch me but his look made me feel that there'd been an obscene exchange."

"You have the Sin Killer to protect you," Father Geoff pointed out. "I shouldn't think you'd need to worry, as long as you behave."

"Yes, if I behave—a big question," Tasmin said. "I wish I knew Jimmy better. To this day I don't really know what he thinks sin is."

"Slaving is obvious enough," the priest said. "He was sold himself, didn't you tell me?"

"Yes, sold by the Osage to a violent preacher, who was struck by lightning and cooked," she said. "The old preacher, though a great fornicator, convinced Jim that sin had to be punished, and he punishes it very firmly, once he identifies it."

"I suppose that *could* make for a nervous married life," Geoff said, with a twinkle of amusement. "Spontaneous sin might occur."

"He considers oaths and curses to be quite sinful," Tasmin mentioned. "I've let slip an oath or two and been slapped for it—nothing like what occurred to Señor Obregon, but they weren't love taps, either. For that reason I try not to speak impurely."

"Or act impurely?" the priest asked. "Doesn't passion thrive on complications?"

"My own passions are direct, but I'm not thriving on them—starving would be more like it," Tasmin told him.

"You shouldn't have fallen in love with a chaste man—I suppose I should have warned you," Geoff said. "Your husband isn't chaste, though."

"No, but that ain't passion, exactly," Tasmin said, brooding. "I *was* much in love with Jimmy once. I wonder where it went."

A cold, cutting wind was blowing—the days had been growing steadily chillier and the night bitter cold. The two babies were snug in their pouches, with their rabbit-skin caps on. Jim, calm and free of his rage now, strolled along with Pomp. Both were of the opinion that it would likely snow that day. They themselves were indifferent to weather—all the mountain men were, except old Zeke, who claimed that cold made his joints ache.

Jim and Pomp were chatting amiably—it annoyed Tasmin greatly, left her feeling discontent. The two men were old companions—so where did she fit? In better circumstances she would have pressed Pomp Charbonneau harder, thrown herself at the marble of his reserve, tried to smash through it with an irresistible force of feeling—the same force that had kept Pomp alive when he lay badly wounded in the Valley of the Chickens. Alone with him she would have yelled and screamed, kicked, bitten, become a wild thing until he opened up to her. But on this chilly prairie, with a tired company plodding along under a slate gray sky, with many watchful gossips in her own family noting her every mood, she didn't dare produce a sufficient fit. All she could do was plod on herself, feeling sour—waiting for her chance.

47

He was slurping up the muddy water . . .

T H E white man had managed to crawl into a mud puddle
in the middle of a shallow lake. He was slurping up the muddy
water, cupping his hands, getting almost as much mud as water.
Greasy Lake recognized the white man—he was one of those
who had been sailing along in a balloon, high above the Platte.
Now he was covered with mud. Even a hog who had just wal-
lowed would not be much muddier than this white man. To
Greasy Lake it all seemed rather peculiar. Probably the white
man had been starving when he crawled into the mud puddle—
obviously he did not know that a clear, bubbling spring was
about a mile distant. The spring had several cottonwoods growing beside it—the trees would have alerted any experienced
prairie traveler that there was water nearby. But perhaps the man
in the mud puddle had poor vision; perhaps he couldn't see the
trees.

Greasy Lake, astride the Partezon's fine white horse, had come
loping quickly across the plains. He had news of the English
from some Pawnees in whose camp he spent a night. There had
been a fight, a great triumph, to hear the Pawnees tell it—four
whites had been killed—Greasy Lake was shown the scalps of
three of them. As he was only a visitor, Greasy Lake remained

noncommittal. He politely refrained from asking whether the
Pawnees had lost any men in the battle—later the boy Rattle
admitted that they had lost three.

In the Pawnees' opinion the whites were headed for the big
trading post that was being built on the Arkansas—so that was
where Greasy Lake decided to go. There was always the likelihood of finding interesting goods around a new trading post. The
whites were always inventing useful things. Though Greasy Lake
had no money he could sometimes get the whites to exchange
goods for prophecies. Usually he just made simple prophecies,
informing them of the location of a nice buffalo herd he had happened to pass. This kind of information might even earn him a
new gun, if the whites were in a generous mood.

The sight of the lost balloonist, drinking muddy water from a
puddle when there was a fine spring in plain sight, reminded
Greasy Lake that there was really no predicting the eccentricities
of whites, and no exaggerating their ineptitude. For one thing
they kept producing watches and clocks, instruments that were
supposed to measure time and break it into units, when common sense should have told them that the notion that time
could be cut up, like a buffalo shank or a fish, was simply absurd.
Time lay all one, open and eternal, infinite like the sky. Of
course, there were seasons, the moon waxed and waned, the
geese flew south or north, and yet all the while time remained
unaffected and unchanged.

The white man in the muddy seep seemed to have no weapon
except a sword of some kind—clearly he would probably starve
unless Greasy Lake rescued him, and if he *did* rescue him the
whites would probably give him a nice reward when he arrived
at the trading post. Once the white man washed the mud off
himself the two of them could easily ride double on the Partezon's big white horse.

"You might walk down to that spring and wash the mud off
yourself," Greasy Lake advised, when Clam de Paty came slog-
ging out of the mud. "Then I can give you a ride to the big new
trading post, down there on the Arkansas."

Clam didn't know what to make of this invitation. He could see no spring. Did the old fool think he would have crawled through the mud if there had been a spring in sight?

"The spring is right over there, by those trees," Greasy Lake said, pointing.

Clam looked toward where the old man pointed. Just vaguely he detected a blur of green, against the dun prairie. Could the old fellow be right? Was there a nice spring where he could get clean? Clam had been lost for five days, and was very hungry. His only food had been a few wild onions. If there was indeed a spring, perhaps there would be a frog in it. In France he had been very fond of frog legs, rolled in flour and served with lots of garlic. The very thought of tender, garlicky frog legs made his mouth water. If he only managed to live to get back to France he intended to eat many frog legs—hundreds of frogs' legs, even.

"Where is the tall man who was with you when you flew in your basket?" Greasy Lake wondered.

"My friend is dead—the Pawnees killed him," Clam told him.

Then he suddenly saw the trees the old man had been talking about—the old fellow had been right. It was merely the fact that he got headaches when he tried to look across long bright spaces that had caused him to miss the trees.

Clam's clothes were matted with mud, pounds and pounds of it. Delighted by the thought of being able to jump into a deep pool and wash off the mud, he began to hurry toward the trees— he kept pace with Greasy Lake on his white horse for the short distance to the water, and when he got there he dove straight in, not bothering to remove his clothes—the spring had a yellowish look but Clam was far too eager for a wash to be deterred by that.

No sooner had he plunged into the water than he rose and staggered out, vomiting, choking, holding his nose: the water he had plunged into was densely sulfuric—it was as if he had jumped into a cauldron of rotten eggs.

Almost fainting from the unexpected stench, Clam managed to stumble back to dry land, still muddy and now yellowish as well. With every breath he choked and retched.

Greasy Lake, in no hurry, came to where the white man stood, choking and gasping. There were some people who enjoyed these stinking springs, but Greasy Lake was not one of them. Some shamans thought the sulfur pools were healthy, but Greasy Lake considered that nonsense. Bad smells did not make one healthy.

"That's the stinking water—the good water is a little farther," Greasy Lake told Clam.

Clam heard the flutter of wings and saw a flock of ducks rising from a pond only a little distance away. Miserable as he was, he felt afraid to hope.

"Are you sure that's clean water, no sulfur, monsieur?" he asked.

"Didn't you see those ducks?" Greasy Lake asked. "Ducks won't land on the stinking water."

A half hour later Clam de Paty had washed himself clean in a pool of clear, icy water. Overhead the ducks circled and squawked, annoyed that he had taken their pond.

48

When he wasn't moaning . . .

" L ᴇ ᴛ ' s just kill him," Ramon suggested to Malgres. "No need to waste a bullet. You can just cut his throat."

Malgres had no fondness for Obregon—no one had any fondness for Obregon—yet he hesitated to adopt Ramon's suggestion. The slavers were stranded, camped by an adequate water hole but unable to agree whether to go on or back. Obregon's moaning was beginning to annoy everyone—he still spat up blood, with now and then a tooth that worked loose. The worst problem was his jaw, which was badly broken. It jutted out at an angle to his chin, and wiggled when he moved or spat.

"Your bad eye points one way and your broken jaw points another," Ramon told Obregon, who lay by a small bush. He was using his saddlebags for a pillow; his money was in those saddlebags.

When he wasn't moaning, Obregon wept at the cruelty of fate. He had never been able to stand pain. Slight scratches that most men ignored he brooded over for hours, coating the small wounds with balms and lotions bought in Santa Fe. Now his jaw was broken, his mouth smashed, some of his teeth knocked out—all this accomplished in an instant because he had been foolish enough to goad the Sin Killer. He had mainly been jesting about the servant girl. His mind had dwelt momentarily on the possibility of stealing one or two of the Englishwomen—while he was calculating how best to do it, he had made his mistake. He knew he should have kept Malgres with him—at least Malgres might have slowed the Sin Killer down, absorbed his charge. In fact, he should have kept all the men with him. Better yet, he should have avoided the English party altogether; that is what Malgres—afraid of the mountain men's guns—had wanted to do. But even Malgres could not have imagined that the Sin Killer would run out and break Obregon's head with a pole. All the renegades had been shocked to see their leader knocked completely off his horse in this unexpected way; and yet, all of Obregon's long experience on the prairies should have taught him always to be ready for the unexpected. Buffalo stampedes were not the expected thing, and yet he had seen three in his lifetime.

Now one man, the Sin Killer, had done him more damage in the course of a second than he had experienced in twenty years of slaving. The slightest movement of his jutting jaw caused him terrible pain—and the pain would go on for months. No one in the group knew how to reset a jaw, and Obregon could not have stood the agony if someone had tried.

Obregon tried desperately to calm his mind, to think carefully about what to do. He either had to prepare to die, or else steel himself against the pain. He hated the pain, and yet he was afraid of the pain of death as well. A bullet wouldn't hurt for long—but still it would hurt terribly, a little nugget of iron tearing through his flesh! Both his options were now distressing, and all because a quick-moving white man had hit him with a stick.

Malgres thought their best bet might be to find the Cheyenne they had been hoping to trade with. The tribes had healers—perhaps one could help Obregon.

He suggested as much to Ramon, who thought it a waste of time.

"I'd rather just kill him—why wait?" he said.

"The Indians like him, that's why," Malgres reminded him. "With Obregon alive, we'll be safe. They won't attack us while he's alive. We're a long way from Santa Fe, and we don't have much food. If we can keep him alive until we're safe, then we should do it."

"Maybe we can tie up that jaw with a piece of rawhide string," Ramon suggested. "It's horrible to look at, the way it wobbles."

They got a string but when they tried to bind Obregon's jaw he screamed so loudly and spewed so much blood on them that they gave the whole thing up as a bad job. All they had accomplished was to make the jaw worse—now it stuck out at an even more startling angle.

Unable to talk, in terrible pain, Obregon moaned and moaned. When anyone looked at him he pointed at his head—he wanted them to shoot him, or at least give him a gun so he could shoot himself.

But the renegades were still debating the wisdom of keeping Obregon alive. The point Malgres kept insisting on was that it was important to have a recognized leader—as John Skraeling had been and as Obregon was—when they went among the tribes.

"*I'll* be the leader," Ramon said. "I'm smarter than Obregon anyway."

"It doesn't matter how smart you are," Malgres argued. "The Indians don't *like* you, but they do like Obregon."

Ramon thought such talk was all nonsense. He thought he knew the business well enough to win the Indians over.

"Obregon never gave them much—just cheap goods," Ramon argued. "If we give them more than he did, then they'll like us."

Malgres ceased to argue. Ramon was too stupid to grasp the point, which was that *liking* didn't have that much to do with the quality of the trade goods.

Obregon would not stop moaning. Around midnight, kept awake by this irritating noise, Ramon walked over and caught Obregon by his twisted jaw, causing him to emit a piercing scream, which was reduced to bloody gurgles when Ramon cut his throat.

In the morning none of the renegades felt energetic enough to dig Obregon a grave, so they stripped him of all his possessions, left him to the coyotes and the carrion birds, and turned back toward Santa Fe.

49

Josefina had always been the bold one . . .

J O S E F I N A had always been the bold one in her family.
Maria might be haughty but she was not one to take chances
when it came to money. She wanted a rich man and she got one
in Charles Bent, the most ambitious young trader to have traveled the Santa Fe Trail. Their mother had not wanted Maria to
marry an *americano* but their father, a practical man, saw the
benefits of such a union right away. The *americanos* were coming—why not recognize reality and form a union with the most
successful of them?

Josefina didn't think of it in those terms—the minute Kit Carson returned and looked at her with his shy eyes, Josefina determined to grab him and get him to marry her. Doña Esmeralda
wouldn't like it and her parents would huff and puff, since Kit
was only a penniless guide, but Josefina intended to point out to
them that if she and Kit got married at the same time as Maria
and Charlie, it would save the expense of a second wedding.
However, if her parents didn't knuckle under, Josefina was fully
prepared to run away with Kit—her father would lose his little
Josie, the child dearest to his heart, the girl who was always willing to fetch his pipe and fill it for him.

Kit had followed Jim's instructions—he walked his horse for

two miles down the gully; he heard no gunfire and supposed the encounter with the Mexican soldiers must have passed off peaceably. He traveled on through the day and through the night and was rewarded not long after sunrise with his first glimpse of the big trading post the Bents were building. Kit would never have supposed those two scrappers, Charlie and Willy Bent, with their fancy partner St. Vrain, would have built anything as large as this huge adobe stockade he was approaching.

No sooner had Kit wandered in awe through the massive gates than Charlie Bent, without so much as a handshake, came over and began to pump him for information.

"I thought you were traveling with a rich Englishman. Where's he at?" Charlie wanted to know. He had heard about Lord Berrybender from Captain Clark—the thought of doing business with a man that rich appealed to his acquisitive instincts, but now Kit Carson, a fellow not worth a nickel, had arrived without him.

"They're coming—they've got an ox, and that ox ain't speedy," Kit told him. "I expect they'll show up in a day or two."

Willy Bent walked up with a grin on his face and punched Kit in the shoulder. Willy and Kit liked to tussle and wrestle, but with Charlie Bent around there were few opportunities for sport.

"Here, Willy—you and Kit get a buggy and a wagon and go bring in that English party. They'll probably be wanting to replenish their supplies, and we can sure help them out."

"But Kit just got here—let him eat at least," Willy said. "Besides, Kit don't work for you."

"Well," Kit said, noncommittally. He didn't want to ignite a conflict between the brothers, and it was easy to do.

While the brothers were facing off, Kit happened to cast his eye toward the parapet and saw two girls—at once he recognized the Jaramillo sisters, the stuck-up Maria and the merry little Josefina, whom he had once been so bold as to kiss.

"What are those girls doing here?" he asked. "I thought they lived in Santa Fe."

"They did, until Charlie decided to marry Maria," Willy said.

Charlie flushed—he disliked casual references to his forth-coming nuptials, but before he could gripe at his brother, Ceran St. Vrain strolled over, looking, as usual, breezy and somewhat distracted.

"Why, Mr. Carson, welcome to our humble post," he said. "I'm glad to see you're unscalped."

"I am, but the Pawnees tried for it," Kit informed them.

"So how was William Ashley's big rendezvous? Profitable, I hope," St. Vrain went on.

Kit was trying to get a better look at Josefina. Here he had just arrived, and Charlie and St. Vrain were already trying to dig out information about business conditions to the north. They wanted him to make a fur report, and do it before he'd even enjoyed a drink of water.

"You see, we're thinking of opening a post on the South Platte," St. Vrain said. "If Billy Ashley survived I guess we could too."

"Nope, you'd all be scalped in about three days," Kit said, annoyed by the persistence of the traders: all they cared about were furs and money.

Ceran St. Vrain was quick to sense the drift of Kit's feelings, but his partner Charlie Bent had no interest in anyone's feelings unless they could be utilized to earn the firm more money.

"You must be hungry, señor," St. Vrain said. "We have plenty—let Willy take you to the kitchen."

"All right, get some grub, I'll hitch the wagon," Charlie said. He himself put work first and grub second, and those who worked for him were expected to support the same priorities. Kit Carson was the only person who knew where the English could be found. After all, there were hostiles all over the prairies—it behooved Kit to make haste on behalf of his friends.

"How'd Charlie get that fair beauty to agree to marry him?" Kit asked Willy, as they were strolling toward the kitchen.

"You know Charlie—he's dogged," Willy reminded him. "When Charlie wants something he don't turn aside till he gets it."

"You're better looking than he is, why didn't you marry her?"

"Not me—I got a fine little Cheyenne wife myself," Willy said—but then he noticed that Kit had stopped listening—Josefina Jaramillo had come down from the parapet and was boldly waving at Kit.

Though he had been ravenously hungry when he rode into the fort, he at once forgot his hunger.

"Excuse me, I see Josie waving—I better go see what she wants," he said.

Willy Bent was startled. Josefina *was* waving, a *very* bold thing for a properly brought up girl to do. But Kit was already hurrying toward her, careless of the proprieties that had to be observed where the well-to-do Mexican families were concerned. One reason he preferred his wife, Owl Woman, was that in Cheyenne life few formalities need be observed. This sudden turn of events made Willy vaguely uneasy—Kit was supposed to be eating, not courting. Charlie would probably have a fit when he found out.

Josie's heart was thumping hard when she saw Kit approaching. She was resolved for a bold strike, one that would horrify her family. It might even horrify Kit. And yet she had long felt that Kit was the man she wanted to marry—if he refused her, she meant to enter a convent and marry no one. Kit had been the first man to notice her, the first to be kind to her, the first to arouse her womanly feelings. Now there he was; Josie felt ready for the gamble of her life: marriage or the nunnery. She did not intend to wither and grow old amid the many neglected old duennas to be seen in Santa Fe.

When Kit was twenty yards from Josefina he looked at her: there she was, smiling her merry smile at him. Between one step and the next he became so shy that he got his feet tangled up. He remembered how clumsy he was and began to feel embarrassed. What if he fell flat on his face and busted his nose again, as he had when he was walking with Tasmin Berrybender up on the Yellowstone? Josie was prone to giggles—no doubt she would giggle until she was out of breath if he fell and busted himself.

But then he was there—he hadn't tripped after all.

"I missed you—I thought you'd never come back," Josie said. "I thought a bear killed you."

"It has been a spell, hasn't it?" Kit said, feeling so shy that he hardly knew where to look.

"What have you been doing? You look older," Kit went on. He wished he could make some witty remark, but none were in his head.

"I been waiting for you to come back so we could get married—I don't want nobody else to be my husband," Josie said.

"Why, that's fine and dandy," Kit said automatically—it had not quite registered that he was answering a proposal. But when it soaked in and he *did* understand what Josie said, he at once turned bright red with shock.

"Say yes, I been waiting a long time," Josefina insisted.

"I guess you're joking—you don't really want to marry me, do you?" Kit asked.

Josefina's hopes collapsed; she felt that her big gamble had failed—her eyes, so merry a moment before, filled with tears at the thought of the long years she would have to spend in the nunnery.

When Kit saw the sudden tears splash down Josie's brown cheeks, he realized that he had somehow said exactly the wrong thing—his tongue had betrayed him, causing him to hurt this little brown girl who had always been his only female friend. If Josie really wanted to marry him, of course he would do it. Josie, in her disappointment, started to turn away, but Kit grabbed her and hugged her close. Her little chest was heaving—he himself was so bewildered that he feared he might faint.

"Don't cry, Josie—you just surprised me," Kit explained. "I been traveling so long I don't have my wits about me. Sure I'll marry you, though, if that's what you want.

"*Is* it what you want—really want?" he asked.

Josie, overcome with relief, could only nod. She pressed her face close against his chest. He wore an old buckskin shirt, filthy from weeks of travel, but she didn't care. She looked up, right into Kit's face. Had he lied? Was he just trying to get her to stop crying? She didn't want her hopes to rise, only to be dashed again. If Kit was going to regret his decision she wanted to know it now.

But when she looked up at him she was immediately reassured. Though still a little red, Kit had a pleased look, and he was still holding her tightly in his arms.

"Josie, you're the best," he told her.

"You mean we can marry? You mean it?" she asked.

"You bet I mean it," he said. "You don't suppose I'd be such a fool as to marry anybody but you, do you?"

Josie stood on tiptoe and kissed his cheek. Happiness filled her like sunshine.

"Maybe we can get married with Maria and Charlie," Josie said. "And then we can have babies. I want five or six."

"Good Lord, where will we put 'em?" Kit asked, blushing again at the thought of the intimacies attendant to having several children.

"Here," Josie said, gesturing at the great two-story edifice still being built.

"Maria and Charlie are going to live here—maybe we could too."

"No, the Bents are too bossy, I'd rather live in Taos," Kit said. He felt it was best to arrive at some practical understanding right away.

"Charlie Bent's apt to rub me the wrong way if I'm around him too much," he explained. "He's already rubbed me the wrong way and I just got here."

"I like Santa Fe better than Taos," Josie informed him. "A lot of mean old women live in Taos—they might pick on me."

"The important thing is to hurry and get hitched," Kit told her. A moment later it occurred to him that he had no money. He and Josie would need a house, somewhere. How would he afford it?

"Let's go tell everybody the news," Kit suggested. He was filled with pride and happiness—he held Josie's hand tightly, as if she were a bird that might escape.

"Maria will be very angry," Josie predicted. "She likes to keep all the attention for herself."

When Willy Bent saw the two of them coming toward him, boldly holding hands, he knew that his moment of apprehension had been justified. Here the two of them came, bold as brass.

"We're getting hitched, me and Josie," Kit announced. "Ain't she something? What do you think?"

"I'm leaving, that's what I think," Willy told them. "Charlie will have a fit—that's another thing I think."

"Charlie's getting married himself—why would he care?" Kit asked.

"He just will," Willy said. "He just will."

50

The men snatched up firearms . . .

MARIA JARAMILLO raced out of her room, screaming so loudly that everyone in the great courtyard of the trading post at once assumed that Indians were attacking. The men snatched up firearms and raced for the parapet. A few sheepherders, just outside the walls, heard the screams, abandoned their sheep, and ran for the great gate, hoping to get inside before it was shut. The small, dark men making adobe bricks hurried to the safety of the arsenal, their arms still covered with mud. St. Vrain, who had been in a storeroom doing his inventories, hurried out, puzzled. Where had the Indians come from? Which Indians were they? He himself had been out that morning on a long scout and had seen no Indian sign at all. It was true that Kit Carson and Willy Bent were expected to arrive with the English party at any time, but if it was them, why did Maria think it necessary to scream at the top of her lungs? Now the sheepherders had left their sheep and the builders their building. Her husband-to-be, Charlie Bent, a man who hated to see work interrupted, would no doubt have sharp words for his bride when he took stock of the situation—but where was Charlie Bent?

"Where's Charlie?" St. Vrain yelled at the distraught young

woman, who was scurrying in and out of the spacious second-floor apartment where she would soon be living with her husband.

"He's dead—I killed him!" Maria cried.

"She didn't—she broke his head a little!" Josefina, her short but usually reliable sister, shouted down at him.

"His head is cut. Maria hit him with a pot," Josefina continued.

"Hit Charlie with a pot? But why?" St. Vrain inquired.

Josefina just shrugged.

"She was angry," she said. "All these pots up here are broken now—every one."

St. Vrain hastened up the main stairway, itself not quite finished, and peeked cautiously into the rooms where the couple planned to live. Charles Bent lay stretched on the floor, bleeding from a gash on his temple. The floor was littered with shards of pottery—the heavy pottery that the local Indians made.

Charles Bent made an effort to sit up, only to fall back.

"Steady now—just rest a minute," St. Vrain advised, kneeling beside his partner. He turned to ask the young ladies for some water so he could bathe Charlie's head, but the two Jaramillo girls were gone. He had to go all the way down to the kitchen to find someone to help him. The cook who brought the water clucked anxiously when she saw all the broken pottery.

Charlie, by this time, was able to sit up, but his eyes were unfocused. St. Vrain washed the cut, which was not serious, and waited patiently for his partner to come back to himself. St. Vrain's first suspicion had been that Charlie had surprised a thief in his apartment and been hit in a struggle—but no. He seemed merely to have angered his beautiful and volatile young bride-to-be. St. Vrain had suspected that Maria had a fiery temper, and here, all around, was the proof.

"I don't go in for this heavy pottery, myself," he said, in order to make a little conversation while his partner was recovering.

"If a woman decides to throw a pot and it's a heavy pot, then heads could get broken," he said.

Charles Bent heard his partner's voice, but the voice, though distinct, seemed to come out of a fog. The fog filled the room. It had been a fine, sunny day when Maria began to throw pots at him, actions which embarrassed Charlie considerably. He didn't want to see his beautiful bride-to-be's face contorted with anger; he had been trying to keep his own temper under control, and so had averted his eyes just as Maria threw the pot that hit him. Now the world seemed foggy, but at least Maria was not screaming at him anymore.

"I expect I can guess why the fair Maria was so angry," St. Vrain told his friend. "It was because of where we decided to put the English, when they arrive."

"How'd you guess?" Charles asked. Kit Carson had informed them that two of the Englishwomen were with child—it seemed in the best interest not only of the travelers but of Bent, St. Vrain and Company to rent the English party quarters for the winter months, rather than allowing them to wander on to Taos or Santa Fe. Kit mentioned that the English party's kit was in bad order: they had few spare clothes, their guns needed attention, they would probably need a new buggy, perhaps a new wagon, blankets, winter coats, cookware, servants, and the like, all things that Bent, St. Vrain and Company could supply for a price. The only rooms yet finished where the English could be properly housed were the handsome second-floor rooms where Charles and Maria had intended to begin their married life. Charles Bent, as Maria should well know, was not a man to put personal convenience over profits. No doubt the English, tired and bedraggled from more than a year of trekking, would be happy to pay well for the lease of such handsome quarters—perhaps they would stay for four months, or even six, in which time, by supplying all their needs, Bent and St. Vrain could recoup a very large part of their expenditure on the post—a large sum made larger by Willy Bent's habit of paying far too much to the laborers—a liberality that horrified Charles when he returned from a trip to Saint Louis and sat down to inspect the books.

Fortunately, there were three small rooms off the stables which, Charles thought, would do quite well for himself and

Maria. Willy could assist the firm's economy by sleeping in a tent—and if he didn't like it he could lump it.

Maria Jaramillo knew quite well that she was marrying a merchant—surely, Charles thought, she would see the sense in vacating their domestic suites for a few months in order to take advantage of this God-sent opportunity to make money—lots of money—off the English party. Surely she appreciated that their position as traders was far from secure. The goods caravans they hoped to operate year-round from Saint Louis traveled at great risk. Any one of them might fall prey to Indians, drought, bandits. Their suppliers in Saint Louis had to be paid, and paid promptly. The concession they had obtained from the Mexican authorities had been expensive, and competition was steadily increasing. Boldness, industry, and economy were required, if Bent, St. Vrain and Company were to hold their position. St. Vrain, convinced that they must expand into untried territories, was already looking at the Platte River country. Their coffers, thanks to the building, were at the moment far from full. Playing hosts, for a price, to this English nobleman and his family was an opportunity that must not be missed. Surely a devoted wife would not object to starting married life in temporary quarters so that this chance for enrichment could be seized.

"Maria was mad anyway," St. Vrain reminded Charles. "She didn't like it that Kit and Josefina included themselves in the wedding."

"I'm mad about that myself—it's a nuisance," Charles told him. But of course, as both Kit and Josefina emphasized, it *would* save on expense, and Kit promised to make himself useful in various ways until the wedding. Maria, when she heard the news, yelled and screamed at her little sister, but Josefina, long used to such displays from Maria, ignored her.

When Maria rushed to Charles to complain, he had little to say. After all, Maria's parents were amenable to the plan—getting two weddings for the price of one seemed sensible to them. Charles refused to contest the decision, which is when Maria's rage flowed through her and pots began to fly.

"I never thought Maria would get so mad she'd hit me," Charles confessed.

St. Vrain, a bachelor, merely smiled. "Women like to throw things. One threw a hammer at me, but it missed."

"A hammer?" Charles asked.

St. Vrain nodded—he did not elaborate.

"Where'd Maria go?" Charles asked.

"I don't know, but I'll find out," St. Vrain promised. "You rest, my friend."

He strolled out onto the balcony just in time to see Maria Jaramillo, mounted on the fine gray mare Charles had given her as a wedding present, go racing off through the great gates of the fort.

Charlie Bent had followed St. Vrain. He stumbled out just in time to see his bride-to-be running away.

"Uh-oh, where's she going?" he asked. "She said she was going home to Taos—but it's in the other direction."

"She won't go very far—let's just go about our business and let her have a nice ride," St. Vrain suggested. "I imagine she'll be more friendly when she comes back."

"If she's any less friendly we'll all be in trouble," Charlie observed.

St. Vrain put his arm around his partner, but did not try to offer advice as to his domestic situation.

"These English won't stay forever," Charlie remarked. "It'll just be a few months we have to live by the stables. What's a few months?"

St. Vrain took a cigar out of his pocket and offered it to his friend, but Charlie shook his head. He didn't smoke and rarely drank to excess. Indeed, he had so few of the common vices that St. Vrain found it worrisome rather than reassuring, since it left Charlie vulnerable to the most dangerous vice of all, an attraction to difficult women—such as the one just racing away on her gray mare.

"Now I've got a dern headache—did you finish those inventories?" Charlie asked.

St. Vrain shook his head. "I would have, but your little bride started screaming so loud she scared the sheepherders," St. Vrain told him. "Then she said she had killed you. I figured the inventories could wait."

"Not for long, they can't," Charlie insisted. "We need to know where we stand—those English will show up soon."

He started for the stairs, meaning to go finish off the inventories himself—but after a step or two he stopped and turned back. His fiancée was now almost out of sight—she was only a dot, far off on the plain.

"Don't you think I should go after her? What if she gets lost?" he asked.

"Don't go after her—she won't get lost," St. Vrain assured him.

Charlie nodded and turned away again, only to stop a second time.

"What if she ran into some Pawnees?"

"There are no Pawnees around. Your bride will return, I assure you. She's just riding off her fit."

Reassured, Charlie Bent went back to work. St. Vrain stayed on the balcony, smoking. What he had not thought wise to suggest to his partner was that the worst threat to their partnership was not Indians, or the bandits, or blizzards, drought, grizzly bears, or any of the other normal dangers of the frontier. The worst threat to the company was an unsettled woman, the very one his sober partner was so in love with: Maria Jaramillo, belle of Santa Fe. If only she *would* get lost, St. Vrain thought. Then our business might have a chance.

51

In a cluster near the gate . . .

" J I M can do as he pleases—I'll be damned if I'll winter in a tent again," Tasmin declared. "Why should I, when we've been offered these fine spacious rooms?"

She stood with Mary and Buffum on the wide balcony of the big stockade, while below them various workmen went about their tasks. In a cluster near the gate the mountain men seemed to be in a serious discussion with the Bent brothers and St. Vrain. Jim Snow had informed Tasmin only that morning that he didn't believe he could tolerate the noisy bustle inside the walls—nor could Jim Bridger or the Broken Hand. Their intention was to make a separate camp a little distance downriver, a plan Tasmin made no effort to oppose. In any case, Jim hadn't come to her for permission; he came to tell her what had been decided. Of course, if she and Monty wanted to bunk indoors, where it was warmer, that would be all right with him.

"Frontiersmen cannot seem to accept any kind of enclosure—I suppose they're too used to wandering around where it's open," Buffum said.

"High Shoulders was raised in the open, just as they were, and yet you don't see him camping out—the man hardly leaves your side."

Buffum merely smiled.

"Soon we'll have our babe, and you yours, and Vicky hers," she said.

"I wouldn't call it soon—we've the damn winter to get through," Tasmin reminded her. "I intend to be comfortable, myself—I can tell you that."

The Berrybenders had been lodged with the Bents for a week. After such a long time spent outdoors, all of them, at first, had found even the spacious rooms provided for them rather stifling; but soon, once again, they had become used to the comfort of roofs and walls, of bedding that was clean, if rather coarse by English standards, and ample meals, wine, and even a set of small, quick, dark women assigned to them as servants. A buggy had been put at Lord Berrybender's disposal, with a nice pair of mules to pull it and a skilled hunter—an ancient fellow named Lonesome Dick—to help him locate game. Amboise d'Avigdor, his boss presumably dead, was being trained as a valet. All the old patterns of aristocratic life were swiftly resumed; once again Lord Berrybender, restored by claret, made frequent demands on his wife. Cook soon took command of the post's big kitchen, scattering the small women like quail and instructing them, by means of signs, how to prepare the various dishes. Mutton was frequently served. Cook's only vexation was the chilis, which the dark women insisted on putting in every dish; but the Berrybenders turned out to like the chilis—well-spiced food had ever been a Berrybender favorite—only Father Geoffrin complained. Icy winds were blowing from the north, the plains were often powdered with thin snow, and the group as a whole were only too happy to be provided with warm housing and ample food.

Mary Berrybender had quickly made friends with Josefina, although not with her haughty sister, who refused absolutely to have anything to do with the English party.

"Josie likes us but *that* one hates us," Mary said, nodding toward the tall beauty who stood with her sullen aunt outside the low adobe buildings where the Jaramillo girls now resided.

Every time Maria saw one of the Berrybenders enjoying what had been her quarters, her black eyes flashed with scorn.

"I suppose it's normal," Tasmin remarked. "After all, we've taken over her bridal suite and kicked her down to the stables."

"But it was her own husband-to-be who proposed it," Mary said. "I find him rather venal. No need to hate us—Charles Bent himself suggested it."

"Still, here *we* are and there *she* is, breathing the odors of the stables," Tasmin replied. "No doubt these Mexican beauties have their pride."

"You didn't mind stables when Master Tobias Stiles was tupping you in ours, back home," Mary reminded her, wickedly.

"Why should you remind me of those ancient efforts?" Tasmin asked. The time when she had eagerly offered up her innocence to the vigorous Master Stiles seemed very distant indeed. Now she was attached to a husband who lived by his own rules, not her rules, and she was in love with Pomp Charbonneau, a calm man who lacked Master Stiles's lusty enthusiasm. The one thing that struck her, on reflection, about her early connection with Master Stiles was how uncomplicated it had been. She had been a happy young woman then, being had by a servant in the stall of her father's stallion. It had not seemed wicked at all. That her virginal little sister kept bringing it up was annoying.

"It's time you stopped talking about such things, Mary," she said. "Here we are, comfortably quartered, and we're likely to be here all winter. It's time you and Piet got down to it—just do it!"

"I will try, but Piet is sadly reluctant," Mary admitted.

"Once you wean him from flagellation I'm sure he'll do well enough."

"He fears inadequacy," Mary confided. "He is only a short, fat botanist—and he's not a man of our class."

"Ha—does he suppose my husband, Jim Snow, or Buffum's finely made Ute are men of our class?" Tasmin asked. "We're in a raw trading post on the American frontier. Who knows what horrors await us? Since you obviously love him, who cares whether he's a man of our class?"

"Piet cares. After all he is a European, brought up to show due respect for his betters.

"I'm afraid I'm one of his betters," Mary said, rather sadly. "I don't know what to do."

"If you can get the man alone I'd suggest undressing," Tasmin advised. "You've a pretty little body. It might be that thoughts of class will recede."

"Possibly," Mary allowed, "but my new friend Josefina reports the same problem with Kit. She wants to start right in making babies, but Kit won't cooperate."

"Kit was mine, you may recall," Tasmin mentioned. "He used to respond to my every whim—now he'll scarcely look at me."

"Selfish Tasmin—you already have two men," Mary chided. "It is certainly only fair that you surrender Kit."

"I prefer to decide what's fair," Tasmin told her. "Go make a man of Piet and leave me alone. It's only to a limited degree that I have any man. Even Monty, on the whole, prefers Little Onion."

"That's because you scare him, Tassie," Mary said, as she left the balcony.

Tasmin stayed where she was, reflecting on Mary's charge. When in a bad temper, she did scare Monty; when in a lustful state, she embarrassed Pomp; and when generally out of sorts in a demanding way, she exasperated Jim. Three men, and yet not one that really knew what to do about her.

Annoyed by that conclusion, she stared insolently down at Maria Jaramillo and her aunt, who, no less insolently, stared back. Tasmin didn't flinch from these hateful looks. Here at least was direct emotion, one she could meet just as directly; no need to peer into the shadows or examine complications where Maria was concerned. Hate, Tasmin could readily understand; it was hesitancy she could not tolerate, particularly the hesitancy of men.

As usual when she was filled with hot annoyance, Father Geoffrin appeared at her elbow—angry vibrations seemed to draw him.

"Now's there's a fine enemy you've made," he remarked. "That girl would cheerfully see you dead."

"So what? I'd rather have an open enemy than a sneak like you, Geoff," Tasmin told him. "What do you think of Monsieur St. Vrain?"

"Very handsome, if somewhat cynical," Father Geoffrin declared. "What are you thinking, my sweet?"

"I ain't your sweet and I'm not thinking, I'm merely looking," Tasmin said.

52

. . . he felt that few of their rivals . . .

" L o o k at Charlie," Kit told Jim. "His face is red as fire—I think he's about to throw a fit."

"Let him—it won't be his first or his last," Jim Snow said. He had secured an awl and some tough sutures of deer gut, and was repairing his moccasins. Charlie Bent's hot temper didn't interest him.

"Charlie's had at least one fit every day when I've been around him," Jim Bridger observed. "He was never taught to control himself."

"How would you teach a fool like Charlie to control himself?" Kit wondered.

"By beating the tar out of him every time he acts up," Jim Bridger suggested. "Willy's not big enough to get the job done."

"I'll whop him, if he throws one with me," Jim Bridger assured them. "I won't waste no time."

"Well, he's had a setback—you can't blame him for being a little hot," Jim Snow reminded them. "He's got eight wagons ready to go east and now he's lost his best guide. At least, he has if Hugh Glass is telling the truth."

Hugh Glass had appeared only that morning, wandering off the prairie minus the Sublette brothers, whom he had been

scouting with. Hugh had passed through Taos on his way to the
post, where, by pure chance, he witnessed the abrupt end of
Teddy Tomball, Charlie Bent's head caravanner—a man who had
safely guided several commercial expeditions to Saint Louis,
with the loss of only one man and a few horses.

"Teddy was dancing with a plump señorita," Hugh reported.
"Some fool had left a rifle leaning against the wall and a
caballero kicked it and it went off. The dern bullet went right
through Teddy's heart."

Charlie Bent, on hearing the bad news, suspected conspir-
acy—he felt that few of their rivals would scruple at murder.

"I wonder who that caballero was working for," he said.

Hugh Glass didn't care for Charlie Bent—in fact he resented
the rooster of a fellow, pecking at him with questions about
everything.

"Where's Abby, Mr. Glass?" Tasmin asked innocently, looking
around for the young bear.

"Dern, we et Abby," Hugh admitted; the news shocked everyone within hearing distance. Even Jim Snow was surprised.

"We was for four days without food," Hugh Glass explained—
everyone wore horrified looks. The Broken Hand turned white
at the news, and Pomp Charbonneau, who had caught the bear
cubs in the first place, let slip a sigh of sadness.

"It was that or eat one of ourselves," Hugh went on. "Of
course, she didn't suffer none—she was sound asleep when we
shot her—never opened her eyes."

Then the old trapper gulped and looked strange.

"It was wrong—I'll never live it down, for that bear trusted me!"
he said. "We should have et Billy Sublette, but Milt didn't believe
he could help eat his brother, so poor little Abby it had to be."

Then, overcome, the old man howled like a wolf and burst
into tears—seeing the rough old trapper so broken brought
tears to many an eye. Kit Carson, who had loved the little bear,
cried like a baby himself—all the weeping astonished the Bent
brothers, who could not quite grasp the tragedy. All these tears
because Hugh Glass and the Sublettes had eaten a bear?

"You never met her—you fool!" Kit Carson stammered. "She was our pet."

Charles and Willy, startled by the fact that everyone was looking daggers at them, were about to walk off when Hugh recovered himself sufficiently to mention the fate of Teddy Tomball, a man acknowledged by all to be a very superior wagon master, after which it was Charlie Bent's time to be upset. There was just time, in his view, for the wagons to make it across the barren lands without the handicap of seriously bad weather; but that was hardly the only consideration. Teddy Tomball had not been sent to Taos only so that he could indulge his taste for dancing with plump señoritas. He had been sent to collect a cartful of silver work from the pueblos along the Rio Grande. It was Charles Bent's opinion that pueblo silver would soon catch on with their customers in the East. Belts hung with conchas of silver, heavy rings with turquoise stones set in them would someday be fetching a pretty price once they were distributed to fashionable merchants in Cincinnati or Philadelphia. The loss of reliable Teddy Tomball was bad enough, but the loss of a cartful of salable silver was an outrage that had Charles Bent hopping mad. None of the merchants in Santa Fe, Mexican or American, would be averse to fleecing the Bents should they get the chance. Where was their silver now? Charlie tried to question Hugh Glass in detail, but Hugh was not much help. He kept breaking into loud sobs at the memory of the dead bear cub. When asked if he had seen a cart, or any silver, Hugh—in Charlie's experience a tricky old fellow himself—grew extremely vague.

"I didn't see no cart," he insisted, "and didn't even know the dead man was Teddy until they turned him over."

Even when primed with a cup of brandy, Hugh Glass was little help. In no time he drank himself into a stupor and stumbled off to have a nap in the rear of the blacksmith's shop.

Under the circumstances, Charlie felt the need of an immediate consultation with his partners, Willy and St. Vrain.

"We need that silver—you better go, Vrain," Charlie said. "They trust you in Taos."

St. Vrain shrugged. "The silver is gone, and you're wrong about the trust," he said. "No one trusts anyone in Taos."

"We need that silver," Charlie repeated.

"Dern it, you've said that sixteen times," Willy scolded. "It's gone, Charlie—what you ought to be thinking of now is who's going to lead this wagon train to Saint Louis."

"That's simple, you are," Charlie said. "I'm getting married in two weeks—I can't do it," Charlie continued. "And I need to keep Vrain here to help out with the politics."

Willy had expected some such answer—his brother could always be counted on to pick him for irksome tasks—and struggling across the plains, with winter coming, drought already there, and the Indians troublesome, was as irksome as any task could be. In his opinion it was already too late in the season to safely start such a journey; and the reason it was late in the season was that Charlie kept cramming peltries and anything else he thought might sell into the wagons. Six wagons would have been plenty; eight were too many to protect.

"I don't want to go," Willy said, though without heat. The wagons were loaded and ready; somebody would have to lead them, or a whole season's profits would be lost.

"I'd send Kit but the little fool's getting married too," Charlie explained.

"Weddings can be postponed," Willy pointed out.

"Not this one—the governor's coming," Charlie reminded him.

"I'll go if I can have Jimmy Snow to help me," Willy said—he saw no reasonable way out of the dilemma.

"Jimmy would do—but his wife's with child," Charlie said. "He may not want to leave her. Why not take Jimmy Bridger?"

"Nope, I need Jimmy Snow," Willy insisted. "He's the Sin Killer—the Indians know better than to crowd him. At least the Cheyenne won't, nor the Osage."

"For that matter you could take both Jimmys," Charlie went on. "I have no reason to keep Jimmy Bridger here all winter, eating my grub. He eats enough for five or six men—it's a pointless expense. Take 'em both."

"I won't—Jim Bridger's too unpredictable," Willy said, firmly. "He don't follow nothing but his own nose. He's likely to turn off and head for Texas, or China. I won't have him."

Charles didn't argue the point. Jim Bridger *was* known among the mountain men for his abrupt, even whimsical departures from whatever route he had been set.

"What if that bossy English girl won't let Jimmy Snow go?" he asked.

"Jimmy may *be* married but he don't *look* married," Willy told him. "You look a dern sight more married and you ain't even had the wedding yet."

Charlie sulked at that. There was no doubt that Maria's hurtful action with the pot had cost him a certain amount of face—also, though he tried not to show it, a certain amount of confidence. He had assumed that once Maria had agreed to marry him, she would comport herself properly, become a docile wife. But now he wasn't so sure, and besides that, there was the expense of a big wedding to be borne. With the English occupying the main suite of rooms, the governor of New Mexico would have to be housed in a first-class tent, which was even then being set up in the courtyard, as far from the English quarters as possible, so as to minimize friction between the testy old Lord Berrybender and the equally testy governor. The governor was bringing a military escort, which was only prudent, but there was no guarantee that he wouldn't turn it on the Bents. Relations with the Mexican government were never entirely smooth—it was mostly through St. Vrain's diplomacy that mutual distrust was kept at a handleable level.

Under the circumstances the last thing Charles Bent needed was to lose a cartful of silver—and all because the otherwise trustworthy Teddy Tomball had been too fond of dancing. It was vexatious, all of it, but one thing Charles Bent had learned was not to waste time brooding about matters that could not be changed. Action was what had got him what he had—action would enable him to get more, and to secure it. The eight wagons were ready to move out. It was time to start them.

Charlie was headed across the courtyard to put a proposition to Jim Snow when he saw, to his intense vexation, that his brother Willy was mounted and almost out the gate of the stockade. With a roar Charlie just managed to stop him. Willy, looking annoyed, turned his horse and trotted over to his brother.

"What in hell do you want now?" Willy asked.

"I want to know where you think you're going—that's what!"

"To visit my wife, where else?" Willy told him. "I'm going to see Owl. You didn't suppose I'd head off to Saint Louis without visiting my wife first, did you?"

"But the wagons are ready to start—can't you see that?" Charlie protested.

"So? Do you suppose I intend to walk every step of the way with them?" Willy countered. "Hire Jimmy Snow, get him started, and tell him I'll catch up with him in three days. Nobody's likely to bother him in that length of time."

Charlie would have liked to pull Willy off the horse and give him a good thrashing, but of course there were several idlers watching, so he shrugged and turned away.

In a moment Willy was out the gate and gone, heading for the Cheyenne village where Owl Woman lived with her family—as a respectable young woman of the Cheyenne she had found it impossible to tolerate the cramped, close ways of the whites. She had spent only two nights in the trading post—she did not like the smells of closed-in people and had insisted on returning to the plains, where the cleansing winds soon blew away bad odors. Owl Woman was very fond of her husband, Willy Bent, but that was no reason to lead a smelly, closed-in life, with a lot of terrible odors in one's nose. Owl Woman, rather fastidious, didn't see why she should change her healthy way of living for one that was obviously not as good.

53

Tasmin had been yawning . . .

" G o ! Go! Go immediately! You have my fondest blessings!" Tasmin said, when Jim came into the room and told her that Charles Bent had just offered him money to lead the goods caravan back to Saint Louis—or, if not all the way to Saint Louis, at least to the Missouri River, by which point the worst dangers would have been passed. She had stretched out on her bed, attempting to read Mr. Goldsmith's *The Vicar of Wakefield*, a copy of which had been discovered in the trading post—Tasmin found the work so bland and tedious that she had laid it aside and was about to nap when her husband entered. Monty and Talley had been taken by Little Onion to inspect a tiny lamb which the sheepherders had brought into the trading post, judging it too weak to survive outside.

Before the drowsiness induced by Mr. Goldsmith's bland prose had come over her, Tasmin had been vaguely wishing that Pomp might appear. She had been thinking restless, vaguely carnal thoughts. But it was Jim, not Pomp, who entered to inform her that he had just been offered a job that would take him away from her for two months.

"I didn't make no promises about Saint Louis—just to help get them to the river," Jim said. "Once they're on the river, Willy can manage it well enough, I expect."

Of course, Charles Bent *had* pressed him to go all the way, the reason being that he considered Jim's judgment, on the whole, to be better than his brother's. But Jim remembered how irked Tasmin had been when he left her while she was pregnant with Monty. He knew she would be irked again if he was gone when the second child came—but he felt he could easily make it to the Missouri River and back with time to spare—and Charlie had offered him more money than he had ever expected to make. It had become more and more obvious to Jim that he would need to begin to earn money at some point. Sooner or later he and Tasmin would probably find themselves in a place where the frontiersman's subsistence skills were not enough. Here was a chance to earn cash, something he had rarely had before.

Tasmin had been yawning when Jim entered—he supposed she would be angry, as she generally was when he proposed to leave. The other two times he had just gone off—this time he thought he had better deliver the news himself. He was very surprised when Tasmin indulged in another great yawn and merely waved her hand, as if his impending departure was a thing of little moment.

"I knew as soon as we got here and I saw all this bustle that you'd soon be leaving," she told him. "You don't enjoy company much, Jimmy—it's rather amazing that you still seem to like me. Besides, there's really no reason why you should spend the winter watching my belly get bigger—it can't be a particularly attractive sight."

Tasmin was right—the bustle of the trading post did irritate him—but that was not the main reason he had accepted Charlie Bent's offer. The main reason was money.

"It's not your belly, it's just the wages," he said. "With two little ones we'll be needing cash."

"That we will—if we live," Tasmin said, feeling her spirits sink. She had rarely felt more mixed, more confused. Her first thought, when Jim announced his news, had been a wicked one: with Jim gone she could at last have a shot at Pomp in reasonable privacy. With Jim gone perhaps she could coax Pomp into being a lover. He could be a wonderful lover, she felt, if she could just get him started.

And yet it was only Jim she felt really safe with; she was touched by the fact that he had broken his pattern. Instead of letting her find out from some of the men that he was leaving, he had taken the trouble to inform her himself, and had even explained that he was leaving in order to earn money that his family would in time surely need.

All this bespoke concern; it was a development she would certainly have welcomed happily a little earlier in their marriage, as any wife would have.

And yet, now, her first thought had been vain, selfish, adulterous. She wanted her lover, and yet she could not but feel new admiration for her husband. What could be rarer than to have a husband change his ways for the sake of his wife and children?

For a moment Tasmin felt so crowded with confusing feelings that tears came into her eyes. Jim saw them and felt he might as well go. At least he had informed her of his intention, as he had been asked to. But when he turned to go Tasmin grabbed him, pulled him down, and hugged him tightly, her cheeks now shining with tears.

"We'll be wanting a house, I guess," he said, hoping to soothe her. "Might find a cheap one in Taos."

"Not Taos—Santa Fe. I've such a preference for capitals, if there's one handy," she said, hoping she hadn't offended him by brushing aside his suggestion.

Jim was amused by Tasmin's switch—sobbing one minute, she became picky the next.

"All right, Santa Fe," he said, hoping to leave her happy. Mindful that Charlie Bent was an impatient man, he gave Tasmin a quick kiss and started to get up, but Tasmin was staring at him in obvious invitation.

"Shut the door—a little peck won't do—let's have a good rut," she said. "I know your Mr. Bent is very impatient, but there *are* situations where wives come first. Besides, by the time you come back I'll be so big you'll hardly be able to get in me."

"Oh, I doubt that," Jim said.

But he obeyed, got up, and closed the door.

Tasmin's habit of speaking bluntly about conjugal matters still took him aback. And she was just as direct physically as she was in her speech. She simply extracted him from his pants and handled him until he was nearly ready to shoot before allowing him entry. Then, once he *had* shot and they were done, she locked him in with her legs in such a way as to suggest that perhaps they *weren't* done.

"Stay awhile, my sweet—stay awhile," Tasmin said. Her eyes seemed to grow very wide at such times. Jim knew Charlie Bent would be fretting—nonetheless he stayed awhile.

the lamb gave a surprisingly loud bleat . . .

M O N T Y never knew when his father might show up and tickle him in his fat little ribs, reducing him to a cascade of giggles. Often, if Talley happened to be nearby, his father would distribute his tickling impartially, tickling Talley too, while Talley's mother watched and smiled. Talley would giggle so uncontrollably that he would grow red in the face and have to gulp in order to get his breath.

On this occasion both boys had been absorbed in an inspection of the tiny lamb the sheepherders had rescued. When they reached out their hands to touch the white, soft fur, the lamb gave a surprisingly loud bleat, causing them at once to jerk their hands away.

Then Monty's father came, and his mother. Across the courtyard the great oxen were mooing. Monty feared the oxen but could not stop looking at them. Then there was a round of tickling—his father held Monty high above his head, and spun him round until he was dizzy. When his father sat him down Monty toppled into Little Onion's lap, where he often napped.

"I consider small children to be the only honest people," Vicky Kennet remarked. Since reaching the trading post her cheeks had filled out, her beauty returned. Her hair was very long again.

"I suppose they may be the only sincere people," Tasmin agreed. "The poor little things can't help it."

Jim, about to lead the small caravan out of the gate, turned and waved at his wife and son.

"Wave at your father, Monty," Tasmin commanded. When Monty just looked puzzled she held up his small hand and waved it for him.

"Say bye-bye," Tasmin ordered, but Monty did not say bye-bye. Although he was interested in the small lamb, he wished Little Onion would take him away. When his mother spoke to him in a certain tone he felt confused and didn't know what to do. He didn't know why she insisted on waving his small hand at his father.

"Now I've confused him, as usual," Tasmin admitted. "Look at him, hopelessly trapped in his small integrity."

"But it doesn't last long, this early honesty," she said. "I was an accomplished liar by the time I was five, and the skill has stood me in good stead."

She smiled, and Vicky smiled too.

"How else is one to manage two men?" she asked, smiling.

"How else is one to manage even one?"

Monty, tired of the lamb, yawned and began to wave. It became a new trick he could do—he waved at his father, he waved at his mother—he waved and waved, giggling at his own brilliance. He even waved at the frightening oxen as they were going out the gate. He waved at Talley, who waved at him. Delighted with this new skill, the little boys waved and waved.

55

No wife could possibly be as cozy . . .

"QUIT pestering me, Owl," Willy Bent muttered, to his wife. It was just dawn—soon he would have to pull himself out of his warm robes and away from his even warmer, bright-eyed wife and head across the frosty prairie to join Jim Snow and do what he could to see that the big eight-team caravan, packed with a fortune in trade goods, made its way safely to the company's warehouse in Saint Louis. It was never easy to leave Owl. No wife could possibly be as cozy and good as she was; it seemed that she anticipated his every need and did her best to satisfy it before he himself even realized that he was needing anything. It might be a good rubbing with some fragrant grease, or it might be tender tidbits of dog, which Owl plucked from the stew pot and fed him with her fingers. It might be some new moccasins, which fit perfectly, or it might be some husband-and-wife activity, which was usually followed on Willy's part by a long, deep nap.

Willy Bent was happily convinced that he had the best wife in the world: a pert, pretty wife who in his opinion was much to be preferred to the long-legged bossy English girl Jim Snow had married. Owl was a steadier companion than the violent Mexican beauty his own brother was about to take to wife. Willy could not imagine that Owl would ever embarrass him to the extent of hitting him in the head with a heavy pot, as Maria had hit Charlie.

And yet, of course, no wife was likely to be entirely perfect or always easy to accommodate. This morning, as always, disagreement arose as he was enjoying the coziness a few more minutes, trying to work himself up to departure.

"I can't be an Indian all the time, dern it, Owl," Willy protested.

"You are an Indian all the time," Owl reminded him, in a pleasant voice. "My own father, Yellow Wolf, made you a member of our band. My father wants to take us on a buffalo hunt, and I want you to stay with us—we're going on a buffalo hunt."

Willy didn't answer. It was true that Yellow Wolf had made him a member of the band, but it still didn't mean he was free to live the Indian life all the time. He had begged Owl to come live at the fort, but she wouldn't—she didn't like the smells, or really anything about the white man's ways. It was a puzzle to her how her Willy, whom she loved deeply, who had tried both ways of living, could not see how clearly superior the Cheyenne way was. And yet, with the beautiful prairies all around them, he still insisted on going away to do some foolish white man's business of some kind.

"I like being with the tribe," Willy assured her, not for the first time. "Maybe I can spend all summer with your people next year, if Charlie can find someone else to supervise the hauling. But I still ain't an Indian and there's times when I have to go to work."

"You're an Indian, my father says so," Owl repeated—she was stubborn when she had her mind set on something.

Willy thought it would have been wiser of the Almighty to create women without tongues, since even Owl, the most agreeable woman he knew, still didn't scruple to use her tongue to create unease in his breast.

Owl didn't press her case, but she didn't like it that Willy was always wearying himself trying to please his brother. She had seen for herself how happy Willy was when he could be with the tribe for a few weeks, hunting, racing horses, letting her tend to his needs. Willy never got a bad look on his face at those times; some nights he slept so deeply that even the bright morning sun didn't wake him. Owl felt that if she could just keep him with the tribe long enough, as they moved around following the buffalo herds and enjoying life, Willy would soon lose the habit of thinking so much about money. Of course, it was all right that Willy and his brother had brought white man's goods to the People. She herself loved colorful beads and cloths, blue particularly, and was quick to put to use the various awls and needles Willy brought her. But all it took to procure those goods was a few skins, and with buffalo so plentiful, skins were easily obtained. Just because the whites had attractive goods was no reason to exchange the cool, airy Cheyenne life for some smelly trading post. In her opinion, being crowded together, as white people were, led to disputes and quarrels that were unlikely to arise where people were free to spread out and go where they pleased.

Still, when Willy got a big frown on his face, Owl desisted. She gave him a tickle or two in an intimate place and then popped out of their robes and helped him get his gear together. There was no point in trying to stop a husband from going away—of course, even Cheyenne husbands often went away when they felt like raiding a little, or just riding around without the impediment of womenfolk.

Indian or no Indian, Willy could never leave his Owl without an awareness of how much he was going to miss her in the chill, hectic months of trekking that lay ahead. Never once had he made the long trip across to Westport Landing without various kinds of trouble presenting themselves. Sooner or later Indians of one band or another would show up, demanding presents and hoping to steal a horse or two, or a gun. The weather would either be too hot or too cold, too wet or too dry. Sometimes animals would sicken inexplicably; other times men would turn up gimpy. But despite the troubles and perils of the road, the company was prospering. They knew the route well now, and were more efficient trekkers than their rivals. Willy wasn't quite as single-minded about commerce as his brother was, but Willy wasn't lazy, either, and he meant to be rich someday.

Owl stood demurely by Willy as he saddled up and prepared to leave.

"I'll be quick to track you down when I get back," Willy assured her. Owl did not like for him to touch her in public, so he gave her the briefest of hugs, mounted, and loped away.

For an hour or more Willy traveled with a lump in his throat. He had a lonely feeling and also a worried feeling. Owl could say all she wanted to about the good Cheyenne way of life, but there were no guarantees in the Cheyenne way of life, or the white way either. It was common knowledge that smallpox had wiped out the Mandans and the Arikaras, strong tribes both. The same disease might come to the Cheyenne—besides which, the Cheyenne were a fighting people. Owl might get snatched in a raid, or killed in a battle, in which case he might never again lie with her in their comfortable robes, enjoying being man and wife. Willy always worried when he left Owl—his mind seemed to conjure up nothing but bad images, some of them rather unlikely. Buffalo were unusually plentiful that fall, and the old bulls were unreliable. What if Owl were off doing some chore and got gored by a buffalo? Also, there were panthers that lurked around Indian camps, hoping to snatch a colt or a young mare— what if one got Owl? Such thoughts were so worrisome that it was all Willy could do to keep from turning back—and he might, in defiance of all commercial good sense, have turned back had he not spotted a horseman far ahead on the prairie. The horse was white, an unusual thing in itself. As Willy approached—not before checking his pistol and his rifle—he saw an old Indian man, sitting on a scrap of blanket, chanting. A white man sat astride the horse. As he came closer Willy saw that the white man wore a look of dejection. Perhaps he had been traveling with the old Indian long enough to grow tired of listening to him pray.

When the old Indian finished praying and stood up, Willy recognized him—it was old Greasy Lake, a prophet he and Charlie had encountered several times in their first years as trappers on the upper Missouri. The old man had even helped them out once by informing them of the approach of a large band of Pie-gans. Willy would not have expected to meet old Greasy—a man of splotchy complexion—so far to the south.

"Hello, Greasy, who's your friend?" Willy asked, nodding toward the white man, who was gaunt, with dark circles under his eyes.

"I am Clam de Paty, monsieur," the white man said. "I am from France and I want now to go back."

"I don't know about France, but I expect we can get you to Saint Louis," Willy told him. "I have eight wagons up ahead—we're Saint Louis bound."

"He was one of the men who could fly," Greasy informed him, nodding at Clam. "He was with the Sin Killer and the Broken Hand and all the English. I don't know where they are."

"I do," Willy said. "They're with my brother at our new trading post, all except Jimmy Snow, who's helping me with the wag-ons."

"You could make the trading post in a day, if you'd care to, sir," he added.

Clam shook his head. He did not want to rejoin the English and the Americans—he wanted to be out of the wild, to live again in a place where there were cafés and theaters, newspa-pers and *jolies laides*. Yet he wasn't in such a place: the wild still surrounded him, and he was almost too tired to hope. If there was a chance to make Saint Louis, he wanted to take it.

In late afternoon, as dusk spread over the prairies, they caught up with the caravan—the white horse turned out to belong to Greasy Lake—he was merely sharing it with the white man.

When Jim Snow, like Willy Bent, expressed surprise at finding Greasy Lake, the old prophet revealed his reason for traveling south.

"It's because of the white buffalo," he told them.

"A white buffalo?" Willy said. "Now that's something I've never seen, and I've seen a passel of buffalo."

"I've not seen one either. Where is it, Uncle?" Jim asked.

"With the Comanches," Greasy Lake told them. "It was born on the night when many stars fell—it is still just a calf. All my life I have waited for this white buffalo, and now it has come."

Though the old man accepted a little food, he refused to stay the night. He mounted his white horse and rode on by moonlight.

Clam de Paty ate only a mouthful or two of venison. He was really too tired to chew. A space was made for him in one of the wagons and he was soon asleep.

Willy and Jim sat up most of the night, not saying much, just watching the fire flicker. Willy had a question he wanted to ask Jim, and yet when he tried to come out with it, he grew embarrassed and kept putting it off. And yet, the question nagged him so that he finally asked it.

"Do you miss your wife much, Jimmy?" he mumbled, finally.

Jim Snow *was* surprised. Why would Willy Bent care whether he missed Tasmin? He remembered how wide Tasmin's eyes had been when they made love just before his departure.

"Some," he allowed, finally. "I miss her some."

What he mainly wished was that Willy Bent was less talkative.

"Then you're like me—I'm already missing my Owl," Willy admitted. He felt better for having said it.

He was hoping Jimmy Snow would talk a little about the way it felt to miss a wife, but Jimmy didn't. He just stared into the fire—his manner seemed so stiff that Willy did not pursue the matter.

In the night Clam de Paty had a painful dream. In the dream his old colleague Benjamin Hope-Tipping was in their balloon, hovering over Paris. Now Ben was over Notre Dame, over the Invalides, over the Seine. Ben was trying to make the balloon descend, so Clam could climb aboard. Clam went running along, underneath the balloon, from which Ben had dangled a small ladder for Clam to climb up. But the balloon never quite came low enough—the small ladder dangled just out of reach. Clam jumped for it but missed; he jumped for it a second time, but missed again. Too tired to jump a third time, he fell back and watched helplessly as the balloon rose and rose, above the Hôtel de Ville, above Notre Dame, above Montmartre. Clam could no longer see Ben; the soft shadows of Paris were replaced by a wide white sky, as vast and empty as the prairies. The sky turned the color of blue ice—in it great yellow bears were flying like birds. The bears had long beaks, like the birds that had hit their balloon. Clam squeezed his eyes shut; he did not want to see the long-beaked bears, or the ice blue sky. He felt a swirling around him, he felt birds beating him with their wings, then he felt nothing.

When Willy tried to shake Clam de Paty awake in the morning to offer him coffee, he at once found that he was shaking a cold, stiff leg, the leg of a man who had died during the night.

"I guess he was just plumb wore out from all the traveling," Willy said, as he and Jim dug the grave.

"The man said before that he was finished—he wasn't lying," Jim said.

56

It was chill on the parapet . . .

I T seemed to Venetia Kennet, now Lady Berrybender, that she had never played the cello so well. With no trekking to do, she was free to practice; though her technique was undoubtedly rusty, her tone seemed to her to have deepened. In the evenings particularly she liked to sit on the parapet and play, the somber sounds of the cello mingling with the other sounds that came at dusk: the bleating of sheep, the neighing of horses, the calls of night birds. It was chill on the parapet, and yet Vicky warmed as she played. Sometimes, coming in late from a hunt, Lord Berry-bender would hear the strains before he was even within the gates.

"Fine girl, my Vic, fine girl," he often said—sometimes he even wept.

"Don't know what I'd do without her," he mumbled.

"You don't have to do without her," Signor Claricia pointed out, with a wink at Amboise d'Avigdor. "She's your wife."

"By God, you're right—keep forgetting she's no longer a mistress," Lord B. said. "Threatened to tear my throat out at one point, but now she's docile as a kitten, on the whole."

Signor Aldo Claricia did not think the cellist was docile as a kitten, or ever would be, but when he heard her stroking her cello he too was sometimes moved to tears. The music made him long for olive trees and little yellow songbirds and carriage wheels rolling over cobblestones. Would he ever see an olive tree again? Aldo Claricia was far from sure. But when he heard the cello he could not but remember the many beauties of his home.

Another listener who invariably wept when Vicky played the cello was Maria Jaramillo; if the concert was a long one she would usually be sobbing uncontrollably by the end of it, to the puzzlement of her little sister, Josefina, herself happy as a lark, mainly because in only a few days she would be marrying her Kit.

"Why, Maria? How can you be so sad when it's almost time for the wedding?" Josefina asked.

"I don't know—leave me alone—what if I made a mistake?" Maria sobbed. It was not lost on her that the one person in the post who was wholly unmoved by the rich, sad sounds of the cello was her husband-to-be, Charles Bent, who generally did his accounts just before dinner—Charlie let nothing interfere with the vital work of his accounts. It seemed to Maria that he might have let the accounts wait, for once. He might have come to their little room by the stable and asked her to dance, or tried to kiss her, or at least held her hand.

"What if I'm not happy when we marry?" Maria asked, grabbing a mirror to assure herself that her beauty, which had brought her nothing but compliments her whole life, was not lost. The mirror did reassure her—though, at the moment, she was rather puffy from crying. It irked her that her plain little sister was so radiant with happiness at the prospect of marrying her Kit. Maria wanted to box Josefina. She wanted to feel what Josefina felt, and yet she didn't.

"The governor is coming in three days," Josefina reminded her. "You better not cry like this when the governor is here— Papa will be angry."

"Go away," Maria ordered. But she knew that Josefina's warning was accurate: the wedding was approaching. She had allowed herself to be put in the path of an august event and would now have to play her part in it as best she could. And yet, when Josefina left, Maria lay on her narrow bed and sobbed, troubled by the great uncertainty she felt. She had said yes to Charles Bent, but would she like him, once the deed was done? Why had she bargained away her freedom? Why couldn't she be happy, as her sister was? None of the questions really had answers—hearing the Englishwoman's music only made her sadder and more perplexed.

"I do believe that's Handel she's playing," Father Geoff remarked to Tasmin. They stood on the balcony, not far from Vicky. The goats and sheep were being brought into the courtyard for safety—several of the goats wore little bells, which tinkled in melancholy accompaniment to the notes of the cello.

"What's the longest spell of happiness you can remember enjoying, Geoff?" Tasmin inquired. "Think hard before you answer."

"If you really want hard thinking, I fear I'm not the man for you," the priest warned her. "But I imagine about twenty minutes is as long as we mortals can stay in a state of pure happiness. Can you copulate for twenty minutes, Tasmin?"

Tasmin shrugged. "Possibly, if I am indulged—but I'm not indulged," Tasmin allowed. "My husband's an honest rambler, he can rarely be persuaded to tarry for twenty minutes, but Pomp is something worse—he's so elusive that I'm not sure why I'm still bothering to try."

"Ah me, the slippery fellow's eluded you again—gone off with St. Vrain to attempt to recover the Bents' lost silver—and just when your husband's gone off too," the priest said. "I suspect you thought that at last you'd have Pomp to yourself."

That was exactly what Tasmin *had* expected—it was one reason she had immediately acquiesced to Jim's departure, only to have Pomp hurry off almost at the same time as Jim. It had made her so angry that she had kicked a footstool, and now had a swollen big toe to show for it. Why would *Pomp* leave, just when they might have enjoyed a bit of privacy?

"I've sometimes felt that your young Monsieur Charbonneau would make a better priest than I make," Father Geoffrin told her. "What's certain is that I'd make a better libertine than him. You wouldn't find me running off to look for a cartful of ugly silver if I had white loveliness available to me."

Tasmin shrugged again.

"I'm no longer very white, thanks to the sun," Tasmin reminded him. "And I'm pregnant. Perhaps that puts him off."

Below them the two little boys were playing with their tiny lamb. Signor Claricia had become fond of the two little toddlers and had made them whistles, which they blew piercingly and incessantly. Pomp himself had made the lamb a collar and a lead, so the boys could lead him. The lamb's only escape was to collapse from exhaustion, which it did often, bleating weakly. Yet when the little boys proposed to let it alone for a bit the lamb followed them, just as the bear cubs once had.

"Look, Tasmin—I believe I see an *amitié* forming," Father Geoff said. He was referring to the bond which seemed to have lately formed between Signor Claricia and Little Onion. The two could often be seen sitting together in the evening, listening to Vicky Kennet play the cello. Tasmin had noticed this bond herself. Signor Claricia, who had been very gloomy since the death of his friend Señor Yanez, had perked up a little of late, partly because Little Onion had taken it upon herself to assist the quiet gentleman in small ways—mending his moccasins when they frayed, or finding him a better pipe. In return Signor Claricia had given the modest young Indian woman a tortoiseshell comb. It was mainly a silent bond—Little Onion had acquired a few words of English; Signor Claricia had not many more. And yet it was clear that the two derived a certain comfort from merely sitting together, quietly observing the life of the post.

"I don't think I know a better person than our Onion," Tasmin said—and she meant it. "She has been given very little choice in her life, and yet her behavior meets the highest standards. Those two little boys would vex a saint, and yet she is rarely cross with them—and she's never cross with us Berrybenders, though we're certainly capable of vexing a great many saints. She's neither a troublemaker like me nor a cynic like yourself."

"Goodness in human beings seems to be where you find it," Geoff said. "I too have the greatest admiration for Little Onion. I had that boil on my foot and she made a salve to cure it."

"Perhaps she's so good because she's never read a novel," Tasmin suggested. "You and I, of course, have read far too many and they've done much damage to our characters, I suspect. I have no particular right to Little Onion's loyalty, and yet she's given it."

The two of them looked down at the quiet couple.

"Selfishness in human beings is where you find it, too," Tasmin said. "It's when I think of our Onion that I feel worst about myself. I ought to be modest, like she is, and yet I'm not. And I ought not to care where Pomp Charbonneau goes, or what he does—and yet I care intensely."

"I wonder if Jim would let Little Onion go?" the priest asked. "She and our lonely Italian might make a promising couple, if Little Onion were free."

Tasmin had begun to wonder the same thing.

"Of course Jimmy would let her go," Tasmin said. "I'm all the wife he wants and maybe more wife than he wants. But there's Monty to consider. He loves Little Onion absolutely. He'd be stricken if she left."

"Well, it seems we'll be here all winter," the priest remarked. "I guess we'll see what we see."

Impulsively, since he was standing so near, he tried to give Tasmin a kiss, but she anticipated the move and drew her head back just slightly.

"None of that, you disgusting wretch," Tasmin warned. "I'm in a bad mood already and even if I were in a better one I wouldn't want to kiss you. If you want kisses, why don't you try Eliza—I've suggested it before."

"It's those great bosoms—the thought of them frightens me," Father Geoff admitted.

At that Tasmin walked off. Discussing carnal matters with Father Geoff was not an activity likely to raise her spirits or lessen her self-annoyance. She knew she ought to give up on Pomp Charbonneau, and yet she could not bring herself to.

As she was passing the room where Mary stayed she happened to see her sister sitting on a low chair, silent, perhaps even dejected; tears shone on her cheeks.

"Hey! What's wrong with you?" Tasmin asked. Behind her she could hear the two little boys, excited by their ability to mount the stairs one by one. They were being followed by Kate Berry-bender, who sometimes condescended to play with them.

"My virginity is taken—Piet has gone to ask Papa for my hand," Mary said glumly.

"Then why are you sad?"

Mary gulped a little before replying.

"Piet got dreadfully out of breath while he was about it," Mary told her. "His face turned quite purple—for a moment I was afraid he might die. I rather think the brambles might be a better method, on the whole. I should wish to die at once if I lose my Piet."

Kate and the boys made a noisy arrival.

"Why's this person crying?" Kate at once wanted to know. Monty clamored to be picked up, while Talley ran to his mother, who was at once forced to stop playing her cello. Tasmin, thinking it was not a good time to explain to Kate why Mary was sad, said nothing.

"I don't wish to speak to this brat right now—you tell her, Tassie," Mary said.

"The flesh is heir to many sorrows," Tasmin said to Kate. "Why don't you go put these little boys to bed, so their mothers can enjoy a moment of peace?"

"*You* haven't been looking after them anyway," Kate pointed out. "*I* have been looking after them, along with Little Onion and Signor Claricia."

"Need you brag?" Tasmin asked. Mary's eyes were still leaking tears. Tasmin thought she might offer a few words of comfort, if only the tiresome Kate would move along.

"It's unfortunate that Mr. James Snow is not here," Kate remarked. "I don't like it that he's gone. If you were a better wife you'd know how to keep him close."

"Unfortunately I'm not a better wife," Tasmin informed her. "I'm a thoroughly troublesome person, though hardly more troublesome than yourself, you impertinent midge. Get out of here and let your sister have her cry. A good cry now and then is something we all need, as I believe I explained to you before."

With a frown Kate grabbed Monty and, though he wailed in protest, carried him inside.

"I wouldn't worry too much about Piet," Tasmin told Mary. "The conjugal process will soon grow easier, once you've had a little practice."

"It was rather a jerky business—somewhat like hiccups. I stopped but Piet couldn't."

Below her in the thickening dusk Tasmin could just see Little Onion standing with Signor Claricia. The blacksmith had just pumped his bellows; the forge flared brightly for a moment. Two billy goats from the large herd, annoyed with one another, were butting heads, as the young Ute woman and the old Italian stood watching, not speaking, not touching, and yet at ease in their comfortable proximity. When the billy goats tired of jousting, Little Onion and Signor Claricia walked off toward the big kitchen—no doubt Little Onion would soon fill her friend a plate of whatever Cook had made. Tasmin felt a stab of envy, followed by remorse. Wasn't that what she wanted herself, a friend to stand close to her, serenely watching whatever there was to watch? And couldn't she have had that very thing with Pomp, if she hadn't insisted on forcing passion on a man who didn't want it? But she had done what she'd done—would she now ever have a friend to stand with her at dusk, watching two goats butt their heads?

57

Outside they could hear the music . . .

"I MERELY hoped you'd treat me like a woman," Tasmin said, weeping.

Outside they could hear the music and sounds of the wedding feast. Musicians had been hauled all the way from Santa Fe, costing Charles Bent money he was reluctant to spend; but with the governor there, for once he dared not economize. In the end he had ignored Maria's objections and invited the English to the wedding. Lord Berrybender was a nobleman, after all—he and his family could not be simply ignored. Wine and champagne were flowing—even before the nuptials began Hugh Glass got so drunk that he rolled off the parapet and broke three ribs—though even that didn't keep him from dancing. Lord Berrybender was no soberer—soon he was hopping around on one foot, attempting to dance.

Tasmin cared for none of it. She was correct with the governor and the various dignitaries and only a little cool with Kit Carson, whom she considered to be something of a traitor for having married without her permission. His bride, Josefina, was such a friendly, winning little person that Tasmin unbent and kissed her. Maria, the haughty sister, looked rather chalky—she had cried all night and had had to powder heavily.

Horse races were to follow the dancing; the handsome Monsieur St. Vrain was expected to win them all, but Tasmin didn't stay for the races. Once she had drunk the proper number of toasts she went at once to Pomp and persuaded him to follow her upstairs, into her bedroom, where a good fire had been laid. With her door firmly locked behind them, well above the clamor of the festivities, Tasmin was determined to have a long, slow, amorous joust of the sort she had been wanting ever since she had fallen in love with Pomp. At last, she thought, I'll have you—and Pomp followed without reluctance—at first he looked rather amused, which was not exactly what she wanted. Tasmin was determined, now that she really had Pomp alone, to break through the amusement and the politeness and arouse a passionate Pomp. She was ready to do anything—hit him, bite him, fondle him, probe, kiss—anything to break down his pleasant, accommodating reserve. She had had enough of merely being tolerated, obliged. She meant to be *wanted,* as much as this man could *want.*

And yet their fiesta was ill timed; just when Tasmin wanted them to be slow, they were quick. But Tasmin refused to quit. She wouldn't let Pomp up. She meant to keep him in the stained and tangled bedsheets all day and all night, if she could. She bit and she caressed—she insisted on long kisses, for it was when they kissed that she was able to feel that she had at last found him. With her mouth on his she whispered that she loved him and he began to kiss back. He was a young man, easily rearoused after a short interval. Tasmin urged and they enjoyed a longer rut; she was beginning to feel that she knew how to please him—and yet finally she jumped out of bed so abruptly that a long spill of seed came trickling down her thigh; she stomped around the room naked, furious, hurt, sobbing in confusion. She stood in front of the fireplace for a moment and then slumped back on the bed and dried her tears with one of the too coarse sheets. Instead of being filled with feeling, as she had hoped to be, she felt drained of it—she felt blank, felt it was all impossible, couldn't understand why she always had to be the one to start the fiesta with this man—why must she do everything? If she wanted to be touched in a certain way she had to take his hand and move it, much as she had taken Monty's hand when she wanted him to wave at his father. Pomp was a grown man—why must she direct things as if they were actors on a stage?

"I guess I'm not learning very fast," Pomp said, wrapping her in his arms. Tasmin, angry, tried to shrug him off but he tightened his arms around her and held her. Too tired to go on the attack, she rested in his arms.

"I *want* you—it's not something I *learned*," Tasmin said, though listlessly. "It's something that is. I have no one to blame but myself. You told me that night on the Yellowstone that you were not really troubled by desire. I've merely been forcing myself upon you. Why should you want me? I'm married to Jim—and I'm pregnant, probably by you. I've made a thorough-going mess, married to a man who constantly leaves me and in love with you, another man, who refuses to arrive. Thank God for Little Onion—she has been more help to me than you and Jimmy put together."

Pomp didn't say anything, but he continued to hold her.

"I wasn't seeking expertise from you, though I wouldn't scorn it," Tasmin said. She had begun to feel comfortable in his arms, though, and when he kissed her lightly she didn't object. It showed that he *was* fond of her, at least—she had always known he was fond of her. Why had she been unable to leave it at that? But she hadn't, and now they were lovers, although only one of them was in love. If pressed, Pomp might claim otherwise, but that was loyalty, not love. Fond he was, loyal he was, attracted he could be, in love he was not. Now that she had touched and considered every part of his body, she could not allow herself to believe that Pomp was going to fall in love with her.

"It's very discouraging to a woman to have to force these things," Tasmin told him, trying not to sound reproachful—it was just something she wanted him to know.

Pomp continued to hold her—she was feeling more and more tired.

"What am I to do, Pomp?" she asked in a low voice. "Sooner or later, unless we're all killed, my father will hunt his way to an ocean where there are boats that go to Europe. By then I'll have my child by Jimmy and my child that I suspect is by you. *What* am I to do then? Stay with Jimmy Snow, who can't bear much domesticity? Pester you, a man who doesn't really need a woman? Leave you both and go home and marry some fop? Stay in America, where, sooner or later, I'll probably get scalped? At least you would fit in my world, if I do go back to England, as I must if my children are to be properly educated. I care for my Jimmy but there's no pretending he'd like England—he wouldn't put up with it for a week. And you don't really want this—*that's* not likely to change."

"That's a big bunch of questions," Pomp said. He looked at her fondly, and twined his fingers in hers.

"Yes . . . a bunch of questions, and you're not helping me answer any of them," Tasmin said.

She sighed, started to sit up, found that she lacked the energy, lay back.

"The worst of it is that I *do* love you, even if I have to teach you everything," she said. She reached for his crotch and held him, and was still holding him, her questions unresolved, when the two of them went to sleep.

58

Tasmin was sitting quietly . . .

T A S M I N was sitting quietly in her room with Vicky Kennet, the two of them passing a mirror back and forth, when the Mexican cavalry, forty-five strong, swept into the courtyard of the trading post. At first the two women tried to ignore the clatter. Both were contemplating cutting their hair, and for the same reason: resignation, utter resignation. Life—or at least romantic life—had arrived at a stalemate; neither woman could foresee a time when they could be happy with their lovers, Lord Berrybender in Vicky's case, Pomp Charbonneau in Tasmin's. The two women, amiable as sisters now, were agreed that they paid much too dearly for whatever driblets of pleasure they derived from these two men.

"Let's cut it off—let's be drab—they can hardly like us less," Tasmin complained. Then, intolerably vexed by the clatter from the courtyard, she strode across the room and flung open the door, meaning to shout down whoever was making all the noise below. How were ladies contemplating the decisive step of cutting their hair to be expected to complete their deliberations when there was such a racket outside?

When Tasmin yanked open the door she almost charged straight into two bayonets, which were attached to muskets

aimed at her. As a result of her momentum she only just avoided
having her bosom pricked. Both soldiers, though uniformed,
were mere boys; both looked shocked when Tasmin came charging at them. Both immediately lowered their muskets. Tasmin,
for her part, was so startled at being unexpectedly confronted
with naked bayonets that she dropped her mirror, which, fortunately, didn't break.

The boy soldiers who faced her seemed frightened, as if they,
not she, were under attack. She saw their legs trembling when
she stooped to pick up her mirror. Beyond them, down in the
courtyard, she could see a great many mounted soldiers milling
around. Her father had evidently been prevented from leaving
on his hunt. Red in the face with outrage, he was surrounded by
cavalrymen. Signor Claricia and Amboise d'Avigdor were with
him, the former looking resigned, the latter looking pale.

"Heigh-ho, Vicky—no barbering today," Tasmin told her.
"There's a bunch of soldiers here and they've made bold to interfere with Papa."

Before the two of them could leave the room to investigate, a
trim young officer stood in the doorway—after glancing around
the room to make sure no men were in hiding, he bowed cour-
teously to the ladies.

"I'm Lieutenant Molino, please forgive my discourtesy," he
said. "I'm afraid you are now to consider yourselves prisoners of
war."

"War? Us? What war?" Tasmin asked.

Lieutenant Molino, who was quite handsome, smiled at them
pleasantly—as if he himself was aware of the absurdity of what
he had just said.

"There are angry wars and polite wars," he said. "I hope this
will be a polite war. For the moment it would be best if you come
with me."

"Now? But we've not made our toilette," Tasmin protested.

"If I may say so, you both look very presentable," Lieutenant
Molino replied. "Right now Captain Reyes is about to make a
speech—his humor will not be improved if we keep him waiting."

He bowed again and swept his arm, indicating that the two of them were to go ahead of him.

"Let's go, Vicky—how exciting. I guess I ain't been a prisoner of war before," Tasmin said.

Once on her balcony, Tasmin saw that the whole courtyard was filled with Mexican soldiers, the sun glinting off their bayonets. All along the balcony the Berrybenders and their servants were being herded along by boy soldiers such as the two Tasmin had almost charged into. In the center of the courtyard, a small, wiry captain with a ridiculous plume on his hat sat on a large sorrel horse, impatiently popping a small quirt against his leg. Charles Bent, red in the face with vexation, was remonstrating with the captain, who appeared to be unmoved by whatever appeal Charles was making. Lord B., still in his buggy, was red in the face too, but he had stopped shouting and was attempting to follow the argument.

"This means Jimmy was right all along," Tasmin remarked, going down the steps. At the bottom Little Onion waited with Monty and Talley.

"Jimmy said we'd be arrested before we got to Santa Fe—now it seems he's proven right. And yet we're not very near to Santa Fe, and we're guests of the important Bents. After all, we just danced with the governor at the wedding. Surely we can't be intended for slaughter."

"It is a pity Monsieur St. Vrain left us," Buffum observed. "He is far more the diplomat than Mr. Bent."

St. Vrain had left that very morning, taking Hugh Glass and Jim Bridger with him, his object to scout out possible locations for a trading post on the South Platte.

"I expect this is just silliness of some sort," Tasmin said, picking up her son. "Papa will have to pay bribes, I expect—that's likely all it will come to."

"No, Tassie, look!" Buffum said. "They almost shot High Shoulders and now they are chaining him, along with Pomp and Mr. Fitzpatrick. If I hadn't begged High Shoulders not to fight, I fear they would have killed him."

Tasmin realized, with a chill, that her sister was right. Nearly half the Mexican soldiers were clustered around the blacksmith's forge, their rifles at the ready. High Shoulders was being chained first—Pomp and the Broken Hand were trying to calm him. Tasmin looked around for Kit but couldn't spot him. As soon as the English party was assembled, Captain Reyes began to speak, rapidly, angrily, and in Spanish. Charles Bent, looking grim, had stalked away—it was clear that it was only with difficulty that he controlled his temper.

At the smithy Pomp was now being chained. As soon as the captain finished speaking, three wagons were brought into the courtyard. Tasmin caught Pomp's eye—he did not seem disturbed, but when she started to walk over to him the soldiers looked at her menacingly. Lieutenant Molino stood nearby, so she approached him instead.

"I had hoped for a word with my friend Monsieur Charbonneau," she said. "Do you suppose that would be permitted?"

Lieutenant Molino shook his head.

"Monsieur Charbonneau is a particularly dangerous spy," the lieutenant told her. "You must not try to speak to him. You must leave him to his fate."

"Leave him to his fate? Surely that's rather portentous, Lieutenant," Tasmin said. "He's no spy at all. He's been our guide for the past year and a half."

"I'm only a soldier, madame," the young officer said. "I only know what I'm told, which is that Monsieur Jean Baptiste Charbonneau is a particularly dangerous spy."

"It's so odd that anyone could think so," Tasmin said. "We had a big wedding last week and Monsieur Charbonneau, the dangerous spy, danced frequently with the governor's wife—and many ladies of the capital as well. Why would the governor's wife allow herself to dance with a dangerous spy?"

Lieutenant Molino permitted himself a smile.

"I cannot speak for the governor's wife, or the other ladies," he said, "but if I were a spy like your friend, *I* would try to dance with the governor's wife. At a grand dance a woman, even a governor's wife, might become incautious. She might tell a clever spy exactly what he wants to know."

"I'm sure that's logical—it's just that it's wrong in Pomp's case," Tasmin assured him. "He's been so busy keeping us alive these past months that he can't have had time for spying. But I fear I'm trying your patience, Lieutenant. I have no Spanish—I couldn't understand your captain. What's supposed to happen now?"

"You are all being taken to Santa Fe—you'll have a few minutes to get your things," Lieutenant Molino told her. "It would be best if you hurry—Captain Reyes does not like to wait.

"In Santa Fe you will be under house arrest—I think you will be quite comfortable until certain matters can be resolved."

"Oh no! The brutes! I can't bear it!" Buffum cried. A cart had been brought for the three prisoners. Pomp and Tom, urged by a thicket of bayonets, had already climbed in, but High Shoulders was prostrate on the ground—a soldier stood over him, threatening to hit him again with the butt of a musket. Before he could, High Shoulders managed to struggle to his feet—he was rudely shoved into the cart, which at once turned and made for the big gate of the stockade. Wild with apprehension, Buffum tried to run to him, only to be blocked by the soldiers, who crossed their muskets and made a kind of fence.

As the cart went out the gate Pomp turned and smiled at Tasmin—he seemed not the least disturbed, though his fellow prisoner the old Broken Hand looked grim.

An escort of ten cavalrymen fell in behind the cart. It was a windy day; dust soon hid the prisoners and their escort too.

Tasmin hurried to her father, who had calmed down. He was talking with Charles Bent.

"I have no influence, not yet," Charles Bent told them. "I hope to have it someday, but right now I'm just the Mexicans' milk cow—what they're milking out of me is money."

"But what's this nonsense about Pomp being a spy?" Tasmin asked. "Of course he's not a spy."

"Captain Reyes thinks otherwise," her father said. "Probably thinks all Americans are spies."

"But where are they going with Pomp?" Tasmin asked.

"Santa Fe . . . let's hope he gets there," Charles Bent told her. "Maybe I can catch Vrain and bring him back—Vrain's better at managing the governor than I am."

"I don't understand—a few nights ago Pomp was dancing with the governor's wife—and now he's under arrest," Tasmin protested. "Why wouldn't he get to Santa Fe? What's going to happen to him?"

"A capricious people, the Spanish—too aloof for my taste," Lord Berrybender declared. "Never forget a slight. I was their prisoner myself, you know, on the Peninsula. Exchanged before any harm was done, although the claret was filthy and the rats big as cats."

"Father, do answer me," Tasmin pleaded. "What's going to happen to Pomp?"

She felt, suddenly, a deep apprehension—what had first seemed merely a bewildering charade, in which a straggly group of English travelers were suddenly required to be prisoners of war, had become something much more serious, at least where the three chained men were concerned.

"The firing squad, probably—usual fate of spies," Lord Berrybender said.

In shock, Tasmin stared at him.

"Usual fate of spies," he repeated, thinking she might not have heard.

59

In her determination to catch the cart . . .

T A S M I N could never clearly recollect her own actions
that morning, once her father had quietly revealed that Pomp
Charbonneau might face a firing squad—might, in fact, be shot
as a spy. In her determination to catch the cart and rescue Pomp
she ignored the soldiers with their crossed muskets—in fact, to
the great annoyance of Captain Reyes, she burst right through
them, knocking three of them down, and ran out the gate, only
to stop in despair when she realized that the cart with the prisoners in it was already merely a dust cloud in the west, so far
away that she had no hope of catching it. Then a man grabbed
her and she began to scream and curse—her curses were so violent that even Captain Reyes, who had started toward her,
stopped his horse in surprise.

The man who grabbed Tasmin was Kit Carson, who had been
hiding in the woolshed, where the sheep were sheared. When he
saw Tasmin make her desperate dash out the gate he raced to
her side and managed to pull her back.

"Stop it, Tasmin—you have to go get your kit, else they'll
chain you too and throw you across a horse," he said, giving her
a good shake, not unlike the one she had given him when he
descended into their camp in the balloon.

Tasmin realized, despite the shaking, that she was very glad to see Kit. Perhaps he could make sense of the whole confusing business. Besides, she wanted him to try and catch Jim and bring him back. When it came to saving people she put her best trust in Jim. Though her bosom continued to heave she managed to calm herself somewhat. With Kit's help she hurried upstairs and got together as much kit as she cared to be burdened with. The others—Cook, Eliza, Buffum, Mary, Kate, Vicky, and Little Onion and the babies—were already in one wagon, waiting for her. The menfolk, in another wagon, were already proceeding out the gate, with an escort of soldiers all their own.

"I hid because I thought they might take me too," Kit said. "I thought I could be more help on the loose—but it don't look like they want me. I guess they figure Charlie's got to have some help running the post, with Vrain gone north and Willy gone east."

"Besides that, you married a girl of good family—that must have helped," Tasmin told him. "Anyway, I want you to go find Jimmy and bring him back."

Kit had to shake his head. "Can't do it," he said. "Jimmy's long gone—it'd take a month to get him back, if he'd come. Vrain's closer, and Vrain knows the Mexicans better anyway."

Before they could talk more, Lieutenant Molino politely led Tasmin to the wagon where the other women waited. Monty and Talley were both crying, unsettled by it all.

"We must hurry," Lieutenant Molino said, as he helped Tasmin into the wagon. "I fear it may snow—it might be difficult to get over the pass."

"I don't care about snow," she said. "I only want to know why your captain thinks Pomp Charbonneau is dangerous."

The old captain with the plume in his hat made an angry gesture with his quirt and the wagon with the women prisoners at once started for the gate. Charles Bent was talking to Kit Carson, who was saddling his horse. Kit looked up as Tasmin went by, but he didn't wave.

"These soldiers are mostly just boys," Buffum observed. "It's too bad all our good fighters left. I suppose they had no notion that we were to become prisoners of war."

The wind increased in force. Soon flakes of snow mingled with the swirling dust. Tasmin kept hoping for a glimpse of the cart that held Pomp but could scarcely even see the wagon her father was in. Little Onion tried to keep the little boys warm under a blanket, but they kept popping out, excited now.

"At least Lieutenant Molino seems rather sympathetic," Vicky remarked.

"Yes, I like the lieutenant, but he's not the one we have to worry about," Tasmin said. "It's that old captain who's in charge, and he could hardly be described as sympathetic."

The snow began to fall more thickly, swirling beneath the wagon, shortening the horizons so drastically that the women could scarcely see their escort, though they could hear the horses tramping just behind them. The women huddled together, pulling blankets around them for warmth. Tasmin's mind was racing—she scarcely felt the cold. The worsening weather seemed to her an advantage. With visibility so limited perhaps Pomp and the others would escape—jump out of the carts and vanish. Their boy captors would never find them in such weather. Surely they could hobble back to the post, where they would soon be rid of their chains. This notion—of Pomp's escape in the storm—gave her hope. If only he'll try, she thought. If only he'll try.

60

Captain Reyes rode with a light heart . . .

CAPTAIN Antonio Reyes, like Tasmin—the English-woman who had cursed him so violently he thought he might have to shoot her—paid little heed to the worsening weather, as the three wagons, the forty-five cavalrymen, and the huddled captives inched across the whitening plain toward Santa Fe. Captain Reyes rode with a light heart, indifferent to the whirling snow, the reason for his lightness of spirit being that in capturing Jean Baptiste Charbonneau he had caught and perhaps would even execute the protégé of his worst enemy, the famous explorer William Clark.

Captain Clark had never met Captain Reyes, or even heard of him. He would have been surprised that this aging soldier in the Mexican army hated him so—but it was true.

In his youth Antonio Reyes had been the best cadet in his school. In only two years he was made captain, in part because of a brilliant campaign he had led against the intractable Indians in the pueblos west of the Rio Grande.

But that well-earned promotion was thirty years behind him, and there had been no other. Antonio Reyes was still a captain, not a general and not a governor, possibilities that had been well within his reach when he was a rising young officer. Then, for one reason only, his promising career had stalled: the much-heralded expedition of Captain Lewis and Captain Clark to the western ocean, across the great rich territory that had once been Spain's and should have been Spain's forever. Napoleon had interfered, selling the Americans a vast region that should not even have been his to sell. But it was Captain Lewis and Captain Clark, pushing into lands where they had no right to be, that had done the damage, both to Spain and to Antonio Reyes.

The Spanish authorities in Mexico City and Santa Fe had not been stupid men. They were well aware that President Jefferson had dispatched the two captains across the country and were not blind to the implications for Spain if they succeeded. Official opinion was unanimous: Lewis and Clark must be stopped! And who better to stop them than the brilliant young Captain Antonio Reyes?

Proudly and confidently, Captain Reyes set out with a company of cavalrymen to intercept the two explorers—set out and failed, not once but four times. These failures, in Captain Reyes's view, had nothing to do with his own skill. He failed because of the difficulty of the land, coupled with the miserliness of his superiors. The soldiers he led were inexperienced, the horses he was given were indifferent, the supplies were pitifully inadequate. The native tribes were uniformly hostile. The weather was severe, the drought extreme, their marksmanship poor, the buffalo elusive. Many of his soldiers faltered and then simply died. At the end of his second attempt, Captain Reyes was forced to limp back to Santa Fe with only six men. On the fourth and final trip the survivors had *literally* to limp back, every single horse having been stolen by the sly savages.

After this ignominy, Captain Reyes was sent out no more, nor was he promoted. The American captains returned in triumph, having crossed the continent with the loss of only one man. Captain Lewis and Captain Clark became big heroes—Captain Reyes was set to drilling cadets. He rejoiced when, a few years later, news reached him that Captain Lewis was dead; but Captain Clark was not dead. He held an important position in Saint

Louis, where he constantly urged Americans of all kinds to press on into the country he and his partner had opened.

A few of Clark's successors, like young Zebulon Pike, were captured and expelled. Captain Reyes himself was given the job of escorting Zebulon Pike out of Spanish territory; but these were only small victories. Many more Americans came: trappers, traders, scientists, military men, all with greed in their eyes. Mexico broke with Spain and became a republic, but in the vast distances of the West, it made little difference. More and more Americans came, ignoring Mexican claims. Soon they were taking beaver out of every stream and pond. From the East there were frequent rumors of plots against Mexico. Old General Wilkinson, governor of Upper Louisiana, was said to be intent on invading Santa Fe. In Texas waves of immigrants were beginning to challenge the Mexican authorities north of the Rio Grande.

To Captain Reyes, who knew how hard it had been to do what Lewis and Clark did, Mexican defeat seemed inevitable unless stern measures were adopted. If he had been governor he would have summarily executed every American who entered Mexican territory illegally. Half measures would never stop the Americans. But the governors were themselves too wishy-washy, too attracted to American merchandise as well as the handsome bribes the traders were willing to pay. Now the authorities had even capitulated to the Bents and St. Vrain, allowing them to build their big trading post on the Arkansas. To Captain Reyes it meant that the end of Mexican rule was near. In ten years, perhaps, or twenty at the most, the Americans would take the whole West, slicing off Texas here, Oregon there, California in good time. Santa Fe, poorly defended, with soldiers who were no more than half-trained boys, would fall to whatever American general chose to invade it.

At last, though, by sheer luck, Captain Reyes had been presented with a chance for revenge. It had been known for some time that Pomp Charbonneau, whom Captain Clark regarded almost as a son, was in the West, guiding a rich Scotsman, himself perhaps a spy. It was known, too, that an English noble family—and the English after all still held the rich northland—were traveling south from the Yellowstone. The English had arrived at the Bent's just as the governor arrived to attend the wedding of the Jaramillo girls.

The minute the governor got back and spread the news that he had seen the English, and Pomp Charbonneau as well, Captain Reyes had seen his chance. He went at once to the governor—it was easy enough to persuade him to send a troop of soldiers to capture the English party and bring it to Santa Fe.

The old lord was known to be very rich—once a munificent ransom had been arranged, the English could be escorted out of the country, as Zebulon Pike had been. Since the governor seemed to enjoy socializing with them, perhaps they could be kept in Santa Fe through the winter and sent on their way in the spring.

Captain Reyes said nothing to the governor about his hatred of William Clark. The governor, in his view, lacked firmness; against the taciturn and treacherous Indians he might employ strong measures, but if Americans or Europeans were involved he sometimes wavered. Pomp Charbonneau, educated in Europe, was said to excel at the social graces. As a dancer he had made a great hit with the ladies who attended the wedding. If he were allowed to reach Santa Fe, social pressure might be brought to bear—Pomp might escape the fate all spies deserved. In Captain Reyes's mind Pomp Charbonneau was just as much a spy as Zebulon Pike. If allowed to return to Saint Louis, he would certainly inform Captain Clark about how weak the Mexican defenses were. There would be more plotting and, very soon, an American army would advance on Nuevo México.

Despite the bitter frustration of his truncated career, Captain Reyes considered himself a patriot. He loved Mexico, hated America. He knew the American temperament, knew they would not stop until they had all of the West. They would eliminate the Indians and the Mexicans as well. Allowing the Bents to build their trading post was, in the captain's view, an act of supreme folly: it was like handing them the keys to the treasury.

Far away, in Saint Louis, Captain Clark lived the life of a hero—while he, Antonio Reyes, no less gifted, had spent his life as a failure, drilling indifferent cadets on a dusty parade ground. He was too old to expect the kind of glory that Captain Clark had enjoyed so long. But the gods were not entirely unfair. Unexpectedly, he had been presented with a chance for revenge. He had Pomp Charbonneau and he meant to put him before a firing squad as soon as they reached Taos—as good a place as any to line up a firing squad.

Of course, there would be an outcry. Captain Reyes didn't care. Let them court-martial him, strip him of his rank, take away his few decorations. If worse came to worst he might have to face a firing squad himself—Captain Clark had powerful friends, and the death of his favorite was not something he would take lightly. Even without Captain Clark's long reach, there would be annoyance. Why had a lowly captain taken it upon himself to kill a young man the governor's wife had been pleased to dance with? But Captain Antonio Reyes was willing to face whatever came. Across the prairies, by the wide Mississippi, Captain Clark would soon know that his favorite was dead. A lowly captain in the Mexican army, a man he had never heard of, would at last have taken his revenge.

61

. . . with the snow still swirling . . .

"COME ON, boy—it's our chance!" the Broken Hand whispered. "It won't snow much longer. Kit's out there—he won't be far. I tell you he gave me a sign."

In the night, with the snow still swirling and the wind keening, High Shoulders had chewed the flesh off his own wrists and slipped his chains. With the same chain he strangled their two guards, boys so young and so frozen that they scarcely realized they were dying. High Shoulders took the boys' muskets and at once disappeared into the swirling snow. The Broken Hand, still chained but convinced that Kit Carson would soon rescue them, was about to follow the Ute. But Pomp Charbonneau hadn't moved.

Tom Fitzpatrick couldn't understand why Pomp wasn't hurrying. Their own lives might be forfeit if they didn't flee while there were a few hours of darkness left.

"You go on—find Kit," Pomp told him. "I'd better stay."

"What? Why stay—our Ute practically chewed his hands off to give us this chance," Tom Fitzpatrick whispered.

"If we all three escape, Captain Reyes might take it out on the others," Pomp said. "He might shoot some of them."

Tom Fitzpatrick heard a rustling from the soldiers' campfire, not thirty feet away. He wasted no more time on debate—unless he could find Kit and get his chains knocked off, he himself would probably be retaken anyway. On the great plain east of Taos there were not many places to hide. But Kit was a loyal man, and he had given a sign—he wouldn't be far. With no more said, the Broken Hand disappeared into the blizzard. He kept his legs wide apart, so his leg chains wouldn't clink.

Pomp slid down from the wagon and laid the two dead boys side by side, closing their eyes when he finished. They had been huddled together sharing a ragged blanket when High Shoulders, an apparition out of the blizzard, threw the deadly chains around both their necks at once. Now, at least, the storm would not annoy them. Pomp spread the blanket over both their faces and weighted it down with rocks, so the howling wind wouldn't uncover the dead boys. Then he pulled his own blanket close around him and waited for what the morning would bring.

62

She shook her head . . .

"Something about you makes me very uneasy—it always has," Tasmin said.

"What?" Pomp asked.

She shook her head, uncertain but deeply worried.

"It's a struggle to keep you in this life, that's all I know," she said.

In the confusion she was able to slip over and talk to Pomp, the only person in the whole company who wasn't confused. Captain Reyes, discovering the escapes, at once dispatched Lieutenant Molino, with fifteen cavalrymen, to try and recapture the fugitives. The remaining soldiers, seeing their two dead comrades, were fearfully guarding the other prisoners, many of them pointing their guns at the half-frozen captives. Bayonets were brandished, although none of the captives were doing anything other than trying to stay warm, feeding small bits of brush into the flickering campfires. Captain Reyes was staring to the east, expecting at any moment to see the captives being brought back.

"I wish you'd run—I don't know why you didn't," Tasmin argued. "You're the one they're convinced is a spy. Why didn't you go?"

"Captain Reyes is quite upset," Pomp told her. "If we'd all escaped, he might start shooting people."

"All right—but what's to stop him from shooting you now?"

Pomp had been watching Captain Reyes closely—every time their eyes met, the captain's flashed with hatred. Something had him stirred up, something that went well beyond the routine matter of arresting trespassers on the Santa Fe Trail. But Pomp had never been to Santa Fe—the two of them had never met. The captain's hatred was inexplicable, unless he just hated all *americanos* on principle, which of course could be the case.

"I wish you weren't always so calm—it's maddening," Tasmin told him. "I ain't calm, I can tell you. I don't want you to get shot."

Pomp tried to put his arm around her but Tasmin shrugged it off.

"You can't jolly me, Pomp, not today," she said. "You should have escaped."

Pomp was beginning to think she might be right. There was something excessive about Captain Reyes's anger. Dimly he remembered a dream in which his mother warned him about a feathered man. He had not had such a dream for years. But here was an angry little soldier with a plume. Was he the feathered man?

And yet he had not wanted to go with High Shoulders and the Broken Hand. He had wanted to stay with Tasmin. Probably Kit had the other two safe by then.

Tasmin's irritation with his calm made Pomp wonder. The captain hated him—the other two he had arrested because they were too dangerous to transport unchained. But the captain didn't really want them; the captain wanted *him,* and there *was* something deadly in his intent. He should have fled, but he hadn't. He should be poised to fight, and yet something in him lazed, *was* calm, as if he had come to a place and a moment that had been long prepared, in which his own part had been fixed by powers greater than himself. Jim Snow, in his place, would have killed Captain Reyes somehow, and taken his chances. But Pomp was not inclined to do that.

"You're quite the strangest man I've ever known," Tasmin told him, bitterness creeping into her tone. "You *won't* help your-self—you *won't*. When Geoff took that arrow tip out of you he said you could live if you wanted to, and I assured him that I'd see that you wanted to. God knows I tried my hardest, but I failed and I don't know why. It wasn't enough—it didn't work!"

Again Pomp tried to put an arm around Tasmin but she jerked away, crying, and stumbled back toward one of the campfires.

To the east Pomp saw puffs of snow rising like a cloud, as dust had risen the day before. Lieutenant Molino was on his way back. In a few minutes he arrived with the soldiers he had left with but without High Shoulders and the Broken Hand.

"They were met by someone," the lieutenant said at once—he knew Captain Reyes was not pleased.

"We saw the tracks of four horses—someone followed us in order to save them," he added.

"It was Carson, the one who married the little rich girl," the captain declared. Then he pointed at Pomp.

"The fourth horse was for him, but he didn't run," Captain Reyes said, fury in his voice. "Why didn't you run, Monsieur Jean Baptiste Charbonneau?"

Pomp was surprised that Captain Reyes knew his full name, but he replied politely.

"I am not a spy, Captain," he said. "I merely worked for Señor Stewart, who was collecting animals for his zoo. When he was killed I helped guide these people to safety, that's all. I don't believe your governor considers me a spy. He was quite courte-ous at the recent wedding. Why should I run when I have com-mitted no crime?"

Captain Reyes looked at him soberly for a moment, but his jaw was twitching, and when he spoke he was almost shouting.

"You have made a misjudgment—a fatal misjudgment," he said. "You are not in a court, and the governor is far away. I am a military man. You are the protégé of Captain William Clark—undoubtedly his spy, sent to appraise our defenses. Under mili-tary rules I am allowed to shoot spies wherever I find them."

He turned and walked through the ranks of soldiers, tapping

this one and that. Soon eight soldiers, nervous and uncertain, were drawn up in a kind of line: an uncomfortable, fidgety firing squad.

The captain walked over to Pomp.

"Get out of the wagon," he ordered.

Assisted by two soldiers, Pomp got out and took an awkward step or two. The inept-looking firing squad was in front of him, the great empty plain behind. Despite Captain Reyes's evident distemper, Pomp still considered that it was a bluff—a bluff designed to get him to make some admission about Captain Clark's intentions—or the American government's, or some-body's. Or was he wrong? Was the captain the feathered man his mother had warned him that he must avoid?

Tasmin and Lord Berrybender, at the same moment, realized what was happening. Lord B. at once stumped over on his crutch.

"I say, Captain, surely this is rather abrupt," he said. "I can vouch for our good Pomp—he's no spy at all. No good to shoot him—I fear I must insist. Surely we can work out an exchange."

Captain Reyes took a musket from one of the trembling sol-diers and swung it like a club, smashing Lord Berrybender's crutch, hitting his peg leg, and sending Lord B. crashing into the snow.

"Do not interfere again," Captain Reyes said. "You are not a lord here. I consider all Englishmen spies. It would not trouble me to shoot you too."

"Not trouble you? What sort of a captain are you?" Lord B. asked, as Vicky Kennet helped him to his feet.

Several soldiers stopped Tasmin, but she struggled free and rushed over to the nice, sympathetic Lieutenant Molino, who was clearly startled by what his superior had just done.

"Lieutenant, can't you stop this?" Tasmin pleaded. "Your cap-tain is too upset. He has no reason to shoot anyone."

Lieutenant Molino looked worried—he had not expected the usually calm Captain Reyes to do anything so unexpected.

"It is not correct," he said, hesitantly. "We were to bring all prisoners to Santa Fe—I heard the order myself. Santa Fe is where we deal with spies."

"Then hurry—stop him before it's too late," Tasmin urged.

With some reluctance Lieutenant Molino stepped forward. The firing squad had just raised their muskets—Pomp, still calm, stood watching.

"Wait, Captain," Lieutenant Molino urged. "We were to bring all prisoners to Santa Fe. The governor said so himself. I fear this is not going to please him."

Captain Reyes carried a long pistol. Without a word he raised it and shot Lieutenant Molino directly in the forehead. The dead man fell back against Tasmin, knocking her into the snow. Father Geoffrin ran over to shield her—who knew who this mad captain might shoot next?

Pomp knew then that he should have been quicker to heed his dream. It was, after all, the feathered man he faced, the man his mother had known he would meet someday. The feathered man had just killed his own lieutenant, who was acting properly.

Tasmin's head was ringing—she had hit the ground hard and was bleeding from a cut on her temple. She tried to stand up but her legs gave way.

"Get a knife, Geoff—stab him!" she begged. "We have to do something or he'll kill us all."

Father Geoffrin watched as the shaky, cold little firing squad attempted to prime their weapons.

"This is a very inept firing squad," he told her. "Maybe they'll all miss."

"There's eight of them, Geoff—they won't all miss!" Tasmin yelled. She struggled to free herself, but the priest hung on to her grimly, fearing the captain would shoot her if she broke free.

At Captain Reyes's signal six muskets blazed. Two misfired completely. A bullet hit Pomp in the leg, another nicked his shoulder. The other bullets kicked up snow well beyond their target.

"Now that is a rare novelty for you," Lord Berrybender remarked. "A whole firing squad—and they missed."

For Captain Reyes what had just happened seemed a last

humiliation, the crowning ignominy of his many wasted years. His handpicked firing squad had failed to kill or even seriously wound Jean Baptiste Charbonneau, who still looked at him without alarm. Worse, he himself, in a moment of terrible disdain, had impulsively killed a fine young officer, a soldier whose promise was not unlike what his own had once been. This, the captain knew, meant the end. He would be court-martialed and very likely executed; and he deserved to be. At a supreme moment of crisis he had allowed his personal feelings to override the necessary discipline of a soldier. He had, in every way, disgraced himself.

But if he must die, Jean Baptiste Charbonneau, the favorite of Captain William Clark, would die too. He snatched a musket from a young cavalryman's hand and walked toward Pomp.

"Kill him, one of you! Your captain's mad!" Tasmin cried. "He may kill us all! Mutiny while you can."

The shivering boys did not understand her. They were too cold to act, too puzzled.

Captain Reyes advanced toward Pomp until he stood at point-blank range. Only then did he raise his musket. For a moment he allowed his gaze to meet that of the young man he was about to kill. The young man's eyes were unfrightened, undisturbed. Once he looked into his intended victim's eye, the captain, to his great surprise, could not turn away, for in the young man's eyes he seemed to see understanding—even sympathy—neither of which Captain Reyes had ever been offered in his life. It was as if the condemned man, the favorite, saw it all: the early glory, then the bitter failure on the plains, the stalled career, the dull cadets, the dust. He saw it all; he understood.

Then, while Captain Reyes was considering the possibility that he *had* misjudged this quiet, sympathetic young man, a gun went off. Pomp Charbonneau fell, as Lieutenant Molino had fallen. The understanding eyes went blank. Captain Reyes turned, to see what fool had fired, and realized, to his shock, that the drifting smoke came from his own musket. *He* had fired.

Tasmin Berrybender screamed—a scream long and terrible, echoing off the distant mountains. Her scream caused a nervous black gelding to rear up and throw its rider. Tasmin broke free of Father Geoffrin and ran to Pomp; her sleeve brushed that of the stunned Captain Reyes as she ran.

After a moment Captain Reyes walked over to the nearest soldier and handed him the musket.

"Corporal, I require your pistol," he said. The corporal fumbled for a moment, then drew the pistol and handed it over. Captain Reyes at once put the gun under his chin and pulled the trigger. He fell under the corporal's horse, his blood soon reddening the thin snow.

With Vicky Kennet's help, Lord Berrybender limped over to where Tasmin knelt by Pomp.

"Why, it's like the bard," Lord Berrybender said, looking around him. "Dead men everywhere you look. Exeunt omnes, or pretty nearly."

Tasmin removed her cloak and spread it over her dearest love.

"Is he gone, our Pomp?" Lord Berrybender asked Father Geoffrin.

"He's gone, Your Lordship," the priest said. "Gone as gone."

The women came slowly round: Buffum, Vicky, Mary, Cook, Eliza, Little Onion—she still held both the little boys.

"Oh no, not him . . . not Pomp," Eliza cried. "He was ever so kind to us girls . . . dear Milly and me, I mean."

"Not a fighter, though, Tassie . . . not like your Sin Killer," Lord Berrybender said, putting his hand on his daughter's shoulder. "Jimmy would have scattered these poor shivering Spanish boys like quail, if he had been here."

"He wasn't like Jimmy, no," Tasmin answered, sad, beaten, yet not really surprised. "I expect Pomp might have been a saint, if he hadn't met me."

The ground being judged too hard for grave digging, the five bodies were put in the cart where the prisoners had ridden. Tasmin insisted on riding in it too, with Pomp. Monty clutched Little Onion tightly—he was afraid of his mother when she looked so. The snow had stopped falling. Cold sunlight sparkled on thornbush and sage. Ahead, hidden in cloud, lay the rising road to Santa Fe.